HUGO DUCHAMP INVESTIGATES:

le bateau au fond de l'océan

BY
GN HETHERINGTON

First Published in 2022 by GNH Publishing.

The right of Gary Hetherington to be identified as the author of this work has been asserted by him in accordance with the Copyright, Designs and Patents Act 1988.

Copyright © Gary Hetherington

All rights reserved. No part of this book may be reproduced, stored in a retrieval system or transmitted in any form or by any means, electronic, mechanical, photocopying, recording or otherwise, without the prior permission of the publisher.

www.gnhbooks.co.uk

Merci

Thank you very much to my lovely girls June Russell and Jackie Waite who are always there to support me. Their daily love means the world to me. I'm grateful to my beaux parents, Bill and Chris and my friends who support me all the way - Joy Edwards, Jennifer Trieb, Suse Telford, Sandra Scott, Kathleen Pope, Margaret Cox and Pam Pletts. Extra special thanks to my French teacher Bastien Greve for his constant help and encouragement and for always allowing me to ask such bizarre questions…

As always, merci to Sheena Easton & Julien Doré.

For my family. My amazing husband Dan and our furry babies.

Notes:

Montgenoux and Beaufort-Sur-Mer are both figments of my imagination, based loosely upon various regions of France. The story and its characters are also a work of fiction.

For further information, exclusive content and to join the mailing list, head over to:

www.gnhbooks.co.uk

We are also on Facebook, Twitter and Instagram. Join us there!

The artwork on the cover, website and social media accounts were created in conjunction with the incredible talent of Maria Almeida and I'm indebted to her for bringing my characters to life.

For Charlie, Seth and Dawn. Tu me manques.

Previously in the "Hugo Duchamp Investigates" series of books:

Hugo Duchamp, a Frenchman by birth, has spent much of his adult life living and working in London and has risen to the rank of Detective Superintendent in London's Metropolitan Police. He lives a solitary but content life. In 2015 in **Un Homme Qui Attend** (A man who waits) Hugo finds himself ripped out of his organised life and supplanted back in the country of his birth when he is seconded to a small town called Montgenoux, a town reeling from the brutal murder of a young girl and a corrupt police force. Warned against getting involved, Hugo is soon embroiled in the investigation when a second girl is murdered and he finds himself in a race against time to catch a murderer that culminates in a fiery and deadly confrontation.

Months later, Hugo is thrown into another investigation, **Les Fantômes du Château** (The Ghosts of the Chateau) while still reeling from the aftermath of his previous investigation and trying to balance a new life in France and a blossoming romance. Following the murder of a maid working in a grand Château on the outskirts of Montgenoux, he finds himself pitted against two new adversaries and a family at war in an investigation that forces him to face his own mortality.

Battered and bruised, Hugo faces the prospect of a serial killer in Montgenoux in **Les Noms sur Les Tombs** (The Names on the Graves). A spate of apparent suicides share an unusual link, a mound of soil at the feet of the deceased and before long Hugo realises that there is someone in Montgenoux who is following a dangerous and baffling plan that threatens the lives and safety of those he has come to love.

The fourth instalment in the series **L'hombre de L'isle** (The Shadow from the Island) picks up after the shocking conclusion of Hugo's last investigation and the action switches to Ireland where Hugo races has to solve the brutal murder of a priest in his most personal investigation yet which will leave him questioning everything he thought he knew and believed in.

* * *

In **L'assassiner de Sebastian Dubois** (The murder of Sebastian Dubois) Hugo's two worlds collide. His new life in Montgenoux is affected by an investigation from his past, and he has to deal with a past he thought he had left behind and a pair of criminals who are determined to wreak their revenge on him. As he attends a crime scene at the newly opened Montgenoux prison, Hugo and Dr. Chapeau find themselves taken hostage and face a battle with violent criminals with only one thing on their minds - Hugo's death.

The discovery of a thirty-year-old skeleton buried under the Beaupain vineyard in Montgenoux (**L'impondérable**) (The Imponderable) triggers a horrific series of events in the modern day, resulting in the murder of a prominent citizen and a murder/suicide. It all appears to be an open and shut case. Hugo faces a complex web of lies and crimes dating back to the eighties, which have devastating effects upon Hugo and those he loves.

Fulfilling a promise, Hugo and his family journey to Moscow, Russia (**Le Cri de coeur**) (The Cry of the Heart) but soon find themselves in mortal danger when Hugo is called upon to assist the local police following the discovery of a mysterious box and its grisly contents. After a body is discovered on the grounds of the Chinese Embassy, Hugo finds himself trapped inside with his family in danger on the outside. The clock is ticking, and the killer has only just begun their deadly game.

After a fire tears through Montgenoux, Hugo and his team must deal with the shocking aftermath of the death of an entire family (**La Famille Lacroix**) (The Lacroix Family) and the fallout as racial tension erupts through the town. When the prime suspect is murdered, Hugo must put aside his own grief to unravel one of his most complicated and heartbreaking investigations.

After decades away, Hugo returns to Paris (**Les Mauvais Garçons**) (The Bad Boys) after a request from the Minister of Justice, Jean Lenoir, following the death of a young man who apparently threw himself from the Eiffel Tower. Hugo soon finds himself face to face with his past as he tries to save the lives of a group of young people whose lives are in grave danger.

A horrific accident in 2010 triggers a chain of events in present day Montgenoux (**Prisonnier Dix)** (Prisoner Ten). When the body of a young medical intern is discovered on the grounds of a scientific research institute, Hugo discovers she had a very difficult past, and the investigation leads to a family torn apart by a deadly secret and an evil murder. Hugo and his team must race against time to protect the innocent before a deadly killer strikes again.

Also available:

Hugo Duchamp Investigates:

Un Homme Qui Attend (2015)
Les Fantômes du Chateau (2016)
Les Noms Sur Les Tombes (2016)
L'ombre de l'île (2017)
L'assassiner de Sebastian Dubois (2017)
L'impondérable (2018)
Le Cri du Cœur (2019)
La Famille Lacroix (2019)
Les Mauvais Garçons (2020)
Prisonnier Dix (2021)
Le Bateau au fond de l'océan (2022)
Chemin de Compostelle (2023)
Hotel Beaupain (2023)

The Coco Brunhild Mysteries:

Sept Jours (2021)
Métro Boulot Dodo (2022)
Cercueils en spirale (2022)
Quatre Semaines (2023)

Also available:

Hugo & Josef (2021)
Club Vidéo (2022)
Hugo & Madeline (2023)
Josef (2023)

PART ONE

MONTGENOUX

u n

Hugo Duchamp shuffled uncomfortably on the plastic benches which lined the swimming pool at the heart of Montgenoux Grand École. Despite his natural reticence against sport, based solely upon his own apparent inability to compete, Hugo found himself caught up in the drama and the emotion of the event.

He was not at the swimming competition in his official capacity of Captain of the Police Nationale, rather as the proud father of one of the competitors, Baptiste Beaupain. The title of father was still not something Hugo had become used to. He had imagined his life would end as it had begun, staid and sterile, and though he might have love affairs, none of them was likely to last. He was not a man prone to fancy, or melancholy, rather a man who had, from an early age, learned his limitations. He had not been taught to love properly, and the act of love was not something that came naturally to him because he always assumed it was fleeting, because it was the only experience he could relate to.

He had been born to a wealthy family, in an arrondissement of Paris proud of the fact it was not fashionable because it meant it managed to keep out those inhabitants the residents would consider undesirable. Hugo had been born to Pierre Duchamp, a stoic man who had inherited his mother's steely determination and irreverence, and nothing at all from his father.

Pierre had, for reasons no one had ever quite understood, chosen to marry a foreigner, an actress and a singer. The match, for whatever reason it had occurred, had produced Hugo and little else, other than contempt and hatred between all those involved. Hugo was barely grown before his parents had divorced, his mother flitting to America to pursue a career no-one believed in but her.

Pierre, as was the want of a man of privilege and distinction, had decided he had no interest or desire to raise a child. He had,

Hugo had always assumed, hoped that he would hand over the child to a nanny who would return him fully grown and entirely compatible with the Parisian highlife Pierre had grown accustomed to. It had not worked out that way. Hugo was never destined to be the perfect child for high society.

Hugo had been taken in by his Grand Mère, Madeline Duchamp, a woman entirely unaccustomed to raising children, but had taken on Hugo because her vanity decreed it. Between the two of them, Hugo and Madeline had forged an entirely unorthodox life together, until her death, when Hugo was barely eighteen years old. She had left him as she had found him. Devastated and alone. But she had done one thing for him. She had left him independent and an adult of means. He knew it was her way of showing her love to him. She was not demonstrative and, accordingly, had never shown him how to be. He did not blame her, primarily because he did not know where he would have been were it not for Madeline. Of all he had lost in his life, her loss was the one which he still carried. He had left France after her death and vowed never to return.

However, everything had changed several years later when Hugo, then a superintendent in the London Metropolitan Police, had been called back to his native France to assist in a tragic and politically sensitive series of murders. The murders had been solved, but somewhere along the way, Hugo had found himself unable to run away any longer. He had been caught in a trap as if he had fallen into a spider's web, and the more he tried to extract himself, the more difficult it had become. Despite it being against everything he wanted, he had been shown a glimpse of a life he had never imagined could be his.

Hugo shook his head, realising he had drifted off into melancholy again. In such circumstances, he did as he normally would - he moved his knee to the left, immediately feeling the reassurance of the person who had changed everything. The man who had taught him that love, and lasting love, was achievable.

Hugo and Ben Beaupain had been together for seven years, sharing a ramshackle Swiss-style cottage on the outskirts of Montgenoux, and although they had encountered their fair share of troubles, they had emerged together, growing stronger all the time. They had married and adopted Baptiste, even though he was already an adult, but still in need of a family to love him.

Hugo and Ben had first encountered Baptiste when he was enrolled in a home for troubled teenagers in Ireland, but when they returned to France, he came with them. Despite his difficult start in life, Baptiste had recently completed his baccalauréat and had now enrolled at Montgenoux Grand École, where he was studying business administration, with a view to one day running the vineyard Ben had inherited following his father's death. Hugo was immensely proud of the young man who had fought through such adversity.

Since enrolling in Montgenoux Grand École, Baptiste had continued his studies, but also joined the school swim team, and their training had paid off. If they won the latest heat, then they would move into the national finals, competing with schools from all over France. Hugo was sure Baptiste was keeping himself busy following a love affair that had ended badly. His young adopted son talked little about Chen Gao, the girl he had met in Ireland and who was now living in China with her husband. At the time, Hugo had witnessed Baptiste's despair, but had been unable to get him to discuss it further.

Baptiste jumped in front of them, bending over and shaking wet hair in Hugo and Ben's direction, covering Hugo's glasses with chlorinated water. He pushed them into his long blond hair, fixing Baptiste with an almost stern glare from piercing emerald green eyes. Baptiste chortled, running his hands through his hair. As usual, he wore his dark hair long on top, with shaved sides. He was also prone to wearing bow ties, but Hugo had noticed that since Chen Gao was out of his life, so were the ties.

'Did I do okay?' Baptiste asked.

Despite the casual tone, Hugo could tell the young man was keen to impress his parents. 'You did an amazing job,' Hugo said.

'And we kept the whooping and cheering to a dull roar so as not to embarrass you,' Ben added.

'You two could never embarrass me,' Baptiste smiled. 'And I know this isn't your kind of fun, but I appreciate you coming out to support me all the same.' He pointed to the enormous clock on the auditorium wall. 'There's only one more round and then we'll be done.'

'And then we'll take you for pizza to celebrate,' Hugo said.

Baptiste patted his stomach. 'Papa, I'm in training. I can't be eating pizza,' he sighed despairingly.

Hugo raised an eyebrow. He was not sure he had ever seen such a firm stomach, and certainly not one with so many squares on it. 'You have to eat,' he sighed. He had never played the father card, because the truth was, Baptiste had been practically an adult when they had met. But somehow, somewhere amongst the confusion of their nuclear family, they had found a way to function as a family. There was never a case of testing boundaries, because when they had come together they had done so by choice, and therefore whatever came after they had somehow always understood it was from a place of love and respect.

Baptiste exhaled and nodded, fixing Hugo with a warm smile. 'Can my buddy come? He's kinda here on his own. His family doesn't live in Montgenoux,' he replied. 'And,' he paused, his mouth twisting, 'as you know, I know what it feels like to be in a weird school away from everyone and everything you know.'

Ben smiled, squeezing Hugo's hand. 'Bien sûr, you can bring your friend. We'd love to meet him.' He pointed toward the pool. 'Now, go swim and make us even prouder.'

Baptiste winked at them and jogged in the direction of the swimming pool.

Ben dropped his head on Hugo's shoulder. 'I like being a Papa.'

Hugo smiled. 'Me too,' he replied, realising he meant it more than he ever thought possible. *I have a family.*

deux

Arienne Shelan slinked across the floor of the Café she owned in the centre of Montgenoux, winking and throwing comments at her patrons as she passed them. She stopped at a table in front of the window, dropping two pizza trays onto the table. She took a step back, placing her hands on her hips and shaking her head, an abundance of red curls bouncing onto her shoulders. She leaned forward, thrusting amble bosoms forward. Arienne Shelan was not a woman who was prone to demureness.

'Do you know how happy it makes an old broad like me to have four such handsome fellas in my establishment?' she exhaled, her voice as heavy as the air of perfume surrounding her.

Ben chuckled, dropping his arm around Hugo's shoulders. 'And two of them are married, and the other two are...' he looked at Baptiste and his friend, 'young enough to be your...'

Arienne clenched her left fist. 'I would choose your next word very carefully, Benoit Beaupain,' she chastised. There was no maliciousness to her tone, just playfulness. 'I've decked you once or twice before when you've given me lip, and I'll do so again if need be.' She turned to Baptiste. 'You're looking even more handsome than ever. You obviously take after both of your ridiculously handsome fathers.'

Baptiste looked to Hugo and Ben.

'I've found it's best not to argue,' Hugo stated.

Arienne moved to the bar and returned with a tray. 'Ice cold beer for the big men,' she said, before adding with a shudder, 'and iced water for the athletes.'

Baptiste's friend lifted his t-shirt, revealing a perfect set of abs. 'You don't get to look like this by drinking those,' he said, pointing to the beers.

Arienne covered her mouth. 'Put that away, jeune homme, or else I'll forget I'm a lady.' She smiled at Hugo and Ben. 'Just call out if you need anything else, bon appétit!' she added before sidling back into the Café.

Ben chuckled. 'Don't take Arienne seriously, her bark is worse than her bite…'

'It's not her bite I'm worried about,' Baptiste mused.

Ben looked at Hugo, who was staring at his drink. 'What's up, cher?'

Hugo picked up his beer, sipping it slowly. He looked down at his stomach. He was not overweight, but whatever Baptiste and his friend had beneath their t-shirts, Hugo's own was hidden far away. 'Peut être, I should have water as well,' he mused, not entirely convincingly.

Ben reached over and kissed his cheek. 'You look perfect to me, you *always* look perfect to me.' He stopped, turning to Baptiste and his friend. He bit his lip. 'Désolé,' he said.

Baptiste frowned. 'Pourquoi?'

Ben turned to Baptiste's friend. 'It's just I don't want to make you uncomfortable in front of your friend. Not everyone likes public displays of affection, especially when it's "oldies" doing it.'

Baptiste cackled. 'Vincent doesn't mind, do you, Vincent?'

Vincent sipped his water. 'Of course, I don't mind. I've read all about you both. Baptiste is lucky to have two such cool fathers.'

Ben slapped Hugo's shoulder. 'You see? We're cool.'

Hugo tipped his head. 'Well, I never thought I'd be described that way, but I'll take it.' He looked at Vincent. 'Baptiste told me you're not from Montgenoux.'

The change in the young man's face was instant. Like Baptiste, he was tall and lithe, his face tight and tanned. He fixed Hugo with a piercing stare with clear blue eyes. His hair was shaved close to his head, much like Baptiste's. 'Non, I'm not from Montgenoux,' he said. His voice had lost the playfulness it had shown earlier, and there was a bite to it.

'Oh,' Hugo replied, picking up his drink again.

'Désolé,' Vincent said, shaking his head. 'I didn't mean to sound rude. It's just a weird time for me, right now.'

'That's okay,' Hugo replied. He did not want to pry, but he could see the young man was troubled by something.

'I don't know about you lot,' Ben interrupted, 'but, I for one, can't wait any longer for some of Arienne's famous pizza.' He picked up a slice and took a bite. He chomped happily. 'Yummy.'

Baptiste pulled a slice and devoured it in two quick bites. Hugo picked up a slice and placed it on a plate. He then picked up a knife and fork and begin cutting up the pizza.

'Oh, yeah, we're indoors,' Baptiste said. 'We're supposed to be polite, aren't we?'

Vincent reached over and took some pizza. He placed it on a plate and began cutting it up, all the while staring at Hugo.

'I won a scholarship,' he said. 'That's the only reason I'm here.'

'And you won it because you're an amazing student, and an even better swimmer,' Baptiste interjected. 'It's true, Papa. I don't think I would have gotten through this term without his help.'

'That's not true,' Vincent replied. 'You're really smart.'

Baptiste snorted. 'Ha, bless you for saying it, but I'm not. But I am trying, and the fact I got my baccalauréat is only because of Hugo and Ben, and if I pass this course, it will be because you're all helping me.'

'And because you're a really hard worker,' Hugo smiled. He turned to Vincent. 'So, where are you from originally, Vincent?' he asked.

Vincent exhaled. 'Beaufort-Sur-Mer.'

'Beaufort-Sur-Mer?' Hugo questioned. 'I don't think I know it.'

'It's on the Atlantic coast, I think,' Ben said.

Vincent nodded. 'I used to hate it when I was growing up, mais now...' he trailed off. 'I think I miss it. I miss everything I used to hate. The quietness, the annoying tourists who descend every summer. The fact everyone knows everyone and all the houses look the same. And for most of the year, the only girls you can kiss are the same ones you've been kissing since kindergarten.' He sighed.

Hugo nodded. 'Still, I imagine you must miss your parents.'

'Papa is dead, et,' Vincent trailed off, 'Maman *isn't*.'

Hugo frowned. There was something about the way Vincent spoke which troubled him. He shook the thought from his head, realising it was most likely his suspicious nature and nothing more.

Baptiste clapped his hand. 'To hell with only eating good stuff, let's have more pizza!'

Ben grabbed another slice. 'I couldn't agree with you more.'

trois

Quentin Arquette threw his bag onto the ground and pulled off his regulation school shirt, buttons flying as he did so.

Behind him, Baptiste laughed. 'There are easier ways of taking off your shirt, Quentin, you know?'

Quentin tipped his head to his left. 'Then the chicks won't get to see me do it, will they?'

Baptiste smiled. Although Quentin was an excellent addition to the swim team, he was the sort of young man most girls seemed to ignore. Not that there was anything wrong with him necessarily, Baptiste reasoned. It was just he was small, with clumpy black hair which he appeared to cut himself, and a tiny snub nose. He was also awkward and prone to inappropriateness. Despite the fact he was barely in his twenties, Baptiste realised that more often than not he forgot that his own teenage years had been spent in a school where his behaviour was monitored and any deviation was likely to result in a punishment that never matched the crime.

'Brigitte's definitely got the hots for me,' Quentin added with a wink. He removed his underwear, standing proudly naked in the changing room.

Baptiste moved in front of him. 'Quentin!' he cried. 'These are communal changing rooms, you idiot!'

'Je sais,' Quentin shot back, nudging his head over Baptiste's shoulder. 'We have an audience,' he added with a wry smile.

Baptiste turned around. Someone was clapping behind them.

Brigitte St. Pierre stepped out of the darkness of the shower cubicles. She was draped in a towel. She smiled when she saw Baptiste and Quentin and, with a swift flick of her wrist, removed her own towel. Baptiste turned away quickly, covering his eyes.

Brigitte laughed. 'Don't be so shy, Baptiste,' she said. 'Haven't you seen a big, beautiful black goddess in all her glory before?'

Baptiste gulped, but could think of nothing to say. Quentin stepped in front of him. He was still naked.

Brigitte moved her head slowly up and down, appraising him. 'What a let-down,' she said with obvious disappointment.

Quentin puffed out his chest defiantly. 'Isn't your Papa a drug baron or something, Brigitte? Can't he buy you some acne treatment and liposuction?'

If she was upset by what he said, Brigitte did not show it. Instead, she slapped her ass; the sound echoing around the tiled room. 'Yeah, sure he can. And then maybe he can suck some fat out of my fat ass and stick it in your scrawny, tiny body.' She paused before adding. 'And especially into your tiny limp dick.'

Baptiste stood rigid, unsure of what to do. He understood Brigitte's bravado. It was something he had got by on himself for most of his life. *Extend your chest. Don't show them they've got to you.* It had worked. *Sometimes.* But often, the insults pierced like an arrow through armour. He liked Brigitte. She was not an obvious athlete, and her physique was not necessarily indicative of a competitive swimmer, but she had something in abundance - determination. She was in the pool hours before classes began and for hours after they had finished. She was determined, and she was unwilling to accept defeat.

Quentin pointed behind her. 'Vincent's over there. Why don't you get your Papa to buy him some special glasses, so that he might finally find you as attractive as you think he is.' He shrugged. 'Or else, you could pray to Dieu for a miracle…'

Baptiste glared at Quentin. *Quit it.*

Brigitte pulled on her towel and spun around. Her mask had slipped, the hurt on her face clearly visible.

Baptiste sighed. 'I'm going for a swim,' he grumbled. 'Cos, after all, that's the real reason we're here.' He moved towards the pool, waving at Vincent.

quatre

Baptiste threw himself over the brick wall, dropping onto his haunches. Vincent gawped, clearly startled by his friend.

'You skipped class,' Baptiste said. 'And that's not good for me. It was English, and it might as well of been Arabic for all the sense it makes.'

Vincent smiled sadly at him. 'Sorry, Baptiste.' He glanced at the cell phone he was cradling in his hands. 'I was talking to Maman.'

'Ah,' Baptiste nodded. He could think of nothing else to say.

'Your folks are dead, aren't they?' Vincent asked softly.

Baptiste closed his eyes, a barrage of images immediately flashing in front of him. A woman with hair the colour of sand, a man with soft lines which creased his eyes when he smiled. It was all he remembered of the couple who had created him. 'My parents died when I was a kid. My grandfather raised me until...' he paused, before adding with a shrug, 'he didn't.'

Vincent nodded. 'But you got lucky in the end?'

Baptiste grinned. 'The first time I met Hugo Duchamp, I thought he was a pervert,' he laughed. 'It's true. What an asshole I was. I couldn't imagine an adult was being nice to me, trying to help me, and wanted nothing in return. But he didn't. He didn't want a thing, other than to help me. He and Ben have saved me and given me a life I never imagined possible. I don't know how that happened, but Dieu, I'm so happy it did.' He bit his lip. 'Désolé. I guess it's tough for you with your dad dying and all that...' He shrugged helplessly. 'Man, I don't know what to say. But I'm here. I'm not sure I'm much use at "talking" but if you need to, I can string together a few words. Ben and Hugo have taught me to do that. I'm not sure how good they are at it themselves, but we all seem to manage to communicate well on a regular basis.'

Vincent smiled with a sadness that hurt Baptiste. 'You're so lucky.'

Baptiste's eyes widened. 'Don't I know it.' He leaned closer to his friend. 'And what about you?'

Vincent turned his head. 'Did you ever wish you could just disappear?' he asked, changing the subject.

Baptiste snorted. His life had continued with a myriad of disappointments. The death of his parents, the indifference of his grandfathers, the cruelty of the teachers who were supposed to look after him. The breaking of a heart. He could still see her beautiful face. Chen Gao. He wished he could not. He had tried to erase her, but it had not been as easy as tearing up her photographs and throwing them in the trash. She was still there when he closed his eyes. He wanted to forget her as much as he did not.

'Life is shit sometimes, Vincent,' he offered. 'And I was the king of wanting to disappear. But take it from someone who knows. It can get better. It *does* get better.'

'You think?' Vincent asked doubtfully.

'I know, for certain,' Baptiste said. 'Your life can't be so bad, can it?'

Vincent shrugged. 'Sometimes it feels okay, and then other times...'

'You miss your father, I get it,' Baptiste said.

'I don't just miss him,' Vincent cried. 'I MISS him.' He stabbed his finger against his heart. 'I miss him dragging me out of bed every morning at five o'clock to go fishing for mussels. I miss yelling at him when I could be bothered, or just pouting at him when I couldn't. I just miss... I just miss it all.'

'Je suis désolé,' Baptiste sighed. 'I live with two gay dudes. If you asked me if I would want to do that three years ago, I'd tell you, you were crazy. But I live in this crazy house, with a cop who is always solving murders and a nurse who is always saving lives, and from the second we wake up, we're all thinking about getting through our day just so we can get back together in the evening, having food and booze and fun, and then starting again the next day. It's the most ridiculously best feeling in the world. I love my life. I *love* it. It's that simple. I never imagined it would happen to me.' He reached over and touched Vincent's arm. 'All I'm saying is things will get better for you as they did for me.'

Vincent threw off Baptiste's hand and jumped to his feet. 'Non, it won't!' he screamed. 'They killed my father and nobody cares. But I care. I fucking care!'

Baptiste's face creased in confusion as he watched his friend disappear into the distance.

cinq

Vincent threw his cell phone to the ground with such force it bounced across the cobbles and smashed into several pieces. Baptiste stepped out of the doorway and moved quickly towards his friend.

'What's going on?' he asked.

Vincent stared at what remained of his phone. 'It's never going to be solved,' he whispered.

'What isn't?' Baptiste asked in apparent confusion.

'My father's death. The police don't care. All they say is, *case closed*,' Vincent spat. 'The police are lazy pigs! And even worse, they're liars and only interested in taking bribes!'

Baptiste stepped into the sunlight, moving next to Vincent. 'That's not true. Not all of them, at least. Hugo is one of the best, most decent people I know. He's not lazy, and he's not dishonest.'

Vincent pivoted until he faced Baptiste directly. 'Is that true?' he asked.

'Is what true?'

'Is your Papa as good as you say he is?'

Baptiste nodded proudly. 'I'd bet my life on it,' he said, before adding, 'not that I'd need to.'

Vincent pursed his lips. 'You mean that?'

Baptiste frowned. 'I'm not sure what you're asking me, Vincent?'

Vincent shook his head irritably. 'Are you convinced Hugo is a good man? That he would solve a crime no matter what?'

Baptiste nodded. 'Sure. No matter what. He's done it before.'

Vincent turned his head. Minutes passed before Vincent turned back to Baptiste. 'You've been a good friend to me, Baptiste,' he stated.

Baptiste shrugged. 'So have you.' He turned his eyes. He had never really had any friends, nor known how to make them. His early teenage years had been spent with much older boys who were only interested in girls and the trouble they could get into. It had suited Baptiste at the time because he had known no different and it had been an escape from the tragedy of his life. But it had cost him dearly.

Ripped away from everything he had known and thrown into a school for troubled teenagers. It was there he had met the love of his life. A girl he thought he would love forever. It was not lost on him that even though she was now gone and belonged to another, he believed he would still love her forever.

Everything had changed the day Hugo and Ben had come into his life, and he had finally imagined a life ahead of him worth living. He had a family and a future career, and with school and the swim team, he could see a very different life. He looked at Vincent. They had become good friends, but Baptiste could sense the melancholy in Vincent because it was a mirror image to the one which had once threatened to consume Baptiste himself.

'I don't know exactly what is going on,' Baptiste stated softly. 'But you have to know I'm here whenever you want to talk, if that's what you want.'

Vincent moved across the path and picked up the remnants of his cell phone. 'Do you ever wish you could just disappear?'

Baptiste shrugged. 'Not really, not anymore at least.'

Vincent looked over Baptist's shoulder, his eyes widening as if he spotted someone. 'I have to go,' he blurted.

'Is there anything I can do?' Baptiste asked.

Vincent stared at him. 'You have no idea,' he whispered. 'Au revoir, mon ami.'

Baptiste frowned again. 'Au revoir, Vincent. I'll see you at class tomorrow.'

Vincent took a deep breath. 'À demain,' he exhaled, as if his life depended on it.

six

Hugo awoke with a start. He had become accustomed to lying in bed in an almost upright position, as if he needed to be ready to jump into action when his cell phone began vibrating on the nightstand. It appeared Ben had become accustomed to it as well, lying next to Hugo, his arms wrapped across his chest.

'Your phone,' Ben mumbled incoherently.

Hugo shook his head, blond hair falling over his face. He lifted his hand and brushed it away. 'What about it?' he muttered.

Ben stabbed his finger towards the bedside table. 'It's there… noisy… making a noise… bothering us…' he groaned.

Hugo reached over and snatched the cell phone. 'Allô?'

'Ah, Captain Duchamp. C'est Lieutenant Garrel.'

'What is it, Markus?' Hugo retorted. Markus Garrel was one of the two Lieutenants who worked with him at Montgenoux Police Nationale. A young, often impetuous officer, he was nevertheless loyal and keen. Hugo liked him immensely and imagined he would one day become a very effective investigator once he was able to curb his natural exuberance. He pulled his legs from the bed, knowing there would be only one reason why Markus would call in the middle of the night.

'You'd better get down to Les Grandes Écoles,' Markus said.

'There's been a murder?' Hugo asked, the hairs rising on the back of his neck.

Markus did not answer immediately. 'Well, yeah, maybe…'

Hugo frowned. 'What do you mean, maybe? Is it a murder, or not?' he demanded.

Markus took a deep breath. 'You really need to see it for yourself, Captain, and then maybe you can tell me.'

Hugo nodded. 'I'm on my way.' He disconnected the call, glancing over his shoulder towards a dazed Ben. 'Ben. I have to go. Check on Baptiste and make sure he's okay. But don't wake him if you can help it. I'll call you as soon as I know what's going on.'

Ben dropped out of the bed, shaking the sleep from his head. 'D'accord. Je t'aime,' he said robotically.

Hugo climbed out of his car, a beaten-up old Citroën he was fairly sure he had no business still driving because it was most probably dangerous. He stretched, pressing his hand into the crook of his back in the same way he always had to when he alighted the vehicle. He sucked happily on the remainder of his cigarette, casting his gaze towards Les Grandes Écoles. It had only been a matter of days since he had been there, proudly watching his son competing in a swimming competition, and it bothered him immensely that he was back again for something which he was sure was going to be quite horrible. His cell phone beeped, and he yanked it from his pocket. He flicked on his glasses to read the message.

Baptiste is fine. Snoring like a baby. Won't wake him. But I'm now WIDE awake, so there's no point in trying to sleep before my shift. Alors, I am here waiting for you. Text or call when you can. Tu me manques. BX.

He smiled, placing the cell phone back in his pocket. It was the ammunition he needed, a shot of adrenalin in his arm to propel him towards what lay ahead of him. He ambled slowly, his eyes flicking to the left and to the right, above him and below him. He knew it was important to gauge a first impression. There would be photographs and video evidence later, no doubt, but this moment, the first moments, were crucial. There were images he would forget, smells which would dissipate, but he had learned enough over the years to know they would return, and they would return when least expected and often with little notice or explanation. It was his one and only chance to survey a crime scene while it was still that. In a matter of minutes, it would be swarming with people intent on understanding what had taken place, being careful not to disturb anything, but the fact remained. The more people who moved among the shadows of a crime scene, the less easy it became able to see what lay beneath.

He stopped. The door to the swimming pool was open, and he could already see the illumination of crime scene lamps glaring at him. They hurt his eyes, but he understood their importance. Like his first impressions, they were there to catch everything his eyes, and the eyes of the forensic team, could not. He took a tentative step towards the door, his fingers touching the cell phone against his thigh, reminded of the message. *Baptiste is fine.* It did not make him feel proud, but he could not deny that he was filled with a sense of grace knowing that whatever he would face walking through the door, it would not be Baptiste.

Hugo stepped over the threshold. There was something about the way in which Lieutenant Garrel was standing, his hands on his hips, staring directly into the pool. His eyes were wide as he shook his head. 'I've seen nothing like this before,' Markus whispered.

Hugo took a tentative step forward. He stopped dead.

'Yeah,' Markus smiled. As usual, his keenness at a fresh crime scene was clear. Hugo found himself admiring his reticence because all Hugo saw was a human tragedy at its worst. 'Etienne and the doc are on their way. We're going to need them, aren't we?' Markus added, clapping his hands together.

sept

Etienne Martine's eyes widened. He turned his head several times, seemingly unable to take in what he was seeing. 'Have you ever seen anything like this before, Hugo?' he asked.

Hugo was staring into the swimming pool, as he had been for the entire fifteen minutes it had taken Etienne and the forensic team to arrive. He was still having trouble processing it. 'Non, jamais,' he answered.

Etienne lowered himself onto his haunches. As usual, the forensic expert who worked with Hugo was dressed in his "uniform" of wide board shorts and flip-flops. His thinning hair was standing on end, ruffled by being roused from a heavy sleep. He stood up, moving around the pool, snapping photographs with his camera. He looked at Hugo, pointing at his shorts. 'You want me to go in? I'm practically already dressed for it.'

Hugo shook his head. 'Non, not yet at least,' he responded. 'We'd better wait for the doctor to get here.'

Upon hearing the word, *doctor*, Etienne visibly winced. It was no secret Etienne had been involved with Dr. Irene Chapeau, Montgenoux's pathologist, but after a series of personal setbacks, Irene had taken extended leave from her position and was travelling with her infant son. She had sent Hugo and Ben regular postcards, but he was unsure if she was doing the same for Etienne. Whilst he considered Etienne a friend, Hugo had long since accepted he was not the sort of man prone to sitting down and sharing emotions with others. At that moment, he felt bad because he was sure whatever was happening between Irene and Etienne, it must have hurt Etienne that Irene had chosen to go without him.

'Ah, so what do we have here?' a voice called out from the doorway. Dr. Viellen stepped into the auditorium. He was an elderly, well respected physician, tall and thin, with pinched features and fair, thinning hair most often shoved under a forensic skull cap.

He had taken over Dr. Chapeau's duties in her absence, and although Hugo liked him, it was not the same as working with Irene, who had become one of Hugo's few friends.

Dr. Viellen stopped in front of the swimming pool, tipping his body into a bow. 'Well, I've seen a lot in my seventy-two years on this planet,' he announced, 'but it still finds ways to surprise me.' He looked at Hugo. 'I do hope you're not expecting me to get in the pool, Captain Duchamp, are you?'

Hugo sent him a tired smile. 'We were waiting for you…'

The doctor lifted his cane, pointing it into the pool. 'Well, I think it's safe to say that we are looking at a deceased person.' He shook his head. 'The strangest thing.'

Hugo turned to Etienne. 'Etienne, can you make sure this is video recorded before we dismantle it all?'

Etienne nodded, moving to his bag and extracting a video camera. He pointed it towards the pool.

'Markus,' Hugo said. 'Can you describe the crime scene as Etienne records it?'

Markus nodded. 'We are at the swimming pool in Les Grandes Écoles Montgenoux,' he began. He glanced at his watch. 'At approximately 12H05 on the morning of March 11th, the night cleaner was finishing her rounds. She entered the swimming pool auditorium via the communal changing rooms. She reports there being no one around, but she noticed a red item, probably a towel, on the ground in the far left corner of the auditorium. She walked around the pool to retrieve the towel. With only the nightlights on, it was only when she turned to face the left side of the pool that the moonlight illuminated the area and she saw what was in the pool for the first time. The witness reports moving slowly across the tiles because at that stage, she imagined it was some kind of student prank and that they had left a dummy in the pool.'

Dr. Viellen peered into the pool. 'Let's hope it is. I'd rather be called from my bed for a prank than the alternative that this is real.'

Hugo flicked on his glasses, agreeing with the doctor. He could see how the cleaner could have imagined it was some kind of elaborate, sick prank. He narrowed his eyes, sadness enveloping him when he realised they were most certainly looking at an actual crime scene. At the bottom of the pool was a large metal desk, and attached to one drawer by a handcuff was a young man, his lifeless body sitting on a chair, his legs under the desk. From his viewpoint, all Hugo could see was the young man was wearing a tracksuit and had a very short haircut. He could not see the victim's face as his head was forward, pointing down at the desk.

'After a minute, the cleaner called for the janitor,' Markus continued. 'And between them, they called the police. I, Lieutenant Markus Garrel, officer in charge of the night shift, attended the scene, arriving at 12H48. As the body had been in the water for at least an hour by then, I decided not to disturb the scene and await backup.'

Hugo nodded. 'Do we have any idea where the desk came from?' he asked Markus.

'Oui,' Markus replied. 'While I was waiting for the rest of you to arrive, I had a look around.' He gestured for Etienne to follow him. 'If you look over to the right side of the pool, you can see there are drag marks on the tiles as if something heavy and dirty has been dragged. I followed the scuff marks into this anteroom to the back of the auditorium. The sign on the door says it's the office of the swim coach.' He led Hugo and the others into a small, cramped office. 'Et, ta-da!' Markus cried triumphantly.

Etienne focused the camera on the corner of the room, where there was a gap the size of a desk, with four small marks in the carpet.

Hugo followed the scuff marks, moving back into the auditorium. 'So, someone dragged the desk and threw it into the pool. And then what? Dragged a body into the pool and handcuffed it to the desk?'

'We don't know if we're looking at a murder here, Captain Duchamp,' Dr. Viellen said.

Markus scoffed. 'Well, he didn't handcuff himself to a desk at the bottom of a swimming pool, did he?'

Dr. Viellen shrugged. 'I don't know that for certain, and nor do you, Lieutenant. This could all be an elaborate suicide.'

'I don't buy it,' Markus shot back.

The doctor turned away from the young Lieutenant as if he could not care less about his opinion. 'Captain, I'll supervise the removal of the body, but if it's all the same with you, I'll go home and get a few hours sleep and we can schedule the autopsy for later this morning. Is that agreeable?'

Hugo nodded. 'C'est bien, Dr. Viellen, merci.'

The doctor smiled and moved towards the entrance to the auditorium. 'I'll just go and wait for my team.'

'What do you want me to do, Hugo?' Etienne asked.

'Keep filming the removal of the body and the desk. I'd like you to go over the chair and desk and also the coach's office.'

'Bien sûr,' he replied.

Hugo stepped back to the pool, tapping his chin as he considered. He reached into his pocket and extracted a cigarette. He knew it was a habit he should break, but he had found over time that it was something ingrained in him, something which he would always have trouble moving away from. He reasoned it helped him think, and to concentrate on what lay ahead of him, but he supposed he was just making an excuse. He sucked on the cigarette as if his life depended on it. His eyes flicked slowly and carefully around the auditorium and pool itself. He knew he would have the video to look back on, but at that moment, he wanted to be sure to take it all in with his own eyes.

'Wait,' he blurted. 'What happened to the red towel?'

Markus appeared by his side. 'What red towel?'

'You said the cleaner spotted what she thought was a red towel, and that's what made her walk around the pool,' Hugo replied. He pointed in front of him. 'There doesn't appear to be anything lying around the pool, a towel or otherwise.'

Markus bit his lips as if chastising himself for missing it. 'I don't know,' he mumbled. 'Maybe she picked it up.'

'Peut être,' Hugo whispered. 'Where is she now?' he asked.

'I put her and the janitor in the staff room until we could take their statements. I left a Gendarme with them,' Markus replied.

'Bon,' Hugo said. 'Let's go and talk, but first, let's have a look around and make sure the red towel isn't around here somewhere.'

huit

Hugo looked at the cleaner and instantly recognised the expression on her face. It was the face of a woman who would be forever haunted by something she had seen. The janitor, an elderly man with a kind, lined face and a mess of white hair, was sitting next to her, his hand placed protectively over her shoulder.

'Bonjour Madame, Monsieur. I am Captain Hugo Duchamp,' Hugo began. 'I am very sorry for what you have gone through this morning.' He pointed at Markus. 'Lieutenant Garrel will shortly take your formal statements and then you will be free to go home.'

'I can't leave my post,' the janitor interjected, panicked. 'Not until the day janitor arrives at least.'

Hugo shook his head. 'Non, you can go home. I'll clear it with your employer if I need to, but in any event, the forensic team and the Gendarmes will be here all night.'

The janitor nodded, seemingly reassured.

'I just wanted to ask you both a few questions before you make your statements,' Hugo began.

The cleaner slowly lifted her head. 'Who is he? Who is the poor boy?'

'I'm afraid we don't know yet,' Hugo said. 'We're just about to move him and take him to the hospital. We'll begin the process of identifying him then.' He paused. 'When you spoke to Lieutenant Garrel, you mentioned there was something on the ground near to the pool.'

She nodded. 'A red towel.'

'Oui,' Hugo continued. 'What did you do with it?'

She frowned. 'What do you mean?'

'What happened to the red towel?'

'I don't know,' she answered. 'I didn't get that far before I… before I…'

Hugo turned to the janitor. 'Did you remove it?' he asked.

He shook his head. 'I never saw it.'

Hugo exchanged a look with Markus. *Then where is it, and is it important?*

'Are you sure you saw a red towel?' Markus demanded of the cleaner.

'Absolutely,' she said decisively. 'That's why I walked around the pool to pick it up.'

Hugo smiled gratefully at her. 'Did either of you see anyone around the school this evening?'

The janitor lowered his head, seemingly embarrassed. 'I was in my office. I do my rounds on the hour, every hour, regular as clockwork. It takes me approximately fifteen minutes to complete a full circuit. Other than that, I watch the television in my office.'

'And you have CCTV?' Markus asked.

'On the front and back entrance to the school. I have screens in my office,' the janitor answered.

Hugo nodded. 'And you saw no one come or go yesterday evening?'

'No one at all,' the janitor said quickly.

Apart from the possibility, someone could enter unseen during your rounds, Hugo thought.

'And is the school alarmed?'

He shook his head. 'Not until after the cleaner has gone. She comes to me; I escort her to her car and then I secure the building and turn the alarm on,' he answered. 'It's the way it's always been done.'

'And you saw nothing either, Madame?' Hugo asked.

'Non,' she breathed.

'There is one thing,' the janitor said cautiously. 'Afterwards, I looked around. I didn't understand how… how the boy found himself in the auditorium. I know he didn't walk in through the front door, nor the back door, so I checked the other exits. The auditorium has its own exit.'

Hugo frowned. 'And it's not covered by a camera?'

'Non, but there's no need,' he answered. 'You see, it's a fire exit. There is no lock as such, just a bar that you push to open. Therefore, it can't be opened from the outside. However, when I went to check on it a short while ago, the bar was down, and there was a brick outside. I don't know what it means, mais…' he trailed off and shrugged.

'How does the door work?' Hugo asked.

'You push the bar down to open the double doors,' the janitor answered. 'And to lock it, you pull it up until it clicks back into place.'

'So it wasn't locked in place?' Hugo pressed.

The janitor nodded.

'And that's why there was a brick outside, holding the door, so it didn't blow open,' Markus added.

'Someone may have left it unlocked after they left the auditorium so they could sneak back in later,' Hugo added. 'We'll ask Etienne to dust for prints.' He pursed his lips. 'Is it normal for the door to remain unlocked?' he asked the janitor.

He shook his head. 'Non, mais…' he trailed off.

'You don't always check it?'

'Non,' he answered quickly. 'There's no need, really. As I said, there is no handle on the outside and there's never been a problem before.' He shook his head in dismay. 'I'm in trouble, aren't I?'

Hugo did not answer. 'And what time did you last check the pool and the auditorium?' he asked.

'At 23H00,' he replied. 'I hadn't yet made my way to the pool during my midnight patrol.'

'Hmm,' Hugo considered. 'Then the pool would have been clear and empty for an hour.' He looked at the cleaner. 'You always clean the pool area at midnight, Madame?'

'More or less,' she replied. 'It's the last job. Often the pool is used until nine, or ten, sometimes later, so I always clean it last.'

Hugo continued making notes on his pad. 'Merci, Madame et Monsieur. The Lieutenant will take your statements and then we'll make sure you both get home. We'll be in touch if there's anything else.'

The cleaner nodded. She was clearly on the verge of tears. Hugo moved forward and reached out, gently touching her arm. 'Madame, I know your distress may feel insurmountable at this moment,' he said gently. 'And I can't say it will disappear completely, but it will fade. You may not forget what happened tonight, but what you have experienced will become easier to bear. Please believe me.'

She smiled gratefully at him, tears falling down her cheeks. 'That poor boy,' she sobbed.

neuf

'I'm afraid, I don't have an identification for you yet,' Dr. Viellen said.

Hugo moved to the head of the gurney. He shook his head in disbelief. 'You don't need to. I know who he is,' he said, his voice cracking.

Juge Renaud Deshors moved swiftly across the morgue floor. 'You do?' he questioned. His voice was deep and smooth. He touched his head, fingers pressing against meticulously cut and styled salt and pepper hair. Hugo had been working with him since his arrival in Montgenoux and though they locked horns occasionally, they had also formed a relationship based on mutual respect.

Hugo nodded. It broke his heart to see the young man lying on the gurney. He wanted to reach over and touch his hand, but he did not dare. It was not because he was afraid of tampering with evidence, as he could tell he had already been washed and prepared ready for autopsy, but rather because he felt as if it would make it even more real.

'Oui. I had supper with him two evenings ago at *Arienne's*,' Hugo exhaled. 'His name is Vincent Roche. He is a student at the school and is on the swim team with Baptiste.'

'Are you are positive it is him?' Renaud asked.

'I'm afraid so,' Hugo answered.

'Tres bien,' Dr. Viellen added. 'Mais, I'll still need a formal identification. His prints aren't in the system, according to your colleague Monsieur Martine. Can you find his next of kin?'

Hugo turned away from Vincent's body. 'If I recall correctly, he's not local. However, the school should have his details, I'm waiting to hear from them.'

Dr. Viellen nodded. 'Shall we proceed with the autopsy?'

'Oui,' Hugo agreed, wondering how on earth he was going to

break the news to Baptiste. At least it was Saturday morning, and there was every chance he was still sleeping.

Dr. Viellen's hand moved slowly and decisively as he sowed up the Y-incision on Vincent Roche's body. Hugo shuffled uncomfortably in his seat. He wanted to retch; he wanted to run into a field to get the stench of death from his nostrils. He also desperately wanted a cigarette, but he knew it was strictly forbidden in the morgue. He looked at the rows of jars and trays lining the table, all containing various parts of what had once been Vincent Roche's internal organs.

Juge Deshors glanced discreetly at his watch. 'What are your conclusions, Dr. Viellen?'

Dr. Viellen sighed. 'I will send the blood and other samples to the lab as that might provide an insight into what lead to this poor young man's demise.' He looked at Vincent's remains. 'All I can really tell you at this stage is that death was most certainly by drowning.'

'Then he died in the swimming pool?' Hugo questioned.

'Oui,' the doctor replied. 'The water in his lungs is chlorinated. We can ask the lab to compare it with a sample from the swimming pool, mais it's most likely where he died.' He turned to Ben, who had been assisting with the autopsy. 'Nurse Beaupain, can you load the photographs on the shiny screens?' the elderly doctor asked, pointing at the bank of monitors behind him.

Ben smiled, nodding as he clicked several buttons on the computer in the corner of the room. Moments later, the screens were filled with a line of photographs. Dr. Viellen moved to the first. He retrieved a pen from his pocket and pointed at it.

'As you can see here, on the first slide,' he began. 'There is an extensive amount of froth present around the deceased's nostrils and mouth. The second slide shows it was also present in the upper and lower airways. The third is of the lungs, note the marbled appearance.' He moved his pen. 'The dark red areas are linked with collapsed alveoli. Most importantly, the lungs weigh significantly more than normal, most certainly because of the water inhalation.'

Juge Deshors sighed. 'So, he drowned. The question is. How and why?'

'I'm afraid I can't answer that, in any great detail at least,' Dr. Viellen conceded.

Renaud turned to Hugo. 'Did he, or did he not tie himself to the desk?'

Hugo shrugged. 'Etienne and the team from Nantes found, quite literally, hundreds of fingerprints and footprints in the auditorium. It would take an age to try and make sense of it, even if it was possible, I'm not sure what they would tell us.' He moved across the morgue, stepping backwards and forwards between the images on the screens. He pointed to one of them. 'What are these abrasions on his forehead?'

Dr. Viellen moved next to him. 'Ah, now those abrasions tell a story too.'

'They do?' Renaud interacted. 'Quoi?'

'Because I believe our young man banged his head repeatedly on the desk as he struggled.'

'To free himself?' Hugo asked.

'Or because he changed his mind,' Dr. Viellen reasoned. 'If this was a suicide, there is a likelihood he changed his mind and tried to free himself. I've seen it more times than I care to remember.'

Renaud nodded slowly. He turned to Hugo. 'What do you think?'

Hugo did not answer immediately. After a few moments, he exhaled. 'There isn't a lot to go on, for either suggesting a murder or a suicide.' He paused. 'Mais, there is something very troubling about this.'

Renaud snorted. 'There is always something troubling in our line of work, Captain. And more often than not, it makes no sense.'

Hugo continued staring at the screens. 'There's nothing here to suggest murder as such, but I've never seen a suicide so… *elaborate.*'

'Then you think it's murder?' the Juge posed.

Hugo shrugged. 'I'm not saying that.' He pointed at the original photograph of Vincent when he was still in the pool. 'Mais, if Vincent killed himself, he arranged it very, very carefully, and that tells us a lot.'

'It does?' Dr. Viellen asked, surprised.

Hugo's mouth twisted into a grimace. 'I believe so, I can't say what at this moment, but I just can't imagine this wasn't a message of some kind.'

Ben appeared by Hugo's side, gently touching his arm. 'Speaking of messages,' he said, pointing at the cell phone in his hand.

Hugo narrowed his eyes.

Hey Papa. Are we having lunch? I can't remember. I have to get to the pool by 14H00 for practice. Let me know. I'm jumping in the shower right now. Bx

Hugo looked at Ben. 'Désole, Juge Deshors, Dr. Viellen,' he said. 'We have to take care of something.'

Juge Deshors nodded. 'I have to get to a meeting as well.'

Dr. Viellen moved across the morgue. 'I'll make sure these samples get to the lab.'

Hugo nodded. 'I'll chase up the school, so we inform his next of kin.' He turned to Dr. Viellen. 'Can you send me a photograph I can show them?'

'Bien sûr, I'll email it to you right away.'

'Merci.' Hugo slipped his hand into Ben's. Together, they moved in front of Vincent's body. 'In the meantime, we need to tell le bateau au fond de l'océan

Baptiste, before someone else does,' Hugo whispered.

dix

Baptiste retched, throwing back his head. Ben leapt across the room and pulled a bin from the corner, tipping out its contents as he ran back to his son, just in time to catch the trail of vomit.

'That was quick,' Hugo whispered.

Ben's eyes flashed. 'Breaking bad news is an occupational hazard, so catching the results is a reflex.'

Baptiste wiped his mouth with the back of his hand. 'He's really dead?' he looked imploringly at Hugo.

The desperation in Baptiste's eyes broke Hugo's heart. 'We still need formal identification,' Hugo replied, 'mais, oui, I'm afraid there is little doubt. Je suis désolé mon fils, vraiment.'

Baptiste reached across the sofa and touched his hand. 'Merci, Papa.'

'I'll get you some water, and a napkin,' Ben said, moving back to the kitchen. He returned momentarily, gently dabbing Baptiste's mouth.

Baptiste looked at him, wide-eyed. 'Is that normal? To throw up?'

Ben shrugged. 'There's nothing normal about grief, Baptiste. Mais, it's not unusual to react like that. He was your friend, and it's only natural you're going to be upset by his death.'

Baptiste nodded, gulping the water. 'I don't deserve to be upset,' he spat back at Ben. 'I'd only known him for a few months, and that was only really through swim club.'

Hugo touched his arm. 'But you WERE friends. We could all see that, especially the other night at Arienne's.' He exhaled. 'Take it from someone who knows, friendship can't be measured just by time, but my moments shared. If we're lucky, moments shared can last for a long time, just because sometimes they don't, doesn't detract from their importance. You could have known Vincent for a week, or for four decades, but if you impacted each other's lives, you will feel the loss, and the length of time you knew one another can't take away from that.' He took a breath. 'The length of time makes it harder, but loss is never easy.'

Baptiste stood, moving across the living room, past the dining table. He pushed open the patio doors, gulping at the fresh air. 'This is my fault,' he shouted into the air.

Hugo took a step forward. 'What do you mean?'

'How could it be your fault?' Ben asked.

'Because he told me, in one way or another, how unhappy he was. How desperate he was,' Baptiste cried. 'And I, being the stupid asshole I am, didn't know what to do about it, and the truth is, I probably didn't even take him seriously. Mais, if I had then...'

Hugo pulled the young man into an embrace. As unusual as it felt for him to engage in such intimacy, it also felt in that moment as if it was the most natural thing in the world. 'Don't go through that door,' he whispered into Baptiste's ear. 'It won't help, but more importantly, it's not true.'

Baptiste turned, kissing Hugo on the cheek. 'Merci, Papa. Je t'aime.'

Hugo kissed him back. 'Moi, aussi.'

Baptiste stared at Hugo. 'I know you need to ask me questions about him, but can it wait? Can I go for a run? I just need to feel the wind in my face and,' he stopped, 'I want to be able to cry on my own for a while. D'accord?'

Hugo nodded. 'We'll be here when you need us.'

Baptiste took a breath and then exhaled. It seemed to last for a long time. 'You always are.'

onze

Hugo stared numbly at the clock on the crowded mantelpiece. It was filled with photographs and keepsakes the three of them had amassed during their time together. Hugo could see there was a thin layer of dust, and it surprised him that it did not bother him. He had lived a staid existence in a white, clean apartment in London where the dust never had a chance to settle.

He supposed his need for cleanliness and lack of clutter had derived from his childhood. Hugo smiled, reminded again of the woman who had taken him in following his parent's divorce - his grandmother, Madeline Duchamp. While she was often a cold, abrasive woman, Hugo had always felt safe with her. She was not demonstrative, nor affectionate in any way, but somehow, underneath all the Chanel, she made him feel loved. Her death had devastated him, but he had, as per strict instructions on her deathbed, not shown it.

And now, all he had of her was a small portrait in a gilded silver frame. It took pride of place in the centre of his mantelpiece and was the only thing that remained of his London home. Her lips were pulled into a regal smile. It was not a smile of happiness, rather one of veiled tolerance. She had tried to teach him love, but it had never been enough. Before coming to Montgenoux, Hugo's love affairs were rare and often doomed to fail before they had even begun.

'You're watching the clock,' Ben whispered, appearing by Hugo's side. 'You need to get to the station, don't you?'

Hugo started, brought back from the memories of his past. Hugo shook his head. 'All I need to do is to be here, with you and Baptiste.'

Ben kissed Hugo's cheek, running his hand across his chin. Hugo closed his eyes, the memory of why Ben's fingers were scarred appearing before him. They had come close to losing each other on more than one occasion, and it still haunted Hugo.

'Baptiste could be gone for a while,' Ben said.

'It doesn't matter,' Hugo said. 'I want to be here for him. Markus and Marianne know what they're doing, they can hold the fort for a while.'

Baptiste appeared in the doorway. He was sweating, his face red and his eyes swollen from crying. 'I'll have a shower and then we can talk, okay?' he said.

Hugo nodded. 'Take as long as you need. We're not going anywhere.'

Baptiste sipped a beer, staring straight at Hugo. 'Do you really think Vincent killed himself?'

Hugo considered his answer. 'I don't know how to answer that, Baptiste,' he stated, 'not yet, at least. It's too early to say for certain. We didn't find a note, but nor did we find anything pointing towards foul play. All we know is he drowned.'

'Tied to a desk at the bottom of the pool?' Baptiste cried. 'What kind of fucked up shit is that?'

'I've seen staged murders before,' Hugo added cautiously. 'Mais, we just can't say at the moment. What can you tell me about Vincent?'

Baptiste shrugged. 'Not a lot. As I said, we were buddies, but not for long. We shared beers, a few laughs, talked about girls, that sort of thing.'

'Then he was happy?' Ben asked.

Baptiste stared into the garden, his eyes straining to see the corner of their swimming pool. 'I don't think I'll be able to get into the pool at school again. Not after... not after...' He took another gulp of the beer. 'Happy?' he considered his response. 'This isn't my speciality, but if I had to describe it, I'd say Vincent's moods were a bit up and down.'

'Up and down?' Hugo repeated.

'Oui,' Baptiste replied. 'Happy one minute, down the next. It was a bit annoying, if I'm honest. Dieu, doesn't that make me sound awful?'

Ben shook his head. 'Non, of course, it doesn't.'

'What sort of things were troubling him?' Hugo asked.

'Stuff from home,' Baptiste replied. He pressed his fingers against his skull. 'I can't remember half of what he said. But I do remember his father died, and he thought there was something off about it.'

'Off?' Hugo questioned, his voice rising sharply.

'He asked me twice yesterday if I ever wished I could just disappear. I thought it was an odd thing to say, but just put it down to him feeling sad about his Papa. But then yesterday, I think he'd been talking on the phone with his mother. And he was really angry, kept saying things like the case was closed, and the police were useless.' He looked at Hugo. 'He asked me if you were a good flic and I said yeah.' He shook his head irritably. 'I knew something was off with him, I truly did, but I just never imagined this…'

Ben put his arm around Baptiste's shoulders. 'You couldn't have known this was going to happen.'

Baptiste shook his head. 'I could. In some ways, I did. He'd been skipping classes more and more, wanting to be on his own. As I said, he was up and down but that phone call, whatever news he got, it's as if it just tipped him over the edge.'

Hugo said nothing because he could think of nothing positive to say.

'But why did he do it that like that? It was an awful way to go.' He stared desperately at Hugo. 'It must mean something. The handcuffs, the desk. Don't you think?'

Hugo exhaled. 'If he took his own life,' he began slowly, 'then it is likely how he did it meant something to him, mais Baptiste, we, you, have to prepare yourself than unless he left or a message of some kind, we may never know his reasons. And his reasons could be because of the imbalance of his mind.' He sighed. 'What I'm trying to say, badly, is that we may never exactly know what happened to him and why. Sometimes, there are just no answers which make sense.'

Baptiste pivoted his head. 'But you won't give up, will you?' he asked desperately. 'I said you weren't the kind of flic to give up.'

Hugo smiled. 'I will do whatever I can, whatever it takes, to try and understand what happened to Vincent, I promise you that.'

'Have you checked your phone, Baptiste?' Ben asked. 'Did he leave you a message?'

Baptiste pulled out his cell phone. 'Nothing new.' He stood. 'I have to keep busy. I'm going to the Vineyard. We're short on grape pickers this year.'

'Are you sure?' Ben asked.

Baptiste nodded. 'I need to keep busy.'

'Would you like us to come with you?' Hugo asked.

Baptiste moved across the room and kissed Hugo on the cheek. 'Merci for asking, but non. I need to be on my own. Picking grapes with my headphones on will do me good for now. Besides. Don't you have to get to the station? All I need from you is to tell me what happened to Vincent, good or bad. D'accord?'

Hugo nodded, hoping he could do what was asked of him.

douze

Hugo closed his eyes, his head rolling back as he puffed contentedly on a cigarette. After a minute had passed, he opened his eyes again, staring at the computer screen. The call button was illuminated, and he knew that once he clicked it, it would only be a matter of moments before he was faced with someone whose life he was sure he was about to shatter.

He knew he should not postpone it a moment longer, for their sakes, not his own. But it always felt as if he should give them that one extra moment of peace before the world came tumbling down around them. A second is just a second, he reasoned, but it was his duty to make them aware of what they had lost. He was not sure if it was easier via a computer screen. There was certainly less awkwardness, but despite his own reticence for physical contact, he knew and understood that if it was needed; he was able to reach out and touch the arm of someone who might need some kind of reassurance.

At that moment, it was not possible. Etienne had retrieved Vincent Roche's records, and they confirmed he was from Beaufort-Sur-Mer, a small seaside town on the French Atlantic coast, about a hundred kilometres from Montgenoux. Hugo had contacted the local police and asked them to arrange for a face-to-face video call with Vincent's nearest relative - his mother. Hugo stubbed out his cigarette, reached forward and pressed the CALL button.

The video call seemed to take a very long time to connect, the entire time Hugo held his breath. Finally, the static of the screen cleared and Hugo was faced with three people, all staring expectantly at the screen.

'Bonjour,' he began. 'I am Captain Hugo Duchamp of Montgenoux Police Nationale.'

'Bonjour, Captain,' a man to the left of the screen said. 'We spoke earlier on the telephone. I am Captain Franc Comtois of the…' he smiled, 'well, I AM the Beaufort-Sur-Mer police. We don't have a lot of crime here in our little slice of heaven. We call on the big city a few miles down the road, if we need help. I haven't done that in a long time,' he added proudly.

Hugo nodded. He imagined Captain Comtois was in his early sixties, a tall, thin man with what appeared to be a nervous twitch, which meant his left eye moved involuntarily when he spoke.

Comtois pointed to his left. 'I am here with Madame Avril Roche and Monsieur Jasper Connor.'

Hugo frowned, unsure why the police captain had invited someone other than Vincent's mother.

'Bonjour, Captain,' Jasper Connor spoke. His voice was deep, and his face darkened by the sun. His hand moved slowly across a jet-black beard. 'I am here because I am a close, personal friend of the Roche family, and to support Avril through this tragic time.'

Avril Roche moved to the centre of the screen, staring into the camera with cold, dead eyes. Her hands were moving anxiously around a shell necklace, grey hair pinned to her head falling onto her face. She did not try to move it. 'Is it true? Is he really dead?'

Hugo sucked in a breath. 'I'm going to share a picture with you now, but I want you to prepare yourself for it,' he said. 'I'm afraid I need you to confirm whether or not this is a photograph of your son, Vincent Roche.' He took a breath. 'Are you ready to see the picture?' he asked.

Avril Roche nodded. 'Oui,' she whispered.

Hugo clicked send and a moment later, a photograph was displayed of Vincent lying in the morgue. Avril Roche screamed, falling backwards out of the chair she was sitting on, her upright legs filling the screen. Captain Comtois and Jasper Connor scrabbled to pull her to her feet.

Avril crawled back into the chair, her nose pressing against the screen. She touched it, her hand shaking as she did. 'Vincent,' she cried. 'Mon beau petit fils.'

'How did he die?' Jasper Connor asked.

'I'm afraid we're still early in the investigation,' Hugo answered.

'Did he kill himself?' Avril whispered.

'What makes you think that, Madame Roche?' Hugo asked.

'I spoke to him yesterday,' she answered slowly. 'And he was angry and upset. Deeply upset.'

Hugo tipped his head. 'About what?'

Captain Comtois and Jasper Connor exchanged an anxious look. Comtois coughed. 'Three months ago, Vincent's father, Arthur Roche, died in a tragic boating accident,' he stated.

A sob escaped Avril Roche's mouth. Her hand moved quickly to cover it. Hugo could see Jasper Connor placing his arm around her shoulders and pulling her to him.

'An accident?' Hugo questioned.

Comtois nodded. 'A tragic, tragic, unfortunate accident, mais,' he paused, his hands moving together in an exaggerated way, 'Vincent was devoted to his father, he never really came to terms with it.'

'He was at school, you see,' Jasper Connor added. 'And we thought it best he didn't know, in case it affected his studies.'

Avril turned to Jasper. 'We should have let him come to his father's funeral. If we had, then maybe he wouldn't....'

Jasper touched her hair. 'We can't think like that, cherie. Arthur and Vincent are dead, and as awful and difficult as that is, we have to move on.'

'Move on?' she questioned, wide-eyed.

He nodded. 'Move on,' he repeated. His tone was firm.

Avril turned back to the screen. 'When can I have my son back, Captain Duchamp?' she asked.

Hugo's fingers tapped against the cigarette packet, but he knew he could not smoke at that moment, no matter how much he needed to. 'I'm afraid, I can't answer that either, at this moment,' he replied. 'I can tell you that as soon as we are able, we will make sure your son comes back to you. In the meantime, we are looking after him.'

'Really?' she asked hopefully.

Hugo's lips twitched. 'We are.'

Captain Comtois moved in front of the camera again. 'I think I should take care of Madame Roche now, Captain Duchamp, if there is nothing else.'

'I understand,' Hugo said. 'I'll be in touch.'

Avril Roche smiled at him with the sad, grateful smile of a woman whose heart had just been broken.

treize

Etienne placed several folders on Hugo's desk. Hugo inhaled on his cigarette, eyeing the folders suspiciously. He imaged that whatever was contained within the pages would one way or another inform his next several days, if not longer.

'I'll give you the short version,' Etienne began. 'I have nothing. I can't find how Vincent Roche ended up at the bottom of the swimming pool. There are prints, *hundreds* of them, all around the auditorium, but that is to be expected. As for the table and the chair itself, the chlorinated water destroyed any evidence on them.'

'And the handcuffs?' Hugo asked.

Etienne shrugged. 'Nothing special, the sort you can buy online. They click into place, so there's no actual way of telling whether Vincent put them on himself or if someone else did.'

Hugo shook his head. 'I just don't understand it. He dragged a desk and chair into the pool. For what reason?'

'It's elaborate, I'll give you that,' Etienne replied. 'We both know if the balance of someone's mind is disturbed, they often do things which are hard to understand.'

Hugo gave a resigned nod. 'And what about the exit door?'

Etienne shrugged. 'Nothing but smudged prints. I might be able to extract a few partials, if I spend a bit of time on it, but as far as I can tell, nothing stands out. Someone likely wedged the door so it was almost shut, but not quite, so they could get back in. It's not inconceivable to imagine the poor kid did it himself, so that he could get back in and drown himself.'

'And the blood test?' Hugo asked.

'Rien,' Etienne answered. 'There was no drugs in his system, so I think we can rule out him being drugged or having taken drugs. There was, however, a lot of alcohol in his blood. Enough to push him well over the legal limit, but who knows if that means anything? It could have just been Dutch courage to go through with it.'

'Anything in the pool?' Hugo asked.

'Nope,' Etienne answered glumly. 'If there was, chlorine does a pretty good job of removing anything which might have been useful.'

'And the coach's office?'

'Same. Lots of prints, but nothing obvious. Marianne is busy taking statements. As far as we can tell, there was some kind of celebration that night in *Arienne's* after the event. The coach and half the staff from the school, and a fair few students were all there until well past midnight.' Etienne flopped into a chair. 'The CCTV footage from the school doesn't tell us anything either.'

Hugo stubbed out the cigarette and immediately lit another. 'Then what are we thinking? Vincent either never left the pool, or he left the door unlocked and came back later because he knew everyone was gone and he could be alone.'

'I admit the whole thing is weird,' Etienne retorted. 'But I'm not seeing anything here to suggest anything other than a suicide.'

'You're probably right,' Hugo conceded. 'Mais, I'd still like to try to understand why he did it in such a way.' He paused. 'And there's one other thing still bothering me.'

'You're talking about the red towel?'

Hugo nodded. 'I realise, it's not a lot to go on, mais as you know, I hate loose ends.'

Etienne smiled. 'That's what makes you so good at what you do.' He shrugged. 'I checked and double-checked. There was no red towel. There were plenty of towels in the changing rooms, but they were all clean and they're white with the school logo on them.'

Hugo sighed. 'And the cleaner didn't actually see it up close. She thought it was a red towel, but it could have been a red t-shirt, or jumper, or coat, or…'

'Or she made a mistake,' Etienne added glumly. 'Either way, we don't have a damn thing to go on.'

Lieutenant Marianne Laurent appeared in the doorway to Hugo's office. 'Excusez-moi, Captain,' she said. As usual, her face was serious, dark hair pulled into a tight ponytail. 'Vincent Roche's teammates are here to make their statement. Do you want to talk to them?'

Hugo rose to his feet. He knew he could leave it to the young, efficient Lieutenant but if he was to have to tell Baptiste there was no likelihood of understanding what had happened to his friend, Hugo wanted to make sure he had exhausted every avenue personally. 'Oui, I'll speak with them,' he said.

The first thing which struck Hugo was the stark difference between Vincent Roche's teammates. The young man was small, with a stubbed nose and cold, dark eyes. The young woman was much larger, with wide hips and wavy hair teased into an afro.

'Merci for coming into the station,' Hugo said. 'My name is Captain Hugo Duchamp. And you are?'

The young woman pushed herself forward, shoving the man out of the way. 'I'm Brigitte. Brigitte St. Pierre.'

'And I'm Quentin Arquette,' the young man called from behind her. His voice was dry and lighter than Brigitte's.

'I'm very sorry for the loss of your teammate,' Hugo said.

'Vincent was a cool kid,' Brigitte sighed. 'He had good vibes.'

'There are just the four of you on the swim team?'

Quentin shook his head. 'Nope. We have two other teammates, but they're on a different course to us. Their class is on a field trip to Germany, I think.'

'Since when?' Hugo asked.

'They left on Thursday after Wednesday's heat,' Brigitte answered.

Hugo scribbled a note on his pad to double-check. He knew it was unlikely to be relevant, but he had always been a great believer in three little words when it came to assessing whether something was relevant to an investigation and worth spending time looking into. *Just in case.*

'Did he really kill himself?' Quentin asked. He tipped his head. There was something about his tone which, while not quite malicious, was certainly cutting, Hugo imagined.

'At this stage, we're still trying to make sense of it all,' Hugo answered. 'Shortly Lieutenant Laurent will take your statements, but I just wanted to speak with you informally first. I want firstly to let you know we have resources available if you need someone to talk to. I know how difficult it can be to lose someone, no matter if they were a best friend, a family member or just a normal friend you saw from day to day. I have been a police officer for half of my life, and the only thing I can tell you with utmost certainty is that grief holds no prisoners, and is unexpected.' He took a deep breath. 'And asking for help, is never, *never* a bad thing.'

'I'm fine,' Quentin snipped. 'I hardly knew him, and we certainly weren't friends.'

Hugo assessed the young man. He was not sure it was true. He was chewing on his bottom lip. He turned his head to Brigitte. Her eyes were wide, but she was playing with her hair with the fingers of her left hand.

'As I said, the dude had good vibes,' Brigitte added. 'But he was only really into class, swimming, hanging out with his buddy Baptiste. He wasn't really interested in…' she trailed off, 'anything else.'

Hugo studied her face. The reality of life was clear on her face. Bravado. Pain. It did not really matter. He was dealing with young people, and their emotions were likely to be myriad and complicated. He was not sure if she was upset by the loss of a lover, or the loss of a potential lover, or someone she was entirely indifferent to.

'Is there anything you can tell me about the last few days?'

Hugo asked.

The two students exchanged a look, but neither answered.

'You want a minute by minute account?' Brigitte said with a smile. 'Because, if you do, it might get a little saucy,' she added with a wink.

'Not at all,' Hugo responded quickly, hoping his cheeks were not flushing. 'I'm just wondering if there is anything which stood out for you, anything unusual, par example.'

'Vincent didn't tell us he was going to kill himself, if that's what you mean,' Quentin replied. 'I didn't say, *hey, see you tomorrow, Vincent,* and he didn't shout back, *no you won't, I'll be dead at the bottom of the pool!*'

Hugo turned to Brigitte. There was something about Quentin's flippancy which irritated him, but he did not what him to see it. 'And you, mademoiselle?' he asked.

Brigitte shrugged. 'I guess he was sad. His father died, I think. But he was okay. He swam, he drank, he was funny when he felt like it. He didn't seem interested in girls,' she added. 'Not that I think he was gay.' She moved her hands. 'I don't know what else I can tell you.'

Hugo nodded. He gestured through the window for Marianne to join them. 'Merci for your time. Lieutenant Laurent will now take your statements.'

'Is that all?' Quentin asked, evidently surprised.

Hugo's eyebrows creased. 'Oui. Unless there's anything else you might like to add?'

Quentin pushed himself back in his chair. 'Non, rien.'

Hugo stared at him, unsure if he was telling the truth. 'Bon,' he said after a moment. 'Merci, for your time. And again, I am sorry for the loss of your friend.'

quatorze

Maître Alberte M Piscar smiled cheerfully. 'Hugo, Ben - it has been a long time.'

Hugo looked anxiously at Ben. Piscar was the Beaupain family lawyer. He had dealt with the entire Beaupain estate for decades. He had also been close friends with Ben's father, Louis. It was a part of their collective past, which Hugo and Ben had agreed to put behind them. However, it had always appeared the past was not done with them, and that it would continue to come back to them in one way or another, forever.

'Is this about *Hotel Beaupain*?' Ben snapped, with clear irritation. 'I have my own avocat, and as far as I know, I can do what the hell I like with my own name and the money that was left to me.'

Piscar fixed Ben with a sad look. His eyes were watery and tired. The eyes of a man who was ready to put everything behind him. He smiled. 'I think *Hotel Beaupain* is a fine idea,' he said.

Hotel Beaupain. It was something Ben had been working on for several years, ever since the death of his father, and having to deal with the vast legacy he had been left. Ben had never wanted to carry on the Beaupain name, certainly not in the way it had been handed down to him. The only solution that had made sense to him was to use it on his own terms.

And in the end, he had decided upon *Hotel Beaupain*. Something he planned to be a place for young and disenfranchised people seeking refuge - they would be met with no questions and no hassle. A safe haven for a night or two, with someone always on-site to help them, should they need it, and if they felt able to ask for it. A decent, safe room, at a price which could be afforded, even if payment was not always possible. It had not been a straightforward path to bring it to fruition, but Ben was determined the privilege he had been born into would be extended to others who needed it. It was a complicated process, but it was moving closer to the end. He hoped it would be open in less than a year.

'You do?' Ben questioned.

Piscar smiled. 'I'm one of the few people still alive who knew your father, Louis,' he continued. 'And despite what you might believe, I imagine he would have been very proud of you.'

Ben shrugged. 'Proudness after death is irrelevant. It's always bored me when people say my father was incapable of saying this or that. It doesn't matter, and it's not an excuse, and more importantly, it doesn't help me now.'

Hugo cleared his throat. 'Maître Piscar, why did you ask to speak to us this morning?'

'My apologies,' he said. 'I know it's the weekend, mais, I was instructed to contact you as soon as possible by my client.'

'Your client?' Hugo questioned.

Piscar glanced over his shoulder. 'Your son, Baptiste, is he here?'

Ben nodded. 'He's in his room. I'm afraid he's had a terrible shock. His friend died suddenly, and Baptiste has taken it quite badly.'

'Bien sûr,' Piscar agreed. 'Mais, I need to speak to you all, I'm afraid.'

Hugo and Ben exchanged a concerned look. Ben rose to his feet. 'I'll get him,' he said.

Hugo watched as Ben moved towards Baptiste's bedroom. 'Can I get you anything, Maître?' he asked.

Piscar shook his head. 'Non, merci.'

A few moments later, Ben and Baptiste returned to the living room. Baptiste flopped huffily onto the sofa. 'What?' he grumbled.

'Allow me to explain why I am here,' Piscar responded. He opened his briefcase and extracted a folder. 'First, I would like to say, that had I known…' he stuttered, 'had I known what was going to happen, I would have acted upon this information sooner. But really, there was no way of me knowing.' He stopped. 'All the same, I want you to know, I am very sorry for the loss of such a young life.'

Hugo frowned. 'You're talking about Vincent Roche?'

Piscar nodded slowly. 'Oui. He came to see me two days ago. He had,' he stopped for a moment, 'certain legal questions he wished to ask me.'

'What questions?' Baptiste interrupted.

Piscar sighed. 'I'm afraid, our conversation was very brief. I had to get to court, you see, and he was not exactly clear in explaining exactly what it was he wanted from me.' He lifted the folder. 'He asked if I would represent him. I said, bien sûr, but I would need to understand in what capacity it was. And then he handed me these two letters and asked me to read them and then act accordingly. I said I would. He left my office, and I left for court. With it being the weekend, I thought I would look at it next week, but then I heard the news, and I realised it was something I could not ignore.'

Hugo looked at the two envelopes. 'And you've read them?'

'One was addressed to me,' Piscar responded. 'And the other to Monsieur Baptiste Beaupain.' He took a breath. 'I'm sure you can understand. I am in a difficult position. I did not agree to be the jeune homme's avocat, and nor did he hire me as such, mais, I feel a certain obligation, because I told him I would discuss the matter further with him when I wasn't so pressed for time.'

Baptiste grabbed the letter with his name on it. He pushed his finger under the flap, but stopped, biting his lip as he stared at it. He looked to Piscar. 'What was in your letter?'

Piscar sighed. 'Instructions. Legal instructions.'

'What kind of legal instructions?' Ben asked.

'Monsieur Vincent Roche was a legal adult,' Piscar began. 'And therefore, able to explicitly lay down his instructions.'

'His instructions?'

Piscar smiled. 'He included a cheque for fifty euros to engage me as his avocat.' He paused. 'My fees are *slightly* higher, mais under the circumstances, I feel obliged to take it as a final retainer. And, his requests are quite simple.' He turned to Baptiste. 'He instructed me to hand you this letter and to ensure I followed a few formal procedures. For one - his body is to be cremated as soon as possible, and his ashes handed over to you, Baptiste. It seems he has instructed you in your letter what you are to do with them. And he also instructed me to come and talk to you, Captain Duchamp, as soon as I could.'

Hugo pursed his lips. 'Why did he feel the need to involve you?'

Piscar frowned. 'I cannot share with you the entire contents of my correspondence, but I feel comfortable in telling you this: Monsieur Roche wanted to make sure he was treated as an adult and there was no misunderstanding in his last requests. Not from any family member, par example. And that is what I will do.' He shrugged. 'I can offer the boy nothing else, other than to honour his one, final request.' He turned his head. 'It saddens me that I was one of the last people who may have seen him alive and that I may have been able to do something more to assist him when he so obviously needed it.' He turned to face Ben, his face clouding. 'However, it is not the first time I feel regret for not having intervened sooner.'

'What did he ask you to do, exactly?' Baptiste snapped.

Piscar pointed to the letter. 'Read your letter, and then we will discuss it further.'

une lettre

Cher Baptiste

Yeah. So I'm dead. *Hopefully*, at least. Ha. Sorry. Is that a bit weird? I don't know, cos I'm dead, but as I'm writing this, I don't think it's weird, I just think it's funny. I'm sorry I didn't ask you to help me, and I'm sorry for keep saying sorry, but at this point, it's all I've got.

I'm sorry. Let's start with that, okay? If I say I didn't have a choice, I guess you'll not understand what I mean. But it's the truth. As the saying goes - it is what it is.

So, let's cut to the chase. You were a good friend. One of my best. I have a buddy back home. Dax is his name, who I've known since I was a baby. I guess he's always been my best friend, but you came pretty close, too. Enough of the sucking up. I have a favour to ask of you. And your Papa. I know it's a lot to ask, but I think you're both the kind of men who will honour the last request of a poor dead kid.

Before we move on, let's talk about that. A bit extreme? Handcuffed to a desk at the bottom of the swimming pool? I admit, the idea only actually came to me today (Friday), but I guess I've probably been thinking about this whole shit for a long time. At least since Papa died. I wasn't even there. He'd been dead for two weeks before I even knew about it. What about his funeral, I asked? He was buried at sea they said - because that's what he wanted. I asked how he died, and they said it was an accident, but when I kept asking, they said he'd killed himself. Drowned, attached to his boat, which had sunk years ago. There was no investigation. There was nothing. Everyone accepted he was just dead and moved on. I spoke to my mother and told her the last thing he'd said to me was: *'I'm so proud of you son, once you finish your course, you have to come back to Beaufort-Sur-Mer and we'll put that education to good use! We'll make a killing with all the tourists - with your smarts, and my charm, we'll have them eating out of our hands! We'll be rolling in money, and your mother will come back to us. More importantly, we'll be able to buy back the hotel that robbing bastard thief, Jasper Connor, stole from us.'*

Baptiste. I realise I have no right to ask anything from you. But you told me that Hugo Duchamp had saved your life and how grateful you were. Didn't you say you wished you could do the same for someone else? Some Oprah shit about paying it forward, or something? Well, guess what? This is your chance. My life might be over, but the truth is what is important to me now. Make my death count for something. You and your Papa.

I've asked the avocat to make sure my mother doesn't get involved. She stopped having rights the second she dumped me and Papa. And I'll never forgive her for not letting me say goodbye to him. Luckily I'm an old boy in my own right now, so she can do fuck all to stop me. But that only works if I have someone, i.e. YOU, to do what I ask.

That's why I have to ask you to step in. What I want you to do is to take me home. Make them turn me into ashes and then leave me in the ocean next to my Papa on his boat. And then, ask your own Papa to do what no one else wants to do - find out what really happened to my father. This is all too much to ask, but I'm asking it, anyway. I'm hoping you guys have a strong sense of moral justice and granting the last wishes of someone who has gone.

You were a good pal, Baptiste, and I guess under different circumstances we would have had a lot of fun. I wished we'd lived that different life - girl, alcohol, parties, a bit of the harder stuff if we felt like it. I am sorry for dragging you into this, but I knew as soon as I met you, you weren't the sort of man who would turn his back on someone asking for help.

Live a long happy life on your vineyard, Baptiste. Not just for you, for me. Oh, and while I'm at it - forget about that Chen Gao chick. Forget the past and move on. There are plenty more girls out there and though it won't be your Chen, there will be someone who can become as important as she was. You just have to stop being stubborn and give someone else a chance. There, lecture over. You're lucky in ways I'll never be, but that doesn't make me sad, it makes me incredibly happy. Smile for me and I'll see you on the other side.

Vincent
X

quinze

Piscar looked at Baptiste. 'Once his death is officially declared as suicide, I can petition the court and have his remains cremated,' he stated. 'Your friend was an adult, and in lieu of a last will and testament, I think we can accept that as his wishes. I can,' he stopped, taking a breath, 'make it happen.'

Hugo looked at the letter. 'It's typed, and there's no signature,' he said. He looked to Piscar. 'Is that legal?'

Piscar studied the letter. 'There could be legal problems if there were any explicit instructions, but the letter he gave me, his instructions, included his signature. I don't think there would be an issue with following the young man's instructions.'

Baptiste turned to Hugo. 'Papa?'

Hugo shrugged. 'I don't know what to say, but more importantly, I don't know what I can do.'

Baptiste smiled. 'I've known you for a long time now, and I feel extremely comfortable in saying this. You can be a good Papa AND a good detective. You've done it before for me.'

Hugo shook his head. 'We do not know what happened to Vincent and his family,' he said.

Baptiste snorted. 'But you heard what he said in his letter. Nobody cares what happened to his Papa. Can you imagine how awful Vincent must have felt if the only way he had to draw attention to his father's death was to kill himself in the same way?'

'It's not that simple, Baptiste,' Ben interrupted.

'It's exactly that simple!' Baptiste cried. 'I knew he was in trouble and I should have stopped him. This is my fault.' He raised his hands. 'Don't do the whole reassuring thing. I know you mean well. But I have to do something. He asked for my help.' He turned to Hugo. 'He asked for *our* help.'

Hugo opened his mouth to speak, but thought better of it. He knew there was no reasoning with Baptiste at this moment. He looked to Ben. Ben smiled. *You have to go.* Hugo exhaled. 'I'm not promising anything,' he began cautiously, 'but I will have Etienne look into what happened in Vincent's hometown and we'll take it from there.'

Baptiste pulled Hugo into a tight embrace and kissed the top of his head. 'Vincent was right. I am lucky and I am going to live a good life FOR him once I've done what he asked of me.'

'Let's take it one step at a time,' Hugo replied. 'Wait and see what the forensic report tells us.'

'And then we'll take him home?' Baptiste asked.

'And then we'll take him home,' Hugo replied with obvious reticence. He suspected whatever lay ahead would not be easy for any of them.

seize

Hugo flicked on his glasses, narrowing his eyes to read the email which had just appeared on his screen. He raised his hand and gestured for Etienne to join him. 'Vincent Roche's final forensic report just came through,' he announced.

Etienne moved next to him, his eyes quickly scanning the screen.

Hugo stood up and began moving back and forth behind his desk. He lit a cigarette. 'Other than the alcohol, and lack of drugs in his system, there is nothing to suggest a crime was committed.'

'And now Dr. Viellen has officially labelled his death a suicide,' Etienne added. 'With no evidence to suggest otherwise, there was no other choice, non?'

'Non,' Hugo agreed.

Etienne frowned. 'I don't understand. You don't look happy. You can't have wanted it to be a murder?'

Hugo shook his head quickly. 'Non, not at all.' He took a draw on the cigarette. 'I suppose it's just the entire business has made me feel very sad. He was the same age as Baptiste, and I can't help but see the similarities between them…'

'Whatever problems Baptiste had, they're all behind him now, thanks to you and Ben,' Etienne reasoned. 'He's not the same person he was.'

Hugo sighed. 'You're right, I know that, but Baptiste has never really gotten over Chen Gao, and I just worry that after what happened with Vincent, it's going to set him back again.'

'Then you have to do what they asked you to, non?' Etienne asked.

Hugo's face contorted. 'What if it doesn't give Baptiste the outcome he needs? You and I both know, these things are never cut and dry, or straightforward.'

Etienne held up a folder. 'I was on my way to give you this,' he said. 'It's everything I could find about Vincent and his family.'

Hugo took the folder and sat down. He opened it. 'There's not much here.'

Etienne shrugged. 'Vincent was right. There wasn't much of an investigation. Arthur Roche had been missing for several days, according to the police report. No one reported him missing because, well, there wasn't really anyone to notice and they were used to his erratic behaviour. His wife, or rather his ex-wife, Avril Roche, said in her statement that he'd been depressed for some time since losing the family business, a hotel. She claimed his suicide did not surprise her.'

Hugo nodded. 'And his suicide? It was as Vincent described?'

'More or less,' Etienne agreed. 'There's a statement from a local tour guide, Dax Chastain. Apparently, he was taking a group of tourists scuba diving at Arthur Roche's sunken boat. It had been there some time and was a bit of a tourist attraction. They'd painted it to make it look as if it had sunken treasure, a skull on the stern, that sort of thing,' he added with a smile. 'Only on that particular day, they got more than they bargained for. Arthur Roche was tied to his own boat.'

Hugo grimaced, stubbing out his cigarette. 'That must have been a horribly macabre sight. And they ruled it a suicide?'

Etienne pointed. 'The autopsy report is in there. It's practically a mirror of Vincent's. No drugs in his system, but a lot of alcohol. Other than that, there was nothing to suggest foul play, so it was deemed a suicide, and,' he concluded, 'case closed.' He paused. 'And while I agree with Vincent's belief that there wasn't much of an investigation, under the same circumstances, I'm not sure we'd do much different.'

Hugo snorted. 'We are under the same circumstances, and you're right, there's not a lot to go on.'

'Then you'll do as Vincent asked?'

Hugo considered his answer for a long time. 'I don't know.'

He reached forward and lit another cigarette. 'I mean, to begin with, I just can't impose myself into another police jurisdiction…'

'It's not stopped you before…' Etienne said with a smile, counting off on his fingers. 'Ireland… Russia… Paris.'

Hugo raised his hand. 'I get your point, Etienne. But those were different…'

'Were they?' Etienne questioned. 'You saw something was wrong, and you used your skills to help right that wrong, non?' He paused. 'And really, all you're going to be doing is accompanying your son to scatter the ashes of his friend as per his last request…' he trailed off, 'if you were to see anything suspicious, then it would be entirely your right, your *duty*, to investigate.'

Hugo clicked his teeth. 'And lock horns with the local detectives.' He shuddered. 'My favourite thing to do.'

Etienne smiled. 'But more importantly, this is about your son. This is what he needs.'

Hugo sighed. 'You're right.' He rose to his feet. 'Then I guess I'm going to Beaufort-Sur-Mer.' He picked up the telephone. 'Mare-Louise,' he addressed the receptionist. 'Can you call Captain Comtois again for me and have him set up another video call with Madame Roche? Merci.'

dix-sept

'There is no doubt, Captain Duchamp?' Captain Franc Comtois asked.

'I'm afraid our pathologist has now ruled it as a suicide,' Hugo replied.

'And the forensic report?'

'There is no evidence of anyone else being involved,' Hugo continued, all the time staring at Avril Roche. She was huddled in a seat in the corner of Comtois's office. She seemed as if she had shrunk into herself since he had last seen her. She did not lift her head.

'There was no trace of drugs in his system, only alcohol,' Hugo continued.

'Just like his father,' Avril whispered. She lifted her head slowly. 'When can I have my son home? I want to bury him.'

Hugo sucked in some air. 'I'm afraid that's rather complicated.'

'Complicated?' Comtois asked sharply.

'Oui,' Hugo nodded. He stared at Avril Roche. 'Madame Roche, I must tell you that shortly before his death, your son contacted an avocat here in Montgenoux, giving him strict instructions concerning his wishes as to what was to happen after his death.'

'Instructions?' she asked, clearly confused.

He nodded again. 'He asked for his remains to be cremated and that his friend from school here, Baptiste Beaupain, bring the ashes and place them next to Vincent's father, on his boat.'

Her eyes widened in horror. 'What are you talking about? I couldn't do anything about Arthur's choices, but Vincent is my son. He can't be buried that way. It's cruel.' She shook her head. 'Non. He must have a grave. I must have somewhere to visit him.'

Hugo swallowed. 'I'm sure you can have some sort of

memorial for your son, mais, these were his wishes, and I'm afraid legally, there isn't anything we can do about it.'

'But I am his mother!' Avril shouted. She turned to Captain Comtois. 'Franc. Is this possible? Can they do this?'

The Captain touched her hand. 'Vincent was an adult, Avril,' he answered. 'If he made his instructions clear to a legal representative, then I don't see you have any recourse to question it. And in the end, isn't it about what he wanted, really?'

A line of tears tricked down her cheek. 'He always said he would never forgive me, and now he's had his revenge. They both have.' She snorted. 'And they are right to because after what I did, I deserve it.'

Captain Comtois twisted his head back to face Hugo. There was something about his expression which caught Hugo by surprise. It appeared to be a mixture of fear and concern. His normal involuntary eye-twitch became more rapid and pronounced.

Comtois recovered his composure. 'Keep me informed of your plans, Captain Duchamp.' He reached forward and disconnected the call, cold eyes staring at Hugo. 'Au revoir.'

dix-huit

Baptiste stared at the wooden box on Hugo's desk. His Adam's apple vibrating as he struggled to find the words to speak. 'That's all there is of him?' he croaked finally.

Hugo looked at the simple box. He had seen too many of them before and it had always filled him with the same sense of disbelief which Baptiste was now experiencing. It was always the same thought. How could a person who had once been living, so vibrant, so big, suddenly be nothing but dust? Hugo had always imagined people found solace in it, but he was not sure it was true.

When his grandmother, Madeline Duchamp, had died, her instructions had been abundantly clear. She was not to be embalmed. She was to be cremated and her ashes interned in the family mausoleum. She had also requested that a small portion be given to Hugo. He had been carrying them with him ever since, afraid to lose them, and yet unsure of what to do with them. They were on his bedside table, and when he saw the box each morning, it reminded him of her, which he supposed was the point. It gave him no comfort, but he wondered whether it did her, as she lay dying, to know that she would live on, next to someone who had cared about her.

Baptiste stared at Hugo. 'That's all there is of him?' he repeated.

'Oui,' Hugo answered softly.

'And it's all him?' Baptiste pressed. 'I mean, they don't just light a furnace and throw everyone in together?'

Hugo shook his head. 'Non, they don't do that.' He touched the box. 'This is all Vincent.'

A week had passed since Dr. Viellen had ruled Vincent's death as suicide, and despite further investigation by Hugo and his colleagues, they had found nothing to suggest otherwise. Except for the red towel. Hugo knew he should not let it bother him, reasoning it was a mistake. But it troubled him nevertheless because it was a loose end. And in his experience, loose ends could turn out to be vitally important.

'When can we go to Beaufort-Sur-Mer?' Baptiste asked. 'You haven't changed your mind, have you?'

Hugo shook his head. 'Non, bien sûr, I haven't,' he replied.

Baptiste smiled. 'Bon.' He moved towards the door. 'I have to get back to class.' He paused. 'Oh, Brigitte and Quentin from the swim team have asked if they can come too.'

Hugo frowned. 'Is that a good idea, Baptiste? We don't know what we're walking into at Beaufort-Sur-Mer. His mother is clearly unhappy about it all.' Avril Roche had sent several emails to the police, the procurer, the doctor and even the government following her son's death. But in the end, it had all proved futile. Everyone had agreed Vincent Roche had the legal right to have his wishes fulfilled.

'I don't care about her,' Baptiste hissed. 'Peut être if she'd cared so much about Vincent and his feelings when he was alive, then he wouldn't be... wouldn't be...' He shrugged. 'Brigitte and Quentin knew him, and as far as I'm concerned, no one has the right to say who can or can't feel sad that he's gone.'

Hugo stepped from behind his desk and pulled Baptiste into an embrace. It still did not feel natural to Hugo. He had spent his life wary and uncomfortable with physical contact, but it was becoming easier for him. 'I just meant that having strangers around might cause extra tension.'

'And as I said, I don't care,' Baptiste pulled away. 'Brigitte and Quentin have the right to say goodbye to Vincent if that's what they want to do. They knew him for the same amount of time as I did.'

Hugo nodded. 'Je comprends.'

'Then when can we go?'

'Ben is busy with the hotel renovations, but he says he can

get away by the beginning of next week.'

Baptiste shook his head. 'I don't want to wait that long. Can you get away tomorrow?'

Hugo looked at the pile of reports on his desk. There was nothing which could not wait, or be looked after by someone else, he reasoned. 'Oui. We can go tomorrow.'

Baptiste kissed his cheek. 'Merci. Je t'aime, Papa. I'll see you tonight.' He stared at the box. 'You're going home tomorrow, Vincent, just like I promised, and then we'll make this all right, you'll see.'

Hugo watched his son leave the office, and he sank into his chair. He sighed and reached for a cigarette.

PART TWO

BEAUFORT-SUR-MER

un

Hugo stepped down from the train, shielding his eyes from the sun. He stopped in front of a large ornate sign on the platform.

Bienvenue à Beaufort-Sur-Mer. Faites place aux souvenirs!

He dropped his bag, shook his head, and glanced over his shoulder. He could hear Baptiste and his friends making their way towards the train door. They appeared to be in the middle of an argument, as they had for most of the journey from Montgenoux. Brigitte St. Pierre, as far as Hugo could tell, was a vivacious and opinionated young woman, but he liked her. Her eyes shone a brightness he saw infrequently. It told him she was keen to engage, and that life was something she was interested in living and experiencing as much as she could.

He was not, however, as sure about Quentin Arquette. Unlike Baptiste, who was of a similar age, Quentin shared none of the humility or reverence. He was surly, antagonistic and often prone to inappropriateness. His comments were soundbites, quips meant to land with the maximum effect on the person he directed them at. He had made Hugo feel very old indeed. And more importantly, Hugo did not know why either of them had insisted on accompanying Vincent Roche on his last journey.

In the end, Hugo supposed it suggested they were young adults, unsure of how to deal with the loss of one of their peers, and that the fact they wanted to embark on such a journey showed how they were only trying to do something they felt was expected. Hugo vowed no matter how much they argued or fought, he would do his best to understand they were likely experiencing a loss for the very first time, and he should do whatever he could to help them. Loss was never easy, no matter how close or distant you were to a person, he reasoned. And they had both decided to accompany Baptiste on his mission.

Baptiste stepped into the bright sunshine, tired, bloodshot eyes narrowing. He noticed the sign and snorted with obvious disgust. 'Let the memories begin! Well, that's a fucking joke, for a start.'

Hugo suppressed a sigh. He was used to Baptiste being surly, but at that moment, he seemed unreachable, and it troubled Hugo because he had seen it before and he knew how disastrous it could be. Baptiste appeared, locked in a spiral of sadness and guilt.

Hugo and Ben had made immense progress with Baptiste since meeting him in Ireland. They had also rescued him from a potentially dangerous situation when they had travelled to Russia. Upon their return, Baptiste had been training to take over the vast and world-famous Beaupain Vineyards. Hugo had felt sure his young adopted son had finally turned a corner and was moving forward with his life. However the guilt over his friend's death and what he could have done to save him was in danger of returning Baptiste to the dark place which had once almost consumed him. Hugo knew all he could really do was to be present for the young man and offer support and love. He hoped it would be enough, but he knew a lot of it would depend on what they discovered in Vincent Roche's hometown.

'Will you stop pushing me, Quentin Arquette, or so help me, Dieu, I'm gonna take off my heels and stab you through the heart with a stiletto.'

Hugo rolled his eyes as Brigitte St. Pierre struggled from the train, dragging a Louis Vuitton trunk behind her. Quentin Arquette pushed past her, tutting loudly. At nineteen, they were younger than Baptiste, who had gone to college late, but Hugo thought they acted much younger. They had bickered continuously on the train journey from Montgenoux, finally forcing Hugo to spend most of the journey alone in the bar. In the time they had spent together, Hugo did not believe they had ever mentioned Vincent Roche, nor the reason for their trip to Beaufort-Sur-Mer. He reasoned that everyone dealt with death in different ways. Baptiste was still locked in a battle with the guilt he felt, and no amount of reassurance seemed to alleviate his pain.

Hugo cleared his throat. 'According to the tourist guide, the hotel is "only a short walk across a nineteenth-century boardwalk."' He ignored the condescending look shot in his direction from Quentin. 'Shall we head over there first and check in?' he asked.

Brigitte pointed to a large suitcase. A suitcase so large, Hugo was convinced it would fit everything he owned, with room to spare. He could not imagine how or why a person would need so much for what was likely to be a brief trip. 'Yeah, I'd like to go to the hotel first, Captain Duchamp,' Brigitte replied. 'I want to get rid of this.'

'Please call me, Hugo,' he said. 'I'm not on duty. I wish you'd let me take it for you.'

She smiled. 'That's very kind of you, but I'm fine.' She shot a dirty look at Quentin and Baptiste. 'At least one of you men has a bit of decency.' Baptiste and Quentin gave her a, *do we look like we care*, shrug of their shoulders.

Hugo finally released a sigh, realising that however long they spent in Beaufort-Sur-Mer, it was going to feel longer, and with Ben still in Montgenoux, it was going to feel even more difficult. He gestured with his finger. 'D'accord, shall we go then?' he said.

Baptiste stepped in front of him, throwing his backpack over his shoulder and clutching Vincent's ashes to his chest.

Hugo followed him into the street. In a lot of ways, it reminded him of Montgenoux. Uneven cobbles leading into a large square, filled with stalls of fresh food, mainly fish it seemed, but unlike Montgenoux, the cobbles lead down to a large jetty and a narrow boardwalk which sliced between the two sides of the harbour. The sea was crystal blue, and the smell hit Hugo instantly. He loved the sea and despite his natural reticence; he wanted nothing more than to jump into it.

His eyes locked on to a family playing on the sandy beach and he ached for memories such as those. He had none. But the one thing life had taught him was, it was never, *ever*, too late to begin making new memories. He shook the thoughts from his head. He was not here for a holiday, no matter how beautiful or picturesque Beaufort-Sur-Mer might be.

Brigitte dropped her bag, wiping her brow with the back of her hand. 'Jeez, it's hot here.'

Quentin put his hand on his hips. 'And as boring as fuck. No wonder Vincent decided to…'

Baptiste stopped dead in his tracks. He turned around, glaring at Quentin.

Quentin's mouth contorted apologetically. 'No wonder Vincent decided he wanted his eternal resting place to be here.'

Baptiste clicked his teeth irritably. He stopped and then moved across the cobbles towards the railings which lined the dock. He pulled on them. 'Papa, where do you think the boat is?'

Hugo moved quickly to his side. He glanced over the side of the dock. The sea was so clear he could see fish moving around. 'I don't know,' he whispered.

'But it's down there?' Baptiste questioned.

Hugo shrugged. 'I imagine so. We'll find out later, I suppose.' He touched Baptiste's arm. 'Let's just get settled into the hotel, and we'll take it from there.'

Baptiste spun around. At the end of the boulevard was a tall, imposing building with shuttered windows. *Hotel Roche*.

'Vincent's Papa's hotel,' Baptiste whispered.

Hugo nodded. He was unsure of the story behind the problems which had led to Arthur Roche's suicide, other than it appeared it may have resulted from having lost the family hotel.

'We shouldn't be staying there,' Baptiste stated.

'It's the only hotel in this damn hick town,' Quentin said,

sweeping past him.

Hugo nodded. 'I think he's right, Baptiste,' he agreed. 'Mais, if you're uncomfortable, we could look elsewhere… We don't even have to stay in Beaufort-Sur-Mer. I'm sure there's a hotel in a nearby town,' he added. 'I can check if you like.'

Baptiste ignored him, striding purposefully towards the hotel. 'Non, let's see what the hell they have to hide.'

'Baptiste, s'il te plaît…' Hugo cried wearily, trying desperately to catch up with him.

deux

Jasper Connor smiled warmly at Hugo, Baptiste, Brigitte, and Quentin. He was dressed in a smart, pinstripe grey suit, a jet-black beard at odds with greying temples. His smile was even and tempered, brilliant white teeth contrasting against sun-darkened skin. 'We've been looking forward to your arrival,' his voice was cool, the lilt of a practised, considered host, 'and I hope your journey was comfortable.'

While the young people looked bored, Hugo stepped in front. 'Oui, merci,' he replied. 'Your town is very beautiful.'

'We think so,' Jasper retorted. 'And thankfully, so do most of the tourists who come year after year. Luckily we're not in high season just yet, therefore I was able to reserve four rooms and all with a sea view, each with their own private veranda overlooking the harbour.' He glanced at the screen. 'There's just a question of payment,' he added delicately.

Brigitte and Quentin turned their back, staring out of the revolving foyer doors. Hugo sighed and pulled a carte bancaire from his wallet and handed it to Jasper.

Jasper took the card, his lips twisting as if he was used to cards of a different colour. 'I'm sure this will be fine,' he said, swiping the card through the machine, staring at it as if he expected it to be declined.

Hugo gulped. He knew there was money in his account, but there was something about Jasper's mannerisms that made him doubt it.

The machine bleeped, and Jasper removed the card. 'There, that's all done. You're all booked in until the end of the week.'

'Merci,' Hugo said. 'We'll just go and get settled in then.'

Jasper nodded. 'Bon. The service is set for 10H00 tomorrow.'

'The service?' Baptiste questioned, pushing past Hugo.

'Oui. The service.' Jasper retorted. He frowned. 'Our small

community is in mourning, Monsieur. We need to pay our respects to Vincent and find a way to mark his passing.'

'*Mourning,*' Baptiste repeated as if the word pained him and he was not at all sure of its validity.

Hugo touched his arm as if attempting to relay a message. *He is right.*

Baptiste reached over the desk and snatched the card keys. 'I'm going to my room,' he said sulkily.

Hugo smiled at Jasper. 'Merci, Monsieur Connor.'

'I wish I was with you,' Ben announced sadly.

Hugo stared at the screen. 'Moi aussi, but you have to deal with the hotel, and really, this has nothing to do with us. We must support Baptiste, but as for the rest, it's none of our business. I feel awkward being here, but somehow or other I seem to have become involved.'

Ben smiled. 'You were asked to help, and you never break a promise.'

Hugo shrugged. 'I'm not sure what good that sort of promise can do. I'll do what I can, but if there's nothing to investigate, then I can't investigate. I can't make something out of nothing.' He paused. 'And despite how Baptiste feels, there are most likely people here who have known Vincent Roche for all of his life. I can't undermine that with insinuations, even if it is to placate our son. Baptiste isn't a child. He has to accept our limitations, and if we have to be the ones to teach him it, then that's what we have to do.'

'You mean, life's shit and often makes no sense?' Ben sighed.

'Sometimes,' Hugo replied.

Ben emitted a sad sigh. 'What's Beaufort-Sur-Mer like?' he asked, changing the subject.

'It looks lovely at first glance,' Hugo answered. 'If you were here. *I wish you were here.* Then we could explore, but under the circumstances, I don't feel as if I should. It feels inappropriate.'

Ben sighed again. 'Oh, je suis tres désolé. I knew I should have come, even if just to keep you company. But right now, I'm sitting in a shell of a hotel that is costing me more money to build than I have, and which, if I listen to my mother, will always be a money pit, unless I charge a decent amount.'

'She probably has a point,' Hugo responded.

'Bien sûr, she has a point,' Ben conceded. 'But MY point is, I'm using Papa's money to build this hotel. You know I wanted nothing from him. But if I do, then it has to count for something. Growing up, I used to see all the migrant workers who came to pick the grapes in the vineyard. If they were lucky, they'd have a tent to sleep in because they certainly couldn't afford to stay in a hotel. I want them to be able to finally stay in a Beaupain hotel. To be safe, have an excellent breakfast and still have some money left over. And not just them. Kids who are running away. Hookers who want to escape their pimps. My father left me money I didn't want or need. It feels only right to give it back one way or another.'

He laughed. 'I warned the old fool I would do something like this, so I hope he's looking down, or,' he paused, 'up, and sees I'm a man of my word. I hope he'd understand, but if not, then it's no great loss. He never understood me when he was alive, so why should it change now. If I fail, I fail. As long as I have you by my side, I just know I can do this.'

Hugo smiled. He was not sure how well Ben's plan would work, but it did not matter. They would try their best to make it work, and that was all that really mattered.

'Ecouté,' Ben said. 'Go and get Baptiste. Drag him out. Go for a walk, have dinner, just the two of you. Don't talk to him if he doesn't want to talk. Just sit with him. Be with him. Drink beer. Eat some food and just be together. That's all he needs.'

Hugo nodded. 'I'll have a shower and then get him. Je t'aime.

I'll see you in a few days.'

Ben smiled sadly. 'You'd better. I always hated sleeping alone, but without you in my bed, it feels unbearable.'

trois

Hugo and Baptiste moved in silence, walking hip to hip up the steep stairway which had been carved into a hill leading from the tower square, towards the fortress which had given Beaufort-Sur-Mer its name.

Hugo cleared his throat. 'I read the brochure about the town in the hotel gift pack,' he said.

'Bien sûr, you did,' Baptiste retorted. There was a mocking to his town, but it was playful, not malicious. 'Désolé, Papa,' he whispered. 'I know I'm in a foul mood, and the last thing I want, or intend, is for you to bear the brunt.' He rubbed Hugo's shoulder. 'I know it probably doesn't feel like it, but I never take you and Ben for granted. I hope you know it because I sure as hell don't show it as much as I should.'

Hugo nodded. 'We know it.' He continued reading from the brochure. He pointed behind them. 'The boardwalk leading from the sandy beach, past the hotel, and up to this path, is from the nineteenth century. Most of the houses are all from the early twentieth century. The Mayor at the time stated they all had to be uniform to impress and encourage tourism. White bricks and red roofs. Apparently, it's written into the by-laws that the houses can't be changed, or that new houses can only be built using reclaimed materials and following the strict guidelines.'

Baptiste stopped and tapped his chin. 'And is there anything else?' he asked with a wink.

Hugo ignored the wink. 'Well, seeing as you asked, there is. The fort after which Beaufort-Sur-Mer takes its name was used during World War One and it was finally practically destroyed by bombs during World War Two. Only ruins still exist. There have been many attempts over the years to repair the fort, but in the end,' he exhaled, 'it's probably just that a ruined fort is probably far more attractive to tourists.'

Baptiste shrugged. 'Sure. What's the point in rebuilding a fort that can never be used? Surely it makes more sense for people to come and look at a fort that was once something and saved people?'

Hugo nodded. He could not fault Baptiste's argument. 'And then in the early…'

'Jesus, Papa!' Baptiste cried. 'How fucking bored were you?'

Hugo laughed. 'I shower quickly and get bored easily without crime reports to read. And despite what everyone thinks of me, I do suffer from separation anxiety.'

Baptiste touched his arm. 'You should never be anxious. You'll never be alone again. I'll always see to it.'

'That's not a promise you can make,' Hugo retorted. 'Or one any of us can make.'

'The hell it is,' Baptiste cried. 'We're the same you and I. We'll grow old together, probably with Ben looking after us, because that freak never seems to age, but we'll always be together.'

Hugo smiled. 'That's sweet, Baptiste,' he said. 'But I still want you to have a family of your own. A wife. Children. Whatever you want.'

Baptiste pulled Hugo to him. 'I have you and I have Ben. I want nothing else. Not anymore.'

'Baptiste…' Hugo cried.

Baptiste raised his hands. 'Don't lecture me, Papa Duchamp. Unless you want to talk about *Hugo Duchamp - the London years?*' He laughed. 'Huh? You wanna do that?'

Hugo laughed, shaking his head. 'Non, I don't want to do that. Using my past as an example isn't an argument winner.' He stared at Baptiste. 'So, just because you don't play fair, doesn't mean this conversation is over, you do understand that, don't you?'

'Sure I do.'

'Bon. Then let's try to make the most of a horrible situation.' Hugo said. He stopped and looked back. The houses were lined up in a uniformed row of matched colours, differing only by curtains, planters and the cars parked outside them. He sighed. 'For as long as I've lived, I've imagined living somewhere like this.'

'Then why don't you?' Baptiste asked.

'I always imagined small town wasn't for people like…' he paused, before adding sadly, 'me.'

'Pfff,' Baptiste retorted. 'It's 2022. That shit has changed.'

Hugo nodded. 'It has. And yet, sometimes, in some places, it hasn't. I don't need friends or comfort, but I do need to feel comfortable. It's not just about "fitting in" and for your neighbours accepting you as being "okay." It's about feeling as if you have a place, regardless of who or what you are.' He shrugged. 'Anyway, let's keep going. The ruins are just a few steps away, and according to the brochure they are spectacular.'

They continued in silence, plodding up the steep stairway. Finally, they cleared it, stepping onto an uneven grass verge.

Baptiste threw back his head and guffawed. 'Well, you're certainly right, Papa. These views are spectacular, et,' he paused, 'a bit more modern, non?'

Hugo flicked on his glasses. Darting in and out of the ruins of the fort were several teenage boys and girls on skateboards and rollerblades. Hugo's eyes locked on a trio of young adults, sat in front of the ruins, sucking contentedly on cigarettes that smelled very different to the ones Hugo was used to. He looked to Baptiste.

Baptiste shrugged. 'Well, at least they're having fun, and the old place is getting used.' He touched Hugo's arm. 'Let's go into the town and eat and get wasted.'

'Baptiste…' Hugo said wearily.

'The only way I'm going to get through this is if I get wasted,' Baptiste replied.

Hugo moved back towards the descending stairs. 'D'accord. But I'm not just your drinking buddy, I'm also your father.'

'Thank fuck for that,' Baptiste said happily. He flicked his long hair over the top of his head. 'You can hold my hair when I'm vomiting later.'

Hugo watched as Baptiste skipped down the stairway. 'Lucky me,' he mouthed.

quatre

Quentin Arquette moved away from the bar and placed a drink in front of Brigitte St. Pierre. 'Your long, slow screw, Mademoiselle,' he said.

Brigitte glared at him. 'It had better be a gin and tonic, or else the only screw you're going to see tonight is the one I hammer into your thick, stupid skull.'

Quentin flopped onto the chair opposite her. 'Wow. The black goddess is also a bitch.'

Her eyes widened. 'And you're a racist, sexist, ugly pig. What's your point?'

'Hey, are you the kids from Vincent's school?' a voice called from a table behind them.

Quentin turned his head. 'Yeah. And?'

'Je m'appelle, Dax Chastain,' the young man answered. 'Vincent was my oldest friend,' he answered, his voice cracking.

The man sat opposite him, reached over and touched his hand. 'It's okay, Dax,' he said.

Quentin smiled. 'Ah, you "boys" must be really sad,' he mouthed in a camp manner.

Dax slapped the hand away from him. 'What are you talking about?' He stood. He was tall, his body lean and his face dark with the sun, blond hair bleached by the sun. His companion was shorter, with brown hair pulled into a ponytail.

Brigitte smiled. 'Ignore Quentin, he is,' she shrugged, 'stupid. Oui. My name is Brigitte St. Pierre. We were at school with Vincent and we wanted to…' she stopped, 'well, it seemed like the right thing to do, to come back with him.'

Dax looked at his companion. 'This idiot is Gregoire. Gregoire Comtois. He thinks he's important because he's the police Captain's son,' he stopped, staring at him, 'but he just isn't…'

Gregoire snorted. 'So you say, dickhead,' he said, playfully punching his friend's arm.

'You both knew Vincent?' Dax asked.

'He was my best friend,' Quentin snapped.

Brigitte gasped. 'In this life? He hated your guts, you delusional prig.'

Quentin ignored her. 'Ignore her,' he spat, throwing his hand towards Brigitte. 'Vincent and I spent every day together for the last year. We *were* best friends.'

Brigitte's eyes widened mockingly. 'As far as I know, your name isn't Baptiste.'

'Ah, Baptiste,' Dax interjected. 'Vincent spoke about him a lot.' He glanced around. 'Is he here?'

Quentin's eyes flared with irritation. 'He WAS my best friend. We laughed at the dyke professeur who stunk of garlic. We swapped notes and between us tried to figure out which chick was likely to put out. If that's not best friends, I don't know what is.'

Dax ignored Quentin and turned to Brigitte. 'Is Baptiste with you?'

She shrugged. 'Oui. He's here, and he's probably not doing well. He and Vincent were tight.'

Quentin snorted. 'Not tight enough for Baptiste to actually save his life…'

'Quentin!' Brigitte shouted. 'And where the hell were you? We all knew he was down. We all have reasons to be ashamed.'

Dax raised his hand. 'Hey, don't go there. There's plenty of guilt to go around,' he lowered his head. 'We were best friends. I don't even remember a time when I didn't know him.'

'I used to be jealous of your friendship,' Gregoire stated. He was staring at Dax, but his head was lowered as if he could not keep eye contact.

Dax looked surprised. 'You were? Why?'

He shrugged. 'We all went to school together, and I had friends, sure, but no one I was as close to as you two were.'

'Odd that he never mentioned either of you,' Quentin quipped.

'Quentin!' Brigitte hissed. 'Do you have to be a prick *all* the time?'

Dax sighed. 'He's probably right. We haven't been friends for a while. He was angry. I think he blamed me for his father's death.'

Quentin raised an eyebrow. 'He did?'

Dax nodded. 'Yeah,' he said, but did not elaborate further.

'Hey guys,' Baptiste appeared in the doorway, Hugo a step behind.

'Baptiste,' Brigitte cried, immediately biting her lip as if chastising herself.

'Baptiste,' Dax repeated, his head rising sharply. His face softened, his lips pulling into a smile.

Baptiste took a tentative step towards him. 'Are you Dax?'

Dax frowned. 'You know me?'

Baptiste flopped into the seat opposite Dax. He slugged the beer he was carrying nervously. 'Yeah, sure. I mean, not really. I saw your photo. Vin…' he gulped. 'Vincent had a photo of both of you as his phone screensaver.'

'He did?' Dax exhaled. The breath was slow, and it appeared as if it hurt him.

Baptiste nodded. 'He did. And he talked about you all the time.'

'He did?' Dax repeated with obvious uncertainty. 'He didn't blame me for his father's death?'

Baptiste shrugged. 'I don't think so. At least, he didn't say so, not to me anyway.' He sighed. 'Listen, he was angry, furious and maybe he said some things he regretted, but all that aside, he still spoke about you, and always about how much he liked you.'

Gregoire poked Dax. 'See, I told you.' He extended his hand. 'Salut, by the way. Je m'appelle, Greg. Gregoire Comtois.'

Baptiste smiled. 'Baptiste Beaupain,' he pointed over his

shoulder. Hugo was lurking by the doorway smoking a cigarette. 'The anti-social one with the cancer stick is my Papa, Hugo Duchamp.'

'Duchamp? As in Captain Duchamp?' Gregoire questioned.

'Oui,' Hugo called out.

'My father is Captain Comtois,' Gregoire replied. He grimaced. 'And I can tell you, he's none too happy about Captain Duchamp coming to Beaufort-Sur-Mer.'

'Then he's an idiot,' Baptiste retorted. 'Hugo is one of the best people I know.' He grimaced. 'Désolé, I didn't mean to insult your father.'

Gregoire shrugged. 'Don't apologise. He is an idiot.'

Baptiste finished the remains of his beer. 'Well, I don't know about anyone else, but I'm going to get completely wasted. For Vincent.'

Dax raised his hand to signal the server. 'I like your thinking.' He swallowed. 'For Vincent,' he repeated in a whisper.

cinq

Hugo stifled a yawn. It had been a long night at the bar, but in the end, he supposed it had been worthwhile. It had probably done Baptiste good to unwind in the company of two people who had probably known Vincent Roche the most. But Baptiste had also fulfilled his promise to get very drunk. Luckily, the vomiting had not followed. *Yet*. Hugo shuffled slowly along the harbour alongside Dax Chastain and a barely coherent Baptiste squeezed between them, an arm thrown casually over each of their shoulders.

'Merci for helping me get him back to the hotel,' Hugo said.

'No problem,' Dax replied. 'It was a good night, wasn't it?' He stopped. 'Shit, what a stupid thing to say after what's happened.'

Hugo shook his head. 'When my grandmother knew she was dying, one of the last things she said to me was that there had better be no sad faces at her funeral. She wanted people to laugh, be happy and tell shocking and outrageous anecdotes about her.'

He sighed. 'It was hard, but it's what we did, and you know, I think it was as much for us as it was for her, and I think it was her way of leaving a parting gift. She didn't want anyone to be sad on her behalf. It's the same one I want to leave when it's my time. I don't want anyone to be sad, just maybe if they feel like it, to spend a little time reminiscing about me in a way to celebrate our time together.'

He smiled at Dax. 'It's not such a hard thing to do, is it? And being happy for a moment or two in grief isn't such a terrible thing. In fact, I'd go so far as to say it's compulsory. I'm sure Vincent wouldn't want you to feel guilty about anything, especially because of him. He felt unable to carry on, and I imagine he would hate anyone to feel as if they were in some way responsible, or that they could have done something to prevent it.'

'You're very wise,' Dax said softly. 'Baptiste got lucky with you as a father.' He appraised Hugo. 'But you can't be much older than him.'

Hugo laughed. 'Well, technically I am old enough to be his birth father, but oui, we actually adopted Baptiste a few years ago.'

'A few years ago?' Dax asked, surprised.

'Oui. He was already an adult - it is, as they say, complicated,' Hugo replied with a smile. 'Mais, you know it worked out for the best. We became a family of choice and it has been pretty marvellous.'

'That's cool,' Dax added sadly. 'My father skipped town before I was born. I think impending fatherhood was such a shock to him that he's still running.' He shrugged. 'But it doesn't matter. Maman is pretty spectacular, and that's always been good enough for me.'

Baptiste muttered something incoherent and fell back into his stupor. Hugo and Dax laughed.

'Let's put him down for a moment,' Hugo said. 'I'm not as young, or as fit as I used to be. Not that I've ever been fit, mind you.' He pointed to a bench opposite the marina and they manoeuvred Baptiste into it. Hugo stretched his back and lit a cigarette, savouring it. The moon was bright, illuminating the clear, calm water. He looked around. Beaufort-Sur-Mer really was beautiful. The sort of place where he had always dreamed of living. He hoped he could revisit it one day under happier circumstances. 'This must be an amazing place to live,' he said.

Dax nodded. 'It can be.' He pointed behind them. 'That's our house over there. Maman says if she could turn the kitchen around to face the hill she would because after thirty-odd years of looking at the same view every day has gotten old.' He faced the gentle lapping water. 'As boring as it sounds, I can't ever imagine growing bored with it. I realise I'm probably in the minority there. Vincent couldn't wait to get out of here. He used to joke that I'll end up like one of the wrinkled men, with creases as deep as fingernails on my face and skin the colour of tar. I agreed and told him, as far as I could tell, it wasn't so bad a life.'

Hugo laughed. 'I can imagine it is a good place to grow up. I know as adults we all get jaded. We feel claustrophobic and imagine the grass is greener somewhere else, and sometimes it is, but sometimes it isn't.'

'Where were you born?'

'Paris,' Hugo answered softly.

'Wow! I take back what I just said. I'd give everything to have grown up in Paris.'

Hugo shrugged. His life in Paris had never been something he considered to have been happy. He supposed with hindsight; it was not as bad as he remembered. As a teenager living with his grandmother, he had first experienced love and loss and what would eventually become his career and his vocation. He had returned to Paris a year earlier and had discovered, to his surprise, it had not scared him as it once had. The ghosts had dissipated, or more importantly, their power over him had.

'Hey, Dax,' a voice called from the shadows.

'Oh, hey, Guy,' Dax replied. 'Guy, this is Captain Duchamp.'

'Ah, I heard he was coming today,' he replied, approaching the bench. 'Enchanté, Captain Duchamp. Je m'appelle, Guy Fallon.'

'S'il vous plaît, it's Hugo. I'm not here in any official capacity,' Hugo stated.

'Guy is a fisherman,' Dax said. 'He supplies the town and most of the excellent restaurants around with seafood.'

Hugo nodded. He imagined Guy Fallon was older than Dax, most likely in his late thirties, with dark hair lightened by the sun and the same weather-beaten face which seemed to afflict most of the people he had seen in the town. Lined faces which told the story of the lives they led. Simple warm days and soft balmy evenings. Guy shook Hugo's hand with a firmness that caused the muscles in his arms to flex. Hugo felt weedy by comparison.

'Nice to meet you, Hugo,' Guy said. He pointed at Baptiste, who had slipped on the seat and was now snoring contentedly, a bubble of spittle on his lip. 'He looks like he's had a good night,' Guy laughed.

'He's not normally like this,' Hugo offered.

'Baptiste was Vincent's pal at school,' Dax said.

Guy looked sadly at Baptiste. 'Poor kid.'

'You knew Vincent?'

'Sure. I was friends with both him and his father,' Guy answered. He exchanged a look with Dax, which confused Hugo. Guy noticed it. 'Arthur was the one who gave me my big break. He showed me where all the best mussels could be found. He used to get them for himself, but then he taught me how I could make a living out of it.' He laughed. 'For a kid with limited intelligence and the inability to work in a dead-end job, it was a lifesaver. Arthur was a lifesaver.' His mouth tightened. 'No matter what people might say about him.'

Hugo looked between the two men. He was still not sure how far he should go, or whether he should conduct any kind of investigation at all. In the end, he supposed it mattered little. Arthur and Vincent Roche were both dead, and it appeared understanding the reasons was going to prove important. 'I was sorry to hear about Arthur's death,' he offered.

Guy nodded. 'I was the one who found Arthur.'

'We both did,' Dax added.

Hugo recalled what Etienne had told him of the suicide of Arthur Roche and its similarity to the way in which his son ended his own life, and he wondered whether Dax and Guy were also aware of it.

'I'll never forget it for as long as I live,' Guy continued. He stared into the water.

'I'm the tourist guide, you see,' Dax stated. 'And I often take the visitors out scuba diving,' he added. 'And Guy usually comes with us, especially when we have a lot of tourists in town.'

'I'm an experienced diver. I think I've been in the water practically before I learnt to walk,' Guy said. 'And because of that, believe me, I've seen some crazy things down there, but I've seen nothing like that in my entire life.'

The three men lapsed into silence. Hugo had read the reports, but he did not want to pry. He imagined both the men, not to mention the tourists accompanying them, were likely still traumatised by what they had seen. He did not wish to push them in a recollection that might trigger something they had not yet learnt to reconcile.

'He was there. Floating, like some bloated pig,' Guy hissed through gritted teeth. 'Tied to his damn boat. He always said he would die in the sea. I just never thought or imagined it would be that way.'

Dax turned to Hugo. 'Is it true? Is that how Vincent died too?'

'I can't talk too much about it,' Hugo answered softly. 'Other than I believe there were similarities between the manners of death.'

Dax threw back his head and laughed. 'Vincent certainly was one prone to being overly dramatic,' he said. 'But even by his standards, that was...' he trailed off, searching for the words.

'Poetic,' Guy finished.

'Poetic, my ass,' Dax snapped. 'It was weird and selfish and,' he clenched his fists as if he was ready to punch something. 'Why the hell didn't he come back here and do it? Why do it a hundred miles away in a place he barely knew, surrounded by complete strangers?' He stared imploringly at Hugo.

Hugo tried to hold the young man's gaze. He had no answers for him which he imagined would satisfy him. 'All I can really say,' he began, 'is that maybe he found it easier to be away. Peut être, he thought, it would be too difficult to return to Beaufort-Sur-Mer. I'm afraid we may never know for sure.'

'He didn't want to come home,' Guy interrupted, 'because he knew we would never let him throw his life away in such a ridiculous, pointless way. We just wouldn't. He just knew it would be easier to end it all with a bunch of strangers.' He stepped away. 'He was always weak and selfish, and just because he's dead now, I don't see the point in rewriting history.' He nodded at Hugo. 'I'll see you at the memorial tomorrow.'

Hugo and Dax watched as Guy left.

'He's right, I suppose,' Dax stated. 'At least I hope he is. If Vincent had come home, I'd like to think I'd see how much pain he was in, and at least be able to do something about it.'

Baptiste lifted his head. 'I think I'm gonna hurl,' he spluttered.

Hugo stubbed out the cigarette and moved quickly towards his son. 'Come on, Baptiste, let's get you to your room.'

six

Clementine Bonheur pulled back a sheet, revealing the painting beneath it. Behind her, Avril Roche gasped. She stepped forward, her hand shaking as she moved near the portrait. Hugo took a deep breath. Vincent Roche stared into the room, his likeness created on canvas with oil. Hugo could feel Baptiste shaking next to him. It had taken Hugo an hour to rouse his heavily hungover son, and he only managed to by finally dragging him fully clothed and throwing him under the shower.

'I don't know what to say, Clementine,' Avril mouthed. She steadied herself against the side of a chair and raised her other hand, tracing it around the portrait.

Jasper Connor appeared by her side. 'You've outdone yourself, Clementine,' he said, placing his hand on Avril's shoulder. 'Hasn't she, Avril?'

Avril raised her hand. It was still shaking. She traced around Vincent's face, without actually touching it. 'Vincent,' she sighed. 'My beautiful boy.'

Clementine kissed Avril's cheek 'I tried my very best to do him justice,' she said. 'I've spent the last forty years painting docks and the ocean for tourists, so it's good to see I can still paint something real.' She stepped back. She was a large woman, with frizzy auburn hair and a rosy complexion. She was dressed in a floor-length floral caftan, which she moved continuously with her fingers as if attempting to move air around her body.

Jasper moved to a table and picked up a glass of champagne, tapping the side of the glass with a ring. 'Bonjour mes amis,' he began. 'I want to thank you all for coming today to pay tribute to our very dear Vincent.'

Hugo looked around the room. He recognised most of the people who had gathered. Dax Chastain and Gregoire Comtois were seated with the fisherman Guy Fallon, next to the man Hugo recognised as Captain Franc Comtois. Another man was staring at the portrait. He was older, with tired and watery eyes and thin, wispy white hair. There were several other people at the back of the room. Some of them already in tears. Hugo swallowed. He touched Baptiste's arm and studied his face out of the corner of his eye. He could sense that he was on the verge of breaking down.

Jasper Connor cleared his throat before continuing. 'Vincent was only with us on this earth a very short time, but he made his time count.' He touched Avril's hand. 'He was a dear friend to us all, but more importantly, he was a loyal and devoted loving son to his mother and…' he paused, lowering his voice, 'his father.' He rubbed his hands together. 'I don't want today to be a sad occasion. Vincent would have hated that. He would want us to come together to help support each other. He believed in family and he believed in helping one another. So, let's do that. Raise a glass, enjoy the food and the company and celebrate the life of a young man who touched us all and was taken from us far too soon.'

He turned away, moving Avril Roche to the corner of the room. She refused. Instead standing stock-still in front of the portrait of her son. Hugo watched as Brigitte and Quentin moved swiftly towards the table of food and he gently guided Baptiste towards a chair. 'A beer?' he asked.

Baptiste lifted his head, his pale face contorting. 'Don't be cruel, Papa, not even if I deserve it.'

'I know it's probably the hundredth time I've asked this,' Hugo replied, 'so forgive me for that, but it's what we do under such circumstances.' He exhaled. 'How are you doing?'

'I'm okay,' Baptiste answered. 'I'm sad, but I guess being here has put things into perspective for me a little. The truth is, I barely knew Vincent. I guess I felt guilty for not doing more to help him, but I have to get over that. I have to believe I would have done more if I'd any actual idea how bad things were for him.'

'Bien sûr, you would,' Hugo said. 'We all would have.'

Baptiste took a deep breath. 'As weird as it sounds, being here has helped. Not just because it was what Vincent wanted, but because you can see how loved he was. These people have almost twenty years of memories with him.' He stared at Avril Roche. 'Should I talk to his mother?'

She was still standing in front of her son's portrait. Her body was rigid. Jasper Connor was still next to her, refilling her glass as soon as she emptied it.

'I'd give her a moment,' Hugo answered. 'She looks like she needs time alone.'

Baptiste stood. 'I'm going outside, I need a cigarette.'

'Shall I come with you?' Hugo asked.

'Non, I just need some air.'

Hugo nodded. 'I'll be here if you need me.' He watched Baptiste leave and unsure what to do, Hugo headed towards the Captain. 'Captain Comtois,' he said. 'It's nice to finally meet you in person.'

Comtois shook his hand. 'You too, Captain,' he responded, as if he was not entirely certain. 'I just wish it were under better circumstances.' He turned to his side. 'May I present a dear find of mine. Dr. Jacques Oppert.'

The man who Hugo imagined being in his eighties struggled to raise himself from his chair. Hugo moved forward quickly and lowered his hand in an attempt to stop the doctor from standing. 'Bonjour. Je m'appelle Hugo Duchamp.'

Oppert pushed himself back in his chair. His eyes were cloudy, and it was clear he was having trouble focusing. 'Duchamp?' he asked. 'Tell me, you're not one of the Parisian Duchamps, are you?'

Hugo smiled. 'I imagine there are a lot of Duchamps in Paris,' he answered.

'Jacques was a pathologist in Paris for over forty years,' Captain Comtois said. 'He retired to Beaufort-Sur-Mer ten years ago, and he likes to keep his hand in.'

'You're still working?' Hugo asked sharply.

Jacques laughed. 'Don't sound so surprised, Captain,' he said. 'I've always been a firm believer that us professionals never really retire. We just slow down. And when I wanted to slow down, I came here to the place I remembered so fondly from my childhood. I have been very happy here.' He stared at Hugo. 'I can't for the life of me think where I know you from.' He smoothed a stray white hair from the top of his almost bald head.

'Je suis désolé,' Hugo said. 'I don't recall meeting you before.'

'Where were you born?'

'Faubourg Saint-Germain,' Hugo answered.

Jacques clapped his hand. 'I knew it!' he cried. 'You look just like her.'

'*Her?*' Hugo questioned.

'Madeline.' Dr. Oppert spoke the name as if was a mantra.

Hugo's eyes widened. 'You knew my grandmother?'

The doctor snorted. 'Oui. I knew Madeline Duchamp. Not well, mind you,' he answered. 'But she knew me. Well enough to hate me,' he added with a twinkle. 'Oh, how your grandmother hated me with a vengeance.'

Hugo smiled, an image of his grandmother appearing in front of him. 'She certainly would have hated anyone reminding her she was a grandmother, but,' he smiled, 'I wouldn't take it personally. Madeline hated everyone. Even me sometimes,' he smiled, before adding with a chuckle, 'quite often actually.'

'She was a spirit,' Jacques exhaled.

Hugo sighed. 'She was that.' He shook Jacques' hand again. 'I'm happy to meet someone who knew her back then. There was Bertram, of course.'

'Ah, also my dear friend,' Jacques smiled.

'You knew Bertram as well?' Hugo asked.

'For about forty years,' Jacques replied.

'Is he… is he?' Hugo asked cautiously.

Jacques chuckled. 'Oui. The old devil is still alive and well.'

Hugo smiled. He felt bad. Captain Bertram Hervé was someone he had known since he was fourteen years old, and in many respects, he had been his saviour and mentor. But he was a distant man, not prone to affection or accepting compliments. However, he had been there for Hugo when he needed a male authority figure, and there was little doubt in Hugo's mind that he would never have become a police officer were it not for him. They had lost touch when Hugo had graduated from the police academy, exchanging only the occasional birthday or Christmas card. When Hugo had moved to London, they had finally lost touch completely. Hugo had never been good at keeping in touch. It felt like hard work and he had never learnt the line between too little or too much communication. In any case, too little had slowly stretched into never.

'I liked him very much,' Hugo said, with utmost honesty.

Jacques chuckled again. 'As did Madeline, as I recall.'

Hugo nodded. 'Oui. I believe she did. Tell me…' He stopped, distracted by a ruckus behind them. He turned on his heels. Avril Roche appeared to have thrown her glass at the wall and Clementine Bonheur and Jasper Connor were trying to calm her.

'Stop touching me!' Avril screamed. She dropped another glass. It smashed against the floor, breaking into pieces. She moved away, turning her back to the portrait. 'He's dead! My son is dead!'

Clementine moved quickly towards her. She pulled her into an embrace and kissed the top of her head. 'Cherie, you have to calm down. Vincent wouldn't want this. Arthur wouldn't want this…'

Avril pulled away, slapping Clementine's hand away from her. 'They're both dead because of us and what we did.'

Hugo stepped forward. He could not determine who Avril

le bateau au fond de l'océan

was talking to, because there were too many people in front of him. By the time he made his way through, Avril had moved out of the door onto the veranda. He made his way after her. He was not sure how Baptiste would react to being around her. He stopped. Avril was in Baptiste's arms, sobbing into his chest. Hugo turned to go back inside, but Baptiste beckoned for him to come closer. Hugo leaned against the wall and lit a cigarette. It was all he could think of doing.

'I'm sorry about that,' Avril said, wiping her nose.

'Don't apologise,' Baptiste said softly. 'We have to let it out somehow. Bottling this kind of shit up does nobody any good. I've been meaning to come and see you…' he said helplessly.

She touched his face. 'Je sais. And so have I.' She took a deep breath and exhaled very slowly. 'I suppose the truth is, I wanted to prolong it for as long as possible. Seeing you, his friend, would make it even more real somehow. I thought I could pretend, and that it would be enough…' She stared at Baptiste's face, her eyes flicking over him. There was no malice in it, just clear concern. 'Tell me, are you being looked after?'

Baptiste nodded. He pointed to Hugo. 'As usual, I don't know how I'd get through anything without Hugo and Ben. I hope you have someone to turn to as well, Madame Roche.'

Avril moved to the railing, thrusting herself forward and sucking in the warm, fresh air. 'I have exactly who and what I deserve,' she answered quizzically.

Hugo and Baptiste exchanged a puzzled glance. Baptiste shrugged his shoulders as if he had no clue what to say or do.

'It's a lovely portrait of your son,' Hugo said.

She nodded. 'Clementine is a brilliant woman,' she replied tartly. She turned to Baptiste. 'Tell me, what are you planning on doing with Vincent's ashes?'

Baptiste gulped. 'He said he wanted to be on the boat with his father. Je suis désolé, I know that isn't what you wanted, mais…'

'Mais, it's what he wanted,' Avril retorted. 'And that's all that matters.' She stepped away, leaning over the side of the veranda and staring towards the harbour. Grey hair had fallen from the knot on the top of her head, but she did nothing to stop it. It drifted in the surrounding breeze. 'I admit, I would like a grave to visit. That's what we're supposed to do, n'est pas?'

'You still can,' Hugo interjected. 'You can have a memorial. Lots of people do.'

She shook her head. 'Non. He wouldn't have wanted that. He was just like his father. They didn't believe in "all that nonsense," which is why, I suppose, they found it so easy to leave this earth. Non. My son must have his last wishes listened to. It's the very least I can do for him now, to not stand in his way.' She frowned. 'You intend on taking him down to the boat yourself?'

Baptiste's mouth contorted. 'I hadn't really thought about the practicalities,' he admitted. 'I was just focused on getting him here.'

Guy Fallon appeared in the doorway. 'Dax and I can take you down,' he said. 'I teach scuba diving, so I'm used to it. The boat is in the shallow part of the marina, so it's quite safe.'

Baptiste looked at Hugo. 'I don't know. I mean, I've done nothing like this.'

'You're already an excellent swimmer,' Hugo reasoned.

'Will you come with me?' Baptiste asked.

Hugo looked horrified, his hand flying to his mouth. 'Moi?'

Baptiste smiled. 'Oh, it's okay,' he laughed. There was a sadness to it, however, which troubled Hugo. 'I'll be okay,' Baptiste added.

Hugo gulped. 'Non, bien sûr I'll come with you,' he blurted, as if he had to before he changed his mind.

'I wish I could come with you,' Avril said, 'but I'm terrified of the water. Always have been, ever since I was little.'

'Dax and I have a glass-bottom boat,' Guy said. 'We can

moor it near the wreckage so anyone who wants to see, but doesn't want to swim, can.'

'That's very kind of you, Monsieur Fallon,' Hugo said.

Avril looked back towards the hotel. 'I suppose I should go back inside.' She moved to the doors, stopping before she went inside. 'When will you do it?'

Baptiste looked at Guy.

'We can do it tomorrow morning,' Guy said. 'That gives us a little time to practice diving.'

Avril nodded. 'Bon. Tomorrow morning it is.' She stopped, looking anxiously back at Baptiste. 'Jasper has arranged a firework display for this evening.'

Baptiste raised an eyebrow. 'A firework display?' he asked with incredulity.

'Oui,' she replied quickly. 'I know it might seem a little strange, but Vincent loved the firework display we had every year here in Beaufort-Sur-Mer. Jasper thought that…' she trailed off. 'Well, he thought it might be a nice tribute. He's arranged it all, and really it is very nice of him, I suppose.'

'I'm sure Vincent would have appreciated it,' Baptiste mumbled.

'You will come?' Avril asked desperately. 'Vincent would have wanted you there, I'm sure. And I would also appreciate having you by my side. It really would mean everything if you were there with me tonight because, at the moment, I'm not sure I can face it.'

Baptiste nodded slowly. 'I'll be there,' he sighed.

sept

Hugo and Baptiste moved slowly up the steps towards the fort. Hugo lit a cigarette, turning his head towards the sky. The fireworks had begun, and it felt like a joyous occasion. Fireworks always had that effect, Hugo reasoned. Baptiste stopped moving. His eyes trained on the exploding rockets above them. Hugo stole a look at him, the lights illuminating his solemn face. It troubled Hugo he could not reach his son, and that guilt was eating away at him. Guilt which was not his. He did not know what to say, and it reminded him once again how powerless he was because he was sure Ben would know exactly what to say.

Baptiste laughed. 'Non, he wouldn't.'

Hugo looked at him in surprise. 'Pardon?'

'You were thinking how you wished Ben was here because he would know the right thing to say to me.'

'How on earth could you know that?' Hugo asked, flabbergasted.

'Because you're you,' Baptiste answered. 'And I'm here to tell you, you're wrong. Dead wrong. You dropped everything to come with me. Hell, you're even going scuba diving with me tomorrow despite it being the last thing on earth you want to do.' He took a deep breath and reached for Hugo's cigarette. 'And the reason you can't think of anything to say to me is because you know there isn't anything you can say to make me feel better, so you're doing the only thing you can, and that's being with me.'

Hugo smiled. 'You're putting an awful lot of faith in me,' he said.

'Not really,' Baptiste replied. 'I feel safe with you and Ben because I know you'll always have my back. I hope you also know it's true in reverse. I will always be here for you both.'

'I know that,' Hugo whispered.

Baptiste pointed to the illuminated sky. 'What do you make

of this shit?'

Hugo lifted his head to the sky. The rockets were firing and exploding in succession in time to the rhythm of a pop song he did not recognise. It felt like a festival, a celebration of something, and it troubled him. But he realised it was not his right to be troubled by how someone else processed grief. In almost twenty years of being a police officer, he had learned grief came in many guises and needed dealing with accordingly.

'It isn't for me to say,' Hugo replied. 'Or you. Whatever you think, Avril Roche has lost her husband and son in a short period of time.'

'Through her own fault!' Baptiste exclaimed.

Hugo shook his head irritably. 'You don't know that, Baptiste, and nor do I. But we can't understand what went wrong for this family because it all began a long time before we became involved.'

'It bothered Vincent enough for him to kill himself,' Baptiste retorted.

Hugo shrugged. 'And that could be an answer in itself. Vincent was troubled, that much was clear. His choice and how he ended his life, prove it.' He raised his hand. 'I understand he may have had his reasons, but we also have to accept his problems may have contributed to his understanding, or rather, his misunderstanding of the situation.'

'I promised I would help him, and so did you!' Baptiste hissed, throwing the cigarette to the ground.

Hugo picked it up. 'I know. And I will. But what I'm trying to make you understand is that, no matter what we do, we may not get the answers you want.'

Baptiste shook his head. 'I don't just want answers. I want closure for Vincent.'

Hugo touched Baptiste's arm. 'You may not get either of those things, but it won't be for the want of trying.'

'And how are we going to do that?'

Hugo shrugged again. 'We're here until the end of the week. Let's just take it one day at a time and see what we can find.' He paused. 'Once we intern Vincent's ashes tomorrow, we can make some discreet inquiries. And I mean discreet, Baptiste. Because that's the way it has to be. You can't crash into these people's grief just because you think you know something.'

'They're hiding something,' Baptiste interrupted. 'All of them. I can just tell.'

Hugo was not entirely sure he disagreed.

'And you think so too, I can tell,' Baptiste added.

Hugo shrugged. 'I don't know whether that's true. Grief takes many forms, Baptiste, and more often than not, it makes people act strangely or out of character. Ecouté. I will speak with Captain Comtois and ask him about Arthur Roche's death. He may, as a professional courtesy, show me his files. But I will also ask Etienne to make further inquiries. And that's all we can do.'

'And if you find anything suspicious?'

'Then we'll deal with it,' Hugo responded.

'Even if that means upsetting someone?'

Hugo nodded. 'If I believe a crime has been committed or covered up, then I will do what I can to investigate,' Hugo replied. 'It is my duty to do so. But it is *my* duty, and if you want my help, then you have to do it my way. Do you understand? You have to trust me.'

'I do trust you,' Baptiste replied. 'But I have to make this right.'

Hugo inhaled the cigarette, turning back to the fireworks. He flicked on his glasses and could make out Avril Roche standing alone on the dock. He sensed Vincent's mother was troubled, not just by her son's death, but by whatever precipitated it. 'We will make this right,' Hugo whispered. 'For everybody.'

Avril Roche gestured to them. 'You came!' she called out.

'I said I would,' Baptiste responded.

She nodded, turning her back to them. She pointed at the fireworks. 'Jasper has gone to a lot of trouble,' she stated.

'The firework display is very special,' Hugo offered. 'I'm sure Vincent would have appreciated it very much.'

Avril turned sharply, fixing Hugo with a steely gaze. 'You believe so?'

Hugo gulped. 'I do.' He looked at Baptiste.

'I think so, too,' Baptiste added. 'It's a good send-off, if nothing else.'

'Do you mean that?' she asked. The tone of her voice was clear. It was desperation.

Baptiste nodded. 'Oui, I do.'

Hugo craned his neck. The fireworks were illuminating the sky in quick succession, filling the air with noise and smoke. He supposed it created an atmosphere that was not maudlin, and he liked it for that. He stole a look at Avril and realised how selfish he was being. While he could not comprehend her grief, he also did not understand what had led to the horrific turn of events in her life. Arthur Roche and his son had both committed suicide, one suicide caused by the other. He also understood it was most certainly none of his business.

Avril stepped away from them. She was staring into the night. Hugo followed her. She was watching Jasper Connor.

'When someone dies,' she said to Hugo in little more than a whisper. 'Is it normal to think of the strangest things?' she asked. 'Things which have nothing to do with your grief, or anything else important, for that matter. Just random things, things which seemingly mean nothing, but which I imagine in the Freudian world, probably mean a lot.'

'When my grandmother knew she was dying,' Hugo replied, 'she told me that if I didn't make sure her makeup was perfect in her coffin, she would come back from the dead and slap me so hard I would feel it for a fortnight.'

Avril Roche turned to face him. She smiled. 'You really are a strange man, aren't you?'

Hugo shrugged. 'You have no idea.'

'And?'

'I made sure her makeup was perfect,' he replied. 'Or rather, what I thought was perfect,' he added. 'I called the woman who usually looked after her when she had events to attend. She refused to do it, so I kept offering her more and more money until she agreed. In the end, I probably paid her as much as she earned in an entire month. She did Madeline's makeup.'

Baptiste shook his head. His eyes widened as if he was saying, *what does this have to do with anything?*

Hugo took a breath. He was not sure what he was saying, or what relevance it had, but he realised he had committed to something and had to follow it through. 'When I saw Madeline in her coffin, I realised she had lipstick on her teeth. All I could think of was that she would be furious with me, so I took my handkerchief and wiped it away. However, I only made it worse. I smudged the lipstick, and it went onto her chin, up to her nose.' He shook his head. 'It was a disaster.'

Avril studied him. 'And what did you do?'

He smiled. 'I closed the lid.'

Her eyes widened. 'What was the point of that?'

He shrugged. 'There wasn't one. There was no point in her having a perfect face or a perfect outfit. She was dead. And when I saw her with smudged lipstick, I realised that she most likely would have found it amusing. And she would also have liked it. I cared enough to try. She wasn't always tolerant, but she was kind to me, and at that moment I'm sure she would have appreciated it that I'd at least tried.' He closed his eyes. 'And she would have appreciated that I covered her up before anyone else got to see her looking less than perfect.'

Avril nodded. 'Then she didn't slap you?'

Hugo exhaled. 'The next day, I woke up with a very sore jaw. I suppose I slept at a funny angle, mais with Madeline, who knows?' he asked. 'If anyone could come back from the dead, it would be her by sheer force of nature.' He smiled at Avril. 'I realise I have taken the long way round to get to this point, but what I am trying to say is that there is never a right or wrong way to grieve. Those left behind are always filled with the guilt of loss, of what-ifs, of what I could have said, what *should* have been said.' He took her hand. 'All I can tell you is this. You will find peace, and you will find a way to move forward. And you will understand that they forgive you.'

She stared at him. 'I will?'

He nodded. 'You will. I know that because I still see Madeline from time to time. She comes to me in the middle of the night when a noise disturbs me and wakes me up. I look at the clock and see that it's 04H00, too early to get up, but not long enough for a good sleep. As I'm trying to sleep again, that's when I see her. And it's nice. It will be nice for you again, Madame Roche. It won't be what you want, or what you expect. But it will be something.'

Baptiste threw his hand over Hugo's shoulders. 'These fireworks are amazing.' He kissed Hugo's cheek. 'Mais, not as amazing as you.'

huit

'If it's all the same with you guys,' Brigitte St. Pierre declared, 'I'll watch from the bottom of the boat.'

'You've never been scuba diving?' Guy Fallon asked.

'Sure. Lots of times,' she responded. 'It just feels a bit weird to be burying the ashes of someone I knew.'

'And you?' Guy asked Quentin Arquette.

Quentin shuddered. 'I only swim as long as my head is above the water,' he quipped. 'I get claustrophobic if I go under.'

Guy nodded. 'I understand. It's not for everyone.' He looked around. 'Well, what about the rest of you? Are you still up for it?'

Hugo stared at Brigitte and Quentin and wished he could join them, far away from the water. Then he turned to Baptiste. He was struggling with the scuba equipment, anxiety clearly etched on his face, and Hugo knew he had no choice but to go through with the dive.

Dax Chastain rubbed Baptiste's shoulder. 'Don't look so panicked, man. I'll be right there. I won't let anything happen to you.'

Baptiste looked reassured. He pointed at Hugo. 'Merci, but he looks even more worried than I do!'

Guy Fallon secured an oxygen tank to Hugo's back. 'You'll both be fine, and that's a promise.' He stared at Dax. His head was lowered, staring directly into the water. 'Are you okay?'

Dax lifted his head slowly. 'I just figured we should say something before we go down.'

'Like what?' Guy asked with a frown.

Dax shrugged. 'I dunno. Aren't you supposed to like say something poetic when you bury ashes?'

Baptiste moved towards him. 'He was your friend, you can say anything you like.'

Dax touched the box of ashes. 'He certainly was,' he said.

'And he was a damn good one. I'm just sorry I let him down in the end.'

'You didn't let him down,' Guy interrupted.

'The hell I didn't,' Dax hissed. He looked out at the sea. 'Au revoir, Vincent,' he whispered. 'You really were the best friend I could have hoped for. You put up with all my shit. You knew all my secrets, and you never asked for anything other than just to be your friend. And I WAS your friend, and that makes it all the worse I didn't believe you, that I didn't try to help you, if I had… Well, if I had you might still be here, not in some crummy box we're about to bury at the bottom of Beaufort-Sur-Mer. I let you down buddy, but I won't again. I can do one last thing for you.'

'What are you talking about?' Guy asked.

Dax stared at Baptiste. 'Help Baptiste find out what happened to his father, for a start.'

'He killed himself,' Guy snapped. 'We all know that, and nothing is going to change that.' He shrugged. 'I can't say I understand why Vincent did what he did, but in the end, we have to just move on because there's nothing else we can do. For him, for them, for us.'

'We'll see,' Dax said quickly. He noticed the anxiety on Hugo's face. 'Well, we're all set. Are you ready, Hugo?' he asked.

Hugo swallowed, staring at the sea. 'I can't wait,' he replied with as much enthusiasm as he could muster.

Hugo fought the urge to panic, instead dragged himself along the guide rope Guy Fallon had tied from the dock to the boat wreckage. Hugo squinted. The goggles he was wearing made everything appear out of focus, or perhaps it was just because he had removed his glasses. It was all he could do to stop himself from panicking.

He forced his eyes wide open because he knew he had to

resist. He had to try to enjoy the experience. Despite it all, he could feel the serenity of the ocean. There was something soothing about it, and it was almost peaceful. The water was cool against his naked legs and when he moved his feet; the flippers he was wearing seemed to propel him forward in slow motion. The ocean was beautiful; he thought. It was crystal blue and when he strained his neck, he could see the glass-bottom boat floating above them, and he could vaguely make out the misty faces peering down at the divers.

Guy tugged the rope which he had tied from the dock to the boat. He tapped it with two fingers. In the basic training he and Dax had given to Hugo and Baptiste, Hugo remembered it meant they were to hold the guide rope at all times, particularly if visibility ever became difficult. Dax and Guy moved slowly, descending into the deep water. Hugo was still fighting the urge to panic. He just about had it under control, but he knew it was not far away, and that it would only take the slightest scare to bring it, and most likely him, to the surface.

They continued the descent to the wreckage. The water was reasonably shallow, which pleased Hugo immensely. Moments later, the wreckage of Arthur Roche's boat came fully into view. It appeared the boat had been staged since it had sunk, most likely for the tourists. A large, fake skeleton was attached to the stern. Dax had told them it had been Arthur's idea. After his boat had sunk, his insurance company had refused to pay for it to be salvaged, so between them they had concluded they could use it as a tourist attraction. After all, there had been a lot of sunken ships in that area, and unlike most of them, Arthur's had sunk near the harbour. It had proved immensely popular with tourists, particularly when they had concocted an elaborate tale of how it had ended up at the bottom of the harbour, usually a sad tale of a lover's tryst which had gone wrong. It changed each time and was far removed from the simple truth.

Dax tugged on the rope again and pointed to a large metallic lockbox that was attached to the cabin. He had told them that was where Arthur's ashes had been placed, and where they would soon add Vincent's.

Although there was little sound, Hugo imagined he could hear the gasp which came from Baptiste. Baptiste swam ahead. He pulled a small metal box from the bag attached to his waist and handed it to Dax with obvious reluctance. Dax took it from him. He placed a key in the larger box and placed the two boxes together, before throwing the lid down and locking it again. He gave Baptiste the thumbs up. Baptiste turned away, and Hugo could not fail to see the tears fogging his visor.

neuf

Avril Roche stared through the glass-bottom boat, perched on the edge of a chair. Her lips trembled as if she was reciting a prayer. Jasper Connor reached over and touched her back. She recoiled from his touch. His eyes widened in surprise and he shuffled uncomfortably. He lifted his head, noticing he was being watched by Brigitte and Quentin.

'Were you good friends with Vincent?' he asked lightly, as if attempting to cover his embarrassment at being rebuked.

'We were on the swim team with him,' Brigitte answered.

Avril turned to her. 'He loved to swim. Ever since he was a baby.' She turned back to see Hugo and the others moving towards the boat. 'It's lucky his father loved the water because I was no use to him,' she added sadly. 'He swam practically before he could walk.'

'He was very good,' Quentin stated. 'He would have won the championships for us, I'm sure.'

Brigitte pulled back her head sharply, staring at Quentin as if she did not know who he was. He stuck his tongue out at her.

'He was that good?' Avril asked.

Brigitte nodded. 'He certainly was.' She paused. 'Listen. I know you probably didn't get a chance to see him in action, but most of our heats were filmed. I have some on my computer. I could burn you a copy if you like?'

Avril exhaled. 'I would like that very much.'

Brigitte smiled. 'As soon as I get home, I'll arrange it.'

'You're very kind,' Avril replied.

Quentin peered beneath them. 'I almost wish I'd gone down with them.'

'Yeah, why didn't you?' Brigitte asked. 'I've seen you swimming, and you aren't so bad.'

'I just didn't feel like it,' he snapped.

le bateau au fond de l'océan

She frowned. 'Why?'

'Because I quit the team.'

'What?' she gasped. 'Why the hell have you quit? We're already one person down,' she bit her lip, stealing a look at Avril. 'Désolé.'

'That's exactly why I quit,' Quentin cried. 'Now stop bothering me!' He stood and moved away, taking a seat on the opposite side of the boat, burying his head in his hands as he stared into the ocean beneath them.

Brigitte turned to Clementine Bonheur, who was seated behind her. 'I loved your painting of Vincent, by the way.'

Clementine shot a sideways look at Avril, who turned away from her. 'Merci. I hope I did him justice.'

'You certainly did,' Jasper interjected. 'As always, you did an amazing job, Clementine.'

Avril snorted. 'Vincent would have hated it.'

'Avril!' Jasper admonished.

Clementine smiled. 'She's probably right. No kid wants his portrait painted.' She stared at Avril. 'I just wanted to do… to do something. I hate feeling useless, and there's not much else I can do.' She lowered her head. 'I do love you, dear old friend, and if I could take your pain away from you, I would in a heartbeat.'

Avril turned to her. Her face was hard, but after a moment, it softened. 'Je sais. I'm sorry. I seem to be angry with everyone at the moment and taking it out on those who don't fight back.' She shrugged. 'That's the trouble with guilt and shame. You feel as if you have to share it.'

Clementine stood and moved hesitantly toward her. She sat down next to Avril, gently touching her arm. 'You have every right to be angry, Avril. And not just angry. Furious. And if you need to take it out on me, consider me a willing volunteer.'

'This wasn't Vincent's fault,' Avril spat.

'Nobody thinks that,' Clementine reassured. 'Bien sûr, it

wasn't his fault. What happened was…' She stopped, glancing anxiously around the room.

'What happened is in the past,' Jasper interrupted. 'And that's where it has to stay.'

Avril covered her mouth as she watched her son being laid to rest. A sob escaped. Jasper moved quickly to her, putting his arm around and rubbing her shoulder. She pushed him away. 'I told you not to touch me, Jasper. This is all your fault!'

'My fault?' he gasped.

She cornered him. 'You know damn well it is!'

Clementine stepped in between them. 'Stop! This isn't the time, nor the place.'

'The hell it is!' Avril screamed. 'If not now, when? We all deserve to rot for what we did to those two beautiful souls.'

Clementine forcibly turned Avril around, using her hands to turn her head. She gestured towards the scuba divers below them. 'Your son is being layed to rest down there. That's all that matters right now.'

'Mon fils!' Avril cried, dropping to her knees. She touched the glass bottom. 'Mon beau fils!'

dix

Hugo took a seat opposite Captain Franc Comtois. Comtois was regarding Hugo with the exact same sceptical look Hugo was sure he would have himself under similar circumstances. Hugo had tracked him down following the scuba dive. Beaufort-Sur-Mer's police department was little more than a small open-plan office at the top of the harbour. As far as Hugo could tell, there was only Captain Comtois who worked there.

As if reading Hugo's mind, Comtois spoke. 'I have two part-time deputies I can call on if I need,' he said, 'and the nearest Gendarmerie is only fifteen miles away.' He smiled, tipping his head proudly. 'I'm proud to say that mostly, even in summer, there is little crime here.' He narrowed his eyes towards Hugo. 'I'm fairly sure there aren't many captains who can make such claims. I understand your own town has experienced many horrific and catastrophic events, non?'

'Larger towns often do, sadly,' Hugo added tartly. 'But we do what we can to put it right.'

The two men continued to stare at each other. 'You know why I am here,' Hugo began.

'I do?' Comtois questioned.

Hugo narrowed his eyes. He had been hoping the detective would not be difficult because, as far as Hugo could tell, there was no reason to be. Jurisdictional concerns aside, it was in everyone's best interests to ensure no crimes were committed.

Comtois sipped the remains of his café. He had not offered to get Hugo one. 'I've known Vincent Roche all his life, and there is nothing I don't know about him. You, on the other hand,' he added, staring directly at Hugo, 'barely knew him.'

Hugo nodded. 'That's true. I only met him once. But he was a good friend of my son.'

'Your *son*...' Comtois snorted, his voice laced with sarcasm.

Hugo ignored it and continued. 'The point is, Captain, Vincent believed something happened here at Beaufort-Sur-Mer which involved his father and lead in one way or another to his death.'

'His father took his own life,' Comtois shot back. The twitch in his eye flexed quickly several times in rapid succession. 'I had also known Arthur Roche for most of his life. We went to school together.'

'Je suis désolé,' Hugo replied. 'I didn't know that.'

Comtois shrugged. 'There's no reason you should,' he retorted. He sighed again. 'Captain Duchamp, I realise you are a distinguished officer, and I apologise if I seem particularly antagonistic towards you, but please understand this when I tell you. Arthur was a friend. If I believed for a second that there was anything untoward about his death, then I would have moved heaven and earth to discover what it was.'

Hugo nodded. 'I understand.' He paused. 'Then forgive me for asking this. Why was Vincent so convinced there was?'

Comtois drained the contents of his drink. 'Because he was a fool. A nice enough kid, but a fool. He was highly strung, just like his mother, and Arthur himself was no walk in the park. He was a drunk for most of his life. A good drunk, if there is such a thing, but a drunk nonetheless.' Comtois exhaled. 'Unfortunately, Vincent inherited the worst from both of them, as far as I can tell. And even when he was a kid, Vincent always saw demons in the shadows.'

Hugo frowned, wondering what the Captain might mean. It was a strange choice of words, he thought. 'I don't understand,' Hugo said.

'And it's not for me to explain it to you,' Comtois snapped. He held up his hands. 'Désolé, again. You must think me an unpleasant police officer. For what it's worth, I'm not, mais,' a smile hovered on his face, 'I am an old grouch, who always thinks he knows better.'

'There's no need to apologise,' Hugo stated. He returned a smile. 'And often enough, old grouches do know better. I'm fast becoming an old grouch myself and hope being wiser comes with it.'

'As far as I can tell, you're no slouch as you are,' Comtois replied with apparent reluctance.

Hugo smiled gratefully. 'I hope so, and that's why, from one police officer to another, I would appreciate your help. I'm not trying to infringe on your department or to suggest you may have missed something. I suppose I'm just asking you to help me, so that I can, in turn, put Baptiste's mind to rest.' He paused, deciding to take another tack. 'You have a son too, don't you?' he asked. 'I met him the other night. Gregoire, isn't it? I imagine he and Vincent were of a similar age. Were they friends?'

Comtois did not answer immediately. 'They went to school together,' he answered, but did not elaborate further. The defensiveness had returned as quickly as it had dissipated.

Hugo clasped his fingers together, desperate to light a cigarette but conscious of the *pas fumer* sign on the wall. 'What did you mean about Vincent seeing demons in the shadows?' he asked.

'Just that,' Comtois snapped. 'As I said, he and Avril share that trait. And added to what he inherited from Arthur, the poor kid had the cards stacked against him. He was always afraid, always imagining the worst in everyone. And the worse Arthur got, between the two of them, you'd think the devil himself was hiding in Beaufort-Sur-Mer.'

Hugo struggled to reconcile his admittedly brief impression of Vincent, with the one which was being presented to him by Franc Comtois. However, it was clear from what Baptiste had told him about Vincent was the young man was troubled. He cleared his throat. 'Did they have a reason to believe that?'

'What do you mean?'

Hugo shrugged. 'Only that it is my experience, often if someone has that kind of fear, it is sometimes based on a reality, a distorted reality maybe, but a reality nevertheless. What I'm asking you is this - did something happen to Vincent Roche to warrant the kind of fear you have described?'

'Rien,' Comtois snapped, as if the word was difficult for him to speak.

Hugo lowered his head. He knew only one thing for certain at that moment. Captain Franc Comtois was lying to him about something, but whether it was important or relevant, he could not determine.

'Rien?' Hugo repeated. 'What about Arthur Roche?'

'What about him?' Comtois snapped.

Hugo sighed. He was growing weary with Comtois and his reticence. He was sure he would never treat another police officer with such detachment. However, the truth remained. Comtois was most likely twenty years older than Hugo, a generation removed, and his reticence to help could be informed by many disparate factors. 'Did anything happen to him?'

'Arthur Roche was a simple man,' Comtois replied. 'A modest man. A self-made man.'

'What do you mean?' Hugo asked.

'The hotel you're staying in was his. He built most of it himself with his own hands,' Comtois said. He gave a sad smile. 'Hell, we all helped. There wasn't much of a tourist industry in Beaufort-Sur-Mer back then, but we all understood that once we had a hotel right on the seafront, it wouldn't be long before the tourists came and that we could finally put this place on the map.' He sighed. 'And it worked. It was tough at first, but we got there. What you see around you is the result of a once dead town coming together to create something exquisite.'

Hugo nodded. 'It certainly is a beautiful town and hotel.' He shrugged. 'I can't pretend I know a lot about such things. But to me, it seems to be both modern and old-fashioned at the same time, and for what it's worth, I like it very much.'

'The modern part is nothing to do with the Roche's, I can assure you,' Comtois snapped.

'And yet, I suppose necessary,' Hugo responded.

'Says who? Jasper Connor?' Comtois retorted in such a way, it was obvious to Hugo there was no love lost between Comtois and the current owner of the hotel, Jasper Connor.

'It devastated Arthur to lose the hotel.' Comtois added, gulping.

'He lost it?'

'Oui,' Comtois replied. His nostrils flared. 'Oh, it was all legal and above board, you might say,' he snapped. 'But you could also say Arthur was swindled out of his hotel, and all the hard work he and his family had put into it.'

'I'm sorry, I don't understand,' Hugo said.

Comtois shrugged. 'It's all perfectly simple. Arthur wasn't much of a businessman, and he was in over his head. Despite the hotel always being full, he was losing money constantly, and the more he borrowed to stay afloat, the more he fell deeper into a hole. And then along came Jasper Connor. The answer to his prayers.' Comtois snorted. 'Answer to his prayers?' he repeated with a bite. 'Like a shark smelling blood, that's what Jasper Connor is. He travels around France buying up businesses when they're in trouble because he knows he can get desperate owners to sell for a fraction of the worth. Damn that man to hell. Arthur is dead because of him.'

Hugo's mouth twisted. Comtois was right about one thing, while Jasper Connor may be acting unethically, it was perfectly legal, and who were any of them to criticise him for helping someone who was in desperate need.

'It cost Arthur everything, his pride, his marriage, his…' he gulped, before adding, 'his life.'

'Why was Vincent Roche so adamant his father's death wasn't suicide then?'

Comtois glared at Hugo. 'I already told you. The kid was messed up.'

'Then there was nothing suspicious?'

Comtois shook his head. 'Arthur was destroyed. He felt as if he had nothing to live for, so he chose not to. It was that simple.'

Hugo nodded. 'Did he leave a note?'

Comtois shrugged. 'Not that we're aware of. He may have, but I never found one.'

'And his wife? Or his son? Didn't he write to them?' Hugo pressed.

'Vincent was away at school by then and Avril...' Comtois trailed off again, 'had also moved on. I don't think she and Arthur had any contact for quite some time before his death. Remember, it was her business too. She'd been the hotel chef for the whole time it was open, ploughed in her own money, and she walked away with next to nothing either.'

Hugo pursed his lips. There was something about how Avril Roche and Jasper Connor interacted, which suggested their relationship was more than he would have imagined it to be.

'If your next question is concerning Avril and Jasper, I'll counsel you to mind your own business,' Comtois spat. 'Mais, I will say this. Avril convinced Arthur to sell to Jasper. He was reluctant, you see. But Avril told him they had no choice. He always listened to Avril. She was the love of his life, from when they were fourteen years old. I think she'd always had dreams of getting out of Beaufort-Sur-Mer, and the fact she barely got out of the hotel kitchen on most days had worn thin after a while. And then when Vincent left for school, well, I suppose that changed everything...'

He stopped, his eye twitching rapidly. 'The day Arthur signed the papers to sell the hotel, he moved out, and she didn't go with him. It destroyed Arthur, and that's no lie. His drinking got worse, fuelled by the pittance Jasper Connor paid him for the hotel. He had a good few months, I suppose you could say, but it was most certainly masking his pain.'

'And Avril?'

'The first thing Jasper Connor did was to hire a new chef for the hotel,' Comtois replied, 'and the second was to take Avril on a Caribbean cruise. Avril and Jasper feel guilty because they should,' he added. 'They cut their trip short because Arthur killed himself.'

'Then they weren't here at the time?'

Comtois shook his head. 'Non, therefore they could not have murdered him.'

It still does not mean they weren't involved, Hugo considered.

'And why would they, anyway?' Comtois continued. 'They had the hotel. They had taken everything from him. The fact is, if Arthur Roche hadn't killed himself, his drinking would have, in one way or another. He'd have either drunk himself to death, or stumbled over the harbour wall one day as he walked back from the bar.'

'And what about Clementine Bonheur?' Hugo asked. 'The lady who painted Vincent's portrait.'

Comtois snapped. 'What about her?' he snapped.

'I got the impression she was involved in what happened.'

Comtois groaned. 'What happened is none of your business,' he repeated. 'We are dealing here with actual people, with genuine emotions. People I have known for a very long time and I like very much. Jasper Connor notwithstanding. No one escaped from what happened with any sort of pride or dignity.'

Hugo nodded. 'I understand. Avril Roche clearly feels differently.'

'Only now,' Comtois spat. 'Guilt does that. Listen, as I said, everyone did what they did for their own reasons. Avril wanted a new life. Jasper wanted a good deal. Clementine wanted everyone to be happy. She's that kind of dame. She acts all airy, floating around the town like she's a fairy or something. She wanted Avril to get what she wanted, and I think she wanted the same for Arthur. Running the hotel was killing him. I guess she just wanted him to be free.' He shrugged. 'Her intentions were good, and I think she was probably the one who convinced him selling to Jasper was the right thing to do.'

Hugo nodded. He rose to his feet. 'Just one more question. As far as I know, Arthur Roche tied himself to his sunken boat and was later discovered by scuba divers. Was there anything found in his autopsy?'

Comtois shook his head. 'Dr. Oppert concluded there was no evidence of anything other than death by suicide.'

Hugo raised an eyebrow. As far as he could tell, the retired Parisian doctor was likely well into his eighties.

As if sensing his reticence, Comtois said. 'Jacques may be old, but he is experienced, and as far as I'm concerned, still at the top of his game. There's not much in the way of murder here in Beaufort-Sur-Mer, so keeping a doctor has always been difficult. When Jacques retired here, he agreed to step in on such occasions his professional assistance is required. He's not called on often, but when he is, I have little doubt of his skills being as sharp as they once were.' He paused. 'And besides, I always send the report off to the next town, have their doc check over it. They found nothing to disagree with in Jaques report.' He glared at Hugo. 'Mais, if you tell him I do that, you and I are going to have an enormous problem. Understand?'

'Bien sûr, I understand,' Hugo conceded, moving to the door.

'Captain Duchamp,' Comtois called after him. 'Take your son home and get him to put this all behind him, for his own sake, and I'll do the same here. It is in no one's best interest for this to go any further.'

Hugo nodded. 'Oui. Merci for your time, Captain Comtois.'

onze

Baptiste moved his head slowly, turning from the top of the ruined fortress overlooking Beaufort-Sur-Mer, towards the stairway and the ocean beneath them. He tried to imagine Vincent being there as if his disappeared footsteps might bring him closer to them. He knew it would not, but he hoped that if he could imagine him in the space, it might make the guilt and loss seem less acute.

While Hugo was with Captain Comtois, Baptiste had been left cooling his heels in his hotel room, with too much time on his hands. All he had was to dwell on what had happened to his friend. When Dax Chastain had called to suggest he join them at the fort for an impromptu send-off for Vincent, away from the adults, Baptiste had reluctantly agreed to go. He wanted a chance to speak to the younger people who had known Vincent, where they would hopefully share more with him about what had happened. Quentin and Brigitte had joined them and Dax had brought along his friends Gregoire Comtois and Guy Fallon. They had also bought along a lot of beer and the type of cigarettes that even Hugo would not approve of. But for the first time in a long time, Baptiste felt relaxed. He sucked on the joint, staring down at the 19th century boardwalk. The people moving along it appeared like ants; he thought with a smile. A snort escaped his lips, which seemed very amusing to him.

Dax Chastain flopped down next to him and handed him a beer. 'How you doing?'

Baptiste shrugged. 'Dunno,' he answered honestly. 'Et toi?'

Dax contemplated his answer. 'I guess I haven't really gotten used to it yet. I missed Vincent when he was away, but I always figured he would come back, so it didn't matter. Right now, I keep thinking that hasn't changed. He's just away, but he'll be coming back.' He stole a look at Baptiste. 'Stupid, huh?'

'Not at all,' Baptiste answered. He had his own ghosts,

people he imagined would walk back into his life at any moment, even though he knew they never would. *Chen Gao*. He closed his eyes and instantly saw her fine, dark hair and the yellow summer dress she had been wearing the first time he had ever seen her. She had continued to wear the dress, and as they had become tuned to one another, it seemed as if she always knew when to wear it to lighten his mood. He missed her every day, but as the time had moved forward, he had realised that the further time marched on, the less likely she was to come back.

He took a deep breath. 'In fact, that's a good way of thinking about it. He's not gone, he's just away, and he'll be back one day. We live with that hope, even if we know it's never going to happen,' he added sadly.

Gregoire Comtois and Baptiste's fellow students, Quentin and Brigitte, joined them on the edge of the ruin.

'What you talking about?' Gregoire asked.

'Life. Death. Small shit like that,' Dax responded.

Gregoire laughed, pulling his hair back and tying it up with an elastic band. 'Hey, do you remember the last time we were up here together? You, me and Vincent?'

Dax laughed. 'Ah, the American twins and their fat friend?'

Gregoire patted him on the back. 'I wouldn't say your girl was fat,' he extended his hands in front of his chest, 'rather she was curvaceous.'

Dax grimaced, the shadow of a memory passing across his face. 'Well, let's just say her curves nearly suffocated me that night!' He stopped. 'Damn, that was a good night.' He shook his head. 'Wasn't that Vincent's last night before he left for school?'

'Yeah. At least he went out with a bang,' Gregoire added with a wink.

'I only ever knew him sad,' Brigitte St. Pierre announced suddenly.

'Man, that sucks,' Dax said. 'He was so much more than that.'

'He certainly was,' Guy added.

Gregoire sidled up to Brigitte. 'I bet you made him happy though, didn't you, sweetheart?'

Brigitte laughed. 'Well, it wasn't for the want of trying,' she stated huffily.

Gregoire playfully pulled at her afro. 'Then he was crazy AND blind, sweetheart.'

'Or he just had better taste,' Quentin Arquette interrupted tartly.

Brigitte glared at him. 'Jealous, much, Quentin? You want some of this black goddess, don't ya? You always have, but you're dreaming honey if you think I'd lower myself in *any* way for you.'

He snorted. 'I'd rather use my left hand.'

She looked at his hand. 'Honey, I've seen you in a Speedo AND naked. Your left hand is about ten times bigger, as far as I can tell.'

Quentin opened his mouth to respond, but before he could, Baptiste held up his hands. 'Quit doing this dance, you two. Just get a room already!'

Quentin glared at him. 'What are you talking about?'

Baptiste smiled at him. 'You know exactly what I mean, you delusional fool.'

'Dieu, Vincent would have loved this,' Dax sighed.

Baptiste turned to Dax. 'It would have been nice to have met Vincent when he wasn't sad.'

Dax nodded. 'I know you'll find it hard to believe after everything that's happened, but he didn't use to be the sort of person to let things bother him,' he replied.

'He certainly wasn't,' Gregoire added.

'Then what the fuck went wrong?' Baptiste yelled. He grimaced. 'Sorry. I know it's none of my business. I saw the darkness in him. I just wish I'd known something else about him, not just how he got like that, but also what I could have done to help him.'

Dax shrugged. 'You can't think like that. You just can't. I understand it, but we all have to just accept it's done. You had his back when he needed it, but that doesn't mean you could have done anything different. I knew him all my life, and I couldn't. The only thing I'm happy about is that he had a friend in Montgenoux. He needed that, and I have to live with the fact I fucking let him down.'

Gregoire stared at him. 'You were his best friend. You did more for him than anyone else.'

Dax rounded on him. 'Except saving his life? Yeah, I *sure* was a great friend.'

Brigitte cleared her throat. 'Some people just can't be helped, not in the way we want to, at least.'

'What do you mean?' Baptiste asked.

She shrugged. 'Vincent asked you for your help. You may not like the way he went about it, but he asked you for it all the same. He knew you would help him, and it's not the way you wanted it to go, but he asked you. And that's a lot. He knew he could count on you, and you should be proud of that.'

Baptiste finished the rest of the joint and threw it into the night air. 'But there's nothing I can do. He was convinced something happened in this damn town. And he was so convinced it became unbearable for him. Just letting it go, accepting that there was nothing wrong, just seems pointless, and such a fucking waste of time.'

'But that's exactly what it was,' Guy Fallon said. 'It's all just pointless.'

'His father killed himself,' Gregoire interrupted. 'That's all there is to it. There is no conspiracy, or lie, or cover-up.'

Baptiste turned to Gregoire. 'Are you really so sure?'

Dax sighed. 'Arthur was depressed. When he lost the hotel we used to see him around town, always drunk and sad. He'd

le bateau au fond de l'océan

always been like that, but it was worse, and so hard to see him that way. There was nothing any of us could do. I wish there had been, but he didn't want help. I suppose you'd say he was only interested in numbing the pain he felt.'

'This has nothing to do with any of you,' Quentin snapped. 'And frankly, everyone blaming themselves is boring, and actually pretty fucking weird. They killed themselves because they were selfish. End of.'

'You really are an insensitive prick,' Brigitte hissed.

Gregoire sighed. 'As irritating as it is. He actually has a point.'

'He could have said it nicer,' Dax said, glaring at Quentin.

'Maybe,' Gregoire conceded. 'Mais, it's the truth. Arthur Roche was a gambler and a drunk. We can dress it up nicely, but it's what he was.' He looked at Dax. 'You know that's true. Everyone in this damn town talks about how Jasper stole the hotel from him, and that Avril and Clementine helped. But it wasn't their fault. It was Arthur's.'

'In what way?' Baptiste asked.

Gregoire shrugged. 'Everyone knew he was running the hotel into the ground. He owed money to everyone. He kept borrowing more and more and he could never pay it back. The more he gambled to try to raise funds, the more he lost, which meant the more he drank. It was ridiculous.'

'Greg,' Dax cried.

'Don't Greg me,' Gregoire Comtois retorted. 'You know the truth as well as I do. We've sat in this exact same spot more times than I can count. Vincent was always whining about his folks, the fights, the lack of money. But he always found a way to blame everyone but who was actually to blame. Arthur. Vincent hero-worshipped his Papa, and that's okay, but we've all been dragged into it. Vincent is dead. Arthur is dead. It's sad, but it has to be the end of it.' He stood. 'I'm going down to the bar. I want to get drunk and have some damn fun because that is exactly what we should be doing at our age. I hope I'll find a nice chick to have fun with, or,' he stopped, smiling at Brigitte, 'unless I've already found one.'

Brigitte smiled, her hands moving slowly around her afro. 'Is that an invitation?'

He laughed. 'Only if you're prepared to be debauched.'

Brigitte stood, smoothing her hair. 'I'm *always* prepared to be debauched,' she said, sliding away from the men.

Gregoire fell into step behind her. 'I bet you are,' he laughed, licking his lips. 'Let's go and be debauched together then.' He glanced back over his shoulder. 'Wakes are fine for old folks, but we're still young.' He lifted his hand and looked at his watch. 'And so is the night.'

Brigitte snuggled next to him. 'And so is the night,' she repeated.

douze

Hugo stepped onto the boardwalk, inhaling the fresh air of a new morning. The smell filled him with a warmth he had forgotten about. Back in Montgenoux, whenever he could, the first thing he did each morning was to sit by his swimming pool, a café in one hand, a cigarette in the other. It was enough to balance him for the day. He would stare at the gently lapping water, more often than not with his feet in it, and it gave him the strength to do whatever he needed to do in the day ahead.

He did not notice Baptiste had followed him out of the hotel. He smiled warmly at Hugo and wrapped his arm around Hugo's shoulders. 'I heard you pacing in your room. You're worried about something?'

Hugo glanced at his watch. It was barely 07H00. 'Désolé, Baptiste,' he responded. 'Strange bed, strange room, strange times…'

'No Ben,' Baptiste added.

'I don't deal with change well, I'm ashamed to say,' Hugo added.

'Nor do any of us, I suspect,' Baptiste replied. 'Have I thanked you for coming here with me?' he asked.

Hugo nodded. 'Once or twice,' he smiled warmly.

Baptiste rubbed Hugo's shoulder. 'Yeah, but as long as you know, I'm grateful, and more importantly, I owe you.'

'You owe me nothing,' Hugo responded, before adding, 'except possibly for making me scuba dive.'

Baptiste laughed. 'I still can't believe you did that.'

'You can't?' Hugo gasped. 'I think I'll be having nightmares about it for a very long time.' He stopped, flicking on his glasses and narrowing his eyes. Something had caught his attention in the distance. 'Isn't that your friend Brigitte down by the docks?' There was something about the way she was seated, which seemed odd to him.

Baptiste turned his head. 'Yeah, let's go and say bonjour.' He laughed. 'I guess she didn't make it back to her hotel, after all.'

They dashed across the boardwalk until they reached where Brigitte St. Pierre was. Baptiste touched her shoulder.

'Get your damn hands off me!' Brigitte screeched. She jumped to her feet, her eyes wide and panicked.

Baptiste jumped back in horror. 'Désolé, Brigitte. I didn't mean to scare you.'

Brigitte looked between Hugo and Baptiste, her eyes flicking quickly between them as if she was having trouble processing what was in front of her.

Hugo took a tentative step towards her. There was something about her demeanour he recognised and it troubled him immensely. He hoped it was not what he imagined. 'Are you all right, mademoiselle?' he asked gently.

Brigitte moved backwards until she hit the railings. There was nowhere else for her to go unless she turned and jumped into the water below.

'I haven't seen you since last night when you went off with Gregoire,' Baptiste said. 'Did you have fun?' he added gaily.

She glared at him. 'I have to go,' she whispered. She moved away from them without saying another word or looking back. Her hands were wrapped tightly around her chest. Hugo noticed her hair was wild and filled with sand and debris.

'Well, that was weird,' Baptiste said.

Hugo watched the young woman disappear into the hotel foyer. 'Do you think she's okay?' he asked. 'She looked half scared to death.'

Baptiste shrugged. 'Probably a bit wasted still.'

'Wasted?' Hugo questioned.

Baptiste studied Hugo's face. 'Are you a cop right now, or my Papa?'

Hugo's jaw tightened. 'Well, technically I am off duty, right now, but I'd like to think I'm always your Papa first.'

'Bon,' Baptiste replied. 'We hung out at the old fort last night and there may,' he paused, adding a wink, 'or may not have been a little recreational enjoyment, if you know what I'm saying.'

'Drugs?' Hugo asked sharply.

'A bit of weed, that's all,' Baptiste answered. 'And we're all adults, so don't get preachy.' He pointed at the cigarette in Hugo's hand. 'And probably not as bad as the cancer stick you always have between your fingers.'

Hugo lifted the cigarette to his lips and sucked on it defiantly. 'And she took drugs?' he asked.

Baptiste shrugged. 'I guess so.'

Hugo pursed his lips, staring towards the hotel. 'Then maybe that's all that was wrong with her,' he mused.

'Probably,' Baptiste replied nonchalantly. He looked up. Brigitte had appeared on the veranda of her room and was staring down at them. 'Hey, Brigitte,' he called. 'Have a shower and catch some ZZZs and we'll see you in the bar for lunch, okay?'

She glared at Hugo and Baptiste and ran back into her room, pulling the door closed with force.

'Weird,' Baptiste said.

Hugo watched as Brigitte pulled the curtains closed. He could not be sure, but she appeared to be sobbing.

treize

Baptiste followed the line of tourists as they trailed slowly behind Dax. His mouth twitched around his breathing apparatus as he tried to smile. He could see by the way they were clutching the rope that it was their first time. Even though it was only his own second attempt at diving, he felt more confident and had felt himself relax into it, and he was secretly proud Dax had trusted him enough to be at the end of the line.

The water was cool against Baptiste's skin but he realised it was the first time he had actually felt warm in days. It was as if a chill had lifted from his body, a chill he thought he could not eradicate. It reminded him of a time before. A time when he had imagined he would never feel warmth again. But it had passed, and he could only hope it would pass again. At times such as these, it bothered him it was passing, just as it had when he realised the memory of Chen Gao, his one true love was slowly passing. Her face was disappearing, just like her yellow dress appeared to be fading in his mind's eye. As much as he wanted to feel alive again, he was not sure he wanted to do so at the expense of losing those who had meant something to him.

He tried to shake the thought away and moved his body in rhythm with the water, and once again, he felt free. It did not matter that his view was mostly obliterated by the somewhat large rear end of the American tourist in front of him.

They continued for several minutes, snaking and circling the harbour and Baptiste realised that when they passed the next curve, Arthur Roche's sunken boat would once again come into view. He hoped above all else he had done what Vincent wanted in some small way. He realised the outcome was not the result Vincent would have expected, but if they were satisfied Arthur's own death was nothing but a rotten, depressing tragedy, then it was better than uncertainty. Baptiste hoped that wherever Vincent was, he saw that, but more importantly, he was with his father and that they both, finally, had found some peace.

He was dragged suddenly back to the reality in front of him. The guide rope had been pulled rigid, and then, moments later, Dax being jerking it with several taunt, hard tugs. Baptiste immediately recognised it from the training session. *Stop.*

Baptiste strained his eyes to try to see what was ahead, because he was sure it meant there was something wrong. He noticed the fisherman Guy Fallon had let go of the rope and was swimming towards Dax, away from the group. Baptiste's eyes crinkled as he tried to understand what was happening. The swimmers in front of him had also stopped, anxiously treading water. Baptiste tried to assess whether he was strong enough to let go of the rope and swim ahead to see what was going on. He made a split decision and dropped the rope, propelling himself forward with as much gusto as he could manage. It took him a few moments to catch up with Guy. He was treading water in front of Arthur Roche's boat. Baptiste swam past him, curious to see what had caught his attention. He stopped, pushing himself backwards, his eyes widening in horror.

'What the hell's that?' he whispered to himself. His first thought was that it was another prop, like the skeleton. A tourist attraction. But something told him it was not. He swam forward. He felt his stomach churn. It took him a moment to recognise who it was. A young man he had only just met.

Gregoire Comtois was tied to the front of the boat, the chain of an anchor wrapped around him, his eyes gaping open, his tongue wide and swollen. Baptiste fought the urge to vomit into the mouthpiece. He lifted his head, looking towards the surface. *I have to find Hugo.*

quatorze

Clementine Bonheur stepped onto the beach and, with the poise of a woman who had done it a hundred times before, placed her easel in the sand. She pulled a foldable stool from an oversized bag, opened it, and lowered her body onto it. Hugo watched her from a few feet away as she tied frizzy hair into a ponytail before lifting a paintbrush and palette into her hand. Within seconds, her hand was moving as if it had a life of its own. It fascinated him, particularly because he had no such talent.

'I can paint you if you would prefer,' she called out to him, without looking around. 'I get a little bored with painting the same thing all the time.'

Hugo started, his cheeks flushing. He had assumed she was so enthralled by what she was doing, she would not notice him watching her.

'Don't be embarrassed,' she added, still not looking at him. 'With your occupation, I would be more shocked if you didn't people watch. Isn't that how you learn all you need to know about your suspects?'

'I'm not sure it's that simple,' Hugo conceded, 'mais, oui, watching is something I spend a lot of time doing, always hopeful that it will produce the results simply asking questions does not.'

She gestured for him to move closer to her. 'Come nearer. I'm afraid I'm a little deaf on my right side.'

Hugo moved across the beach towards her. After breakfast with Baptiste, he had found himself at somewhat of a loose end. Dax had arrived and invited them to join him scuba diving again with a bunch of tourists. Hugo had politely declined, but Baptiste had seemed keen and Hugo had encouraged him to go, pleased by the flush of adrenaline in his cheeks. He turned his head. Clementine Bonheur appeared to be in the middle of a painting of the historic harbour.

le bateau au fond de l'océan

'Your painting is beautiful,' he said.

She smiled. 'Merci. I suppose a big city boy such as yourself must find it a little tragic that I spend my time painting the same damn things, mais…' she trailed off, with a flamboyant shrug of her shoulders.

'Not at all,' Hugo responded. 'I wish I had such talent, and,' he studied the painting, 'I imagine no matter if the subject matter is the same, that each one of your paintings is different and unique in its own way.'

Clementine smiled, appearing almost embarrassed. She pointed to a house on the hill behind the harbour. 'My studio is there. The door with the red flowers. I willingly accept patrons.' She turned her head. 'I really would like to paint you, though. It would be a pleasant change from seascapes. And you have a face which cries out for immortalising in watercolour.'

Hugo shook his head. 'Merci, that's very kind of you, mais non,' he answered softly.

Clementine laughed. 'Ah, modesty prevents it, I suppose. That's a shame. Peut être I'll do it from memory, anyway. You have a face I'm sure it is difficult to forget. I'm sure you have people who would appreciate it, even if you wouldn't.' She studied his face. 'Oh, and those eyes. They are more beautiful than the sea.' She chuckled upon seeing Hugo blush. 'I'm sorry, I didn't mean to embarrass you.'

Hugo smiled. 'You didn't.' It was true. He had never become accustomed to compliments, and he had never learnt how to accept them. His response had always been to look over his shoulder and say, *are you talking to me?*

She laughed again. 'Ah, well, un peu.' She dropped her brush into her lap, splashing it with paint. She wiped it with the back of her hand, spreading a trail of red paint across her kaftan. The fact it reminded Hugo of blood splatter was not lost on him, and yet another reminder of the darkness he walked through on an almost daily basis.

Clementine stared at him. 'Do you know the real reason I never wanted children?' she asked him. 'I told everyone it was because I hated brats. Bring me a child fully grown and de-snotted and I'll give him love, I used to say. But the actual truth was, I never learnt how to be anything other than I am. My mother didn't want to be a mother, and my father didn't want to be a father. They were told they had to, so they did, and the result was the three of us living together in the same damn home I now use as a studio with a mattress in the corner. We are all told what we should be, but very few of us are told just how to achieve that.' She shrugged. 'Some make a passable attempt at it, others don't, and others,' her mouth twisted, 'shouldn't have bothered. I wasn't sure which category I would fall into, so I thought it wiser to live an entirely selfish life by following my own path.'

Hugo stared at her. He found himself unable to disagree. 'I understand,' he said softly.

She raised an eyebrow. 'And yet you have a son?'

He shrugged. 'Baptiste was fully grown when I met him. His joining my family was a case of three people coming together who didn't know how to be a family. I take no credit in it, other than between the three of us we made it work.' He stared at her. 'Had I never met Baptiste, or my husband Ben even, I am sure I would still be in London, most likely alone, except for the times when I could not bear it. And those times would be brief, and they would be fleeting before I would return to the person I was before.' He stopped, biting his lip, realising he had said too much.

Clementine nodded. 'You got lucky.'

'Oui,' Hugo exhaled.

'Mais, so did they,' she added.

'Did you never think of leaving Beaufort-Sur-Mer?'

She laughed. 'Only every day, ten times a day,' she answered. She stared at him. 'I expect a man from the big city must think this

le bateau au fond de l'océan

town to be strange and tremendously boring.'

'Not at all,' he replied. 'Montgenoux isn't much bigger.'

'Well, it is boring,' Clementine retorted. 'The truth is, and it's a truth it has taken me a long time to admit, is that I never left because I was too afraid. It was easier to be a square peg in a round hole. Besides, I'm talking about Paris,' she retorted.

Hugo shrugged. 'Paris isn't much bigger either, in real terms. Each arrondissement is its own little town, and believe me, it is filled with all the shame, gossip and problems of any other small town.'

She stepped into the sand, kicking off her shoes and stepping into the water. 'Ever since I was a child, I've been plagued with terrible insomnia. I barely sleep four or five hours, if I'm lucky. However, what is fortunate is that I can step out of my studio, throw on a kaftan and walk around this town in the middle of the night, if I feel like it, and I can do so and feel completely safe.'

'I'm not sure that's advisable in Paris,' Hugo interjected, 'or Montgenoux sometimes,' he added with a wary chuckle.

'I can imagine,' Clementine continued. She turned her head, tired eyes flicking over the harbour and the water. 'All signs of life are present here. I can walk any night and be constantly surprised. One night I can see lovers in the moonlight, caught in a tender, sometimes passionate embrace. Other nights, the lovers could be different, male, female, sometimes both,' she added with a chuckle. 'Sometimes happy, sometimes sad, sometimes caught in the throes of passion, or the types of passion which can spill over into anger. But it's all here, and in this town, you can be part of it, or not. But it is beautiful.' She kicked the water with her feet. 'In winter, it is peaceful. In autumn, it is tranquil. In spring it is exciting, and in summer,' she looked shyly at Hugo, before adding, 'it can be tremendously exciting.'

Hugo laughed. 'But safe?'

'Oui,' she replied with a frown. 'Bien sûr, it's safe. Why

wouldn't it be?' She pointed towards the tiny police office. 'Franc Comtois spends most of his days sleeping in there, and even if he didn't, criminals don't come here unless they get lost, and they move on as quickly. Nothing happens here. Rien.'

Hugo looked to the harbour, reminded again of the incident involving Brigitte St. Pierre. He was still troubled by it, but also torn as to know what he should or should not do, primarily because he did not know what had happened, and it was not for him to speculate. He hoped she would come to him if she needed to.

'You look concerned,' Clementine said. 'Is something troubling you?'

Hugo was not sure how to respond. 'I think we're all a little on edge, that's all.'

Clementine turned her head away from him. 'I expect you have a thousand questions you're probably afraid to ask, or who to ask, for that matter.' She turned back to him. 'Well, ask me. I will answer you, but whether I'm telling you the truth is up to you to decide.'

Hugo smiled. There was something about her which he liked. Like the last time he had met her, she was wearing a full-length floral caftan which moved gently with the breeze and hid her body beneath it. He could not tell if she was small or large.

He dropped into the sand and kicked off his flip-flops. The coolness of the golden sand felt pleasant beneath his toes and he was again reminded it had been a long time since he last had a vacation. For as long as he could remember, his life had entailed moving from one disaster to another. He was not sure he wanted it any other way, but there were times, like that day, when he sensed he was missing out on something, that perhaps something was passing him by.

It barely felt like a moment ago when he was barely fifteen years old and his life had changed inexplicably. He had discovered love and a passion for investigation and he was not sure he had ever really looked back since then, nor taken the time to breathe. It had been as if he was always running, frightened to stop in case he would have to think about what had happened to him, or that it would catch up with him.

'In my job, we are taught to always question the motives of people, and how they say what they say,' he said.

Clementine nodded. She pointed at her easel. 'It's not so different in my line of work.' She pointed at Hugo's face. 'I have spent the last forty years staring at faces, and the one thing I've learnt for certain is that lies show. We all "put on a face" so to speak, but we can't hide it all. It hides underneath the surface and if you look hard enough, you can always see the truth. The darker a lie, the more difficult it is to bury.'

'I agree.' Hugo stared into the sea. 'Isn't it amazing how our minds wander when we stare at the sea? I'm constantly amazed by it.'

'The ocean does that to us,' Clementine interrupted his reminiscence. 'It forces us to stop and to allow the memories to come back. Good and bad. We realise it is pointless to fight them.'

Hugo nodded. 'You're probably right. I'm trying to decide whether it's a good thing, or whether it would drive me crazy.'

She shrugged. 'Well, I've always believed you have to be a little crazy to survive this life, no matter where you are.' She sighed. 'And to make sense of what we must endure, you have to be *really* crazy.'

'I can't stop thinking about Vincent,' Hugo whispered.

'The nicest boy,' she said after a few moments, 'who certainly didn't deserve what happened to him. But then again, none of them did.'

Hugo stared at her. 'I imagine it must have been very difficult for you because you've known them for such a long time.'

'Oui,' Clementine replied. 'All of our lives, really.' She threw back her head and laughed. 'Oh the reminiscing is coming thick and fast now. Believe it or not, there was a time, a million years ago it seems, when I was Arthur Roche's sweetheart.'

'Really?'

She looked at him sharply. 'I haven't always looked like an old shrew, you know, Captain!' she snapped, but there was no malice in her tone, just gentle goading.

'Désolé,' Hugo said quickly, his cheeks flushing. 'That's not what I meant.'

She waved her hand dismissively. 'I'm teasing you. Non, I was his sweetheart, but truthfully my heart was never in it. He wanted a wife, a family, a career, and I wanted to…' She stabbed the canvas with her paintbrush. 'Disappear into a painting. I had imagined a life of travel, perhaps fame and fortune, although I'm never sure if that was something I aspired to, other than it felt as if it was a way out of this town. What I really wanted was a simple life, enough money to get by on a day-to-day basis, and,' she winked at Hugo, 'the occasional secret trysts with lovers young and old, whose names I never cared to learn, and who did not trouble me again once their trains took them back to whence they came.'

Hugo smiled. 'And did it work out as you planned?' he asked.

'Well, I'm still here, aren't I?' she replied with clear sadness, before adding with a smile. 'Mais, it hasn't all been dull. I'd have hated that. A woman of my limited wiles can have trysts, even in places such as Beaufort-Sur-Mer.' She winked. 'Any person can be desirable to someone else when options are limited.' She kicked her feet, bending to the water and splashing it on her face. She smiled as the droplets cascaded down her face. 'The fundamental problem with living in a place like this is that nothing changes. We all know each other. We all know each other's secrets, and we all share in each other's lives.' She took a breath. 'Good or bad.'

Hugo did not wish to pry, but he sensed she would be one of the few people who may be able to help him understand what had decimated the Roche family.

He decided his only option was to be direct. 'Do you have any idea why Vincent Roche may have thought his father's death was something other than suicide?' he asked.

Clementine stepped out of the water and made her way back to the painting. A minute passed. And another.

'Because that's what he wanted to believe,' she answered finally. 'I suppose that's what we all wanted to believe. But the truth is much simpler and much sadder, and one which those of us involved must carry with us for the rest of our lives.'

'I don't understand?' Hugo frowned.

'You must have put together a theory or two by now, Captain, non?'

Hugo shrugged. He was not sure about anything. There seemed to be nothing to suggest anything untoward in Arthur Roche's death, and as far as he could tell anything else was none of his business.

'The reason we all feel so guilty about Arthur's death isn't because of some grand conspiracy,' Clementine continued. 'It's much more mundane than that. In fact, it is immensely boring. Jasper Connor came to Beaufort-Sur-Mer two years ago, and he was like a breath of fresh air, especially for us women of "an age." He had us all swarming around his honey pot.' She stopped, wiping her mouth with the back of her hand. 'Perfectly decent women can be known to make fools of themselves under such circumstances.' She turned her head slowly to Hugo. 'And I always loved honey,' she added with a wry smile. She exhaled sadly. 'Mais, he had his sights set on a bigger prize.'

'Avril Roche,' Hugo stated.

She nodded. 'And I encouraged it, if you can believe that. Well, I've never been a woman prone to bitterness or jealousy and sentimentality bores me rigid. Nevertheless, I am also not a prude. Avril and Arthur's marriage had been over for a long time, just neither of them ever wanted to admit it. His drinking and gambling were one thing. I expect she could have gone on, forgiven him even. However, the longer it went on, the more it rendered him not much of a husband or a father. Avril wanted more.'

She shook her head irritably. 'Non. She deserved more. No matter her feelings now, in the cold light of days filled with regrets, it changes not one thing. She deserved more. Vincent adored his father, but adoration such as that comes with built-in glasses. He saw what he wanted to see.' She stabbed a paintbrush against the canvas. 'The rest of us saw the truth. Avril was never beaten by Arthur, not with his fists at least. But he did beat her down. And it meant that a man such as Jasper Connor was so easily able to swoop in.'

Hugo stepped forward. 'What happened?'

Clementine sighed. 'Jasper Connor wanted Avril, and I helped him get her. It was one of the biggest mistakes I've ever made.'

Hugo frowned. 'In what way?'

'Jasper wanted the hotel, and he knew he could get it cheap,' Clementine replied. 'Arthur owed money to everyone, and he didn't much care. But the hotel was still the major business in Beaufort-Sur-Mer. He had his protectors. Captain Comtois, for one. Jasper wanted the hotel and I think he would have done anything to get it.'

'Anything?' Hugo interrupted.

She shook her head again. 'Not that. Not murder,' she answered. 'He's far too lazy to get his hands dirty, I'm sure. Non, Jasper figured out pretty quickly that if he was to get the hotel, he needed Avril's help, and so he went for it. He wooed her. He seduced her, and of course, she fell for it. I encouraged her to fall for it!' she added with a dismissive shrug of her shoulders. 'Why the hell shouldn't I have? And why the hell shouldn't she have gone for it? Years of impotence and neglect, and then suddenly some smartly dressed stranger, a millionaire businessman, no less, rolls into town and sweeps you off your feet?' She snorted. 'Avril may have changed her mind now, but the truth is, she would have been a fool to ignore him. Any of us would.'

Hugo scratched his head. 'No offence intended,' he began. 'Mais, what was it about Beaufort-Sur-Mer that enticed Jasper Connor? If he really was a successful businessman, a small hotel in a seaside town in southern France isn't likely to be the sort of investment which would interest him, surely?'

Clementine turned to him. 'And therein lies a lot of questions with very few answers.'

He frowned again. 'Désolé, I'm not sure I understand.'

'What do you make of Jasper?' she asked.

Hugo considered. 'I can't say I've had many opportunities to form one opinion or another,' he answered honestly.

Clementine laughed. 'You're being very diplomatic.'

'Not necessarily,' he responded. 'It's simply that first impressions are important, but they are only a beginning. I have barely had a chance to evaluate him for myself, and only have the opinions of others to go on. It's quite clear what Vincent Roche thought of him, but that is not necessarily indicative of the truth.' He moved across the sand. 'Let's put aside Jasper Connor's motive for wanting the hotel, for the moment. How did he go about it?'

Clementine snorted. 'He wooed Avril, that's how. And then he wooed me to talk her into it.'

'Talk her into it?' Hugo questioned.

She nodded. 'Oui.' She put down the paintbrush and stepped away again, sitting on the edge of the water. Hugo moved closer to her, and after a moment, sat next to her, kicking his feet into the water.

Clementine smiled at him. 'I wish you weren't a homosexual,' she said. She laughed at his reaction. 'You get that a lot, I suppose?'

Hugo shrugged. 'I've heard it once or twice, and I have as yet not found a different response other than, *je suis.*'

She laughed. There was a sadness to it, which he detected. He cocked his head. 'Mademoiselle?'

Clementine waved her hand dismissively. 'Not everything is so easily accepted, you know?'

Hugo snorted. 'I think I can safely agree with you on that, Mademoiselle. I have spent a lifetime trying to understand my place in this world. Mais, what is your point?'

She stared at him. 'Only that small towns amplify everything. We can try to hide, but we can *never* hide, as it happens. We wear masks for others; the masks they want us to wear.' She pointed towards the harbour. 'I wonder what some people would do to hide their true selves. To protect themselves from the view of others.'

Hugo clasped his hands. 'I'm afraid I don't understand.'

'Nor do I,' she blurted. 'Other than, I am sure it means something.'

Hugo watched her. He was not sure whether she was being deliberately vague, or rather that she was just the woman she projected herself to be - a bohemian, wandering nonchalantly through her life.

'Or it means nothing,' she added with a shrug.

Hugo pulled a cigarette out of his pocket and lit it. 'You said Jasper Connor was determined to get the hotel. How did he get it?'

'I told you,' she snapped. 'By wooing Avril, and me, and whoever else he needed to, I don't doubt. He promised her a new life, so she did what she had to do. She wanted out of her marriage. She saw Vincent going off to his new life. First to Montgenoux, and then I don't doubt he would have gone even further. What were her choices? Slaving in a hot kitchen while Arthur drank and gambled every penny they made.'

She shook her head. 'Nobody could, *should*, blame her for her decisions, because if we're honest, we would all have done the same. She went to Arthur with the deal from Jasper and she encouraged, or rather, demanded, he sign it. Arthur was a simple man. I imagined he thought it would save their marriage. Avril encouraged that belief, whether she believed it was debatable, and rather pointless now. Jasper told her he would buy the hotel, renovate it, and sell it on for a huge profit. She knew the hotel had potential, so it wasn't too much of a stretch. He said once that was done, they would move on to his next venture together.'

Hugo nodded. 'Yet he's still here. So, they didn't move on,' Hugo continued. 'Pourquoi?'

She shrugged. 'Arthur died, and that changed everything. Avril blamed herself, of course she did. Whether or not she needed to doesn't matter. She had just wanted out of her marriage, and out of Beaufort-Sur-Mer, and the only way she could do that was by selling the only thing she had. The hotel.'

'Mais, with Arthur dead, wasn't that the end of it?' Hugo posed.

'Peut être. Or the beginning,' she replied, quizzically. 'There are no genuine answers to any of these questions. Just the actions of foolish old people who ought to know better.' She clenched her fists again. 'There are a lot of us here like that. People who are old and have lived the same life for decades. We have no interest in changing, but more importantly, we have no tolerance of those who require us to do so.'

'And how does that manifest itself?'

Clementine smiled. 'It manifests itself in ignorance, and intolerance, and indifference.'

Hugo threw the cigarette butt into the water. 'Yet Avril has remained with Jasper, non?'

'Oui. They remain together in hatred, it seems,' she replied.

'Doesn't that strike you as odd?' Hugo asked.

'I told you - Avril blames herself for what happened to Arthur and Vincent,' Clementine responded. 'She also blames me for encouraging the union. She blames Jasper for swindling Arthur.

Somehow that has now amalgamated into us all being responsible for Vincent's death.'

She exhaled. 'And she's probably correct. What do I know? I have as much guilt on my shoulders as I can bear. I can bear no more.' She took a deep breath. 'And now with Vincent dead, we're all going to be haunted by both his and his father's death, and that is as it should be. We should always wonder what we could have done, what we *should* have done to prevent it.'

Before Hugo had a chance to respond, something in the ocean caught his attention. A scuba diver had surfaced and was waving his arms frantically in their direction.

Hugo narrowed his eyes. The diver removed the mask and mouthpiece, and Hugo recognised it as Dax Chastain.

'Help! Help!' Dax shouted hoarsely. 'Call the police! He's dead!'

Hugo ran towards the water.

quinze

Hugo watched aghast as Baptiste rose from the sea, shaking off the water as he plodded towards the beach. He could tell by his face there was something very wrong. He ran towards him. It bothered him that his first thought had been - *Dieu, don't let it be Baptiste!* As normal as it was to feel such a way, he reasoned, it made him feel no better. Whoever was dead belonged to, and was most probably loved by, someone just as much as Hugo loved Baptiste.

Moments later, Dax threw himself out of the water, dropping with a thud onto the beach. He removed his visor and mouthpiece, desperately gasping for air.

Hugo moved quickly towards them. 'What happened?' he demanded.

Baptiste stared at him, his eyes wide with confusion. He removed his mouthpiece. 'He's dead.'

'Who is dead?' Hugo questioned.

Baptiste rolled over, throwing off his oxygen tank. He stood. He stared at the water. Guy had now surfaced and was pulling the clearly traumatised tourists onto the harbour landing bay.

'Did you send for the police?' Dax asked, sucking air into his lungs.

Hugo nodded. 'Oui. Clementine Bonheur has gone to find Captain Comtois.'

'Non!' Dax cried. 'Not Franc. It can't be Franc.'

Baptiste stepped forward. He touched Hugo's arm. 'It's his son down there,' he said, pointing at the sea.

'Down there?' Hugo asked, confused, following Baptiste's gaze.

'He's dead,' Dax whispered. 'Gregoire is dead.'

Hugo's eyes widened in horror. 'Gregoire Comtois?'

Dax nodded. 'He's dead,' he repeated.

Hugo shook his head, a myriad of confusing and disparate

thoughts clouding his mind. 'How?'

'He's tied to the boat,' Baptiste replied with a shudder, before adding, 'with an anchor.'

'An anchor?' Hugo gasped. He stopped, his attention caught by the crowd of people gathering at the top of the boardwalk. Captain Comtois stepped down the walkway.

Hugo turned back to Dax. 'Are you sure it's Gregoire Comtois?'

Dax nodded again. 'I've known him since we were kids.' He stared at the approaching figure of Captain Comtois. 'Dieu. I can't tell, Franc.' He stared at Hugo. 'Will you do it?'

Hugo nodded. He turned, moving quickly towards a man who was just about to have his heart broken.

Franc Comtois stared at the sea. He had not moved since Hugo had broken the news to him. 'I can't be true,' he had cried before sinking onto a bench. They had sat together in silence for almost an hour waiting for the Gendarmes and the forensic team to arrive from the nearest town, then waited as the divers descended into the shimmering harbour water. As long as it took, Hugo hoped it would take longer because he could only imagine how Captain Comtois would feel when his son emerged from the deep.

Hugo cleared his throat. 'Are you sure you want to be here?' he asked Comtois. 'I can wait instead.'

Comtois shook his head with vigour. 'I *need* to be here,' he said, rubbing his eye. The twitch was vibrating angrily and seemed to be giving him pain.

Hugo reached over and touched his shoulder. 'I understand,' he said, 'but you may not want to see this.'

Comtois glared at him. 'Would you leave?'

Hugo reached into his pocket and extracted a cigarette. He lit it, taking his time before responding. 'I can't imagine anywhere I would want to be less, but I also know I wouldn't be able to move from the spot.'

Comtois nodded. 'What happened down there, Captain?'

Hugo shrugged. 'I don't know.' He was relieved to see Baptiste was now in the bar, sitting with Dax and Guy. 'However, as far as I can tell, there appears to be some similarity with what happened to Arthur and Vincent.'

'You're suggesting my son killed himself?' Comtois snapped. 'What on earth would my twenty-year-old kid have to kill himself over? His grades always sucked. He works part-time in a bar and that's enough for him because he lives rent free with me. He spends his summer banging tourists from the four corners of this planet. Gregoire has only two things to fear - his liver and sexually transmitted diseases.'

'Then he wasn't worried or upset about anything? Could this be about what happened to Vincent? They were friends after all.'

Comtois snorted. 'I don't know what kind of relationship you have with your son, Captain Duchamp, but I have never, nor had any desire to, talk with my son about anything other than where the remote control is and when he's going to get his lazy ass off the sofa and do something productive with his life.' He stopped, looking slyly towards Hugo. 'You must think I'm a bastard for saying these things, especially now.'

Hugo inhaled the cigarette as if his life depended on it. He stared at the sea. 'I think you're a man who is about to experience something you can't imagine, and you're dealing with it the only way you can.'

Comtois smiled sadly at him. 'Don't make me like you, Captain. I'm too old and you're too young and too much of a hotshot. Everything I never was and never will be. I should hate you, and I was angry at you for coming here thinking I'd done something wrong. But everything I've heard about you tells me only one thing. I know nothing, and you are the real deal.'

Hugo laughed. 'Merci, for saying it, but it's most definitely not true.'

Comtois rose quickly to his feet. The diving team had surfaced and, for the first time, they saw Gregoire Comtois. He was strapped to a stretcher, but the anchor was still wrapped around his torso. It was macabre, but Hugo knew it was the way it had to be to preserve any potential evidence.

'Call Jacques,' Comtois snapped. He rose to his feet, striding towards the steps. 'He's the only person I want to touch my son.'

seize

Hugo and Baptiste sat in silence on the veranda outside Hugo's room. Hugo's eyes were fixed firmly on the beach. The unmistakable vision of a forensic tent and police tape had done nothing but attract hoards of tourists. The press had also arrived, photographers and reporters talking directly to cameras. It was an occupational hazard, Hugo understood, but it made him sad, nevertheless.

Dr. Jaques Oppert had arrived quickly and quietly, and the elderly doctor had made arrangements for the body of Gregoire Comtois to be moved to the nearest morgue, where he would follow to perform an autopsy. Despite his interest in the case, Hugo had no right to ask to be involved, although Captain Comtois should also be removed from the investigation. In such a small town, though, and with a long service record, Hugo suspected no one would intervene. And under similar circumstances, he would most likely act the same way himself.

Hugo regarded Baptiste from the corner of his eye. He was staring directly at the part of the ocean where the body had been removed. He had not spoken since Hugo had led him back to the hotel. All he had done was taken Hugo's packet of cigarettes and smoked one after the other. Hugo blamed himself for encouraging such an unpleasant habit.

'It can't be a coincidence,' Baptiste said finally.

Hugo knotted his eyebrows. He was not sure what to say. 'It's rare, but this sort of thing happens sometimes.'

Baptiste twisted his head. 'What do you mean?'

'Multiple suicides,' Hugo stated. 'Vincent died as a result of his father's death, and it's entirely possible Gregoire did, too. Sometimes people just aren't able to cope with such tragic events and they don't know how or don't feel able to ask for help. It's awful and I wish it wasn't true, but it is.'

'I can't believe Gregoire did that to himself,' Baptiste shook his head. 'I mean, I was with him the night before. He was happy, he was flirty and funny and high.' He gasped for breath. 'There was nothing to suggest he felt that way.' He looked desperately at Hugo. 'Or is it me? Am I so stupid, so self-centred, I don't see what the hell is going on around me? My grandfather always said I was a self-absorbed prig, and I always thought it was bullshit, but maybe he had a point. Two people killed themselves after spending time with me. I'm the common denominator.'

Hugo pulled him into an embrace. 'You cannot be held responsible for what was going on with those boys.' He closed his eyes, searching for one of the memories he had hidden in a part of his brain he used to protect himself. 'When I was working in London, there was a woman, a very successful woman with a husband and three children she loved dearly. One day, she threw herself off Hammersmith Bridge. She left one note. *I love my life, but it wasn't the one I dreamt of.* Her husband, her family, her friends said it made no sense. She was always happy. She loved her husband and children, her job and her life, they said.' He shrugged. 'But it seems whatever demons she was running from, she couldn't escape them.'

Baptiste grimaced. 'What's your point?'

Hugo shrugged. 'It seems to me as we all get older, we find ways of hiding our true feelings. At least the ones we imagine people around us wouldn't understand. The same could be true for Gregoire. Outwardly he was happy and confident, but underneath, he could have been traumatised by what happened to Vincent and his father.'

'You think?'

Hugo nodded. 'It's possible. Or it could be something more personal. We can't be sure unless he left some explanation. I'm sorry you're having to deal with this, Baptiste, but I have to try to impress this upon you - you can't look back on what happened and imagine scenarios, things you could have done differently. It'll drive you crazy, but more importantly, right now, it's irrelevant. I don't mean that to sound cold, but it is what it is. You have to move forward, not just for your own sake, but also for theirs.'

'I made a promise to Vincent,' Baptiste whispered.

'Je sais,' Hugo replied. 'But again, you may have to accept that you can't do anything about it. Vincent took his own life, and he left you with what may be unrealistic expectations.' He sighed. 'I've spoken with Captain Comtois. Etienne has looked into the paper trail and there appears to be nothing untoward. There may have been an unfair business transaction, but as far as I can tell, it was one Arthur Roche went into willingly.'

'Then why the hell did he kill himself?' Baptiste cried.

'Because it didn't have the outcome he wanted, I suppose,' Hugo mused. Before he could say any more, his cell phone rang. 'Allô, Hugo Duchamp,' he answered.

'I'd recognise that voice anywhere,' the person on the line spoke.

Hugo tried to recognise who was speaking. It was a man, and his voice was deep and with the unmistakable croak of old age. The sense memory appeared, and he was instantly transported back to his fifteenth year. 'Captain Hervé?' he gasped. 'Is that really you?'

Bertram Hervé chuckled. 'I haven't been Captain for a long time,' he said. 'Ah, but now I hear you are. I can't tell you how proud and happy that makes me, son.'

Hugo exhaled. Bertram Hervé was an authentic voice from his past, though it must be over twenty years since they had last seen or spoken with one another, and it was something Hugo felt bad about. Keeping in touch with someone from the past was not something he was good at. But for Bertram Hervé, of all people, he should have made more of an effort.

Bertram was responsible for so much that had happened to Hugo. He had been there for him when Madeline Duchamp had died. This strange, rotund man, with not much hair, or height, but plenty of girth and attitude, had entered his life, and though he had not remained for long, his impression had proven to be one of the most pivotal moments in Hugo's life.

Hugo had never quite understood the relationship between his grandmother and the police officer, other than there was one, and a very bizarre one at that. But what he knew for certain was that when Madeline died, Bertram was the first person to console Hugo. In fact, he was the *only* person to come to Hugo and comfort him.

His parents had not seen fit to be there for him or to offer him refuge. Hugo's father, Pierre, had attended the lavish funeral and wake, holding court and acting as the centre of attention. It had suited Hugo. He preferred melting into the background, and he certainly had preferred being as far away from his father as was possible. When the crowds left, each leaving nothing but warm, pointless, and most often fake platitudes, for a woman they either never knew, or most likely secretly hated, Hugo had found himself alone. Completely alone. He was used to it, but without Madeline, Hugo realised for the first time there was no one else in his life. He had tried to view the path ahead of him as one which was open and could be filled with adventures, but all he had seen was emptiness. On her deathbed, she had foretold it, and for the first time since he had known her, she apologised to him. It had not been necessary, but in those last moments he had seen her love for him, while shielded, had most certainly always shone brightly.

However, Bertram had arrived at Madeline's mansion the day after her funeral, fixing Hugo with a firm, but warm, look. *I shall miss Madeline very much,* he said. *She was a fine woman, and she loved you very much.* Hugo had been unsure of the truth, but he believed she was as fond of him as a high society Parisian grand dame could be. Bertram had then informed Hugo she had insisted Bertram look in on Hugo, and was to help him in whichever way he saw fit. The trouble had been, Hugo did not know what to do with his life. He was still a teenager, but Bertram had made him feel like an adult. Hugo could still hear the words which had changed his life.

'You can be whatever you want to be. The first time I met you, you were lurking in a doorway. A tall, thin, fifteen-year-old, bones and ears not yet grown into your body, but green eyes as keen and alert and shining with an intelligence I have rarely seen. I asked Madeline, does he always hang around like that being nosy? She told me you weren't nosy, you were just learning. Watching and learning. You have a journey ahead of you, Hugo Duchamp, and I am going to help you get there. You listen, but more importantly, you learn and you understand. I wish I had a dozen like you in the **Commissariat de Police du 7e arrondissement.**'

Hugo exhaled. Bertram Hervé had saved him, and it upset him immensely that he had barely thought about him in years. There was another reason, he surmised. He had met someone else at the same time. Someone Hugo had spent twenty years trying to forget. Bertram reminded him of the love and loss Hugo had felt during that period of his life.

'Bertram,' Hugo whispered. 'I can't begin to tell you how good it is to hear your voice after all this time. And also how ashamed I am that I haven't kept in touch with you.'

Bertram laughed. 'Same here. My grandson - a useless pasty kid, but harmless enough, connected me to the "unterweb" or whatever the hell you call it,' he grumbled, with a warm natured lilt. 'Anyway, in seconds he had you on the screen.' He snorted. 'You didn't grow to look like Pierre, so Madeline won't be completely turning in her grave. She even wouldn't have minded the fact you grew up like your grandfather. She loved him after all.' He paused to allow Hugo to regulate his breathing. 'But more importantly, she would see just how much of a fine young man you grew into, and all the wonderful, brave things you have done in your life and career. Some very terrible men and women are in prison because of you.'

'Because of you, too,' Hugo replied. 'I wouldn't have become a police officer in the first place were it not for your encouragement.'

'I dropped you off at the gates,' Bertram quipped, 'and whatever happened behind them was all down to you, not me.'

Hugo frowned. He was not sure how true that was. Bertram Hervé had believed in Hugo when there was no one else who did or cared enough to try. He sighed. His emotions were bubbling beneath the surface and he did not want to give in to them. Not in front of Bertram, nor Baptiste. He cleared his throat. 'How did you even know where I am?'

'Jacques called me,' Bertram replied.

'Ah,' Hugo responded, his left eyebrow arching. 'Pourquoi?'

'He thought there may be trouble.'

'Quoi?' Hugo retorted. 'What kind of trouble?' He wondered why Dr. Jacques Oppert would have felt it necessary to call Bertram to inform him Hugo was in Beaufort-Sur-Mer.

'He didn't say,' Bertram answered.

Hugo sighed.

Bertram laughed again. 'Ah, I see you have inherited more than your good looks from Madeline.' He took a moment. 'Let me begin by telling you I have known Jacques Oppert for longer than you have been on this planet. He is a good man. He is also cut from a cloth you probably wouldn't recognise. We old folk have to grow with the changing times. Often we don't want to, but we try, or else we don't bother. Sometimes one is easier than the other. Jacques left Paris because he wanted an easier life. Like any of us here, he had seen too much, and he'd certainly dissected the bodies of too many people.'

'He wanted an easier life, I get it,' Hugo said crossly. 'What are you saying?'

Bertram sighed. 'Well, for one thing, he's almost as old as Moses,' he said with a laugh, 'but regardless of that, he's a damn

le bateau au fond de l'océan

fine doctor, and any place should be grateful to have him.'

'Mais?' Hugo interrupted. 'Because I know you are getting to a but. What aren't you telling me?'

Bertram sighed again. 'You know what it was like in Faubourg Saint-Germain. Places such as that, and I suppose the town you live in, are ruled by a hierarchy, and be damned anyone who tries to interfere.'

Hugo stole a look at Baptiste. Luckily, he appeared to have grown bored with Hugo's reminiscing telephone call and was staring towards the sea smoking another cigarette. 'What has he told you about the investigation?' Hugo pushed.

'Very little,' Bertram replied. 'Other than, I of all people should understand when discretion must be used. He reminded me of a time, long ago, when I had done something similar.'

'1995,' Hugo whispered.

'1995,' Bertram repeated. 'We won't go into the past, Hugo, it's boring for a man of my age, and probably still too fresh for one of yours.'

'I agree,' Hugo said. He had no interest in revisiting his past. It held nothing for him but sadness and disappointment. It was more that he realised he agreed with Bertram - sadness was boring. It was like a cape made of lead that a person could never shake, no matter how much time moved away from the origin of the sadness. He lit another cigarette. 'Bertram,' he said finally, 'are you suggesting Jacques Oppert covered up something here in Beaufort-Sur-Mer?'

The line went silent.

'Bertram?'

Bertram laughed. 'Your voice has the same intonation as Madeline's when you're chastising me.' He sighed. 'Dieu. I miss that woman.'

Hugo sucked on his cigarette. 'You have no idea.' He paused. 'So?'

'Money is power, Hugo as well you know,' Bertram continued. 'And it can influence the outcome of an investigation.'

'Not for me,' Hugo snapped, more firmly than he intended.

'So I see,' Bertram laughed, 'but we're not all as principled as you.'

'What are you trying to tell me?' Hugo asked. 'Did Dr. Oppert help cover up a murder?'

'Bien sûr, non,' Bertram snapped. 'Mais, he is aware of his limitations and what he is being asked to do.'

'And what is he being asked to do?' Hugo asked.

'Jacques can see the similarity between the other deaths, and the fact that the investigating officer is the father of the deceased,' Bertram added. 'Which of course makes him aware of the problems which could be caused by it all.'

Hugo nodded. 'I agree. Mais, what can I do?'

'Jacques has suggested you request to be involved.'

'I can't do that, Bertram,' Hugo replied. 'And nobody would appreciate it if I tried.'

Bertram coughed. 'Bien sûr, non. Any Captain with half a brain would be appalled and outraged by such a suggestion… mais, would it bother you?'

'Well, oui, un ti peu,' Hugo answered.

'Mais, you would accept it, because you would understand all the usual nonsense - legal implications, the bad guy getting off, etc, etc…'

'What aren't you telling me, Bertram?'

'I'm making a call to an old friend,' he answered. 'Nothing more. What I'm suggesting is that you make an official request to be at the autopsy of the poor boy, just as an official bystander. No one can reasonably deny your request, least of all the poor Captain whose son is gone. Do what you must do, Hugo, because I suspect you must know that you have to.'

Hugo paused. 'What has Dr. Oppert told you?' he pressed.

Bertram did not answer.

Hugo took a deep breath. 'Gregoire Comtois didn't kill himself, did he?'

Bertram coughed. 'Not for me to say, mais in the interest of ensuring there can be no indication of impropriety,' he continued slowly, 'it wouldn't harm for you to be there, would it?'

Hugo sighed. 'D'accord. I'll see what I can do. However, while we are on the subject, I feel as if I should mention the fact Dr. Oppert is perhaps a little old to still be working,' he added delicately.

Bertram laughed. 'If his hand is less steady than yours, then I'd be amazed. Do your job, Hugo Duchamp. That's what I taught you, isn't it?' He said with a gentle scolding. 'Do your job and be damned the consequences. Do you remember the last thing I said to you when I dropped you off at the police academy?'

Hugo did not need to recall it. He smiled. 'You said the only thing I have to do to be a good cop was to be a good cop.'

'I am very wise,' Bertram conceded.

'I did not know what it meant at the time,' Hugo said.

'But you do now?'

Hugo laughed. 'Non, I don't, you old fool,' he replied. 'Mais, what I took it to mean was that I just needed to be like you. Don't take any crap from anyone, rich or poor, young or old, man or woman. You taught me people lie, and that it isn't always a bad thing. You told me to understand what the lie meant, and then move on from there.'

'And has it served you well?'

'Better than you know,' Hugo conceded.

'Then you've done me proud,' Bertram replied. He sounded proud. It touched Hugo in a way that hurt. Madeline had not lived long enough to be proud of him, and his parents had never shown any particular interest in him or what he had done with his life.

'You've done us both proud.' Bertram added. He took a deep

breath. 'That damn grandson of mine showed me what you got up to in Paris last year. That must have been a tough case.'

Hugo remembered it well. It had been tough, but what was harder to face was he had not even given a thought to Bertram Hervé, and he knew exactly why that was. It came back to the same thing. He still could not face the part of his life Hervé was associated with.

Bertram continued. 'Make sure next time you're in my hood, kid, you look me up. I'm eighty-seven years old. There's only so much life left in the old bones. D'accord?'

Hugo exhaled. 'D'accord, Bertram.' He smiled and realised he meant it.

dix-sept

Captain Franc Comtois glared at Hugo, stomping angrily into the corner of the morgue. Hugo and Dr. Jacques Oppert exchanged a worried glance. Comtois flopped onto a metal chair. The scraping of the legs against the slate floor threw a piercing screech into the room.

'If you think for one damn second,' Comtois hissed, 'that I'm leaving this seat, then you're going to have to take out your gun and shoot me through what's left of my damn heart.'

Hugo gulped. 'I assure you, Captain Comtois, that is not my intention at all,' he said in the most reassuring tone he could muster.

Comtois raised an eyebrow. 'Then what the hell are you doing here?' He glared at Oppert. 'Because I know I'm certainly not the one who invited you.'

The doctor shuffled away, seemingly readying himself for the autopsy ahead.

Hugo had thought a lot about what he was going to say on the journey over to the morgue. And he had come to one conclusion. Jurisdiction was one thing, but as a police officer it was his sworn duty to uphold the law. He knew that could be ignored under the right circumstances. He had worked with other police forces before. In Ireland, in Russia and Paris, he had worked well with the local police departments, for the most part. In the end, they had understood, some with more reluctance than others, that cooperation was as much a legal sanctuary as anything else.

He cleared his throat. 'Captain Comtois,' he began. 'You have lost your son. I have a son. You might say it's different because it is. He has only been my son for a matter of a few years. I didn't create him. I didn't change him, wipe his face, his tears, or feed him when he could not do so himself.'

'Your point?' Comtois snapped.

'My point,' Hugo continued, 'is that I would be devastated by his loss, even after such a short time. My point,' he added, 'is that I know what that loss would feel like, but I also know your loss is amplified because of the time, the sharing, the togetherness of decades I can't have.'

'Then why are you here?'

Hugo took a breath. 'Because you shouldn't be,' he replied. He looked quickly at Dr. Oppert before turning back to Comtois. 'But nobody is interested in fighting with you about it. However, and please forgive me for saying this, if your son's death isn't what it appears to be, and if a case was ever to come to court, we both know that some unscrupulous avocat could very well use your presence here to cast doubt upon what Dr. Oppert may say regarding the death and the manner of it.'

Comtois' mouth twisted into an irritated sneer. 'So, what you're saying is your presence, a man with, what is the expression? No horse in the race is likely to counteract my decision to be here? Is that what you're saying, Duchamp?'

Dr. Jacques Oppert slammed his fists on the table. 'Bien sûr, that's what he's saying, Franc, you old fool!' he shouted. 'And it's not him who should say it, it's you.' He rounded on the Captain. 'I should tell you not to be here. Hell, I shouldn't even be here myself, at my age, as they'll no doubt argue if this goes to court, but we're doing what we're doing. Captain Duchamp has to be here, just because it allows you and I to be here.'

'What do you mean?' Comtois shot back.

'Because he's a highly decorated and respected police officer,' Oppert replied. 'And if we allow it, he'll stand up for us when some asshole tries to belittle us. He'll say I did my job as well as any other pathologist he's known, that my hand barely shook while I made the Y-incision and that you,' he pointed at Comtois, 'remained in your chair and kept your mouth shut the entire time.' He took a breath. 'And because the damn procurer told me he had to be here.

That was his condition for allowing me to allow you to witness what I'm about to do, although we ALL know you shouldn't be.'

Comtois opened his mouth to respond, but seemed to think better of it.

Oppert turned away from him. 'Bon. Now that we all understand each other, we can proceed finally.'

Hugo stared at the body of Gregoire Comtois. It filled him with horror and a sense of sadness he could barely suppress. It was the same thought he knew would consume him if he allowed it. He had been taught all death was tragic, and he understood that, but it was impossible to look at flesh unblemished by age, and not feel the intense sadness of loss, of a life not yet lived. Gregoire Comtois was young and smooth, his body lithe and not yet tarnished by an excess of living, and naked for the world to see. He appeared as a child. Franc Comtois had not turned his head to look at his son since Dr. Oppert had placed him on the gurney, and Hugo understood why. He did not need to see it; he did not *want* to see it, he just needed to be there. To be next to his son and share the final space they would share together.

Unlike most of the pathologists Hugo had worked with, Dr. Jacques Oppert was silent as he worked. He gave nothing away, and also, despite his age, he moved swiftly and deftly. Hugo had no doubt he was as good a pathologist as he had been twenty or thirty years earlier when he was likely at the height of his career.

Hugo stared at Gregoire, saddened that he had been in a similar room barely a week earlier. A similar young man. A similar death. But Hugo did not need Dr. Oppert to have spoken to know there was something different. He had been to enough autopsies to see the difference with his own two eyes. He did not need to understand what he had seen, or the technicalities at least. It was the way in which skilled professionals went about their duties. The change in the facial expressions - the taut twisting of lips, the eyes flecking at first with concern, then interest and then, finally, in recognition. Hugo had grown accustomed to such nuances in Dr. Irene Chapeau, the pathologist he worked with in Montgenoux, but he also recognised it clearly in Dr. Jaques Oppert.

'Did he drown?' Captain Franc Comtois asked, finally breaking the silence.

Oppert turned to him, his forehead creasing.

'Ah,' Comtois nodded. The realisation took but a fraction of a second to spread across his face. He lowered his head and muttered something incomprehensible.

Oppert stared at Hugo and shrugged his shoulders helplessly.

Hugo picked up a folder. 'I've been reading the forensic report,' he began, 'and it appears Greg...' he paused, before adding, 'the deceased was tied to the hull of the boat by an anchor. An anchor which was attached to the boat, but was only a prop. A prop placed there for the tourists to see.'

'Your point, Captain?' Comtois snapped.

'I don't have one, as such,' Hugo said demurely, 'rather I'm wondering how he got down to the boat.'

Comtois tutted. 'He swam, obviously.'

Oppert cleared his throat. 'I'm afraid that's not possible, Franc,' he said. His voice was little more than a whisper, as if he was frightened to speak the words aloud.

Comtois pulled himself erect. 'What the hell are you talking about, Jacques?'

Gregoire Comtois was lying on the gurney. Hugo was pleased that Oppert had covered his torso and his skull. But what it had revealed was not lost on Hugo. Oppert had shaved the hair from Gregoire's head and it had shown the tell-tale sign of trauma.

Oppert took a deep breath. 'You know what I'm saying, Franc,' he said, his tone soft and weary.

'Non, I don't,' Captain Comtois snapped.

The doctor clasped his hands together. 'There was no water in his lungs, Franc,' he stated.

Comtois turned his head slowly to stare at his son and quickly snapped it back. 'Are you sure?' he asked hoarsely.

'There was no water in his lungs,' Oppert repeated. He took a breath. 'And you of all people know what that means.'

Comtois' eyes widened. 'There's no doubt…' he trailed off, seemingly unable to finish what he was trying to say.

Dr. Oppert nodded. 'I'm afraid not, Franc,' he said. 'Gregoire was already dead before he went in the water.'

Comtois leaned forward. 'You're positive?'

Oppert nodded again, but said nothing.

'Then how did he die, Jacques?' Comtois whimpered. He was rubbing his chin with such vigour it appeared to Hugo it must be painful, yet Comtois did not seem affected by it.

The doctor pointed to the injury on Gregoire's head. Hugo moved closer to it, lowering his body to study it. The skull was shattered on the right side, a gaping hole clearly showing what had happened.

'He took a hell of a blow to his head,' Oppert said. 'It would have been quick, and it would have been catastrophic.' He stared at Comtois. 'I realise this will make little difference to you now, but the shock will come at some point, so I'm telling you to hold on to this knowledge. Gregoire would have died quickly and he would, if you pardon the expression, have not known what hit him.'

'How long has he been dead, Dr. Oppert?' Hugo asked.

Oppert tapped his chin. 'It's difficult to say with any certainty. I'll send the samples over to the lab. We'll have a better idea then. It will also show us if he had any drugs or alcohol in his system. The water changes things, but I'd estimate he's been dead no longer than twelve hours, and somewhere between ten and twelve.'

Hugo looked at the clock on the wall. 'Then that would make

it between midnight and 02H00 this morning.'

Oppert nodded. 'I would concur with that.'

Captain Comtois stood and moved to the opposite end of the morgue. 'If he was murdered, then how the hell did he end up on the boat?'

Oppert looked to Hugo. 'That is the question, non?'

Hugo stood. He pursed his lips. 'Can we say with any certainty that Gregoire didn't fall from the harbour into the water and then banged his head?'

Comtois slammed his fists together. 'You can't be so stupid as to believe that, Captain Duchamp,' he bristled.

Hugo shook his head. 'Non, but then we have to extrapolate what that might mean.'

Oppert continued. 'If he fell into the water and hit his head, in that case, there would have been water in his lungs,' he added.

'I don't understand what you're getting at, Duchamp,' Comtois replied.

Hugo moved across the room. He reached into his pocket and extracted a cigarette. 'Désolé, I must smoke,' he said.

Oppert tutted. 'That's a disgusting habit, and you'll end up on one of these slabs before your time if you keep it up.'

Hugo lit the cigarette and took a moment to reflect. 'I know, mais…'

Comtois rose to his feet, and seemingly it was too much for him, so he flopped back onto the chair. 'Then he was definitely murdered?'

Oppert nodded. 'There's little doubt. Désolé, old friend.'

Comtois stared at Hugo. 'Then how the hell did he end up tied to the boat?' he repeated.

'Therein lies the question,' Hugo mused. 'And all I can think of is that someone wanted us to believe this was another suicide.'

'They must have known we would have investigated,' Comtois cried.

'But they may have imagined we wouldn't look too closely, particularly considering what happened to Vincent and Arthur Roche,' Hugo added.

Hugo turned to face Comtois. 'We can't deny there is a connection, or certainly an inference of one. Captain Comtois,' he continued cautiously. 'Vincent Roche believed his father was murdered. If that was not the case, then he believed at the very least something was being covered up.' He paused. 'My question is straightforward. Is there something you're not telling me because as far as I can tell, we need to understand exactly what happened before we can figure out whether what happened to your son is connected?'

'We've been through this,' Comtois replied, clearly exasperated. 'There was no cover-up.'

'Then why did Vincent think there was?' Hugo interrupted. 'Because he clearly did.'

'Because he was stupid and crazy, just like this father,' Comtois spat.

'What is it you're not telling me, Captain?' Hugo pushed. 'This isn't about being indiscreet anymore. I believe someone has used what happened to murder your son. And therefore, we need to understand what that could mean, and more importantly, what relevance it may have.'

'These things aren't connected,' Comtois mouthed.

Dr. Oppert coughed. 'Tell the kid, Franc, just tell him, dammit, or I will.'

Franc Comtois lifted his head. 'Arthur killed himself, Captain Duchamp. This was not about covering anything up,' he repeated.

'Then what is it about?' Hugo asked keenly.

Comtois sighed. 'This was all just about protecting Avril and Vincent.'

'In what way?' Hugo asked.

'The evening before he killed himself, there was a fight,'

Comtois replied, 'between Arthur and Jasper Connor. Arthur had been drinking heavily. He'd always been a drinker, but for some time it had gotten out of hand. Especially when Jasper came on the scene. That particular night, Arthur was combative and argumentative with everyone. It started in the harbour bar and ended up at the hotel. He said some terrible things to Avril, and in the end, I think he just pushed Jasper too far, so Jasper told him the truth.'

'The truth?'

Comtois nodded. 'He'd had enough of Arthur badmouthing him to anyone who would listen. Accusing him of nonsense.'

'Nonsense?' Hugo questioned.

'It was all nonsense,' Comtois replied. 'Jasper is many things, but mostly he's just a rich businessman who cares little about people and more about money. Anyway, he finally had enough of Arthur's conspiracy theories and he told him the truth. He and Avril had conspired to get the hotel for a fraction of the cost. Avril would get a cut and Jasper would get the hotel for half of what it was worth.'

He sighed. 'Avril is a fine woman, but she'd had enough. Enough of Arthur and his ways. She knew that if they sold the hotel together, Arthur would keep the money and drink it and gamble it away and she'd end up with nothing. She'd had enough of struggling, of being the only one working, trying to make the hotel work, keeping their head above water. She wanted to make sure she and Vincent were looked after. So, she cut a deal with Jasper. A deal she most likely isn't proud of now, but it was a deal she felt comfortable with at the time. She convinced Arthur to sell by lying to him about a future she had no interest in sharing with him. She swore Jasper to secrecy and promised that once the hotel was his, she would leave Arthur and be with him. The condition was, Arthur could never know the truth. But then he pushed the wrong buttons, so Jasper snapped and told Arthur the whole sorry truth.'

le bateau au fond de l'océan

Hugo frowned. 'What happened next?'

Comtois continued. 'Arthur told Avril and Jasper that he'd make them pay. I'm not sure they imagined what that might mean, or even if Arthur did himself. Avril came to me, desperately worried she was going to be arrested. I told her whatever she had done, it was not a crime. Not a legal one, at least.' He stood and then immediately sat back down, as if he could not make his legs work. 'I'd known them both a long time, but I also knew I couldn't let Arthur keep going as he was. He was making threats. Not just against Jasper, but against me.'

'Even me,' Dr. Oppert added.

Hugo shook his head. 'Mais, pourquoi? Are you saying there were absolutely no grounds for his belief?'

Comtois shrugged. 'The truth is, from a legal viewpoint, I saw no evidence of a crime. When he accused me of taking bribes, I warned him off, but he said he wasn't done. He said he was going to see an avocat in the next town, and that he'd take us all to court. Me, Jasper, Avril, Clementine. He said the avocat had told them he would suggest to a court that we were all involved in a criminal conspiracy to rob him of all his money.'

Hugo nodded. 'It is possible.'

'Je sais,' Comtois agreed. He stole a look at Oppert, before quickly turning back to Hugo. 'And let's just say, I wasn't keen on an investigation into my finances.'

Hugo stared at him. 'And why is that?'

'It's not important,' Comtois hissed. By now, his eye was twitching rapidly.

'The hell it isn't,' Hugo proffered.

Comtois shook his head. 'The two aren't connected.'

Hugo clenched his fists. 'But they could be. You have to see that. If Arthur was going to make sure there was a court case, whether or not he had grounds, whether or not he won, it all becomes very relevant, especially if it becomes clear there were people who had a lot to lose.' He stared at Comtois. 'I ask you again, why did you not want to be investigated?'

'Because I didn't!' Comtois screamed. 'And I'm telling you, it's not relevant.'

Hugo shook his head in disbelief. 'I can't believe you're saying this. You, of all people. When we become police officers, we swear a solemn oath to the Republic...'

'Cut the crap, Duchamp,' Comtois interrupted.

Hugo sighed, realising he was getting nowhere. He paused and decided to take another tack. 'That night he confronted Jasper and Jasper told him the truth. You said Avril came to see you. What happened next?'

It took Comtois a few moments to respond. 'I went to see him. I told you, I'd known Arthur all of his life. I tried to reason with him, make him see sense, but he was hellbent on getting revenge.'

'Then why didn't he?' Hugo interjected. 'If he was hellbent on it, why on earth would he kill himself?'

'Because I told him to let go.' Comtois stated. 'I told him blaming everyone else, fighting with everyone, was useless. That it was all his own fault. I picked at him like a scab, reminding him of every terrible thing he did to Avril and Vincent. And then he was going to do it again?' Comtois shook his head. 'I kept at him. How useless he was, how useless he'd always been and that now Avril had a chance for a real life with a real man. All Arthur was interested in was dragging her back down with him. The last thing I said to him was...' he trailed off.

'What was that?' Hugo pressed.

Comtois dropped his head. 'I told him to do us all a favour and just get lost, and how much better Avril and Vincent would be if he just...' he gulped, forcing air into his lungs, 'disappeared.'

'I see,' Hugo replied. 'And then?'

'They found him the next day,' Comtois continued. A vein

le bateau au fond de l'océan

throbbed in his forehead, and a grim smile appeared on his face. 'Tourists finding him on the attraction he himself had designed, there was something poetic about it.'

Hugo moved across the morgue. He stopped in front of Dr. Oppert, before turning back to Comtois. 'You've just spent time explaining to me exactly why someone might have a very real motive to murder Arthur Roche. Yourself included.' He met Oppert's gaze.

'I had no reason to be part of any conspiracy,' the doctor bristled.

Hugo stared at him, unsure whether that was true. He had no reason to believe the doctor, other than the assurance of Captain Bertram Hervé, a man Hugo respected, yet had no actual knowledge of for the preceding quarter of a century.

'You can study the autopsy report,' Oppert continued calmly. 'Have your own experts look at it if you see fit. But I assure you. I *promise* you, there was nothing to suggest Arthur Roche died of anything other than suicide.'

Hugo considered. Arthur Roche was now ashes at the bottom of the ocean. A report would be of little use to him now. The fact remained. Arthur Roche had both a reason to commit suicide and one to forge ahead seeking revenge on those he thought had trespassed him. Hugo knew, however, that in the end, there was little sense to be made from either explanation. He turned back to Comtois. 'Are you one hundred percent sure?'

Comtois nodded.

'And Avril and Jasper?' Hugo continued. 'When they were informed of Arthur's death, did anything seem odd, or out of place to you?'

'Non,' he replied. 'Jasper stated it was a fitting end to Arthur, and that he had gotten his wish to embarrass him and Avril.' He stopped for a moment. 'If you're asking me, do I believe they murdered him and faked his suicide, then I have to tell you, non, I don't believe that to be the case.'

Hugo nodded. He was not sure what to believe. 'If you were so sure of the facts, then why not just tell Vincent at the time instead of leaving it until he returned in the school holidays?' he asked.

'Because there was no need for him to know,' Comtois answered. 'Avril was mortified. She begged me not to tell Vincent. She didn't want him to know the truth, especially what she had done. She wanted Vincent to go on with his life without always dwelling on the past, so she did not want him at the funeral. And she was worried that if he knew the truth he would disown her. I understood her motive. She didn't want Vincent to lose both parents.' He sighed. 'I like Avril a lot. She made a mistake, but it was a mistake I believe she was pushed into. In my opinion, she didn't deserve to be punished any more than she was already punishing herself.' He rubbed his hands together. 'In the end, we all agreed to keep the truth from Vincent, but how were we to know Vincent would take it the way he did?'

Hugo moved his head between Comtois and Oppert. 'That's all there is?'

Oppert was the first to answer. 'I promise you, I examined Arthur thoroughly. There was nothing untoward about his death. He was a fine swimmer, a healthy man. He swam to his boat and tied himself to it. He made his point.' Oppert added matter-of-factly. He did not look at Comtois. 'Arthur decided his love for his family was worth more than revenge, and that in his mind at least, they would be better off without him.' He stopped, eyes flicking over the remains of Gregoire Comtois. 'What Arthur did has nothing to do with anything this. Arthur was a troubled man and Vincent inherited his melancholy, I'm certain of it. This is a tragedy after a tragedy, but that's all it is.'

Hugo followed his gaze and stared at Gregoire. 'And yet here we are.'

le bateau au fond de l'océan

Comtois finally rose to his feet. 'We are looking at something quite different.'

Hugo nodded. 'I agree.' He turned his head between the two men. 'Have you told me everything?'

'We have,' they cried in unison.

Hugo closed his eyes for a second. They had both just lied to him. He was certain of it. However, the truth remained that if he questioned them on it, the denial would be swift, heartfelt and no doubt mixed with them being offended. The question was - was the lie important, or merely an omission irrelevant to the murder of Gregoire Comtois? All Hugo knew for certain was that he was going to have to proceed cautiously. He stared at Comtois. 'You are going to have to let me investigate your son's murder, in my own way, and without interference,' he warned.

'I will not!' Comtois roared.

'Oh, shut up, Franc,' Oppert interrupted. 'You're not stupid, so stop acting it. Captain Duchamp is a fine detective. I have it on very good authority, and that is exactly what you need. Or are you telling us you want your son's murderer to walk free because you're too damn stubborn to do the right thing?' He glared at Comtois. 'Answer me, you old fool.'

Comtois lips twisted into an irritated, sad smile. 'I hate you.'

'And I hate you, you stubborn goat,' Oppert retorted. His voice softened. 'But we're both too old for this nonsense. Let's leave it to the young Captain Duchamp.'

Comtois stared at Hugo. 'Very well, but on one condition. When you discover who killed my son, I will be the first person you tell.'

Hugo held Comtois' gaze. He nodded. 'Once the suspect is safely in police custody, you will be the first person I tell,' he answered.

Comtois smiled. 'Bon. Then make sure he is <u>very</u> safe, or else...' he trailed off. 'I will.'

dix-huit

'So, you're in charge of the investigation?' Baptiste asked hopefully.

Hugo raised his hands. 'Now, don't get too excited. All I am doing is taking charge of the investigation so that there can be no suggestion of impropriety when any person is arrested and prosecuted.' He stared at Baptiste. 'But I'm still not convinced there is anything to investigate regarding Arthur Roche's death. Despite what Captain Comtois told me, it doesn't change the outcome. If there was any crime committed, it may have been one of fraud, but even that is tenuous.'

'But you'll have access to all the reports?' Baptiste retorted. 'And you can interview witnesses and shake the damn truth out of them?'

Hugo smiled. 'I'm not sure what it is you think I do in my day-to-day life, Baptiste,' he replied. 'Mais, I can assure you, I don't think I've ever shaken the truth out of a witness before.' He paused. 'No matter how much I may have wanted to.'

Baptiste moved across the veranda, staring down to the harbour. 'Then it's true. Gregoire Comtois was murdered.'

Hugo frowned. 'I didn't say that.'

Baptiste smiled. 'Non, you didn't, but I can read you like a book.' He shrugged. 'Anyway, don't worry, you didn't tip me off. Everyone in Beaufort-Sur-Mer is talking about it. Two plus two, and all that.'

Hugo shook his head. 'I can't talk about this, and nor should you be.'

'The fact you're in charge of the investigation now, rather than Captain Comtois, pretty much confirms it,' Baptiste continued. 'Alors, where do we go from here?'

'WE go nowhere,' Hugo replied tartly. 'In fact, I'm pretty certain it would be best if you returned to Montgenoux.'

'I'm not a kid,' Baptiste snapped, 'so, don't treat me like one.'

Hugo exhaled. 'I wasn't. But if you want to be treated as an adult, you should remember that as an adult, you have responsibilities. Not just your studies, nor your place on the swim team, but you are also supposed to be in charge at the vineyard. Those are all adult things, not here, watching over my shoulder. Let me do my job, and you do yours.'

Baptiste tutted. 'I'm not leaving. Not until I know for sure what happened. And you can't make me.'

Hugo sighed. 'Don't be petulant, Baptiste. I'm not suggesting I would make you leave. But you can't have it both ways. If you want me to investigate, then I must do so as Captain Duchamp, not as your Papa, and that requires you keeping away from the investigation. Are we clear?'

Baptise stared at him, nodding finally. 'I always listen to Papa,' he answered with a smile.

'Bon,' Hugo replied.

'But I need to help. I need to do something, or I'll go crazy,' Baptiste pleaded.

Hugo stared at him. He did not want Baptiste to become involved, but he also knew he would do whatever he wanted, anyway. 'There is a dynamic in Beaufort-Sur-Mer that will evade me, but not you,' he said.

Baptiste frowned. 'What do you mean?'

'Well, for a start, you were one of the last people to see him alive,' Hugo stated.

Baptiste coughed. 'You think I'm a suspect?'

Hugo laughed. 'Well, you don't have an alibi as such,' he stated. 'I think I can vouch for your moral character, however.' He shook his head. 'But you mentioned you were all up at the old fort last night. Drinking… smoking…' he trailed off, a shadow of disappointment appearing on his face.

'Yeah,' Baptiste replied. He squinted as if he was trying to recall the events as they happened. 'Actually though, Gregoire went off early with Brigitte, and I didn't see him again.'

Hugo raised an eyebrow. 'Brigitte St. Pierre?'

Baptiste winked. 'Yeah. I think they went off for a little privacy, if you know what I'm saying.'

Hugo moved across the veranda. He reached into his pocket and extracted a cigarette. He lit it, staring at the veranda. 'We saw Brigitte down there this morning,' he said. 'And, as you may recall, there was something off with her.'

'Oh, yeah,' Baptiste replied. 'She did look pretty freaked out.'

'She certainly did,' Hugo retorted pensively. He took a long drag.

Baptiste stared at him. 'Wait. You can't think for a second Brigitte would be involved in what happened to Gregoire? I know her. She's a cool cat. She's not that sort of girl.'

Hugo did not answer immediately. 'But unless I'm very much mistaken, something happened to her.'

Baptiste shrugged. 'Yeah, but that could mean anything... or nothing.'

Hugo nodded. 'I agree. But I have to speak to her. At the very least, as you said, she is one of the last people to have seen Gregoire alive.'

'What do you want me to do?' Baptiste asked.

'Rien.' Hugo replied. 'Listen, I know I can't stop you from doing what you want to do, but for me, just keep a low profile. If you find out what people are saying and you think it's relevant to the investigation, then please tell me, other than that, just keep safe. That's all I need you to do for me.'

'D'accord,' Baptiste retorted, clearly disappointed. He rose to his feet. 'D'accord. I'll keep my ear to the ground for you, Inspector Clouseau,' he said, winking at Hugo. 'But, I'll expect a raise in my pocket money.'

dix-neuf

Hugo stepped out into the harbour. A sizeable crowd was still gathered, and it appeared the same reporters were reporting the same lack of news regarding the death of Gregoire Comtois.

He had just completed another terse conversation with Captain Comtois, who had informed Hugo that the local procurer had decided to withhold the information surrounding the cause of Gregoire's death. Hugo supported the decision. It made sense to rule the death as unexplained because it would most likely allow the murderer to presume their plan had worked and that Gregoire's death was not being investigated as suspicious. It would give Hugo and the police the vital chance, a small window, to gauge the reaction of everyone while their guard was down and when they would presumably be feeling some relief they had gotten away with their crime.

Before leaving the hotel, Hugo had called Brigitte St. Pierre's room, and she had either been out or just not answering the telephone. Baptiste had passed on her cell phone number, but it also appeared to be turned off. Hugo had asked Baptiste to see if he could track down his fellow students and inform them Hugo needed to speak with them urgently.

Hugo moved closer to the dock, stopping in front of the steep walkway which lead directly into the water. Dax Chastain and Guy Fallon were standing in silence, staring into the sea. Hugo stopped next to them and cleared his throat.

'I'm very sorry for your loss,' he whispered.

Dax turned his head. His eyes were red and swollen. His face was pale, covered with the unmistakable greyness of loss and disbelief. He did not respond.

'Merci, Captain,' Guy said. 'Have you seen Franc? How is he?'

'He's as well as can be expected,' Hugo responded. 'I think

he's very much in shock. Dr. Oppert is with him.'

Guy nodded. 'It's good he's not alone,' he replied. His voice was light, and to Hugo, it sounded automatic, like it was a recorded message on an answering machine.

'Why did he do it?' Dax spoke finally. He was staring at the sea 'He was fine last night.' He gesticulated at Guy. 'You were there. He was having a blast.'

Guy shrugged. He ran a calloused hand over his smooth skull. 'And the truth is, who knows how he was dealing with what happened to Vincent?' He shuddered. 'I hate to sound all new age, but aren't we all a bit in denial and having trouble "processing it"?'

'He wasn't even that close to Vincent,' Dax snapped

'What can you tell me about last night and the last time you saw Gregoire?' Hugo asked.

Dax pointed towards the fort at the top of the hill. 'We were up there from about 17H00 until 23H00. We were having...' he paused, before shrugging. 'We were hanging out. Greg left early.'

'Was he on his own?' Hugo pressed.

Dax met Hugo's gaze. There was something questioning about the way he looked, Hugo thought. Dax shrugged. 'I think he walked down with Brigitte. I didn't really pay a lot of attention.' He shuddered, before adding, 'I didn't think I needed to.'

Hugo nodded. Dax had confirmed what Baptiste had told him. 'Et toi, Monsieur Fallon? Were you at the fort also?'

'Yeah, for some of the time, at least,' Guy Fallon replied. 'The rest of the time, I was fishing as usual. I saw Greg later though.'

'And when was that?' Hugo questioned.

Guy considered. 'About 21H00, maybe a little later,' he answered. 'It wasn't quite dark. I had just about finished putting down my nets and cages. I normally finish about 22H00 and then go to the bar for a few drinks before turning in. I start early, 04H00 usually, so late nights aren't a possibility for me.'

Hugo noted the times on a pad. 'And what was he doing when you saw him?'

Guy shrugged. 'He was sitting on the benches over there,' he said, pointing to a row of seats at the far end of the dock. They more or less directly overlooked the area where Arthur Roche's boat was sunk and the place where Gregoire Comtois had ended up.

'On his own?'

Guy nodded. 'Oui. He was just sitting there, smoking.'

'And you didn't speak to him?' Hugo asked.

He shook his head quickly. Too quickly for Hugo's liking. He turned to face the fisherman.

'Well, I didn't talk to him, as such,' Guy said reluctantly. 'I mean, I just called over to him and asked him if he wanted to come for a beer.'

Hugo tried to ascertain if that was the extent of the conversation. It was hard to tell. Guy's dark eyes were wide and cold and expressed nothing. 'And what did he say?' Hugo asked.

Guy coughed. 'He told me to go fuck myself.'

Dax spluttered. 'Sounds like Greg!'

'Does it?' Hugo asked with a frown. 'You saying it was a normal response?' If someone he knew spoke to him in such a way, he would most certainly question why.

Dax's mouth twisted into a sad smile. 'Yeah pretty normal, especially when he was wasted.'

'And you're saying he was wasted last night?' Hugo questioned. He knew it would be a matter of some days, if not longer, before the lab returned the results of Gregoire's blood and toxicology. He noticed the hesitation on Dax's face. 'I'm not interested in getting anyone in trouble, Dax,' he said. 'I just want to try and understand what happened last night.'

Dax nodded. He shrugged. 'We had beers, a few joints. Nothing crazy. Nothing excessive.'

'Then why did he tell Monsieur Fallon to get lost?'

Dax shrugged again. 'Because that's the sort of thing he did when he was wasted, I told you.'

'Or when he got dumped,' Guy added with a laugh.

'Dumped?' Hugo asked sharply.

Dax shot Guy a look.

Hugo continued. 'You said Gregoire left with Brigitte St. Pierre,' he repeated.

'I said they left at the same time,' Dax corrected. 'That's all.'

'And he was on his own when he was over there,' Guy added, pointing at the bench again.

But something had most certainly happened, Hugo reasoned, and it was something which had clearly upset, if not traumatised, Brigitte St. Pierre. It made speaking to her a priority. He did not want to bother Etienne in Montgenoux to ask him to try to track her cell phone, and as it appeared to be switched off, it would likely prove fruitless anyway.

'How did Gregoire get down to the boat?' Hugo asked.

Dax frowned. 'What do you mean?' he snapped. 'He swam, obviously.'

'In the dark?' Hugo interrupted.

Dax and Guy exchanged another look.

Hugo stepped closer to the edge of the harbour and flicked on his glasses. 'Gregoire died during the night,' he continued. 'When it was most certainly dark.' He pointed to the lights in the harbour. There were several lampposts with chains of lights hanging between them. He had seen them at night, and while they illuminated the dock and the boardwalk, he did not imagine they would provide much light in the water itself.

'It's just that I would imagine the visibility isn't great down there,' Hugo continued.

'We must have swum it a thousand times over the years,' Dax reasoned. 'We could probably find our way there with our eyes closed. But we also have torches and headlamps,' he added tartly.

'Most people in Beaufort-Sur-Mer dive, and they probably have their own equipment, not that it matters.' He pointed to the far end of the beach. Hugo narrowed his eyes. He could make out a makeshift stand with a large painted sign above it - *Chastain Diving Tours.* 'That's my place,' Dax continued. 'And I have a storage box there where I keep all my equipment. There's a padlock, but I barely ever remember to put it on, so pretty much anyone could help themselves to diving equipment if they wanted to.'

Hugo looked at him doubtfully. 'Do you keep an inventory of your stock to see if there's anything missing?' he asked.

Dax laughed. 'An inventory? I can barely count, Captain!'

Hugo did not want to divulge what he knew yet, but he still wanted to explore different possibilities and scenarios. 'We didn't find any evidence of any equipment by the boat,' he stated.

Dax shrugged. 'It doesn't mean they're not there, in the sand, by the boat, stuck somewhere...'

Hugo nodded. 'And then what? He swam to the anchor and managed to tie himself to it? All in the dark, or perhaps with a torch or headlamp which has subsequently disappeared?'

'What are you suggesting, exactly, Captain Duchamp?' Guy questioned.

'Rien,' Hugo replied. 'I'm just trying to make sense of what happened.'

Dax spat into the water. He ran his hands through his sun-kissed hair. 'I don't think that's ever going to happen, Captain. None of what happened is ever going to make sense. If I'm sure of anything, I'm sure of that.'

I hope not, Hugo thought. For all of their sakes, he hoped there was a way through the darkness which had descended upon Beaufort-Sur-Mer and its inhabitants.

vingt

Hugo knocked on the door to Captain Comtois' office. The office was sparsely furnished and contained none of the flourishes the police station in Montgenoux had, though little of that was to do with Hugo, rather than the effervescent receptionist, Mare-Louise Shelan. Hugo turned his head. There were no personal touches, no photographs or signs of a life away from the station. The only things on the wall were a row of framed certificates, commending Captain Comtois for long service, fishing and deep-sea diving competitions.

Comtois lifted his head slowly. He was nursing a crystal glass with his left hand, a whisky bottle with the other. His face was ruddy and his eyes glazed. Hugo suspected he had spent a great deal of time alone in his office with the bottle.

'Can I offer you a drink, Captain?' Comtois slurred.

'Non, merci,' Hugo replied. He pointed to a seat opposite Comtois. 'May I?'

Comtois nodded. 'Oui, bien sûr.' He watched as Hugo sat. 'Do you have news?'

Hugo bit his lip. 'Désolé,' he replied. 'I've spent the day going around the harbour. As I'm sure you already know, there aren't any CCTV cameras around.'

Comtois snorted. 'I signed the objection when the mayor tried to have them installed.' He shook his head. 'We all thought it would spoil the "ambience" of the town. And besides, with a crime rate like ours, what was the point? Nothing ever happens in Beaufort-Sur-Mer.' He snorted, seemingly at the irony of the statement.

'One thing is troubling me,' Hugo said. 'We know your son was dead before he went in the water, but how did he get down there? There are no lights in the water. Dax Chastain and Guy Fallon suggested that he could have used a torch or a headlamp and then dropped them. You and I know that's not possible, because somebody else took Gregoire down to the boat and tied him to the anchor.'

'I am aware of that,' Comtois yelled, slamming his fists on the desk. He knocked over his glass and cursed, quickly refilling it. 'What the hell's your point?'

Hugo took a deep breath. 'Only that in the darkness, it can't have been easy. I don't want to upset you, Captain, mais, we have to wonder how someone moved your son's body through the dark water and secured him to the boat.'

Comtois stared at Hugo, his forehead crinkled with confusion. 'What are you suggesting?'

'I'm not sure yet,' Hugo answered. 'We could be looking at two people.'

'Two people?' Comtois interjected, his voice shrill. 'You can't be serious.'

'I'm not saying I am,' Hugo replied. 'Rather, I'm just thinking aloud. Whoever was responsible either had help or…'

'Or?'

'They were experienced,' Hugo continued. 'They knew what they were doing. Or they planned it in advance.'

'What makes you think that?' Comtois shot back.

'Well,' Hugo mused, 'to orchestrate something like this in darkness seems like a lot of hard work to me. They'd have to hold their breath, to know their way down to the boat, where the anchor was, etc.'

Comtois lifted his glass. He watched the ice as it slid around the crystal glass. 'Or he had help, or planned it in advance,' he said, repeating Hugo's theory.

Hugo nodded. 'These are all possibilities. And without cameras, it's going to be extremely difficult to be certain of anything.'

He held up his hand and extended his fingers. 'So, we have

un, an accident. Gregoire is killed by accident, following a fight, or a struggle, par example. Whoever else was involved, panics and in the heat of the moment stages another suicide to try and cover up the accident, or the murder. If we are to believe that, then I have to wonder how he did it? I for one am fairly sure I couldn't drag a body through cold, dark water and somehow or other secure it to a boat with an anchor, at least not without help. Therefore, I can only imagine it was done by someone who is capable and proficient in the water. They must be used to swimming in darkness or holding their breath, or they were able to access breathing apparatus.'

He extended another finger. 'And then we have deux - for some reason, our killer planned to murder Gregoire that night by the dock. And because they knew what they were doing, they had the equipment to hand. Breathing apparatus, torches, those sorts of things.'

Comtois nursed his drink. 'That's all possible, Captain Duchamp, but it all boils down to the same thing, non? Et, it seems to me you have very little to go on.'

Hugo nodded again. 'I agree. But it's a start. I want to find out what happened to your son, and I'm going to need your help to do so. Those scenarios are a start, non?'

'I will most likely murder whoever is responsible for this. You understand that, don't you?' Comtois interrupted.

'I do,' Hugo replied. 'And I will do whatever I can to prevent that. For both your sakes.'

Comtois smiled. 'You can try. Or you can look away. I'm a police officer with almost forty years of service. I have no wife. I have no children now. A long, lonely, depressing life is not something I am planning on or looking forward to. Which makes me very dangerous. Men who have nothing to lose,' he smiled, before adding, 'have absolutely nothing to lose.'

Hugo took a deep breath. He wished he could reach out to

the man he barely knew. While they were colleagues of the same rank, Hugo imagined they had very little in common. Hugo was not used to walking next to men such as Comtois. He hated thinking of it that way, but Comtois was a manly man and while Hugo did not think of himself in any similar linear way, he did not think of himself as anything less manly, such as a man like Comtois. He was just a different sort of man. And that was enough for him. He stared at Comtois and hoped he would have someone to look out for him.

'Gregoire deserves justice,' Hugo whispered.

'Bullshit,' Comtois shot back. 'Gregoire deserves me taking out my gun and making sure his murderer never gets to walk the boulevard again.'

'And I will also do everything I can to prevent that,' Hugo repeated, more slowly and with bite.

Comtois smiled. 'We'll see who gets to pull the trigger first, then, won't we?'

vingt-et-un

Hugo took the steep staircase towards the fort slowly, stopping several times to steady himself on the handrail. He looked behind at the dazzling boulevard and dock now some distance below him. He lit a cigarette and sat on a step. He was reminded again of just how beautiful Beaufort-Sur-Mer was. But in moments such as these, he felt as if he could see and feel the air tinged with so much tragedy and sadness.

There was something amiss about the town. A seemingly quiet, quaint coastal town, revered by tourists, also appeared to be a hotbed of secrets and lies. He supposed all towns were the same in one way or another, and that it was never really possible to know exactly what happened behind closed doors. In that respect, Montgenoux was no different. He had seen first-hand just a few of the secrets people hid, often terrified of being discovered and prepared to do anything to prevent it. It almost always resulted in a multitude of tragedies.

He regarded his cell phone again. The message from Baptiste had been simple and direct:

I've found Brigitte. Come to the fort and come alone. BX

All things aside, Hugo was not sure who he could bring anyway, but it had certainly piqued his interest. He took a long drag on his cigarette and flicked on his sunglasses. He tugged at the linen shirt he was wearing. It was already sticking to his body. He had spent most of his life between Paris, London and Montgenoux, so he had never really become used to warm weather, or acclimated to any sort of weather in particular.

'Papa!' Baptiste called from the clearing. 'Over here,' he gestured.

Hugo cleared the top step and strode across the grass verge. Baptiste was standing on the corner of the fort, standing between two crumbled walls, which Hugo surmised was once the entrance.

He narrowed his eyes. Behind Baptiste, Hugo could make out two figures sitting on a concrete slab.

The slab was covered in graffiti and was most likely hundreds of years old. There was something about the oldness being tarnished with something new which touched him. He knew it should not, but it was like combining two different eras. The younger generation was enjoying the fort, rather than viewing it from behind glass or ropes. The fort had been long abandoned, but it had taken on a new purpose. He was surprised it had been allowed to happen, but to see it being used was something heartening.

He stopped, stubbing out the cigarette with his foot and taking a moment to appraise the scene in front of him. Brigitte St. Pierre and Quentin Arquette, Baptiste's two swim teammates, were sitting on the slab. Quentin's arm was thrown over Brigitte's shoulder in what Hugo only could describe as a protective stance. He frowned, thinking it was odd because, as far as he could tell, the two young adults were not close in any way. Quentin's small stature meant his arm barely stretched all the way across Brigitte's shoulder. Her head was down, but Hugo could see the moistness against her dark cheeks. She had clearly been crying.

'Papa,' Baptiste said, taking a step forward. 'Brigitte has something to tell you, but you have to promise you won't do anything about it.'

Hugo frowned. He shook his head. 'Baptiste, you know I can't make any such promise, especially if a crime has been committed. I'm not an avocat and there's no such thing as police-client privilege.'

Brigitte slowly lifted her head. 'It's the only way I'm going to talk to you.' Her voice was calm and collected, but Hugo could hear the determination in it.

Hugo studied her face. He knew he could not make a promise he could not keep, but he also knew he needed to hear what she had to say. He inched forward. 'Let's just talk and we'll decide what to do afterwards, d'accord? All I can promise you is that I will listen with an open mind and I will do whatever I can to help. You have my word I won't do a thing I don't believe is in your best interests.'

Brigitte looked to Baptiste. Baptiste shrugged. 'I've told you before. I'd be dead, or worse, if it wasn't for Hugo. I trust him more than I trust anyone else in this world, and that will never change.' He reached out and touched her arm. She recoiled instantly, pulling it back inside the sleeve of her cardigan.

Baptiste's mouth twisted anxiously. 'You can trust him.'

Quentin snorted. Baptiste glared at him. 'You can trust him, Brigitte,' Baptiste repeated.

Hugo lowered himself onto a stone opposite Brigitte and Quentin. He leaned forward. 'What exactly happened last night, Brigitte?' he asked softly.

Brigitte sighed. She reached between her legs and picked up a bottle of beer, placing it against her lips, the liquid spilling down her lips and chin. She wiped it away with her sleeve and took another sip. 'When Gregoire was flirting with me, I was flattered,' she whispered, her voice thick and heavy with emotion. 'I figured, why would some cute dude like him go for a fat black chick like me, with bad skin and frizzy hair I can't control…'

'Are you kidding?' Baptiste interjected. 'You're a knockout!'

'Sure you are,' Quentin added. Unlike the last time Hugo had heard him, this time the young man sounded sincere.

Brigitte pulled back her head and stared at Quentin. 'Dieu, that felt weird!' She laughed sadly. 'Don't start feeling sorry for me, Quentin, I couldn't stand that.'

Quentin smiled. He shrugged. 'Well, yeah, you are fat and your skin is like Swiss cheese, but mon Dieu, you've got a hell of a rack and a great ass!'

Brigitte turned away. 'That's better, but keep your eyes off my tits, you pervert, or I'll poke them out!'

The three youngsters laughed. It was forced and sounded fake. Brigitte took another drink. 'Anyway,' she continued, 'when Gregoire suggested we get out of here and go somewhere private he knew, *I thought, sure, why not? What have I got to lose?*' She snorted, snot spraying from her nostrils. 'What have I got to lose?' she repeated. 'As usual, I have zero sense when it comes to men.'

'What happened?' Hugo pressed gently.

'We went down to the beach,' Brigitte replied. 'Gregoire said he had a key for one of the beach huts, and that we could go there together. He said it was the last hut on the beach, so it would be nice and private. I agreed to go.' She swallowed. She began sucking on the air as if she was having trouble getting any words out of her mouth.

'And then we were making out,' she continued. 'After a while, we stopped, had some more beer and weed. It was all very casual and fun. He was funny and cute and a good kisser. I suppose I kinda liked the idea of having a holiday romance - the kind you only ever read about in trashy magazines. Some sun-kissed hunk who is eager to please and horny as hell. The kind you never have to see again or worry about him embarrassing you in front of your family or friends because he's pretty dumb and hasn't got much going for him. Just a happy memory of making out and getting sand in your ass. Do you know what I mean?'

Hugo nodded, although he was not at all sure he did. Those kinds of love affairs had never been on his horizon. 'What happened next?' he asked.

She sipped the beer slowly. 'I woke up alone in the hut this morning.'

Hugo leaned further forward. 'And Gregoire?'

She shrugged. 'I have no idea where he was, or when he'd left, mais...' she swallowed, gulping air desperately into her lungs, 'I knew straight away something was wrong.'

'Wrong?' Hugo asked.

Brigitte nodded. 'My shorts and my underwear were off and it was obvious… it was obvious I'd had sex.'

'You were raped!' Quentin interrupted, his voice bristling with anger.

'Is that correct, Brigitte? Were you raped?' Hugo whispered.

She moved her head slowly but said nothing. It was not clear whether she was nodding or shaking her head.

Hugo gulped, pressing back the bile which was rising in his throat. 'By Gregoire?'

Brigitte swallowed.

'Did Gregoire Comtois rape you last night?' Hugo whispered.

She lifted her head slowly. 'I think so.' She shook her head. 'Mais, I don't know.'

'Tell me what happened,' Hugo replied.

She stood up and moved around the slab, finally leaning against one of the walls. 'I can't be sure,' she responded. 'I don't remember.'

Hugo nodded. 'What is the last thing you do remember?'

She considered. 'We got high and were just sitting, staring out at the sea. The moonlight was beautiful on the water. I've never really seen that before. I'm a town girl, and… well, I guess with the beer, the weed, I just passed out.'

'Or that's what he wanted to happen so he could have his way with you. He drugged you. It's obvious,' Quentin interrupted.

Brigitte glared at him. 'Why drug me?' she questioned. 'I told you I was into him. I'm not saying I would have slept with him, but I'm not saying I wouldn't have either.'

'But you don't remember it happening?' Hugo continued.

She shook her head. 'Non, et…' she glanced down, clearly embarrassed. 'I was sore. It didn't feel right.'

'Because he forced you!' Quentin hissed. 'The bastard raped you!'

Hugo cleared his throat. 'You said you were alone when you woke up, and that you were partially naked. Did you notice anything else in the beach hut?'

'What do you mean?' Brigitte asked.

Hugo shrugged. 'I don't know, any sign of anyone else? Clothes? Beer cans?'

Her lips shook. 'I can't say I noticed anything. All I could think about was getting out of there and getting back to the hotel and having a shower.'

Hugo tried to hide his emotions. 'And that's what you did?'

Brigitte nodded. 'I stood under the shower until I couldn't stand up any longer and then I scrubbed my skin raw,' she responded. She sighed. 'I know what you're thinking - I should have gone to the police right away.'

'Well, to the hospital at least,' Hugo replied. 'You still should. This isn't about anything other than you. You did what you needed to. We would never judge you for acting in the way you needed to.'

She shook her head vehemently. 'I can't talk to the police.'

Hugo took a deep breath. 'I understand, but right now the most important thing is getting you checked out.' He took a moment. 'Brigitte, there are things you have to consider.'

'Consider?'

He nodded again. 'Oui. And I am sorry to be indelicate, but you need to be examined by a professional. You don't know exactly what happened. For a start, you need to see if you are hurt in any way, but also, there are tests which must be administered.'

'Tests?' Brigitte questioned. She stopped and slapped her forehead. 'Oh, Dieu. You mean AIDS, don't you? You're saying he could have given me AIDS?'

Hugo's jaw flexed. 'There are tests which can be run, but more importantly, there is medication which can dramatically reduce what happens to you next. Not just for AIDS, or other diseases, but you also need to know if he used a condom. All of these things can be dealt with, but they do need to be dealt with.' He stopped, hoping the silence would give a chance for the information to sink in. 'I'm so sorry this has happened to you, and I'm so sorry it's me that is having to be the one to talk about this with you, but I beg you to go to a hospital. Everything will be handled with compassion and discretion.'

'And what about him?' she asked. 'What about Gregoire? Is it true what they're saying? That he killed himself?'

Hugo stared at her. If she knew different surrounding the circumstances of Gregoire's death, he did not see it on her face. However, that was a consideration for a different time. 'Let's not talk about that now,' Hugo responded. 'At this moment, we just need to concentrate on you.'

'You can't tell his father,' Brigitte interrupted.

'The hell he can't!' Quentin hissed. 'His son was a rapist! We should be shouting it from the rooftops!'

'His son is dead!' Brigitte screamed at him. 'And you want me to tell his grieving father that his son was a... his son did that?' She shook her head. 'I won't, I tell you. I won't be responsible for a father finding out something like that about his kid when he's just lost him.'

Hugo raised his hands. 'As I said, we can talk about this all later.'

She shook her head again with force. 'Non. I'm telling you. I won't be responsible for this.' She sighed. 'And besides. What the hell COULD we say? That I *may or may not* have been raped by Gregoire? Because, as I've just explained to you all, I don't know what the hell happened.' Her voice cracked. 'I just don't remember.'

'That's because the bastard drugged you,' Quentin snapped.

'I was already high and drunk,' Brigitte retorted. 'And the first thing anyone is going to say is that I was so wasted I can't say for certain what the hell happened.' She wiped the tears from her eyes with intense irritation. 'And they'll say I knew what was going to happen when I went with him to the beach hut, or that I'd instigated it myself. And they'd be right to say that because it could be true.'

She looked at Baptiste and Quentin. 'You both saw me going off last night with him and I bet the first thing that passed through your heads was we were going to hook up.' Neither of them responded. 'And that's what everyone will think.' She faced Hugo. 'And that is why I can't ruin Captain Comtois' life over this. And you can't make me.'

Hugo nodded. 'You're right. But as I said, you have to go to the hospital. Regardless of anything else, you have to be checked out and you have to talk to someone, someone professional who knows what they are doing. This isn't about the police right now, this is only about you.'

Quentin stood up. 'He's right. I'm taking you to the hospital.'

Baptiste moved next to him. 'We both are.'

Brigitte looked between them, her face crinkled with uncertainty and fear.

'And we're not taking no for an answer,' Quentin said softly.

A cloud passed across her face as she seemingly wrangled with a thought. Finally, her shoulders dropped as if she was resigned to what was going to happen. 'Okay.'

Hugo watched the three of them as they passed. He lit a cigarette because he needed to process his thoughts. He could not deny that after what he had just heard, Brigitte St. Pierre had just demonstrated an excellent motive for the murder of Gregoire Comtois, and provided a straightforward case for self-defence. He watched the three of them disappear from view.

vingt-deux

The first thing Hugo noticed was the door to the last hut on the beach was open. He approached cautiously, narrowing his eyes. The night was descending, but he could still see well enough. He stopped by the door and called out. 'Allô, police!'

There was no response. He moved forward, peering around the corner of the door. His heart sank as the realisation hit him. It was obvious the beach hut had been used that day. He could smell the ice cream and the frites. A bucket and spade and various food and drink packaging were strewn around the floor. The scent of innocence and laughter still hung in the air. He sighed. Judging by the remnants of food, it had not been long since the last occupants had left.

He pulled out his cell phone and began taking pictures. He was fairly sure there would be very little forensic evidence to be found, and even if there was, what would it prove, or how could it be used? He glanced around. He could ask for a forensic evaluation, but he had given evidence in court cases enough times to know whatever was found would likely be inadmissible due to what came after it. All the same, he would seal off the hut until he figured out what to do, or rather, whether he could convince anyone to release funds to have the beach hut examined.

His journey to the beach hut had been slow and deliberate. Not because he was in no hurry, but because he needed to understand what he needed to do, and what was required of him. These myriad of thoughts bounced around his head, each demanding his attention.

He knew above anything else, he could not keep Brigitte St. Pierre's accusation of rape to himself. If anything were to happen to indicate she was involved in the murder of Gregoire Comtois, he could find himself in trouble for keeping the secret. But it did not mean he was prepared to put any pressure on her. He had to wait

le bateau au fond de l'océan

until she had been to the hospital and properly examined. All he knew so far was that she was a victim, and he would not change his mind until he had conclusive evidence otherwise.

The question of Captain Comtois was infinitely more complicated. Hugo had already decided to limit what Comtois was told. While a sound enough idea, Hugo imagined in a town such as Beaufort-Sur-Mer, secrets were not always hidden for long. He did not want to risk news of the allegation reaching Comtois ears. The fear of his reaction was very real to Hugo, and because of that, he needed to make sure Brigitte was well and taken care of before the father of the man she believed had attacked her became involved.

Franc Comtois needed to be informed of any accusation against his son, but Hugo knew it had to wait. Therefore, Hugo had decided to call upon Dr. Oppert to ask his advice on how to proceed. Hugo also knew that by the following morning he had no choice but to contact the local Juge d'Instruction and Procurer to inform them what he had discovered. He also hoped that by then, he would have more to go on and more evidence to offer.

'Captain Duchamp, are you in there?'

Hugo recognised the voice of Dr. Jacques Oppert from outside the hut. He stepped out onto the beach. He smiled at Oppert. 'Merci for coming, Dr. Oppert.'

Oppert nodded. 'Bien sûr. You sounded concerned on the telephone,' he replied. 'And I admit, it intrigued me.'

Hugo exhaled. He moved closer to the lapping shoreline and lit a cigarette.

Oppert moved next to him. 'I've worked with enough police officers to know you have a dilemma on your hands. I imagine you know already what you must do, but you want someone older and,' he smiled, *'presumably* wiser, to nudge you in the right direction. Alors, talk to Jacques and we'll see what we can do.'

Hugo took a long drag. He turned to face the doctor. 'How well did you know Gregoire Comtois?'

Oppert's eyebrows crinkled. 'Not well,' he answered. 'We hardly moved in the same circles there being sixty-odd years age difference between us.' He paused to consider. 'If you're asking what I thought of him, I'd have to say very little.' He noticed Hugo's reaction. 'That's not such a bad thing. It means that I heard very little about him one way or another, which suggests he was not a youth prone to trouble.'

'And what about his relationship with his father?' Hugo asked.

Oppert shrugged. 'Franc rarely spoke of him, and he and I don't have the sort of relationship which extends far beyond our occupations. We eat regularly, we drink together most nights, but we do not,' He paused and shuddered, before adding as it if was a dirty word. '*Talk*.' He laughed. 'I got the sense father and son weren't particularly close, especially since the death of Franc's wife. Franc is kept busy enough, and he has his own interests. And he is, of course, of an age, a man who believes his role in a child's life ends when the doctor says, *félicitations*! Subsequently, I suspect he had very little interest in raising the boy.'

The doctor narrowed his eyes towards Hugo. 'Most of this, I'm sure you could have worked out yourself, Captain, so tell me, what is this really about?'

Hugo took another drag of the cigarette. 'There has been a serious accusation made against Gregoire. An accusation which may, or may not have a direct bearing on his murder.'

'Accusation?' Oppert asked with a raised eyebrow.

Hugo nodded. 'A young woman has stated she believes she was sexually assaulted shortly before his death.'

'*Believes?*'

'Désolé,' Hugo responded quickly. 'She knows she had sex, but she does not recall it happening. She either passed out or she was drugged. Either way, she has no recollection of consenting to sex and therefore, she <u>was</u> raped.'

le bateau au fond de l'océan

Oppert pushed a wisp of hair away from his face. 'And you're saying it was Gregoire?'

'It would appear so,' Hugo responded. 'He was certainly with her shortly before, and they were engaged in foreplay.'

Oppert turned. 'In there?' he asked, pointing towards the beach hut.

'Oui,' Hugo replied.

Oppert moved slowly towards the hut. 'This is terrible,' he mumbled. 'Poor Franc.'

'The girl was raped,' Hugo shot back. His tone was harsher than he intended, but it was necessary.

Oppert stared at him. 'Then why are you telling me instead of Franc?'

Hugo sighed. 'At this point, she doesn't want to report it. There is no actual physical evidence since she showered afterwards. She woke up half-naked, so there isn't likely to be any evidence on her clothes. And she also doesn't want to report the rape, particularly because of Gregoire's death and what it might do to his father.'

Oppert snorted. 'And because she knows any avocat would tear holes through her story.' He tapped his chin. 'Nevertheless, she has given us a powerful motive for his murder.'

Hugo shrugged. 'Peut être, mais, then why tell us at all?' he countered. 'There was no reason to mention it if she was implicated in his death.'

The doctor sighed. 'You know the answer to that, as well as I do, Captain Duchamp.'

Hugo nodded. 'She says she had no intention of reporting what happened to her.'

Oppert extended his hands. 'And yet, here we are, and it appears,' he paused, 'she has.'

Hugo fixed the elderly doctor with a glare.

'Don't be cross with me, Captain,' Oppert retorted. 'You

know as well as I do, the young woman could very well be setting up her defence, in case she is implicated in the murder.'

Hugo did not answer.

Oppert moved to a bench and lowered himself onto it slowly. He shook his head. 'What a damn mess,' he said grimly. He looked at Hugo. 'What are you going to do?'

'I've sent her to the hospital,' Hugo replied. 'At the very least, she needs examining and treating. Despite her unwillingness to report the rape...'

'*Alleged* rape...' Oppert snapped.

'I am obliged to take her statement and inform the investigating authorities,' Hugo snapped. 'And it will be called what it is, until we know otherwise, no matter who is involved.' He took a deep breath. 'And the fact is, I believe her when she says she doesn't want Captain Comtois to know. She doesn't want his last memory of his son to be this.'

Oppert nodded. 'She's right. This would destroy Franc. He's a very proud man, and oui, he's just lost his son. This sort of scandal is something no one ever really recovers from.'

'And there's nothing you can tell me about Gregoire?' Hugo asked again. 'Nothing to suggest he could have done something like this?'

Oppert turned his head. He stared at the sea, his eyes watering as the salty air hit them. Finally, he cleared his throat. 'Young people make no sense to me anymore,' he began. 'They are so different these days, and I don't quite understand it.'

Hugo frowned. 'Désolé, I'm not sure what you mean.'

The doctor laughed. 'A few years ago, I went to a sauna in Paris while I was visiting my son,' he replied. 'It was something I used to do often back when I was younger. As age has decided to riddle me with aches and pains, I thought it might be nice to revisit one of my old haunts. Anyway, on this particular day, there I was, sitting as naked as the day I was born, and over from me was a pleasant fellow. Well-groomed beard and hair, a slight body, and then, as I looked down, I realised there was something very different about the two of us men.'

'Quoi?' Hugo frowned again. He stopped, realising what the doctor was suggesting.

'Bien sûr, it didn't bother me,' Oppert added. 'Once I thought about it.' He smiled at Hugo. 'Just because I don't understand it, or the fact I may have appeared shocked, makes me neither judgemental nor phobic. It's another world. I don't need to understand it, that's all. And the fact remains at my age, I don't enjoy seeing myself naked, let alone anyone else seeing me.'

Hugo suppressed a smile. 'I'm not sure what this has to do with…'

Oppert shrugged. 'All I'm saying is that young people are different these days. I know nothing about what they do in their private lives. They even call themselves different things.' He smiled. 'And I think that's marvellous because it's like everything we ever fought for in the olden days. Sticking two fingers up at the "big man" telling them they didn't have the right to date a black girl! Can you imagine?'

'And Gregoire?'

He shrugged again. 'Gregoire was young. As I said, I don't understand the young.'

'Captain Comtois really should be told about this,' Hugo said.

'You're right, of course,' Oppert replied. 'Do you want me to tell him?'

Hugo shook his head. 'Non, but I would appreciate you coming with me. I think we would both appreciate your support.'

Oppert rose to his feet. 'D'accord. But not now. It can wait until tomorrow morning. Let him have one last night to grieve in peace.'

Hugo opened his mouth to speak. He was reluctant to leave it any longer, but in hindsight, it probably was better to wait and see what the hospital report showed concerning Brigitte St. Pierre's rape.

Oppert moved away slowly. He stopped. 'Before we talk to Franc. I have to ask you. What are your thoughts concerning the validity of this girl's report?'

'I believe she was raped,' Hugo answered.

'Then you have to also consider the victim is most likely our suspect.'

'Mais, until we know otherwise,' Hugo shot back. 'she is only a victim, and a witness to the last hours of Gregoire Comtois, and that is the way we will treat her.' He paused. 'That is the way we will all treat her. Especially Captain Comtois. You agree?'

Oppert sighed as he shuffled slowly across the sand towards the boulevard. 'À demain, Captain.'

vingt-trois

Baptiste opened the door and stepped inside Hugo's hotel room. He threw himself onto the bed, emitting a loud, frustrated groan. Hugo moved in from the veranda, staring at his son. His eyes were closed, and he looked pale.

'Are you all right?' Hugo asked. 'Have you been at the hospital all of this time?'

Baptiste opened his eyes slowly. 'Yeah,' he mumbled.

'How is Brigitte?'

Baptiste pulled himself up in the bed. 'Can I have a cigarette?'

Hugo nodded and pulled out two cigarettes and handed one of them to Baptiste. He lit them both and gestured for Baptiste to follow him onto the veranda. 'I'm a terrible father,' he groaned.

Baptiste smiled. 'You're an amazing father, you just make smoking look cool.'

'That doesn't make me feel better. It makes me feel completely ashamed of myself,' Hugo sighed. 'How is Brigitte?' he asked again.

'She's still in hospital,' Baptiste replied. 'Quentin and I stayed, but they kicked us out this morning. It was weird. Quentin is like this whole different dude. He's nothing like how he was back at school. If I didn't know better, I'd say it was almost as if he actually cared about Brigitte. He spends so much time fighting with her, you'd never imagine it for a second.'

'She's been through a terrible ordeal,' Hugo responded. 'And often in times like this, old resentments disappear. You know Lieutenants Garrel and Laurent in Montgenoux? They bicker day in, day out, but when it comes down to it, I have no doubt in my mind that should either of them need support, they would give it to each other willingly. It's just what we do. Quentin is just trying to be there for someone he knows.'

Baptiste tutted. 'Yeah, well, it's weird.'

'Are you saying Brigitte's still in the hospital?' Hugo continued. 'What did the doctors say?'

Baptiste shrugged. 'They wouldn't tell us.' He paused. 'Before we left, Brigitte just said something about,' he lowered his voice, his eyes darting around the room, *bruising,* and that she had to stay in overnight for observation. She seemed better this morning, happier even. Apparently, they gave her lots of shots, and there was a woman talking with her, some kind of counsellor or something. The counsellor made her understand she had been sexually assaulted and that no matter what lead up to it, it wasn't her fault. I guess having a professional say it helped. Brigitte said she'd call when she was being discharged, so we could pick her up.'

Hugo nodded again. 'And has she spoken with her family?'

'Her parents are out of the country,' Baptiste replied. 'I got the impression they're not close.'

'Well, at least she's speaking with a professional, and being looked after by doctors,' Hugo reasoned. He stared at Baptiste. 'Despite what she says, you do understand she needs to make a statement?'

'Non, she doesn't, and non, she won't,' Baptiste relayed.

'Oui, she does,' Hugo said forcefully. 'For many reasons, but most importantly, she was, as far as we know, one of the last people who saw Gregoire alive. We can't just ignore that.'

'That doesn't mean she had anything to do with it,' Baptiste snapped.

'I didn't say she did,' Hugo replied. 'Mais, that doesn't change things. We have to take a statement, there's just no way around it.'

'And then what?'

'And then we'll see,' Hugo answered. He stubbed out his cigarette. 'First, I'm going to speak to Gregoire's father. He needs to know what happened the night his son was murdered.' He rose to his feet, heading towards the door and to give even more bad news to a grieving father.

'You can't be serious!' Franc Comtois screamed.

Hugo shuffled uncomfortably on the sofa in the centre of Comtois' living room. The room was overcrowded, and there was an abundance of plates piled on a table, mouldy contents spilling onto a dirty carpet. The room had the unmistakable musk of somewhere which had not been aired in a very long time.

'My son was not a fucking rapist!' Franc continued. He slammed his fist on the table, a cloud of dust flying into the air. 'I will not allow you, or anyone else like you, to make such an accusation!'

Hugo narrowed his eyes. There was something about the way in which Comtois had annunciated *you*, and *anyone like you*, which bothered him. There was an intimation to the tone. There was disapproval to the tone. Hugo recognised it because it was one he had experienced for most of his life. It was the disapproval of a father who wanted more, or rather, wanted less, which might embarrass him.

Dr. Jacques Oppert raised his hands, stepping between the two men. Despite his advanced age, the doctor was agile and alert. He smoothed the wisps of hair that were animated and stared into Comtois' eyes as if attempting to pacify him. 'Franc, be calm. Think of your blood pressure.' He pointed at Hugo. 'The Captain was suggesting no such thing, but he is doing his job, as you should understand. This can't be the first time you found yourself where Captain Duchamp is now.'

'What exactly is this person claiming?' Franc countered.

'*She's* not claiming anything, as such,' Hugo replied. 'She is very confused and very distressed. But ultimately, we can't ignore it.'

'Do you think she murdered my son?' Franc blurted.

'I honestly can't answer that at the moment,' Hugo replied.

'Mais, you must have a feeling,' Franc pressed. 'Is she making up a lie to cover up what she did?'

'We're getting ahead of ourselves,' Hugo continued. 'Brigitte isn't exactly claiming anything at this point, primarily because she can't remember everything that happened to her.' He paused. 'She is being treated at the hospital, and that should give us a better idea of what happened to her.'

'Nothing, that's what.'

Hugo clenched his fists. 'I have spoken with this girl. I witnessed her shortly afterwards. I knew something was wrong, and I should have trusted my instincts.'

'Captain Duchamp,' Dr. Oppert interrupted. 'I caution you that path is very long, and very tedious, and not one you should embark upon. Take it as advice from a man who has been alive almost twice as long as you have.'

Hugo smiled at him. He faced Comtois. 'Brigitte isn't lying about being raped.' He stated. 'Of that, I am sure.'

'Sure?' Comtois questioned. 'I have seen many women, even a few men, making such a claim, and I have been taken in myself occasionally. Has your reputation made you too bold, Captain?'

Hugo took a step back. He did not want to fight with Comtois, but nor did he want to back down. He had to make Comtois understand what they were dealing with, or else there was little point in him being there. He did not ask for permission, but he took a cigarette from his pack and lit it.

'She was raped. Brigitte St. Pierre was raped,' he stated. 'And I imagine her medical report will confirm someone drugged her. Not that she took drugs, but that she WAS drugged. Drugged to make her docile and drugged so someone could have sex with her. She has said there was a chance she would have had sex with Gregoire that night, so unless there is a pathology to your son which meant he took pleasure from drugging and raping women, then I have to assume what happened was something entirely different.'

The three men stared at each other, and then turned away, each staring at another point in the room. Hugo stared at a photograph of a young Comtois in his uniform, presumably from when he first became a police officer. Oppert stared at a picture of Gregoire Comtois. He was smiling, wild hair cascading down his shoulders. Hugo followed Comtois' gaze. He was staring at a silver frame where the photograph had been removed.

'What is it you're not telling me?' Hugo asked. The desperation was clear in his voice and he wished it was not.

'Rien,' Comtois spat.

Again, Hugo knew he was lying. He felt the anger rising. 'D'accord. If you have nothing to tell me, then I will tell you this. If we are to proceed with the assumption Brigitte St. Pierre could be responsible for your son's murder, then we can only do so by accepting her explanation. I won't talk to her in any other way, and I won't allow you to do otherwise. Either you call your Juge d'Instruction, or I will call mine.' He exhaled. 'Those are the facts now, Captain Comtois.'

Franc snatched the telephone from the table, his fingers stabbing angrily at the buttons. 'Fine.' He waited for the call to connect. 'Anton, this is Franc Comtois.'

'Ah, Franc. Ça va?' the Juge asked.

Franc ignored him. 'I am here with Captain Duchamp and Dr. Oppert. There is something we need to discuss with you.'

'I am at your disposal,' Anton said.

Franc nodded. He took a breath and then relayed what Hugo had told him about Brigitte St. Pierre.

The Juge remained silent. 'You were right to bring this to me,' he said finally. 'There can be no suggestion of a cover-up.'

'What would you like us to do?' Hugo interjected.

'Well, you must take a statement at the earliest opportunity,' the Juge replied. 'The young woman is fundamental to establishing a timeline and could provide valuable information regarding Gregoire's murder.'

'Or she killed him and is lying,' Franc spat.

The Juge sighed. 'Franc. You just told me you don't believe for a second your son could be guilty of something so heinous.'

'Bien sûr he couldn't,' Franc cried. 'My son was a good boy. This girl knows something, I'm sure of it. That's why she's lying.' He stole a look at Dr. Oppert and then looked away.

'Peut être,' the Juge conceded. 'Mais, you have to tread carefully mon ami. The young woman has not yet made a claim against your son. If we accuse her of being involved in his murder, any avocat worth his salt is going to very quickly make a very loud and very public accusation against your son.'

'But it would be a lie!' Franc erupted.

'Oui, mais, you can't have it both ways,' the Juge reasoned. 'You can't claim she was involved in Gregoire's murder and not have her defend herself. Obviously, you won't like it, but it is her right. That is the whole point of a defence, Franc. You know that as well as we all do.'

'And let us not forget the fact, Brigitte St. Pierre was drugged and raped,' Hugo interjected.

'Stop saying that!' Franc hissed. 'All we know for certain is she most likely had drunken sex with someone and can't remember it. That is all.' He spelt out with his fingers. 'That isn't rape in anyone's book.'

'Franc, Franc,' the Juge sighed. 'That's not helpful. As I said, you can't have it both ways. You can't call her a liar and yet attribute it as being a motive for the murder of your son.'

'Then what the hell do we do?' Franc cried.

'You do nothing,' the Juge retorted. 'You and I have discussed this already, and I will not tolerate your involvement. Captain Duchamp - take a statement from the young lady and get it to me as soon as you can, along with any medical reports. I want to

le bateau au fond de l'océan

try to understand exactly what happened to her last night and what she did in the aftermath. We need to either rule her out or rule her in. I'm sure I don't need to tell you this, but you must proceed with caution and carefulness. If this is a dead-end, then rule it as a dead-end and move on. We have a murder to solve. Excusez-moi, Messieurs, I am due in court shortly. Keep me updated.'

Hugo stared at the telephone as Franc Comtois retrieved it and placed it back in its cradle. Comtois slammed his fist again on the table. 'Dammit, I can't just sit here and do nothing.'

Dr. Oppert moved towards him and placed his hand on his shoulder. 'That is exactly what you must do, Franc,' he said. 'Not just for your own sake, for Gregoire's.' He smiled at Hugo. 'Captain Duchamp is more than capable of doing what needs to be done.'

Hugo took a breath, not at all sure he agreed.

Comtois ground his teeth together. 'He'd better. Whatever happens, I will not have my son accused of something he would never, *ever* do.' He stood and moved across the room, yanking open the door. He turned back to Hugo. 'Find out what really happened and why the damn girl lied about my son, or so help me, there'll be hell to pay.'

vingt-quatre

The first thing Hugo noticed about Brigitte St. Pierre was she appeared much calmer and more relaxed than she had the previous day. He hoped it was an indication she was feeling better despite what had happened to her. He knew she was likely never to get over it. But he also knew it was important she received as much help as possible if she was to stand a chance of being able to find a way to move forward.

Brigitte was reclining in the hospital bed, Quentin Arquette draped protectively next to her. There was something about the scene which bothered Hugo, but he could not put his finger on what it was. It felt odd, and out of place. He shook the thought from his head, realising it was an occupational hazard to always see shadows in the light.

'How are you feeling this morning?' Hugo asked Brigitte.

She smiled. The smile was warm, though she appeared tired. 'Bien, merci,' she replied. 'The doctors seem to think I'm going to be okay, they've pumped me full of different drugs and I have to get regular check-ups, mais they say I'll be fine...' she trailed off as if she was not sure at all, 'then I talked with a psychologist and she said it's *okay* to not be *okay*.'

Quentin snorted. 'Fucking quack.'

Brigitte punched his arm. 'Don't be a bitch, Quentin. She actually made a lot of sense.' She turned to face Hugo. 'So, I'm guessing you're here to force me to make a statement?'

Hugo shook his head vigorously, mortified by her choice of words. 'I'm not here to force you to do anything at all, I can assure you.'

Brigitte nodded. 'The shrink said I should talk to you, but only on my own terms.'

'Bien sûr,' Hugo agreed. 'We just need to try to understand what happened to you two nights ago. To you and Gregoire.'

'Je sais, je sais!' she cried. 'Don't you think I know that? I've been racking my brains trying to piece it all together.'

'Did the doctors help with that?'

She lowered her head, her eyelashes flicking demurely. 'Not really, other than I had sex,' she paused, lowering her head further before adding, 'vigorous sex.'

'That's not all. Tell him the rest,' Quentin goaded.

Brigitte lifted her head. 'They ran blood tests on me. They said there were traces of Rohypnol in my system.'

Hugo's eyes widened. 'Rohypnol?' he repeated

'Oui,' she replied.

'And I take it you didn't take it yourself?'

'Non, of course not,' she answered. 'I told you - we had some beer and a bit of weed, but that's it. I wouldn't even know where to get Rohypnol. Weed is as hard as I go.'

'The bastard drugged her and then he raped her,' Quentin hissed.

'We don't know that,' Brigitte snapped. 'And the truth is, we don't know shit.' She turned to Hugo again. 'So, I'll make a statement, but I won't say anything I'm not sure about.'

'I wouldn't expect you to,' Hugo replied. He took out a notepad and began writing. 'Let's begin at the beginning. We know you left the fort with Gregoire around 21H00 two nights ago. Do you remember that?'

She shrugged. 'It's a bit vague, but yeah, as I told you. I sort of remember leaving and going to the beach hut, making out and then getting higher. It all goes hazy after that, and the only thing I remember next is waking up in the morning and realising something terrible had happened.'

'And there's nothing in between?' Hugo nudged. 'No fragments, nothing which makes no sense but you remember it, anyway?'

She shook her head. 'Je suis désolé, mais non. Nothing else

has come back to me.'

'Don't apologise,' Hugo stated. 'There's a chance it will come back to you later.'

'I don't think I want it to,' she replied. 'They say ignorance is bliss, and maybe I'm better off not knowing what happened to me in that beach hut.'

Hugo was not sure he disagreed. 'What about the journey to the hut?' he continued.

Brigitte frowned. 'What about it?'

Hugo tapped his chin. 'Was there anything unusual about it?'

She closed her eyes as she tried to recall; her face contorting unhappily. She opened them again. 'There's nothing. We walked down the steps. He told me a few stupid, moronic jokes, like he was trying to impress me. I got the impression he was pretty nervous, like it was his first time or something. I remember being surprised by that because he was so different when we were at the fort with the others. When he was with the crowd, he was cocky and sure of himself.'

She stole a look at Quentin. 'The way all boys think they have to be to try to impress us girls, and show off in front of each other. But yeah, I remember hoping he wasn't a virgin.' She stopped, staring at Hugo. 'See, I was already thinking about having sex with him then.'

Hugo grimaced. 'That's not relevant to what happened to you later. That was without your consent and can only be called what it was. Rape.'

Brigitte scoffed. 'Yeah, and courts and juries really buy that shit, don't they? I can see it now. *She had it coming. She asked for it. She was a prick tease. She had her bits hanging out.*'

Hugo opened his mouth to speak but could not. As wrong as it was, there was truth to what she said. 'It's not always that way,' he said with as much reassurance as he could muster. 'Sometimes it feels as if nothing has changed, but some things have. There is

le bateau au fond de l'océan

more support for women in your position than there used to be.' He sighed. 'I'm not saying it's perfect, but it is better.'

Her mouth twisted. 'It's all irrelevant, anyway. Even if I wanted to report what happened… he's gone. There's nothing to be done. They aren't going to prosecute a dead man, are they?'

'However, somebody murdered Gregoire Comtois, Mademoiselle St. Pierre,' Hugo spoke softly. 'And while I understand why you don't want to talk about what happened to you, it could have some bearing on what happened after, and I'm afraid we can't just ignore that.'

'The scum got what was coming to him!' Quentin shouted.

'That's not for us to decide,' Hugo interrupted. 'That is a matter for the court.' He moved closer to the bed. 'Mademoiselle, is there anything else you can think of? Anything, no matter how inconsequential it might seem now.'

Brigitte shook her head. 'I told you everything. I was out of it, and when he stopped to talk, all I was thinking was whether it was worth hooking up with a virgin.'

'Stopped to talk?' Hugo interrupted, his voice rising sharply.

Brigitte's face crumbled in confusion, as if it was the first she had heard of it. 'Oh yeah, I forgot about that,' she said finally. 'I went over to the edge of the dock and looked in the water. I didn't feel like making small talk, especially with them.'

'Them?'

She nodded. 'Yeah. When we got to the dock, Gregoire stopped to talk to Vincent's Maman and the creepy bloke who owns the hotel.'

'Avril Roche and Jasper Connor?' Hugo asked.

'Yeah.'

Hugo considered. 'And what were they doing?'

Brigitte shrugged. 'I don't know. Just standing, I think. I didn't want to talk to her when I was drunk, so I stepped away.'

'Did you hear what they were talking about?' Hugo asked.

She shook her head. 'Non. It didn't last very long, that's all I can tell you. I didn't have time to make up my mind, so I figured I'd go along to the hut, anyway.' She gulped several times. 'I've always been a dumb bitch when it comes to making stupid decisions.' She sighed. 'I don't remember anything else until the following morning.'

Hugo leaned closer. 'Do you remember seeing Baptiste and me?'

She considered. 'I guess. I didn't want to see anyone, I just wanted to get to my room and shower.'

Quentin stood and approached Hugo, blocking him from seeing Brigitte any longer. 'I think that's all, Captain Duchamp,' he said. 'The doctors said Brigitte should be resting.'

'Bien sûr,' Hugo responded. He tapped the notepad. 'Mademoiselle, I'll have someone type up your statement and then you can sign it, d'accord?'

Brigitte nodded, shuffling uncomfortably on the hospital bed. 'Okay. For all the good it'll do. As I told you, I remember nothing and I'm not sure I want to.'

Hugo stepped towards the door. 'Mais, if you do,' he said, 'call me right away.'

Brigitte turned her head, staring out of the window. 'Au revoir, Captain.'

vingt-cinq

The hotel receptionist pointed over Hugo's shoulder towards a set of open patio doors. He thanked her and walked outside.

It was lunchtime, and already the outdoor dining area with its panoramic view of the harbour and the sea was full of diners. They were laughing and chatting gaily, and Hugo thought it was as if the horror of the death had already been forgotten. He supposed it had. It was the way of the world to move on, to forget as soon as possible. To relegate the darkness of life to a place in the past where it could no longer touch them. It was easier to dismiss it, to take relief in the pain belonging to someone else than be faced with the realisation that it could have been them.

Hugo twisted his head until he found who he was looking for. Avril Roche and Jasper Connor were huddled together in the far corner of the restaurant, their heads bowed, engaging in a whispered, private conversation. Hugo had always made it his business to not judge anyone unless an investigation especially called for him to do so. As far as he was concerned, everyone was entitled to a private life so long as it did not interfere with or affect others. It appeared to him that whatever had transpired between the Roche family and Jasper Connor, while a tragedy, was not a police concern unless it needed to be.

He made his way towards the dining table slowly, suddenly feeling very awkward. Jasper Connor spotted him, his blue eyes widening with anger. He stroked his jet-black beard and leaned forward, whispering something to his dining companion. Avril Roche turned her head. Hugo noticed instantly how pale she was and how her eyes appeared red and sore. She turned back to face Jasper quickly, the grey hair on the top of her head falling clumsily across her shoulders. She muttered something, pulling the hair back together and securing it with a wooden stick.

Jasper Connor gestured with his fingers for Hugo to

approach them. 'Join us for lunch, Captain Duchamp,' he said, his voice quickly moving into polite-host mode.

Although he had not eaten, Hugo did not want to join them. 'Non, merci,' he said.

Jasper pointed to a seat between him and Avril. 'Well, at least join us in a glass of wine. It's a fine vintage.' Without waiting for Hugo's response, he poured a glass and slid it across the table.

Hugo sat down, his fingers gently touching the glass. 'Merci,' he replied, realising there was little point in arguing.

Avril touched Hugo's hand. 'Franc said you were investigating Gregoire's death. Have you found the monster responsible yet?'

'I'm not really investigating,' Hugo answered. 'Rather, I'm just helping out until alternative arrangements can be made. I have my own job to get back to, I'm afraid.'

'And Franc can't get his hands dirty in this again,' Jasper muttered.

Hugo wondered what the hotelier meant by *again*, but before he could ask, Avril continued.

'We're all very upset by what happened,' she said. 'We've lost so much, I don't think we can take any more.'

Jasper reached across and took her hand in his. Hugo noticed her reticence, but in the end, she did not pull away. Jasper turned to Hugo. 'As nice as it is to see you, Captain Duchamp. I suspect you are here for a reason, non?'

Hugo nodded. 'When was the last time you saw Gregoire Comtois?'

Jasper and Avril exchanged a look.

Jasper shrugged. 'I do not know.'

'Nor I,' Avril confirmed.

Hugo lifted the glass of wine and took a sip. He was not fond of wine, but he wanted the chance to give them a moment to think about what to say to him next because he was sure of one thing and one thing only. They were lying. Not just because of what Brigitte St. Pierre had told him, but for their own reason, he was sure of it. Now, he only had to figure out whether that lie was important to him, or important just to them.

'Peut être on the night of his murder?' Hugo said. 'Peut être on the harbour?' he pressed. He wanted his tone to be clear. *I know you saw him.*

Avril snatched her hand away from Jasper, admonishing him with a look. 'I often go to the harbour in an evening. It's quiet then and I get a chance to be alone.' She sipped her wine. 'Captain Duchamp, you must think me an awful woman.'

Hugo shook his head. 'Not at all. I don't know you,' he responded.

'Mais, you've heard enough about me to form an opinion,' she replied. 'And an opinion you would be well within your rights to form.'

'But one I wouldn't make,' he replied, with as much reassurance as he could.

'I go to the harbour to be near my husband,' she continued. 'You can call it a penance. I'm not sure if that's what it is. It is all I have left to do for him. To hope that he sees me and knows how sorry I am for some terrible decisions I made. My son, Vincent, paid the highest price, and that is something I will have to live with for the rest of my life. I am ashamed and I am embarrassed, but more importantly, I would give everything to rewind time and put right what I did.'

'Avril...' Jasper whined.

She smiled at him. 'And then there is you and I. We will spend the rest of our lives together in the full knowledge of what we did, and why we did it. For money. For revenge. To satisfy an unhappy woman. It's all stuff, and it's all nonsense, and it angers me it has taken me this long for me to realise it. My punishment, I hope, will be a long, long life ahead of me, one filled with regret and shame. It is what I deserve, not an easy life, or a life I choose to cut short. I must pay for what I did in whatever way I can.'

Jasper looked anxiously towards Hugo. 'Avril is very upset.'

Hugo nodded. 'I understand,' he said. 'Mais, I'm not here to talk about that. Rather, I need to know what happened when you saw Gregoire.'

'I told you…' Jasper began.

Avril interrupted. 'It was obvious he was going off somewhere with that girl who came with you.' She smiled sadly. 'That in itself was a bit of a surprise. He stopped to talk to us.'

'I also take a walk at night,' Jasper added.

Avril continued. 'He just said hello, and that he hoped I was doing okay. I'm not even sure what I said, but I kissed him and told him to enjoy himself because life was so short.'

'And then he went off with Brigitte?' Hugo asked.

'I imagine so,' Avril replied.

'And you?'

'We went to our rooms,' Jasper answered.

Avril laughed. 'Don't be stupid, Jasper. Captain Duchamp is no fool.' She smiled at Hugo. 'We went to Jasper's penthouse room, and we got drunk and made love. It's what we do most days because there is nothing else to do, nothing else to fill the void I have created in my life.'

Hugo took a deep breath, fighting the urge to reach across and console her.

Avril rose to her feet. 'Anyway, please excuse me. I must go. I have to keep looking for Clementine.'

'Clementine Bonheur, the artist?' Hugo asked.

She nodded. 'I haven't been able to find her since last night. She's not at her studio and not answering her cell phone. I am quite worried.'

Jasper laughed nervously. 'This won't be the first time she's shacked up somewhere with a tourist half her age.'

'Peut être,' Avril conceded. 'Mais, not now. She has been with me all this time, trying to help me when I didn't want to be helped. For her just to go off somewhere is…' she trailed off, searching for the word, 'odd.' She pulled her lips into a smile at Hugo. 'I hope you discover the truth, Captain Duchamp. It won't help any of us, I'm sure, but it is what you must do. Au revoir.'

Hugo watched as she moved unsteadily towards the exit. He turned back to Jasper Connor, who had moved away and was already speaking hurriedly into his cell phone.

vingt-six

Baptiste burst into Hugo's room. 'It's all over the news!' he cried. He ran across the room and switched on the television, and moments later the local news station filled the screen.

The newscaster, a serious young woman with blonde hair and immaculate make-up, stared down at the camera. 'In breaking news, we can reveal the sordid and devastating last hours of the murdered young man, Gregoire Comtois, son of Captain Franc Comtois of the Beaufort-Sur-Mer police.'

Hugo sank onto his bed, already dreading what was coming.

The newscaster continued. 'It is alleged that late Thursday evening, Gregoire Comtois sexually assaulted a young woman, a tourist. The young woman is currently under the care of a specialist in hospital, where she is being treated for the injuries she sustained during the attack. It is believed she has cooperated with the police regarding her rape and her attacker. We have reached out to the Procurer for a statement, but none has been forthcoming.'

Hugo stood up and turned off the television. 'This is bad, this is really bad,' he said.

'Is it?' Baptiste questioned. 'I mean, if he raped her, he raped her. It's no good covering it up now.'

Hugo shook his head. 'But evidence can be lost, and it can be distorted. And Brigitte is about to become very involved in something she doesn't deserve and is most certainly not prepared for.'

'Then we'll help her,' Baptiste stated.

Hugo tapped his chin. 'The question is - who talked to the press?'

Baptiste shrugged. 'It could be anyone. A nurse, or an orderly at the hospital. They saw a chance to make a few Euros and took it.'

Hugo nodded. It was not unusual, and he had seen it happen

many times before. Before he could say anything else, there was a loud knock on the door. He opened it. Dax Chastain moved into the bedroom.

'I need to talk to you,' he said, pacing back and forth.

Hugo studied the young tour guide. He was pulling at his sun-bleached hair anxiously. 'Have you seen the damn news?'

Hugo pointed at the television. 'We were just watching it.'

'It's crazy,' Dax cried. 'Gregoire wasn't a rapist, he wouldn't… he couldn't be…'

'Things aren't as simple as that,' Hugo stated.

'He wasn't a rapist! He couldn't be!' Dax repeated. 'I know that for a fact.'

Hugo tipped his head. He pointed to a chair. 'I think you'd better sit down and tell me exactly what you mean.'

'We've been friends all our lives. Not close, not *really* close,' Dax began. 'But close enough, if you know what I mean.'

Hugo frowned. 'I'm afraid I don't.'

Dax sighed. 'Gregoire was always a quiet kid. We used to think it was because his Papa was a bit of a hard ass, always on his case, and in a lot of ways, I suppose it was. But when his mother died it got worse.'

'How?'

'He became more and more withdrawn, and at the same time, more and more out there. He took drugs, drank a lot, he tried to hook up with a lot of girls. It was all a bit…' he trailed off. 'Fake.'

'Fake?' Baptiste asked.

'Yeah,' Dax replied. 'Vincent and I knew there was something off about him. We even tried to talk to him, but he just wouldn't. The more we pressed, the more outrageous he got. In the end, I think we just chose to ignore him. He always had money, so he was good to have around because he always had a supply, but then one day, I understood what the problem was. We were at the fort one night and everyone else was sleeping off a great party. Anyway, Gregoire was sleeping next to me and I woke up and found him on top of me. He was kissing me, and his hand was down my pants. I was shocked. I pushed him off and jumped up. He laughed it off, spouting some bullshit about how he thought I was a chick.'

'And couldn't that have been true?' Hugo asked.

Dax shook his head. 'He couldn't even look me in the eye when he lied. And besides, I could tell how into it he was when he was on top of me.'

Baptiste shrugged. 'So, what are you saying? He was gay, or bi? So what?' He winked at Hugo. 'There's absolutely nothing wrong with that.'

'I didn't say there was,' Dax snapped. 'I couldn't care less what he was. But others would. Especially his father.' He stole a look at Hugo. 'Gregoire told me how his father used to laugh at all the gays who came here during the summer, and how he'd use nasty, derogatory words about them. After that night, the next morning, I pulled Gregoire to one side and told him it was okay, that it didn't matter to me, and that we were still friends.'

Hugo nodded. 'How did he react?'

'He denied it at first,' Dax replied. 'Called me a freak and a liar, but he looked into my eyes and we both knew the truth.' He paused, running his hand through his hair. 'After that, we kinda made little jokes about it. We didn't speak about it. I mean, why would we? I think he was pleased someone shared his secret without actually having to speak about it. He relaxed around me, because I hope, in the end, he saw that it didn't have to be a big thing.'

He took a deep breath. 'Then, about four years ago, a family came from Sweden for a holiday. The son was obviously gay, and it was really obvious he had the hots for Gregoire. So, I took

Gregoire to one side and told him. He was angry with me, but really it was because he saw a chance for something us douchebags had every summer with the tourists, and he never did. He said it was impossible, and I told him nothing was impossible. I said between the three of us, Vincent and me, and Gregoire we could make sure nobody knew anything and nobody saw anything.'

He smiled. 'And that's what we did. For the last four years, the Swedish family has come for their two-week summer holiday and we make sure Gregoire and his hunky Swede get to spend plenty of quality alone time together. Nobody ever knew and nobody ever suspected.'

Hugo sucked in a breath, once again reminded of a past that had never happened for him. Of summer romances under a warm sun. His one and only summer romance had ended before it had begun, leaving him devastated and once again alone. He was not jealous of Gregoire, or others like him. He was just sad. 'Merci for telling us about this, Dax,' he said, 'mais, I'm not sure what this has to do with what happened with Brigitte St. Pierre?'

Dax stabbed his finger in the air. 'Because I know for a fact Gregoire could never have raped that girl.'

'How can you know that for certain?' Hugo asked. 'Were you there?'

'Of course not,' Dax snapped. 'But I knew Gregoire. He wasn't just gay. He was a virgin. At least with a girl.' He laughed. 'He once asked me what I would think about seeing a naked man coming towards me, hell-bent on having sex with me. I told him I had nothing against it, but the thought of seeing another naked man made me feel queasy and most certainly turned off. He laughed and said it was exactly the same for him with women. He loved women, he just didn't need to see their "bits." I agreed. It was the same for me.' He stared at Hugo. 'Gregoire was a virgin. We laughed about it, because we were both virgins, me with men, and him with women.'

'Wait a minute,' Baptiste interrupted. 'I was there with you all on the fort that night. It seemed to me he was pretty into Brigitte.'

Dax laughed. 'I told you. That's a game we've been playing for years,' he replied. 'Each summer we find a tourist whose maybe not the prettiest girl, and we get her drunk, he gets drunk, they have fun, they go off. The whole town talks about it the next day, but nobody ever really knows what happened. And the truth is, they both just get wasted and incapable of doing much of anything, and the next day, well, they're still not sure what they got up to.' He smiled sadly. 'It's a tried and tested system that worked well.'

'Then Brigitte was just what? Another cover for him?' Baptiste pressed.

Dax nodded. 'I hate to say it, but oui, probably.'

Hugo recalled what Brigitte had said, about how she had imagined Gregoire was not the type of man she had first imagined him to be. Hugo had his own experiences of trying to be someone he was not. He was not proud of it, but it was what it was. He had been hurt, and he had hurt. There were casualties in love and it made him sad. It made him sad that Gregoire Comtois had to hide, and that he no doubt hurt others in his quest for happiness.

He took a breath. 'I don't know what to say,' Hugo continued. 'The last thing Brigitte remembers was being with Gregoire, and I'm afraid there is little doubt she was drugged and somebody raped her.'

'Then it wasn't Gregoire,' Dax insisted. 'He wasn't capable of that. Sure, he made out with her. Then he would have done what he usually did with the chicks, get high and drunk. They both pass out and wake up the next morning, not sure what kind of crazy night they had. It kept him sane until his summer love came back. He wouldn't rape anyone,' he repeated firmly.

Hugo looked away. 'Then what went wrong? What changed? And more importantly, how did he end up dead?'

Dax stood. 'Find out. But I beg you. Make sure whatever

happens, everyone knows the truth. Hiding being gay isn't worth admitting to something else.'

Hugo frowned. 'I don't understand what you mean?'

'I know Captain Comtois,' Dax replied. 'And if you ask me, I think he'd rather have the town believe his son got carried away and had sex with someone when they were high. He'd say it was drunk kids not knowing what they were doing. He'd rather that be the truth than anyone know his only son was a fag.' He wiped his mouth. 'Désolé, for the language. But promise me you won't let that happen, Captain Duchamp.'

Baptiste stepped in front of Hugo. 'The hell he won't,' he snapped. 'None of us will.'

Hugo closed his eyes and took a deep breath.

vingt-sept

Hugo moved swiftly across the boulevard, annoyed with himself for wearing flip-flops because they did not allow him to move as quickly as he would like. His mind was in a whirl. The message left on his cell phone had been troubling:

Captain Duchamp, this is Avril Roche - could you meet me at Clementine's studio? I'm very worried about her. I looked through the letterbox and it appears as if her home has been ransacked. It isn't like her to just disappear and not tell me, no matter what Jasper says. I'll be waiting outside for you.

Hugo hoped it was nothing but the concerns of a woman troubled by the events she had been forced to live through in recent times and that Clementine Bonheur was, as Jasper Connor was so sure of, merely off somewhere having fun. Hugo realised he was on high alert, but it did not mean there was nothing to be concerned about. He took the steps two at a time, flicking on his glasses to read the street names as he moved.

He had not been to Clementine Bonheur's studio, but he remembered it from when she had pointed it out to him. Whilst all the houses in Beaufort-Sur-Mer shared the same design and colouring, hers was distinguishable by the paintings which lined the walls. He was not sure why, but at that moment, there seemed something very sad about the coastal paintings around her home. He continued as fast as he could, moving across the narrow walkways. He found Avril Roche sitting on a stool between a row of plant pots, brimming with exuberant and colourful flowers. She jumped to her feet.

'Merci, for coming so quickly, Captain Duchamp,' she gushed. 'I realise you must think me foolish. Jasper certainly does, but it isn't like Clementine, really it isn't.'

Hugo shook his head. 'Bien sûr, non,' he answered quickly.

'It's perfectly understandable to be on edge after everything you've been through.'

She nodded. 'Despite what Jasper says, this isn't normal for Clementine. She wouldn't just leave me like this.'

'I understand,' Hugo replied. 'In your message, you mentioned something about her studio appearing as if it had been ransacked?'

'Oui.' Avril stood, moving across the cobbled pavement. She lifted the letterbox. Hugo lowered himself, narrowing his eyes to stare through the small slot. He could see what she meant. The studio appeared chaotic, with chairs and a table upturned and paint and what appeared to be an easel upended. He pulled his body straight.

'Do you have a key?' he asked Avril.

She shook her head.

Hugo glanced around. He knew he should not break into the studio with no actual cause to do so. There were dozens of plant pots, just as there were around his Swiss-style cottage in Montgenoux, and he wondered whether there would be a key hidden under one of them, just like there was at his home. His hand rested on the door handle and he pushed it down. Nothing ventured, nothing gained, he reasoned. To his surprise, the door swung open, and he could see inside the studio.

Avril gasped. 'It was open all the time.'

Hugo gestured to her. 'Stay where you are, s'il vous plaît. I'll go in and have a look around. I'm sure there's nothing to worry about.'

Avril nodded, taking a step backwards.

Hugo stepped into the room and stopped immediately. He knew the smell. It had invaded his throat and chest on far too many occasions. From fifteen years of age to forty, he understood what it indicated. It was the smell of death. He looked behind him. Avril had returned to the seat, chewing anxiously on her lip, playing with the grey hair on top of her head.

He pushed the door behind him, leaving only a slither of daylight exposed. He knew instinctively that every move he made now counted. He had learned it the hard way, often on the receiving end of a scolding from the pathologists and forensic investigators he had worked with over the years. Every step was important because vital evidence was in danger of being eroded or destroyed. As always, he hoped his suspicions were wrong and that his imagination was playing tricks on him.

He stopped as he rounded the corner of the living area. A large armoire divided the living room from Clementine Bonheur's studio - a small white-walled space filled with light and large French windows overlooking the harbour below. White shutters blocked the windows, but the gap between them let in enough light for him to see. But at that moment there was nothing light about the space. It was splattered red. The splatter of blood.

Hugo lifted his head. Clementine Bonheur was tied to a large ceiling fan by a rope tied around her neck, her body limp and her eyes wide open and staring. Hugo swallowed. The last time he had seen her, she had been wearing the same floral kaftan, but now it was sliced in half, hanging on either side of her exposed torso. It was also covered in blood. Clementine had been cut open from her neck to her sternum with such force, her internal organs were exposed. Hugo walked backwards, stepping outside and closing the door firmly behind him. He reached for his cell phone.

vingt-huit

Hugo watched in silence as the forensic team moved swiftly, but with infinite care around Clementine Bonheur's studio. He was standing in the doorway, now covered completely in a forensic suit. Clementine had been photographed, and before they began removing her body, Hugo took the last opportunity to study her as she was.

He was not sure he had seen a crime scene like it before. Of course, he had seen many corpses desecrated. Too many. They were often ritualistic, or sometimes just plain sadistic, but there was something different about Clementine Bonheur. Her chest splayed open as it was, was one thing, but it was the portrait on the easel next to her which troubled him immensely. It was a crude, almost childlike painting. Hugo suspected a paintbrush had not been used, rather he suspected the murder had used their finger to paint a likeliness of Clementine as she hung dead in front of the easel. Forensics would confirm it later, but Hugo was also sure that no paint had been used, rather the murderer had used Clementine Bonheur's blood.

He flicked on his glasses, his eyes moving over the canvas slowly. The strokes were defiantly wide, finger size wide, though he saw no sign of fingerprints, which suggested the killer had used gloves. He noticed several scratches on the canvas, but other than that, it appeared new and unused.

Dr. Jacques Oppert stepped carefully across the room, following Hugo's gaze. 'I rather suspect they'll confirm it was Clementine's blood,' he grumbled, as if reading Hugo's mind.

Hugo nodded. 'Oui. I'm sorry, you must have known her well.'

Oppert shrugged. 'She was a charming lady,' he tapped his head, 'a little scatty, but good company.' He pointed to a row of empty wine bottles lined up across the kitchen bench. 'She liked wine and men, but she was harmless enough.' He shook his head. 'She certainly didn't deserve such an abysmal end.'

'No one does,' Hugo added. He stared at her body. 'Was she alive when… was she alive when he did that to her?'

The doctor considered his answer. 'I'd like to say, we'll know more when I do an autopsy, but because of the amount of blood and her expression, I feel comfortable in saying she was, tragically, most likely alive when the monster butchered her.'

'Then he's a sick bastard,' Hugo hissed.

Oppert shrugged. 'Bien sûr,' he responded, 'mais, that doesn't help us. You and I both know that, for the most part, sociopaths often hide in broad daylight. They appear as you and I.'

'They usually give themselves away in one way or another,' Hugo reasoned.

'We can only hope so,' Oppert nodded.

'Is there anything else you can tell me?'

The doctor shrugged again. 'Not at this stage, I'm afraid. We can hope forensics finds something more for you because I suspect the autopsy will provide little more insight into what we see before us.'

Hugo moved his head slowly around the room. He suspected the forensic team was also likely to have their work cut out for them. The studio, while compact, was overflowing with bric-à-brac, bottles and glasses and plates piled high. It was a home well lived in, a home born of time spent on fun, not routine. Accordingly, Hugo imagined it would be very difficult to discern who had been there, and what was out of place. It upset him tremendously because he wanted to catch the monster who had murdered her so horrifically.

Dr. Oppert stepped away. He turned, staring at Clementine Bonheur once more. He cleared his throat. 'I really want my next autopsy to be on the bastard who did this to dear, sweet Clementine.'

vingt-neuf

Hugo stared at Captain Franc Comtois. He was seated on the same metal chair in the corner of Dr. Oppert's morgue, where he had been barely days earlier, witnessing an autopsy about to be performed on his son. His head was lowered, chin resting on his chest. It was almost as if he had aged twenty years in the time since Hugo had met him a few short days earlier.

Hugo knew he needed to speak with Comtois, particularly concerning the alleged homosexuality of his son. It had been troubling Hugo. If it was how Dax Chastain had suggested that Gregoire was afraid of his father discovering the truth, then it opened up an entirely fresh line of investigation.

Hugo had suspected Comtois did not approve of him, but he had not been sure if his antagonism was down to the fact he resented Hugo investigating something entirely personal to Comtois. Hugo had noted the elder captain appeared less than accepting of Hugo's adoption of Baptiste, but he remained unsure whether that was informed by homophobic undertones, or rather the judgemental nature of an older man, set in the ways of a different generation.

However, Hugo could not shake the feeling that Dax Chastain had seemed to indicate Gregoire knew of his father's feelings regarding homosexuals, which was why he had remained in the closet. Either way, Hugo knew it was a conversation he could not put off much longer.

Dr. Oppert walked quickly into the morgue from the anteroom, snapping on a pair of latex gloves. He stopped in front of the gurney, shaking his head slowly. 'Pauvre, Clementine.'

'I'm going to kill the monster who did this with my own bare hands,' Comtois muttered.

'I can't say I'd stop you,' Oppert agreed. He flicked on a visor and with a swift movement of his hand, belying his advanced age, pulled back the skin which had been folded back across her chest.

As Oppert continued with the examination, Comtois turned to Hugo. 'So, tell me, Captain - how do you think this connects with what happened to my son?' His voice was laced with ice and it was challenging.

Hugo turned his head slowly. 'I couldn't begin to imagine,' he replied. 'Mais, I believe it is too coincidental for there to be no connection.' He narrowed his eyes. 'We're missing something. Or rather, I think I am missing something.' He paused, took a deep breath, and cleared his throat. He had no interest in outing Gregoire Comtois, especially now that he was dead, but he had to know if Comtois knew, as his son had suspected. 'When I told you about the allegation made against your son, I sensed you were sure he was not capable of such an act.'

'And I stand by that,' Comtois snapped.

'Is it because you know different?' Hugo shot back.

Comtois' eyes widened, flecking with anger. 'What are you suggesting?'

It was only a moment, but it was all Hugo needed to know the truth. Franc Comtois knew about his son's sexuality. He exhaled. 'You knew he wasn't a rapist because you know what he was hiding, didn't you?'

Comtois did not answer.

'Are you really more bothered about people discovering the truth than them believing him to be a rapist?' Hugo pushed, unable to hide the incredulity in his voice.

'My son was not a rapist,' Comtois bristled.

Hugo nodded. 'I think you're probably correct. My question to you is a simple one. Are you prepared to allow people to assume your son was guilty of rape, rather than explore the fact, he would not sleep with a woman?'

'Be very careful what you say next, Duchamp,' Comtois growled.

'Franc,' Oppert sighed. 'Don't be a fool. He knows. We all know.'

Comtois glared at Oppert. 'Then if we all fucking know, we don't have to talk about it, do we?'

Hugo took a tentative step towards him. 'I have as little interest in gossip, or speculation, as I'm sure you do.' He took a deep breath. 'However, we can't ignore the glaring fact something happened to Brigitte St. Pierre. Something she doesn't remember…'

'So, she says,' Comtois interrupted tartly. 'We only have her word for it.'

'And the doctor's,' Hugo shot back.

'I read the hospital report,' Comtois interrupted.

Hugo turned to Dr. Oppert. The doctor lowered his head, clearly embarrassed.

'And the only thing clear is,' Comtois continued, 'is that the girl engaged in what they call "rough sex," and that she had copious amounts of drugs and alcohol in her system.'

Hugo shook his head irritably. 'I will not have her called a liar,' he snapped. 'She told me she did not remember what happened to her, and I believe her. Whatever she did that night, whatever she wore, whatever she drank, whatever drug she took, did not mean she deserved to wake up without her underwear the following morning, with no recollection of what happened to her, and to have to imagine what she might have been through. I can't begin to imagine how she feels, but I do know this. I will be her champion if I need to be, and I won't allow her to be called a liar just because it is easy to do so.'

He narrowed his eyes at Comtois. 'As much as you have lost, Captain Comtois, she is also a victim.'

'You've just spent five minutes telling us how she was brutalised by my son,' Comtois snipped.

'Brutalised by *someone*,' Hugo retorted.

Comtois pointed at him. 'Someone she imagined was my son. My son who ended up dead hours later.' He glared at Hugo. 'Now, perhaps you can begin by telling me how exactly this girl is not your prime suspect? Because she is sure as hell mine. I have no doubt in my mind she murdered my son.'

Hugo turned away. He could see Comtois point. But yet, there was something about it that troubled him. There was something they were missing. If only he could see through the fog, he knew it would begin to make sense. Two people had died in Beaufort-Sur-Mer, and he could not ignore the suicides of Arthur and Vincent Roche. He could not imagine what the connection might be, but he had investigated enough crimes to know there was something very amiss in the town.

'Captain Duchamp?' Dr. Oppert called out.

Hugo shook his head, realising he had drifted into his thoughts again. He stared at Comtois. 'If you have no doubt your son is innocent, then what do you think happened?'

Comtois shrugged. 'She believed my son was her attacker, and she sought revenge.' He sighed. 'Really, Captain Duchamp, from what I've heard about you, I imagined you were rather more intelligent than you are displaying now. As everyone keeps telling me, I am too close to this investigation, and as I keep telling them, being a father who has lost his son does not make me less a detective. As I told you, I read the hospital report. Brigitte removed all physical evidence after having taken a shower. She doesn't remember what happened, and the examination provides no further evidence. Then we have to ask ourselves, what do we have?'

'We have a rape and a murder which happened the same night,' Hugo replied. 'I've asked the forensic team to examine her clothes, to see if that provides any evidence. The same goes for the beach hut, but because other people used it the next day, it has obviously been tainted.' He slowed his breath. 'If Gregoire didn't rape Brigitte St. Pierre, then what else does that suggest?'

'He interrupted the rape,' Dr. Oppert replied.

'And it cost him his life,' Comtois exhaled.

Hugo nodded. 'It would seem that way,' he stated. 'Sadly, that doesn't bring us any closer to understanding what happened.'

'Then we have nothing,' Comtois sighed.

Hugo pointed to Clementine Bonheur. 'We have this. *This* doesn't fit.'

'Doesn't fit?' Oppert queried.

'Oui,' Hugo replied. He stood and moved across the room. 'If we were meant to believe Gregoire was murdered either by Brigitte St. Pierre following her rape, or by someone who discovered her, and acted on her behalf, then it would be very difficult to prove, and most likely prosecute.'

'Your point?' Comtois asked wearily.

'Then why was Clementine Bonheur murdered?' Hugo asked. 'We know it can't have been by Brigitte St. Pierre because she was in hospital at the time.'

'Then her accomplice, and/or her rescuer?' Oppert posed.

Hugo shrugged. 'It's possible, but I think unlikely. The murder of Clementine Bonheur has changed the narrative. Did she see something? Was she a witness who had to be removed?' he suggested. 'If that was the case, then why didn't she report what she might have seen? I can't imagine she would keep quiet about something that happened to Gregoire. She'd known him all his life, after all.'

'Then why else would she have been murdered?' Oppert called.

'That is the question,' Hugo replied glumly, 'I can't answer.'

'She may have seen something,' Comtois reasoned. 'And just not have realised it.'

Hugo nodded. 'I think that's a reasonable explanation. The murderer may have suspected she was a witness, and couldn't take the chance she might realise the significance of what she had seen, eventually.'

Comtois shook his head irritably. 'None of this helps us, Captain,' he moaned.

'I agree,' Hugo replied, before adding, 'at least not in a way we understand yet.'

'As I said, I've looked you up on the computer,' Comtois stated.

'Hmm,' Hugo replied. 'And what conclusion did you come to?'

'You're a pain in the ass,' Comtois spat, 'but you're tenacious and you're thorough.'

Hugo tipped his head. 'It's true, I suppose.'

Comtois sighed. 'And then this morning, I spoke with Jacques old friend in Paris,' he continued. 'And he told me he knew of no finer police officer than you, and if he had lost a loved one, he would want you to be the one investigating it.'

Hugo felt his cheeks flushing, but he could think of no response.

'I admit this is beyond me,' Comtois said, lowering his voice. 'Therefore, I only hope it isn't beyond you because you're all I've got.'

Dr. Oppert clapped his hands and turned around. 'There you go, playing nice at last. Then let us deal with this dear lady.' He pointed at Clementine's body. 'It is pretty much as we expected. She was still alive when she was strung up and then gutted like a fish.' He shuddered. 'She was alive when the monster did it. But we must take a modicum of comfort in the fact she would have bled out very quickly, and I believe she would have lost consciousness before she really understood what was happening to her.'

'How can you be sure of that?' Comtois snapped.

Oppert pointed at the rope burns on Clementine's neck and arms. 'She wasn't tied up for a long time before death. I expect she was subdued.' He pointed at her head. 'There's quite a bump there, so I imagine she was knocked out and then strung up. She may have come around, she may not, but I don't believe much time passed before she was murdered.'

Hugo nodded. 'And when was that?'

'Not long,' Oppert replied. 'Sometime yesterday evening, between ten and fourteen hours ago.'

Comtois pointed at the photograph of the canvas painted in her blood. 'And what about that monstrosity?' he pondered.

The doctor omitted a weary breath. 'I'm afraid I have no wise words regarding that,' he answered. 'Other than it appears to be a rudimentary portrait of Clementine, painted using her own blood.'

'We are dealing with a very sick individual,' Hugo nodded. 'Is there anything we know about it yet?'

Oppert shook his head. 'The forensic department has it, but they're backed up. I don't expect we'll hear anything from them for some time. I've studied the photographs, and as nice as it would be for the murderer to leave his prints in Clementine's blood, I don't think he has. He appears to have used gloves.'

'That's what I thought,' Hugo agreed. He shook his head. 'The whole thing seems to make little sense. And it is certainly extreme,' he added.

Comtois snorted. 'The master of understatement!'

'The Captain is correct,' Oppert interjected. 'It is extreme.' He considered. 'Back in the old days in Paris, if I saw anything like this, I would imagine it meant one of two things.' He turned to Hugo. 'Do you agree?' he asked in an almost challenging manner.

Hugo nodded. He moved closer to the photograph. 'I would imagine the killer was either playing with us, wrapped up in his own psychosis, or more likely he is attempting to distract us.'

'Distract us?' Comtois questioned. 'What do you mean?'

'He wants us to look at the portrait because he knows it will attract our attention,' Hugo replied.

Dr. Oppert smiled. 'And stop us looking at something else.'

He moved across the row of photographs. 'Yet I am at a loss as to understand what the distraction could be obfuscating.'

Hugo moved next to him. 'I agree.'

The doctor sighed. 'Messieurs, I cannot put it off any longer. I must complete my examination of this dear lady.'

'Be gentle, Jacques,' Comtois replied, his voice cracking.

'What can you tell us, Dr. Oppert?' Hugo asked.

They had watched him in silence for almost an hour as he moved around the remains of Clementine Bonheur. The elderly doctor had moved quickly but with the consideration of a man who knew what he was doing and had done so before more times than he cared to remember.

Oppert removed his gloves. 'Not a great deal, I'm afraid,' he answered with desperate sadness. 'What I can tell you is the young lady had sexual intercourse in the hours preceding her death. There is evidence of spermicide, so I imagine a condom was used, and to answer your next question, there is nothing to indicate any sort of violence. I've taken samples and will have the lab look at them, but as you know, the actual cause of death is clear.'

He shrugged. 'We can only hope forensics finds something in her studio, but I'm afraid there's nothing I can tell you which I believe would help. She was in reasonably good health, her liver was a little fatty, but nothing serious. She ate three or four hours before her death, a meal of oysters, if I'm not very much mistaken.'

'Oysters?' Comtois interrupted sharply.

Hugo turned to him. 'Is that important?'

Comtois remained silent for a few moments. 'Guy Fallon, the fisherman, specialises in oysters.'

'And supplies them to most of the restaurants in Beaufort-Sur-Mer,' Oppert interjected. 'And I have eaten oysters myself with Clementine frequently, as I am sure have you.'

Comtois stared at him. 'And so has Guy.'

'Franc...' Oppert replied wearily.

'He is half her age,' he stated simply.

A wry smile appeared on Oppert's face. He spread his hands in front of him as if he was saying, *ah; I see what you mean*.

Hugo, however, did not. 'What is the relevance?' he asked.

'It has absolutely nothing to do with this or oysters,' Oppert replied. 'However, it was common knowledge Clementine had… certain *appetites*. And the younger the better, if you know what I'm saying.'

'Talk to the fisherman,' Comtois snapped.

Hugo frowned. 'Because he's young, and is a fisherman who specialises in oysters?' he asked doubtfully.

Comtois raised an eyebrow. 'You have something better to go on, Captain?'

Hugo stared at Clementine. While the connection was tenuous, it was somewhere to start. He moved towards the door. 'I'll catch up with you both later. Dr. Oppert, if you hear anything from forensics, will you call me and let me know?'

Oppert nodded. 'Bon chance, Captain Duchamp.'

trente

After searching for over half an hour, Hugo finally spotted Guy Fallon in a secluded part of the harbour, hidden from view by a large sign.

He was seated on the edge, his feet trailing over, moving in and out of the water, even though he was wearing shoes. Hugo made his way slowly towards him, clearing his throat as he did. Fallon spotted him approaching and Hugo immediately recognised the look on his face. It was fear, and it was also realisation. He had been waiting for Hugo, or someone like Hugo, to come and find him.

'May I join you?' Hugo asked.

Guy pointed next to him. Hugo sat down. He pulled out a packet of cigarettes, offering one to Guy. He shook his head. 'Disgusting habit.'

Hugo nodded. 'I can't say I disagree, but it hasn't stopped me yet. Do you mind if I do?'

Guy shook his head, studying Hugo as he lit his cigarette. 'You really enjoy that,' he said.

'I do, even though I shouldn't,' Hugo replied.

Guy exhaled. 'I suppose in your line of work, you take relief where you can find it.' He stared out towards the sea. 'I know it sounds weird, but I only ever feel happy when I'm in the water.'

'It's not weird at all,' Hugo replied. 'I grew up in Paris and then lived in London. I now live in a town I love very much, but every time I come to the sea I feel as if I'm missing something. When I bought my house in Montgenoux, I only really bought it because it came with a swimming pool. It's not the same as having this every day, but it matters to me. I spend as much time as I can in my swimming pool and it makes me very, very happy.'

They lapsed into silence. A conversation started and finished between two men who barely knew each other.

'I know why you're here,' Guy said finally.

'You do?'

He nodded. 'Clementine.'

The way in which the young fisherman spoke her name told Hugo all he needed to know. However, as usual, he did not know if he was dealing with a bereaved loved one or a potential suspect. 'I only met her this week, but I found I liked her very much,' Hugo said. 'She seemed to be a woman filled with joy and enjoyment of life. I've always found myself envious of such people, but not in a resentful way. I'm always happy for them.'

Guy smiled at him. 'Clementine would appreciate that, I'm sure.' He closed his eyes. 'Did she suffer?'

Hugo took his time to respond. 'Her death was not pleasant, but it is my understanding, it would have happened quickly. Dr. Oppert believes her suffering would have been brief.'

'You'd tell me that anyway,' Guy retorted. 'No matter what happened.'

'I would say it differently, peut être, but it is the truth,' Hugo answered.

Guy turned to him. 'How did you know about me?' he asked.

'I didn't. I don't,' Hugo responded. 'She had oysters for her last meal,' he offered as an answer.

'How the hell do you know that?' Guy snapped. His hand flew to his mouth. 'Oh, shit, that's how you know that.' He leaned over the side of the dock and retched, a mouthful of spittle falling into the water.

Hugo inhaled his cigarette, turning away from Guy, hoping to give him time to compose himself.

'She was a great broad,' Guy said finally. He wiped his mouth with the back of his hand. He smiled. 'You know? Tough, but yet she was soft and feminine. Sexy. A voice that made her sound like a hundred different sailors or fishermen who came through town. And then in the next breath, she was gentle, like a virgin on her wedding night.'

He sighed. 'Those hands that were sore and wrinkled from the sun and grabbing drinks, and smoking cigarettes, and jumping in the sea, and yet they were able to produce the most insanely beautiful things on a piece of canvas.'

Hugo nodded. 'You liked her.' His mouth twisted sadly. 'You liked her a lot.'

He shook his head angrily. 'Non, I loved her,' he shot back. 'But she didn't love me, at least, not in the way we all understand love. She loved everybody at the same time, and for the same reason. She loved a stranger in the same way she loved a lover. That was just her. That was just her way.' He closed his eyes. 'Dieu. I loved her. I never said it. She would have hated for me to say it, but I hope to hell she knew it.'

Hugo sucked on his cigarette. 'She knew it,' he replied with conviction. 'You know she did.' He turned to face Guy. 'And that is why you need to tell me everything, and I mean *everything*, you might know. If you cared about Clementine as much as you say you did, that's all you can do for her now. Her death was horrible and I want to make sure whoever is responsible pays for it.'

'How do you know it wasn't me?' Guy retorted.

Hugo shrugged. 'I don't. But I'm always hopeful the guilty show themselves in one way or another. Either way, it doesn't change what I'm asking you. Tell me what you know, and I'll do what I can to make sense of it.'

Guy snatched the cigarette from Hugo and took a drag. 'What do you want to know?'

'Tell me about yesterday.'

Guy exhaled, his jaw flexed involuntarily. 'You have to understand - Clementine was a free spirit.'

Hugo flashed a sad smile. 'I got that impression,' he replied. He took a moment. 'I only met her briefly, but I tend to know very quickly whether I like someone, and I have to say, I really liked

le bateau au fond de l'océan

her.'

Guy gulped, then his mouth pulled into a grin. 'It wasn't just you. She had that effect on <u>everyone</u> she met. That's why the tourists all flocked to her. It was a ridiculous waste of her talents, but I don't think she minded too much. It wasn't about money for her. It was about enjoying every day. She once told me she had lived her life as if it was her last day on earth. She got up, thanked whoever for the night before,' he pointed above him, 'and whoever else for giving her another day. A lot of people said she could make a fortune if she took her painting seriously, but she always said that would involve,' he smiled, 'taking her painting seriously.'

He shook his head. 'That's not to say she didn't. She was just in the moment. If she painted a honeymooning couple sitting on the beach, she approached it the same way she would if she was painting something that was going to be hung in a museum or an art gallery. It was all the same to her. She spent her day painting and her nights spending the few euros she made that day. It wasn't a fantastic life, some people might think, but it suited her and I never saw her unhappy.'

'Some people only need to live simply, and that's more than enough,' Hugo agreed.

'She loved her life, I think,' Guy replied.

'And what about your relationship?' Hugo asked.

'Don't read too much into that,' Guy answered. 'I'm not trying to diminish it, but the truth isn't really like that. Clementine would certainly never want or look for a relationship. As for the two of us, yeah,' he shrugged. 'We hooked up occasionally, usually when one of us, or both of us, was in the mood, and when there was no-one else around.'

'But you cared for her?'

'Sure,' Guy replied. 'I thought she was fantastic. She was funny, and when she took off the damn floral kaftan she had a killer body.' He coughed. 'Désolé, I sound like a prick, don't I?

Mind you,' he added with a wry smile, 'she would have appreciated the compliment.'

Hugo felt the sadness of a life lost in such a pointless and despicable way beginning to consume him. 'So tell me about the last time you saw her.'

Guy gulped. 'I had some oysters left over. If I don't sell all I catch, I have to get rid of it. As it happens, Clementine was partial to oysters, so I stopped by her studio.' He gulped. 'She opened the door, looked at my basket and said, *what do I have to do for them?* I laughed and replied, *everything*. She stepped back and ushered me in. *Good job I'm good at doing everything then, isn't it?* She laughed and pulled off her kaftan.'

'And then?'

'And then we had sex,' Guy whispered. 'And then the oysters, or rather, a bit of both,' he added demurely.

Hugo nodded. 'What happened next?'

Guy shrugged. 'We said our goodbyes, and off I went.'

'And there was nothing unusual?'

Guy considered. 'Not really. Normally we'd lie together for a while, but she seemed keen for me to go. She said something about having something to do, or somewhere to go, or,' he shook his head again, 'someone to see.' He shook his head irritably. 'I hate to say it, but I can't fucking remember, exactly.'

'Try,' Hugo pressed. 'It could be important.'

Guy closed his eyes and lowered his head. After a minute, he raised it. 'I can't remember. And I really can't be sure.'

'That's okay,' Hugo replied reassuringly. 'How did she seem?'

He smiled. 'Like a woman who'd just had sex and oysters, two of her favourite things.'

'Then she didn't seem worried or concerned about anything?' Hugo pressed.

Guy shook his head. 'Non, I don't think so. We talked a little about Gregoire and how sad it was. She said something about how it was a reminder to always live each day like it was your last, just as she'd always done.' He turned slowly to Hugo. 'I think the last thing she said as I went out the door was - *if this is my last day, at least I went out with a bang and a stomach full of man and oysters, it doesn't get better than that.*' His chest rose and fell rapidly, as if he was fighting back tears. 'I'm a suspect, aren't I?'

'You were the last person we know who saw her alive,' Hugo replied.

'Non, I wasn't,' Guy snapped. 'Because she was very much alive when I left her.'

'That's not what I meant,' Hugo reasoned. 'Rather, you have answered a few questions I had.'

'Such as?'

'Well, according to your testimony, she was alive and well when you left her,' Hugo replied. 'And she didn't seem worried or concerned about anything, which suggests her murder was not necessarily connected to something she may have seen or heard concerning the murder of Gregoire Comtois.'

Guy frowned. 'And how does that help, exactly?'

'I'm not sure,' Hugo answered honestly. 'Mais, it just might. Is there anything else you can think of? Anything, no matter how small or inconsequential you might think is.'

Guy considered again. 'Not really. The only other thing was when I first arrived at the studio, I could hear her talking, so I assumed Clem was with someone. I was about to leave when I heard her say something like, *d'accord, I'll see you later.* Then I knew she was on the phone, so I realised it was safe to knock.'

Hugo nodded. 'And is there anything else you can recall about the conversation?'

Guy shook his head. 'Non, désolé, that's all I heard, just the tail end of it.'

'And what about her tone? Did she sound happy, worried, anything out of the ordinary?'

Guy rubbed his chin. 'I don't think so. I suppose if I had to guess, I'd say she sounded irritated, but I honestly couldn't be sure. Believe me, I wish I could.'

Hugo smiled at him. 'You've been very helpful, merci.' He paused. 'I'm afraid I will have to ask you to go to the police station. You need to give DNA and blood samples and your fingerprints.'

'Then you believe I'm involved?'

Hugo shook his head. 'At this point, I don't think anything. The fact is, you were there, and you had sex with the deceased. At the very least, we need to rule you out. Providing your sample will allow us to do that. Because above all else, I'm sure you want us to be able to tell who else was in Clementine's studio because that person was her murderer. I realise it may be problematic for you, but it's a small price to pay for Mademoiselle Bonheur, non?'

Guy jumped to his feet. 'It's a very small price for that lovely lady. I have nothing to hide, and besides, I really, *really* want you to catch the bastard who did this to her. But I beg you, let me at him first.'

Hugo grimaced. 'Monsieur Fallon, please understand this. I realise feelings are running very high in this town, but I will not, I CANNOT tolerate vigilantism, and if Clementine Bonheur is half the woman I think she was, or half the woman you all tell me she was, then she would not want it either, no matter what happened to her. Do I make myself clear?'

'I just want to feel better,' Guy whispered.

Hugo reached over and touched his arm. 'You will. It won't be for a long time, but you will feel better, but attacking her murderer will not make it happen anytime sooner. Be patient, but more importantly, help me, and help her. Isn't that what she would have wanted?'

Guy smiled. 'Damn, she was great.'

trente-et-un

Hugo stepped onto the veranda and smiled, happy to see Baptiste was waiting for him. His smile extended upon seeing the ice-cold beer and an unopened packet of cigarettes next to them.

'I figured you'd need them,' Baptiste stated.

Hugo flopped into a chair, pulling the glass to his lips. They smacked together contentedly. 'You have no idea,' he said, reaching for the cigarettes and extracting one. He took his time to savour it.

'I'm sorry for dragging you into this complete mess,' Baptiste sighed.

Hugo's lips twisted into a wry smile. 'I do seem to walk into trouble wherever I go, don't I?' He paused. 'Mais, none of this is your fault. I respect you and the promise you made to Vincent.'

Baptiste interjected. 'A pointless promise.'

Hugo shrugged. 'It wasn't pointless to Vincent, and that's all that counts.'

'We've solved nothing, and probably never will,' Baptiste whined. 'I should have listened to you all and stopped acting like a whining, spoilt brat.' He gawped at Hugo. 'I am sorry for dragging you into it though, but I love you immensely for being by my side.'

Hugo reached across and touched his arm. 'You never need to apologise to me. And Ben and I will always be by your side, even when you don't want us to be.' He leaned back in the chair. 'I'm still not convinced Arthur Roche's death was anything but suicide, however, that's not to say I've ruled out what has happened since isn't somehow connected.'

Baptiste frowned. 'How?'

'That's the question I wish I had the answers to,' Hugo responded. 'Mais, there's been a rape and two murders since we arrived, and we have to assume there is a link. Vincent Roche was convinced something was wrong in Beaufort-Sur-Mer. What if he was right? And what if our coming here forced someone to take horrible, drastic action?'

'Then it is our fault!' Baptiste gasped. 'If we'd stayed in Montgenoux, then maybe…'

Hugo touched his arm again. 'Stop right there, Baptiste. We aren't responsible for the actions of others, we can't be.' He stubbed out his cigarette and immediately lit another. 'However, I have to face reality. I can't stay here indefinitely. I have my own department to look after, and the investigation should be handed over to Captain Comtois and the nearest Police Nationale. I fear this will not be solved soon.'

Baptiste nodded. 'You're right, I suppose. When do you want to leave?'

'I'd planned to be here for the week anyway,' Hugo answered. 'It's Friday now. We'll see what we can do, but we have to think about leaving by Sunday. I should be back at work by Monday. There is a…'

Before he could finish, a loud knock at the door interrupted him. Hugo jumped to his feet and hurried into his hotel room. He pulled open the door. His eyes widened in surprise.

'Hey, Hugo. How are you doing?'

Hugo watched in disbelief as Etienne Martine moved into the room, pulling Hugo into a warm embrace. Hugo worked with Etienne in Montgenoux and he considered him to be one of the foremost forensic specialists in the whole of France.

'Salut, Baptiste,' Etienne said cheerfully as he moved onto the veranda, flopping happily into a chair.

Hugo followed him out. 'What are doing here?' he asked.

As usual, Etienne was dressed in his "uniform," of a very colourful Hawaiian shirt, board shorts, and flip-flops. The same clothes he wore, no matter the weather. 'Things were pretty slow in Montgenoux,' Etienne replied. 'And I've been monitoring you down here, and it looked like you had your hands full, so I thought I'd come to see what I could do to help.' He shrugged. 'I have tons of holiday days to use and nowhere to go, so I figured a few days by the seaside would suit me just fine.'

Hugo smiled. He knew Etienne was going through a tough time with a relationship, but he was pleased to see him. He had nothing against the forensic teams in other jurisdictions, but it had always seemed to him that Etienne had a unique ability of discovering facts no one else could. And after what had transpired in Beaufort-Sur-Mer, Hugo knew he needed all the help he could get. He was immensely grateful for the support.

Etienne clapped his hands together. 'Tell me what I can do, and we'll get started.' He pulled a laptop out of his backpack.

'The truth is, I don't honestly know,' Hugo retorted.

Etienne laughed. 'Great! My favourite kind of investigation,' he replied cheerfully.

Hugo grimaced. 'I shouldn't be investigating this as it is. They're not entirely happy to have me here, so I can only imagine how they'll feel about me bringing in my own forensic expert.'

Etienne winked. 'When has that ever stopped us before?' he posed. 'And besides, as you well know, I'm the soul of discretion. I can investigate quite freely with no one knowing I am.'

Hugo suppressed a smile. 'I am aware of that, but it doesn't mean we should.' He sighed and lit another cigarette, flopping back into the seat, clearly resigned. 'D'accord, let's get started.'

'Whoever is responsible for this is a sick son-of-a-bitch,' Etienne said as he studied the crime scene photographs. He turned to Hugo. 'Do you believe the same person is responsible for the murders of Gregoire Comtois and Clementine Bonheur?'

Hugo did not answer immediately. He had been thinking about it a lot and had found it difficult to come to an opinion one way or another. 'I was just explaining to Baptiste, I believe there has to be a connection between the attack on Brigitte St. Pierre, the murder of Gregoire Comtois and the subsequent murder of Clementine Bonheur.'

Etienne tapped his chin. 'Then the first question is - do you think Brigitte St. Pierre capable of murder?'

'Absolutely not,' Baptiste interrupted.

'Everyone is capable of murder,' Hugo reasoned. 'Especially when provoked or deeply hurt. We can't rule Brigitte out, although there is little doubt someone sexually attacked her, and most likely drugged without her permission.'

'And that gives her one hell of a motive,' Etienne added.

Hugo nodded. 'I agree. Mais, I keep coming back to the question - why tell us about the rape? I realise she could have done it to preempt any witness coming forward, but then why not wait until such a witness came forward to implicate her? The result would be the same, and any doctor or avocat would reason she was too traumatised to come forward initially.' He shook his head. 'Non. I believe there's something about it we're just not seeing.'

'Then how about someone came across Gregoire raping Brigitte when she was unconscious?' Etienne continued. 'And they reacted by murdering him?' His eyes scanned the laptop screen. 'According to the autopsy, death was blunt-force trauma.' He scratched his head. 'Then why not leave him in the beach hut, if that's where it happened? Why go to all the trouble of creating such an elaborate show?'

'I have no answer for that,' Hugo replied. 'Other than peut être, it was nothing but a smokescreen to distract from what really happened. The murderer could have counted on us believing it just to be another suicide. I don't like to say it, but it's quite possible that if I hadn't been here, Captain Comtois could have accepted his son's death as another suicide, particularly bearing in mind his secret.'

'Secret?' Etienne questioned.

Hugo lowered his voice. 'According to Dax Chastain,

Gregoire was not only gay, but he was also a virgin and only pretended to go with girls because he was afraid of his father.'

'And you believe him?' Baptiste questioned. 'Dax could have his own reasons for lying.'

Hugo slouched his shoulders. 'It's possible, though it ties in with something Brigitte said to me.' He turned to Etienne. 'Just for the sake of clarity, we could try to find the young Swedish man Gregoire was supposed to be in a relationship with. It may prove nothing, but it could clarify the situation.'

'Mais, we still come back to the elaborate way the body was posed,' Etienne continued. 'How would the murderer have moved the body down to the boat?'

Hugo tapped his chin. 'Also, according to Dax, most people in town know how to dive, and a lot of them have their own equipment, or know someone who does. He also said that for the most part, he doesn't even lock his storage box on the beach because he's never had to.'

'Dax has a lot to say for himself,' Baptiste mumbled.

'I agree,' Hugo replied. 'It doesn't mean he's lying, though. However, I agree with Etienne. When I went scuba diving, it half scared me to death, and that was in broad daylight attached to several others, including two well-trained experts. I can't imagine any scenario where I would go in the water alone, especially in the dark, while dragging a dead body with me and posing it on the boat. Unless…'

'You were an expert,' Baptiste concluded.

'Exactement, or I had help,' Hugo answered with a nod. 'Mais, again it brings us back to the point the entire town pretty much could pull it off. I noticed Captain Comtois himself was an experienced diver. The only person I know for certain isn't a good swimmer is Avril Roche, although,' he paused, 'I only have her word for that.' He lapsed into a glum silence.

Etienne pointed at the laptop. 'And then how does

Clementine Bonheur fit into it all?'

'Isn't it obvious? She saw something,' Baptiste reasoned.

Hugo contemplated. 'You're right, of course. It would certainly make sense,' Hugo conceded. He shook his head. 'Still, the way she was murdered confuses me. The mutilation? The painting of a portrait in her blood? It all seems extreme. Too extreme, and so very different to everything else.'

Etienne snorted. 'That's an understatement! Mais, you're right. If we are looking at the same murderer and he got rid of Clementine because of something she may have seen or heard, then I don't get why they would go about it in such an extreme way. Why not just make it look like a suicide?'

'Unless there is no connection,' Hugo reasoned. 'And we're trying to force one. It may not make any sense to us, because, well, it makes no sense.'

'Is her studio still sealed off?' Etienne asked.

'Oui,' Hugo replied. 'There's a backlog at the forensic lab, so everything is still in situ. Do you want to take a look?'

Etienne jumped to his feet. 'I thought you'd never ask. Let's go.'

trente-deux

Stepping into Clementine Bonheur's studio was no easier the second time around, Hugo concluded, even though she was no longer physically there. Etienne moved out of the daylight into the darkened room. He stopped dead in his tracks when he saw the painting.

'It looks so much worse in real life,' he whispered.

Hugo shook his head. 'It doesn't get any easier,' he conceded. He pursed his lips. 'We've seen a lot, Etienne, haven't we? Mais, this seems particularly deranged, non?'

Etienne shrugged. 'Deranged, oui. Unusual? Non.'

'That makes me sad,' Hugo replied.

Etienne took a step further towards the painting. 'Admittedly, this is unusual. What have forensics told you so far?'

'There are literally dozens of prints and samples throughout the studio,' Hugo replied. 'It'll take a few days, probably much longer, to work through it all. They confirmed it was her blood used in the painting, but there were no fingerprints on the canvas, other than Clementine's, which suggests the murderer was wearing gloves or cleaned up after himself.'

Etienne nodded. 'I'll put in a call to the lab, see if I can't help them speed things up.'

'This wasn't a quick process,' Hugo added. 'The murder, the painting of the portrait. It would have all taken time.'

'I'm not so sure,' Etienne replied. 'The painting's hardly a work of art.' He shrugged. 'The whole thing could have taken only ten minutes if our killer wasn't hesitant.' He glanced around the studio. 'It's a mess, but nothing seems odd, or out of place, does it?'

Hugo followed his gaze. 'You're probably right, but then again, would we even know what to look for, or what might be out of place?'

Etienne moved slowly and carefully around the room, turning his head as if assessing everything he was seeing. 'There was no forced entry?'

'Non,' Hugo replied. 'Mind you, the door was unlocked when I arrived, which probably suggests she didn't always lock it.'

'Many people don't,' Etienne reasoned.

'We may have one thing in our favour,' Hugo continued. 'No one has found her cell phone yet. And according to Guy Fallon, who was here with her the night she was murdered, when he arrived she was on the phone talking with someone. It might mean nothing, but it's pretty much all we have.'

'Have you tried her number?'

'Forensics have, and it's been switched off the entire time,' Hugo replied.

'Or it's been destroyed,' Etienne said, pointing out of the studio window. The sea was a stones throw away from the studio. 'A quick and easy way to dispose of the phone would be to throw it out of the doorway straight into the water. It's doubtful it would ever be found. I'll get on to her service provider and see if we can track her last calls.'

'If their number is even listed,' Hugo reasoned.

Etienne shrugged. 'Still, worth a try when we have so little else to go on.' He pointed to a portrait on the main wall. It was much larger than all the others in the room. 'Who is this?'

Hugo narrowed his eyes and flicked on his glasses. 'I don't know. I don't believe I've seen him before.'

'It stands out more than the others.'

Hugo nodded. 'Oui. She painted one of Vincent Roche in a similar size, and...' He stopped, leaning forward to read what was written in the bottom left corner of the painting. *Arthur*. 'Ah,' he sighed. 'Arthur Roche.'

Hugo studied the painting. Like most of the men and women in Beaufort-Sur-Mer, Arthur Roche had a well-lined face with sun-kissed skin and hair. His eyes sparkled blue and his once blond hair was turning white and pushed smoothly over a wide forehead. 'He looked like a kind man,' he said.

Etienne did not comment, instead moving slowly across the room, casting his gaze from left to right in a way Hugo was used to. He was studying, contemplating, and taking his time to ensure he missed nothing. Etienne moved his hand across a crowded mantelpiece, touching nothing. He tilted his head. 'Do you see this?' he asked Hugo.

Hugo tried to see what he was looking at. 'What is it?' he asked.

'The portrait of Arthur Roche is uneven,' Etienne replied. He pointed to the neat row of smaller paintings. 'See all the other paintings? They're all flush against the wall, whereas this one...' He placed his gloved hands carefully around the portrait and pulled it from the wall. They both looked behind it.

Hugo's eyes widened. 'It's an envelope,' he gasped.

Etienne pulled it from the portrait and handed it to Hugo. Hugo took it from him and took a deep breath. He placed his finger under the seal and carefully opened it.

Une lettre from Arthur Roche

Bonjour.

I was born in Beaufort-Sur-Mer and it is where I will die. It is in my bones. I know it. The smell of the sea, the sand, the fish, the smoke of the night is always on my skin like cologne. And today, it is where I will die. I am leaving this letter behind for my son, and I have asked my oldest friend Clementine to give it to him when he returns from college. I know my death will devastate him, and for that, I am more sorry than I can say. But my death consumes my every waking thought, and if I am lucky enough to sleep, it follows me there too.

I know the disaster of my life is my own fault. I blame my downfall on myself. But I blame those who took advantage of me more. Jasper Connor swindled me out of my life's work, but he did not do it alone. Avril was a willing participant. Her blame is less because she had a lot to put up with from me over the years, but I did not deserve for her to side with a monster like Jasper Connor, and nor did our son. She robbed him of his legacy all for a few pieces of silver.

For the last few months, I have been gathering evidence against Connor and his shady comings and goings. It is not just Beaufort-Sur-Mer that he has corrupted - his reputation precedes him, and he has left a trail of devastation wherever he goes. But he has gone too far this time. He may have destroyed my life, but I won't let him destroy others. That is why I have been gathering evidence, so that in my absence, you, Vincent, can take him down and reclaim what is rightly yours. What you do with this information, and your mother's involvement in it, is down to you. I may have never told you how much I loved you, nor how proud I am of you, but I am now. You are everything I never was and never could be. I'm sorry for leaving you this way, but I hope you understand that my time is done. I love you.

All you need to bring down Jasper Connor and the people he has corrupted is waiting for you, son. I've hidden it in a place only you and I would know. A place where even the sting of a jellyfish couldn't reach.

Au revoir, Vincent. Grow strong.
Papa.

trente-trois

Etienne raised an eyebrow. 'Well, what did you make of that?'

Hugo shrugged. 'Well, I doubt very much it would have been the answer Vincent Roche was looking for. Mais, it is an answer of sorts.' He frowned. 'Mind you, we don't know for certain Arthur Roche actually wrote this letter.'

'You could ask someone who knew him to verify the handwriting,' Etienne suggested, 'such as his wife.'

Hugo met his gaze. 'I couldn't do that. If the letter is real, it's the writings of a man who was very disturbed. A man who was about to kill himself. However, he was quite clear that he believed his ex-wife was involved in some sort of corruption with Jasper Connor. Showing her this letter could tip off Connor into destroying evidence.'

'Vincent obviously never saw the letter,' Etienne added.

'Oui,' Hugo replied. 'Clementine was instructed to only show him upon his return to Beaufort-Sur-Mer. Something he never did,' he added sadly.

Etienne frowned. 'Why didn't he leave it with an avocat?'

'He may have trusted no one,' Hugo reasoned. 'His letter seems to suggest there was corruption in this town. His only choice may have been to trust Clementine. And after Vincent died, perhaps she didn't know what to do with it. She probably didn't know who to trust.'

He shrugged. 'And as far as I can tell, Clementine herself actively encouraged Avril to leave Arthur for Jasper Connor. I believe she felt guilty about that.' He looked again at the letter. 'With both Arthur and Vincent gone, it's not unreasonable to assume she didn't want to destroy Avril's life any more than it already was. And that letter could cause even more problems for Avril, especially if it implicated Jasper Connor in crimes. It's clear that Arthur Roche believed he had been swindled out of everything - his hotel, his money, his marriage… Leaving the papers with a lawyer, or the police, may not have been an option for him, because he didn't know who he could trust, and who had not been compromised by Jasper Connor.'

'Then what can we do about it?' Etienne asked. 'As you said, we have the same dilemma as Clementine Bonheur did. And now they're all dead. The letter is cryptic, and presumably whatever Arthur Roche was getting at was an obvious message to his son, who can't tell us where to look.'

'Peut être,' Hugo replied distantly.

'What is it, Hugo?'

'Nothing, really,' Hugo replied. 'I mean, you're right. All we can do is hand the letter over to the authorities and they can include it in the investigation. It's all we can do, really.'

Etienne gave him a doubtful look. 'There's not a lot to go on, so it'll most likely end up in an evidence locker.' He paused and glanced around the studio. 'Do you think this has something to do with Clementine Bonheur's murder?'

Hugo pursed his lips. 'We certainly can't rule it out. Arthur Roche hid something. Something it appears could be very damaging to Jasper Connor. Someone may have known about it and suspected Clementine had it.'

Etienne pointed at the painting. 'It wasn't exactly well hidden, though. It only took us a few seconds to find it. If someone was looking for it, they didn't try very hard.'

Hugo tapped his chin. 'You're right, it doesn't appear Clementine's murderer was searching for anything specific.'

'And,' Etienne added, 'the letter could just be the ramblings of a very troubled man.'

'Anything is possible,' Hugo conceded. 'But, we can't discount the fact that if someone suspected Clementine was hiding something, and she refused to say what it was, it could have resulted in her murder. And they may not have searched properly because they were disturbed.' He stopped, considering something. 'You're right, though. I have to do something with the letter,' he added. 'I don't know what good it will do, but I hate the thought of it just ending up ignored.'

Etienne nodded. 'If Jasper Connor swindled Arthur out of his hotel and it was illegal, then maybe we can get some sort of justice for Arthur, anyway?'

Hugo stared glumly at the letter. 'It doesn't give us a lot to go on.'

Etienne nodded. 'And with Vincent dead, how are we going to understand what it means?' he asked. 'What the hell does a jellyfish have to do with it?'

Hugo continued staring at the letter. 'Obviously a coded message between father and son.'

'Exactly,' Etienne sighed. 'Only the son's dead, and that's where we are. At a dead-end.'

Hugo looked to the door. A thought occurred to him. 'There may be someone we can ask.'

trente-quatre

Hugo and Etienne stood together in silence on the dock, staring out at the crystal blue sea. He was once again reminded of his swimming pool behind the Swiss-style cottage he shared in Montgenoux with Ben and Baptiste, and he felt the pang of sadness that had been troubling him.

He had spent most of his life alone because he thought he had wanted to, but since his arrival in Montgenoux and the subsequent change in his life, he had come to realise that one of the reasons he had preferred to be alone was because he was sure he would always lose whatever he found. It was not lost on him that since he had met Ben they had both found themselves in mortal danger on more than one occasion. No matter how much he felt as if he was moving forward, he had never been able to shake the feeling danger was but a step behind him, breathing down his neck.

'For such a pretty town, it sure feels like there's a rotten undercurrent,' Etienne broke the silence.

Hugo glanced around. The beauty of Beaufort-Sur-Mer struck him once again. He narrowed his eyes at Etienne. 'Need I remind you what has happened in our little slice of heaven in the last few years?'

Etienne tipped his head. 'You may have a point. We have had our fair share of serial killers, it seems.'

Hugo leaned over the railings. 'The world has changed. I suppose it's always been a dangerous place, but I don't know, it seems to have gathered speed. People aren't the same. It seems to me that a lot of people hide behind computer screens and they say and do things to other people they would never do to their faces, and somehow or other that behaviour had started to spread, extending beyond the keyboard.'

'Thank Dieu you aren't on Twitter,' Etienne laughed. 'You're right. But there are people like you, and as long as that's the case, we still stand a fighting chance.'

'And people like you,' Hugo added.

Etienne smiled. 'I like to call them gatekeepers. Good people to keep balance and check on an abysmal world.'

Hugo snorted. 'We're a cheery pair today, aren't we?' He pointed towards a fast-approaching boat. 'Ah, here he is now.'

Dax Chastain peeled off his wetsuit, frowning at Hugo. 'What do you mean?'

Hugo repeated his question. He did not want to give away all the details because he thought it prudent the existence of a letter not be made public just yet. 'I know it's an odd question,' he began, 'but you're one of the few people who knew Vincent well. All I'm wondering is if you can think of a place where he might have spent time with his father, maybe just the two of them.'

Dax threw a t-shirt over his head. 'Arthur Roche wasn't really the touchy/feely sort of father. Once Vincent could drink, they had that in common, I suppose,' he added with a sad smile. 'Before that, there was only really the boat.'

'The boat?' Hugo questioned.

Dax nodded. 'Yeah. When we were kids, Arthur used to take us all out on the boat. He was one of those cool Papas, throwing caution to the wind. We used to have a hell of a good time out on the sea, diving in, swimming with dolphins, that sort of thing.' He gulped. 'Damn, I never really thought of it, but I suppose I got my love of the water from Arthur. It certainly wasn't from my parents. We were all devastated when it sunk. Mind you, it just started another adventure. Scuba diving. That all came from Arthur and his boat. He encouraged me. I wouldn't be doing what I'm doing if it wasn't for him.'

Hugo considered. 'And Vincent dived with his father?'

'All the time,' Dax replied. 'Unless his father was drunk, even then…'

'What about a jellyfish?' Etienne interjected.

Dax appeared confused. 'A jellyfish?'

Hugo nodded. 'Did anything happen with a jellyfish?'

'I don't think so,' Dax answered. 'As I said, we played with the dolphins and seals, saw a few whales, even a shark once or twice, mais I don't remember anyone being stung by a jellyfish…' he trailed off. 'Oh, wait. Are you talking about Pepe?'

'Pepe?' Hugo asked, his voice rising.

'Yeah, Pepe,' Dax answered with a smile of happy reminiscence. 'I'd forgotten all about him. Dieu, we must have been eight or nine when we painted that.' He turned to Hugo. 'One summer, Arthur bought a big old metal box for storing the fish we caught. It was rusty and dirty and had graffiti all over it, so Vincent asked if we would paint it.'

'So, you painted a jellyfish on it?' Hugo asked keenly.

'Yeah, I'd forgotten all about it,' Dax answered. 'It wasn't a painting like one Clementine would do, but we were pretty proud of it. For kids, it wasn't half bad, or so we thought.' He lowered his head, wiping his eyes with the back of his hand. 'Damn, would you look at me, getting emotional over a stupid painting we did years ago.'

'Je suis désolé for bringing up all these old feelings,' Hugo consoled. 'Tell me, what happened to Pepe?'

Dax pointed to towards the sea. 'He went down with the boat. I guess there wasn't a lot of point in dragging it up. It was fixed to the stern, you see.'

Hugo followed his finger, his face growing pale, the realisation dawning on him of what they may have to do.

Etienne chuckled. 'I guess that means you get to go scuba diving again.'

Hugo raised his eyebrows. 'Maybe, but I couldn't do it without my trusty forensic expert to make sure everything is above board. Make sure all the evidence is extracted correctly, that sort of thing.' He gave Etienne a once over, pointing at his shorts and bare feet. 'Besides, you're already pretty much dressed for it.'

'You don't play fair, Duchamp,' Etienne bristled, his eyes twinkling. 'I've never been scuba diving before.'

'Nor had I,' Hugo retorted. 'And if I can manage it, so can you.' He turned to Dax. 'Could you take us down to the boat again?'

'Sure,' he replied. 'Anything I can do to help.'

Hugo tipped his head towards Etienne. 'I have to make a few phone calls. Maybe in the meantime you could give our amateur here a crash course?'

'You don't play fair,' Etienne repeated, gulping for air.

trente-cinq

As they descended into the water, Hugo realised it sadly did not get any easier the second time around. He could feel how tightly the rope was being gripped by Etienne, and he was especially relieved that Baptiste had joined them. The young man had taken to diving well, and Hugo felt reassured having him at the end of the rope behind them, his eyes trained firmly on the amateur older men in front.

Hugo was unsure what they were heading into, and whether they would discover anything of importance in the wreckage of Arthur Roche's boat. All he knew was they had to at least try to rule it out. While back at the hotel, Hugo had taken the time to speak to Dr. Oppert and the forensic team to see if there was any update. He had not been happy with the response. It appeared to him there was very little progress being made. Despite the numerous fingerprints in Clementine Bonheur's studio, none of them were in the police database. Similarly, the other investigations had stalled.

There was no lead on Gregoire Comtois' murder, nor the rape of Brigitte St. Pierre. It appeared to Hugo they were at a complete dead end. He knew he had to return to Montgenoux and his own duties, but he could not shake the fact that by doing so, there would be very little progress made with the investigations he left behind.

Hugo narrowed his eyes, moving his body gently against the flow of the water. He watched in marvel at the number of different fish swimming near them, curiosity evident. He resisted the urge to reach out and touch them.

The sunken boat was coming into view and he wondered again what secrets it held. If they managed to find a lockbox with a jellyfish painted on it, would they even find anything in it? And if so, would it be something that would alter the direction of the investigation and perhaps finally fill in some of the many blanks? He desperately hoped so, because as much as he wanted to return home, he also wanted some kind of justice for those who so desperately needed it.

Ahead of him, Dax Chastain gestured for them to slow down. They all began treading water as Dax secured the guideline to the boat, as he had the last time. He pulled the rope around the side of the boat, attaching it to the guide rail. Hugo exhaled into his mouthpiece, feeling a little more relaxed that they were now tethered to the boat.

Dax gestured again, and the four of them swam slowly around the boat. Hugo took a moment to study it. He had felt unable the first time because he was experiencing mild terror. The boat was pretty, and he could see why tourists admired it. The skull and crossbones were effective enough, but in the light of what had happened, it all just felt desperately sad to him.

Dax waved his arm, pointing to the stern of the boat. Hugo swam closer until Pepe the jellyfish came into view. He gulped. The painting was rudimentary, but he could see the love and care of the work of two young boys. It filled him with a sadness that caught the back of his throat, and he could feel his chest tightening into a sob.

Dax swam ahead. He pulled a crowbar from his accessory belt and levered against the edge of the box, and with a quick flick, snapped the box open. Hugo, Etienne and Baptiste moved around him. Hugo narrowed his eyes. He could make out several tools all secured to the box with rope. They did not seem out of place. His eyes flicked around the rest of the box. It appeared there was a smaller lockbox in the far corner.

Hugo nodded at Dax, gesturing towards the smaller box. Dax nodded, reached down and unknotted the rope holding the box in place. He swam back to Hugo and handed the box to him. Hugo stared at it. It felt light and heavy at the same time. He could only hope that whatever secrets it held, the contents would help make sense of what had happened in Beaufort-Sur-Mer.

trente-six

Hugo stared at the lockbox. He was almost afraid to open it, but he was not sure why. He supposed he was worried whatever it contained would further complicate an investigation he was already having trouble getting a grip on. His hand hovered over it, his fingers flexing as if he was afraid to touch the box in case it burned him.

'I don't think it's an unexploded bomb, Hugo,' Etienne stated reassuringly. There was no malice in his tone, simply it appeared as if he understood what was causing Hugo's reticence.

Hugo grimaced. 'Bombs can come in many forms,' he replied. He narrowed his eyes. A large padlock was all which stood between them and the contents. 'How are we going to open it?' he asked.

Etienne dragged his bag towards him and rummaged inside it, moments later retrieving a bolt cutter.

Hugo laughed. 'It will never cease to amaze me what you carry around with you.'

Etienne shrugged. 'In our line of business, you can never be *too* prepared.' With a quick slice of the bolt cutters, the lock fell to the ground.

Hugo took a deep breath and pushed back the lid. The box contained one large zipped plastic bag. He lifted it, shook off droplets of water and opened it, dropping the contents onto the veranda table.

'What do we have here?' he mumbled to himself as he sorted through the contents, spreading them across the table. 'A stack of what appear to be bank statements. A bundle of newspaper clippings. A CD, and a dozen or so photographs,' he spoke, his fingers tracing across them.

He lifted the bank statements and flicked on his glasses. 'These appear to be statements for a joint savings and also a current

le bateau au fond de l'océan

account in the names of Arthur and Avril Roche.' He quickly scanned the contents. 'They are for the last three years, ending about eight months ago, around the time of Arthur Roche's death.' He handed them to Etienne. 'I've never been good with figures, so I guess this is one for you to see if you can spot anything important.'

Etienne nodded. 'I'll scan them into my laptop in a moment and see what I can find.' He paused. 'In the meantime, what do we have here?' He picked up the newspaper clippings, his eyes moving quickly across them, his lips twitching as he processed what he was seeing. 'They all seem to concern Jasper Connor and his various business investments in France.' He held up one of them. 'Par example, this one is a report of an alleged investment swindle Connor was involved with in Switzerland,' he lifted another, 'and this one suggests he was investigated for being involved in the illegal importation of drugs from Spain in Marseille.'

He placed the clippings back onto the table. 'I'm going to need to spend a little time on this, and see if I can figure out what is real and what is just speculation, but more importantly if any of it can help us.'

'Why would Arthur Roche have all this stuff?' Baptiste asked. 'He must have thought there was something in it which could bring down Jasper Connor.'

'Or it was the hope of a desperate man,' Etienne suggested.

Hugo picked up the photographs. 'What are these?' He spread the photographs across the table. 'Photographs of Jasper Connor and Avril Roche together - mostly of them kissing.'

Baptiste shrugged. 'Maybe he was intending on blackmailing Jasper Connor?'

'I don't see why,' Hugo responded. 'Avril had already divorced him. There really was no point. At best, he might convince a court that she acted inappropriately, but as far as I can tell, Jasper Connor never actually paid Avril to swindle Arthur, rather to help him get the hotel at a good price. The divorce had passed uncontested, and though I don't know all the details, I'm fairly sure we'll find there was no divorce settlement. As has been clear all along, Avril Roche may have acted inappropriately, but she didn't make a great deal of money from her ex-husband. Non, it must mean something else, but I can't for the life of me…' he stopped suddenly, his mouth falling open.

'What is it?' Etienne asked. He leaned forward keenly.

Hugo passed him two photographs.

Etienne studied them. 'A man handing another man an envelope.' He held the photograph close to his face. 'I can't say for certain, but it appears the envelope is stuffed with cash.' He passed it back to Hugo, pointing to a corner of the envelope. 'It's not the best quality, and without the negative, I'm not sure what I could do with it, but that looks to me as if it's the corner of a euro bill sticking out.' He stared at Hugo. 'Is it important?'

Hugo nodded. 'I believe so.' He pointed to the photograph. 'There on the left, that is Jasper Connor.' He paused, his hand shaking gently. 'And the man he is handing the envelope to is Captain Franc Comtois.'

'Shit,' Baptiste whistled. He grabbed the photograph. 'Jasper Connor was bribing the police!'

Hugo felt himself growing angry. He had inherited a police station ruined by bribery in Montgenoux and it was something he was still battling with. He took it personally for many reasons. He would not allow himself to ruin someone unless he was very sure of their corruption. He stared at Baptiste. 'We know nothing of the sort, Baptiste, and we can't suggest otherwise until we're sure. I won't allow it, and if you want to be here with us, you must remember that. Oui?'

Baptiste's cheeks flushed. 'Oui. Je comprends.'

Etienne pointed at the CD lying on the table. It was a standard, blank case with no writing on it. 'What about that?'

Hugo placed the CD into his laptop. 'Let's give it a listen.' Moments later, a crackling recording began over the speakers.

"This is all you need to do. Slip this in his drink and wait twenty minutes."
"Why do I have to do it?"
"Because he trusts you. He doesn't know me."
"I don't understand. Why do we even have to do this? We have the money. We have the hotel. Isn't that what you wanted? Didn't you say it was all you wanted - to build a life just for the two of us?"
"Oui. Mais - it's not so easy. I owe people. Bad people."
"You owe people? What are you talking about? You told me you were rich."
"I am. I was. Dammit, it's not always so easy. Decisions are made. Some good. Some bad. And sometimes you have to deal with people you wouldn't normally. Bad people. This is our only way out of this. I came to Beaufort-Sur-Mer to start again. To make a new life. I didn't intend on falling in love, but I did. And if you want me to stay, you have to help me."
"Mais, I already have! I've done everything you've asked of me. I'll never be forgiven for what I've done, but I did it because I love you and now you're saying it wasn't enough, that I have to do more."
"This will be it. Once we do this, it'll all be over. I'll have paid my debts and that'll be it."
"Why drag him into this?"
"Because he's the only one who can do it, and he's never going to agree, is he? That's why we have to make sure he has no choice. Slip this in his drink and then leave the rest to me."
"And then it will be over?"
"Then it will be over, my cherie."

The CD stopped. Hugo scratched his head.

'Who were we listening to?' Etienne asked.

'I can't be sure,' Hugo replied, 'because the recording isn't great. Mais, I'm fairly sure it was Jasper Connor and Avril Roche. The voices suggest so, and the conversation seems to confirm it.'

Baptiste nodded. 'I'd agree.'

'Why would Arthur Roche even be recording that?' Etienne pondered. 'Was this about the hotel?'

Hugo shrugged. 'It may not have been about the hotel. Peut être he was just suspicious that Connor was having an affair with Avril and he wanted proof. He not only got proof they were having an affair but had been swindling him out of his money for months.' He frowned. 'Then again, maybe this recording wasn't about him at all. Let's listen again.'

The three of them listened in silence to the CD once more.

Hugo lit a cigarette. 'There's something off in that recording. Something I can't pinpoint. I'm fairly sure they weren't talking about Arthur.'

'What makes you think that?' Baptiste asked.

Hugo considered. 'Well, for one thing, they seem to indicate they already have the hotel and the money belonging to Arthur Roche. What else would they need from him? Jasper Connor seems to be suggesting he needs someone to help him pay off a debt.' He shook his head. 'They don't seem to be talking about Arthur Roche.'

Etienne gave him a doubtful look. 'Then who?'

Hugo shrugged again. 'I wish I knew.' He rose to his feet. 'D'accord. Can I leave you with your investigating to see what you can turn up?'

Etienne nodded. 'Sure. Where will you be?'

Hugo picked up the photographs. 'I'm going to see Captain Comtois and see what he has to say about this. I've known he was lying to me about something, and this might just be it.'

trente-sept

Captain Franc Comtois was on his porch, a drink in his hand, the ice sliding back and forth as his hand gently shook. Hugo walked slowly up the boulevard towards his house. He could see Dr. Oppert was with him again, a drink rested on his chest as he slept. Hugo moved his feet heavily against the ground in an attempt to announce his arrival. Comtois turned sharply, his face instantly clouding.

'You again,' he spat, red eyes narrowing angrily in Hugo's direction.

Oppert lifted his head, his eyes slowly opening, a tired smile appearing on his face. 'Believe it or not, Captain Duchamp, I was just having a dream and guess who was in it? Madeline.'

Hugo stopped. It still shocked him that he had innocently come across someone who had known his Grand-Mère. It was like a lightning bolt. A connection to the past Hugo had long assumed was severed forever. 'What was she doing?' he asked.

Oppert chuckled. 'Slapping me around the head and telling me I'd better look after you and help you, or else she'd be back and I'd be sorry.' He visibly shuddered. 'And I believe she meant it.'

Hugo gulped, suddenly overwhelmed with a loss long forgotten. 'I don't doubt it.'

'Whaddya want, kid?' Comtois slurred.

Oppert gently touched his friend's arm. 'He's doing his job, Franc.'

Hugo studied the Captain and realised it was most probably not the best time to confront him about the pictures. However, he was reluctant to put it off. He would not be responsible for another death just to spare the feelings of a grieving father, especially if that father was hiding something.

Oppert pointed to a seat opposite them. 'Have a seat, Captain. Can I get you something to drink or eat?'

Hugo lowered himself into the chair. He shook his head. 'Non, merci'.

'Have you found the bastard who killed my son?' Comtois slurred.

'Non, I'm afraid not,' Hugo replied. He placed a copy of the photographs they had retrieved from Arthur Roche's boat in front of Comtois. He had decided his only approach was to be direct.

Comtois leaned forward, squinting. 'What in the hell are these?'

'Arthur Roche left them,' Hugo answered.

Oppert picked up the photographs, smoothing thin and wispy white hair as he did. His eyes widened, and he returned them and said nothing.

Franc Comtois picked them up. His nostrils flared. 'I don't know what you think these are, but I'm telling you if you...'

Hugo raised his hands. 'I'm suggesting nothing.'

Comtois balled his fists. 'Bon, or else I'd show you what we do to troublemakers around here.'

Oppert chuckled. 'Oh, for goodness' sake, Franc. This isn't the Wild West and as much as you think you could, I'm telling you, running someone like Captain Duchamp out of town is not an option. Don't test me either, you old fool.' He stared at Hugo. 'All that aside, I must beg your indulgence, and most certainly your ability not to judge. There is an explanation. It may not be one you are satisfied with or even understand, but there is an explanation.'

'You know about this?' Hugo gasped, clearly shocked. He shook his head in disbelief. 'All the time I knew the two of you were lying to me.'

'I never lied,' Oppert retorted.

Hugo's mouth twisted angrily. 'Call it what you will. I'll tell you what I call it - you two withholding information you both deemed irrelevant.'

Oppert bowed his head. 'Je suis désolé, but it really wasn't relevant, or I would have told you.'

'I don't believe you,' Hugo snapped. 'This is bullshit, and I swear if something either of you should have told me earlier could have prevented… could have prevented what happened, then par Dieu, I'll…'

'You'll what, Captain Duchamp?' Comtois interrupted. 'Throw two old men in jail?'

'If I have to,' Hugo shot back.

Comtois snorted. 'You think that works as a threat to me? If you do, you're a stupid f…'

'Finish your sentence, I beg you,' Hugo warned.

Comtois laughed. 'All I mean is, jail is no threat to me.'

'Well, it is to me!' Oppert cried. 'I moved here for an easy life, not to end my days an old lag.' He faced Hugo. 'I helped, that's all.'

Hugo frowned. 'Helped?'

'Shut the fuck up, Jacques,' Comtois hissed. 'Or so help me…'

Jacques slapped Comtois on the arm. 'Don't threaten me, you old fool. I'm not lying to Captain Duchamp, and nor are you. It's too late for that.'

'Too late?' Hugo interjected.

Both men lapsed into silence.

Hugo sighed. 'D'accord. Since you're both going to be obstinate, and I don't have time to waste, I'm going to be direct. And if you're not going to help me, then I have to assume you are part of the problem.' He took a breath and faced Comtois. 'Let's begin with this. How long did you know your son was gay?'

Comtois opened his mouth, outrage appearing on his face, but before he spoke, he seemed to fold into himself as if the fight within him had suddenly dissipated. 'I'm sixty-three years old. I'm not deaf, dumb and blind!' he scolded. 'I probably knew before he did.'

'And what did you do about it?' Hugo asked.

Comtois sniffed. 'What do you mean? I did nothing about it. Gregoire kept his… *peculiarity* away from me and that's all that mattered. He knew better than to parade it in front of me,' he added proudly.

Hugo shook his head angrily. 'For Dieu's sake, this is the year 2022. It's not the dark ages, times have changed, dammit.'

'Not for me,' Comtois snapped back, 'and not for my friends. Gays are people you see on television. They're not the sort of decent people we are.'

'Oh, what rubbish!' Dr. Oppert interrupted. 'Fags have been around forever,' he lowered his voice demurely at Hugo. 'Excusez moi. *Homosexuals* have been around forever, and frankly, they are some of the nicest people I've met, especially in my line of work. They're also some of the worst, but really, that's the point.' He turned to Comtois. 'I've said this to you before, and I'll keep saying it until it gets through your thick skull. They're the same as you or I. Some are good, some are bad, but in the end, WE are all the same.' He shrugged. 'I don't care to think about what they do in bed, any more than they do I.' He smiled sadly. 'If only I had the chance.'

Hugo suppressed a smile.

Comtois blew a raspberry and took another drink.

Hugo pointed at the photograph. 'Tell me what this is about.'

'I will tell you nothing,' Comtois retorted huffily. There was a change to his tone, Hugo noticed. It almost rang with the sound of defeat.

Oppert sighed. 'If you don't Franc, I will.'

Comtois glared at the doctor, searching his face as if assessing if he was speaking the truth. He exhaled irritably.

Hugo tapped the photograph. 'It seems to me this photograph suggests one of two things. Bribery or blackmail. Now, I can't be certain, because I don't know you very well, but I can't

le bateau au fond de l'océan

imagine you'd be swayed by a man like Jasper Connor unless...' he trailed off, 'unless you had no choice.'

'Jasper Connor is a bastard,' Comtois threw back his head and spat onto the ground. 'And I rue the day he rolled into Beaufort-Sur-Mer. If I'd known the trouble he was going to cause, I would have run him out of town before he had a chance to get his foot in the door. He's not what he seems, Captain Duchamp. He is a wolf in sheep's clothing.'

'I'm getting that impression,' Hugo conceded. 'Tell me. How did Jasper know your son was gay?'

Comtois shrugged. 'From Avril probably. I didn't bother to ask. I was just so mad, I wanted to kill him.' He smiled. 'I *almost* killed him, but as I was choking him, I realised he would win if I did. So I stopped.'

'What did he want from you?' Hugo asked.

'He wanted me to turn a blind eye to something that was going to happen,' Comtois replied.

Hugo nodded. 'And what did you think that meant?'

'Nothing good,' Comtois answered. 'Anyway, he had me backed into a corner. I guess he judged by my reaction I didn't want my little family secret to become public knowledge. He had me by the balls and I wanted to punch him in his. But I couldn't. So, I did the next best thing. I told him if I was going to become a dirty cop, he was going to have to make it worth my while.'

'Worth your while?' Hugo questioned. 'Then you were the one who asked for money?'

Comtois nodded. 'Oui, bien sûr,' he replied. 'Mais, I'm not fucking stupid, or in the need of money. I wanted my secret kept, but I also wanted Jasper Connor to be my bitch, not the other way around.'

Hugo scratched his head. 'Then what did you do?'

He smiled at Oppert. 'I went straight to my dear friend. Jacques and I talked about it, and together we came up with a plan.

A simple one, as it happens, but the best plans usually are. We both knew there was only one response. Blackmail works both ways.'

'Then you planned to accept the blackmail, and then use it to blackmail, Jasper Connor, in return?' Hugo asked with a frown.

'Oui,' Comtois replied.

'I don't understand,' Hugo stated simply. He pointed at the photographs. 'Did you know about these?'

Comtois shook his head. 'Non. They don't surprise me, though. I'm guessing you got them from Arthur somehow?'

'Oui,' Hugo replied.

'Arthur was out of control,' Oppert said. 'He was drinking more and more, and his accusations were becoming more and more outlandish. He was out for revenge, mais,' he stared at the photographs, 'if he had these photographs, why didn't he use them?'

'I'm not sure,' Hugo answered. 'Other than he realised that if he used it against Jasper Connor, he would also most likely destroy someone else he probably liked.' He faced Comtois. 'Namely, you, Captain Comtois.'

'Stupid bastard,' Comtois grumbled. 'He was a good man.'

'Tell me what happened with Jasper? What was the plan?'

'To finish him.' Comtois finished his drink. 'And get him the hell out of town. Jacques took our own photographs. A sort of mutually assured destruction, is what I planned to tell Jasper afterwards. He couldn't destroy me, without destroying himself.'

'And yet he's still here,' Hugo reasoned.

'That wasn't my decision,' Comtois replied. 'After Arthur died, Avril came to me and begged me to leave it be. To let it alone. Let her live in peace. She promised me that Jasper would give me no more trouble ever again.' He shrugged. 'I agreed because he wasn't the only one holding the cards anymore. I hate the fact he's still here, but I'm hopeful he'll get bored and move on, eventually.'

Hugo cleared his throat. 'So, Jasper Connor came to you with blackmail in mind. And you saw a way to turn the tables on him, I get that. You said this was about you turning a blind eye. What does that mean, exactly? What did he want you to do?'

Comtois sighed. 'He didn't want me to interfere with a drug shipment coming into Beaufort-Sur-Mer from the Atlantic. He'd arranged it all, he said, so all I needed to do was make sure I wasn't around the harbour on one particular night. He told me it was a one-off. A way to pay off his debts. He swore it would never happen again.'

'And you believed him?'

Comtois shrugged. 'I didn't much care,' he replied. 'Once it was done, I planned on showing him my own evidence and giving him a choice. Keep my secret, but more importantly, to get out of Beaufort-Sur-Mer.'

'Then you're telling me, to keep your son's sexuality a secret, you turned your back on drugs being brought into France?' Hugo gasped.

'What choice did I have?' Comtois retorted. 'He was threatening me, and I couldn't let him get away with it.'

Hugo turned to Oppert. 'And you went along with this ridiculousness?'

Oppert nodded. 'I've always hated bullies. And I've found the only way to deal with them is to beat them at their own game.'

Hugo leaned forward. 'You said he had it all planned. Who else was involved?'

'He and Avril had a plan,' Comtois continued. 'They had the help of someone else. They said it was fool proof.'

Hugo sat. 'Tell me <u>exactly</u> what happened.'

trente-huit

Hugo and Etienne walked side by side in silence up the steep steps towards the fort. Friday evening was sweeping into Beaufort-Sur-Mer and bringing with it a chill. Hugo could taste the salty dampness on his lips.

He had asked Etienne to meet him on the boulevard because he felt like walking and talking. He had been cooped up for too long, and he was sure that with some fresh air and time, he could finally begin to piece together the puzzle and make sense of what had happened in the preceding week. They had done it before, and he hoped they could again.

The conversation with Captain Comtois and Dr. Oppert was also troubling Hugo. It was not necessarily because he did not understand their motives for doing what they had done. He understood Comtois was from an older generation, and one which was not always accepting of lifestyles different to their own. However, it was the fact that somehow Comtois had reconciled allowing drugs into France as an acceptable compromise for keeping his secret.

As far as Hugo was concerned, the two were very different, and Comtois was as responsible as Jasper Connor was for the crime. However, Hugo knew he needed to put it all to one side for the moment, because it was more important to find a way of understanding what the link was to what had occurred afterwards.

The two friends reached the top of the steps. Hugo carried on into the clearing. There was something about the fort, the combination of the past and the present, which appealed to him. It was as if it was made from distinct moments in time, thrown across years, centuries even. He had always believed the past and the present, and for that matter, the future were all linked in one way or another. It was as if everyone walked the same path, and it did not matter at what point in history they walked it, their lives would echo the lives of people before and after.

He realised then his recent trip to Paris, the city of his birth, still troubled him. He had imagined at first it was because he had left it unresolved, with unsatisfactory reunions with his parents, but as he stood on the fort overlooking Beaufort-Sur-Mer, a thought occurred to him. It was not that he regretted walking away from his past, rather that he had not acknowledged it. Speaking with Captain Bertram Hervé had reminded him of that. When in Paris, Hugo should have walked the streets he had left. They had nothing to hide, and they could not hurt him. But they could remind him. Not just of bad times, but of good times.

He had spent his time in Paris running from the people who had hurt him, and that had caused him pain, and most probably them too. In the end, it was not about pain. It was about remembering and moving on. He knew he needed to return to Paris. Not to see anyone. But to acknowledge what it had meant to him.

'You should never go back,' he said aloud.

'Pardon?' Etienne questioned.

Hugo smiled. 'I was just thinking about my recent trip to Paris, and what a terrible job I made of it.'

Etienne's mouth twisted. 'I don't think that was entirely down to you, Hugo.'

He shrugged. 'Maybe, maybe not. I don't think it matters. We spend so much time running from our past that often we miss the point. We're not running from the past, we're running from who we were in those places. The things we did. The choices we made.' He looked down at the harbour below them. 'It's the same wherever we go. We never escape it, and nor should we. I thought I was happy when I lived in London, but it was only because I had left Paris and my family. But I had just exchanged one thing for another.'

Etienne frowned. 'Je suis désolé, I'm not sure I understand.'

Hugo laughed. 'I'm not sure I do either.' He took a deep breath. 'I suppose what I'm thinking, what I think I've forgotten about is the fundamental part of an investigation.'

'And that is?'

He smiled. 'You begin at the beginning.'

'Don't we always?' Etienne asked with a laugh.

'We should,' Hugo replied. 'But often we don't for a myriad of reasons, put simply because everything starts from a different beginning.'

Etienne glanced at the cigarette in Hugo's hand. 'Are you sure you haven't had one of Baptiste's "funny" cigarettes?'

'Ha, non,' Hugo answered. He took a long drag on his "normal" cigarette. 'Mais, I think I am seeing things more clearly. What I'm trying to say, in my usual slow, roundabout way, is that whenever we investigate a crime, we invariably each start from different starting points. We ignore something because we think it is unrelated. Therefore, we move on to the next point, and then we ignore something else because again, it seems irrelevant. But what if we take a step back? What if the first point, the point we thought *couldn't* be important, was actually the starting point, then if we accept that…'

'The second point becomes much more interesting,' Etienne concluded.

Hugo moved across the clearing, stepping between the ruins of the fort. 'I imagine a lot has happened in this very place over the last hundred years or so.'

Etienne eyed a torn condom wrapper. 'I'd say so!' he laughed.

Hugo moved further. Standing next to one of the benches. He leaned forward, taking in the panoramic view of the boulevard, the harbour, and the crystal blue sea beneath them. Beneath them, the people moving around were tiny, stick-like figures and at that moment, it all seemed so far away, so far removed from everything that had transpired.

From this vantage point, it all seemed very innocent. But it was not. Despite the beauty, he knew that behind the façade there was always danger lurking. He had learnt it in Paris, then London, in his new home of Montgenoux, but also in the places where he had travelled - Russia and Ireland. All he knew for certain was that there was no escape from the darkness, no matter how pretty something may appear from the outside.

'That conversation with Comtois has really pissed you off, hasn't it?' Etienne asked, breaking the silence.

Hugo moved his shoulders. 'Not really. I'm irritated by what he and Dr. Oppert did, but I'd be a liar if I said I didn't understand their reasoning. I don't have to agree with it, or support it, but I understand it.'

Etienne nodded. 'Everyone is capable of making stupid decisions for what they believe is the right reason.' He narrowed his eyes. 'The point is - has it helped you understand what happened in this town?'

Hugo lit a cigarette. 'Well, I wouldn't go so far as to say that,' he replied eventually with a tight smile. 'But I have a few ideas.' He turned to Etienne. 'Which means, as usual, I have to rely on you, as I so often do, to illuminate the darkness. Because in my crazy brain at this moment, nothing really makes sense.' He nodded. 'And that is why, in this part of the book, or the movie, I would turn to you, mon ami, and say, *enlighten me, tell me something which will make me say, ah! There we have it. It was Professor Plum, with a candlestick in the library.*'

Etienne guffawed. 'You never cease to amaze me, Hugo Duchamp!' He folded his hands in front of him, lowering himself onto a chair. 'D'accord, so now that you've put *no* pressure on me. I'll tell you what I've found so far, but I wouldn't get too excited if I were you.'

He took a breath and extracted a notebook from his pocket. 'Let us begin with Jasper Connor,' he began. 'There's not a lot to go on, other than he's a pretty shady character. He calls himself an investor, but so far as I can tell, all he's ever really done is gather together several small investors with a view to making an enormous investment. You know the sort of thing, "if fifty of us give five thousand euros and invest it in an up and coming company, we can all make a hell of a profit." It seems not only didn't he invest the money he collected, but he also kept it all for himself,' Etienne added.

'There are a lot of very pissed off people after him,' he continued. 'There are court cases, of course, and a few arrests of people he's worked with, but it seems he knows what he's doing. That's how he's managed to get away with it for so long. A lot of people take the fall for him, and he seems to walk away unscathed.'

'Then what went wrong?' Hugo asked. 'Because I'm assuming something did. Unless Captain Comtois was still lying to me, he seemed to indicate that Jasper Connor was in trouble with a lot of dodgy people and needed to get them off his back.'

Etienne nodded. 'I guess he annoyed the wrong people. Or he hooked up with the wrong people.'

Hugo frowned. 'Then, how did he end up here, Beaufort-Sur-Mer? It's a beautiful town, but it's hardly Paris or the South of France. I can't imagine there's an enormous amount of money for him to make here.'

Etienne pointed to the sea. 'Mais, there's that. A vast ocean. A small coastal town with minimal police. It's an easy way to get drugs into the country.'

Hugo nodded. 'I suppose.'

'His bank account is pretty empty,' Etienne continued. 'Which is surprising because I can't figure out how he paid for the hotel.'

'What do you mean?'

He shrugged. 'He didn't pay for it from his regular bank account, but he is the deed owner. I checked. There is an avocat of note on the deeds, who presumably paid for the hotel on his behalf, but figuring out how he got the money to them is likely to prove problematic, and I can't imagine we'll be able to get access to their records, even if we could get a mandate from a Juge, these people are often very adept at hiding what they think we shouldn't see.'

'Then we have nothing,' Hugo sighed.

'We could have something. If you spoke to the Juge…'

Hugo shook his head. 'You're right. Even if we could get a mandate, it would take a forensic accountant an age to try to figure it all out, and in the end, would it help? We know Jasper Connor is a shady character, but is it relevant to this investigation? We can pass it on to the relevant department and they can look into him, but as for us, as for now, we have little time to waste. Anything else?'

'Not a great deal,' he responded. 'I've had a chance to go through the forensic reports, such as they are, but I'm afraid there isn't a great deal there. There was nothing of any substance found in the beach hut, nor Clementine Bonheur's studio. Lots of fingerprints and fibres. An enormous amount of blood in the studio, but it's all Clementine's.' He sighed. 'The simple truth is there are too many samples, and not enough to go on. They've fed most of them through the databases, but no red flags.'

'What about the phone conversation Guy Fallon overheard?'

'I traced the call to the public telephone on the boulevard overlooking the harbour,' Etienne answered. 'And as you know, there are no CCTV cameras around, so again, we have a bit of a dead end.'

'The public telephone?' Hugo repeated. 'Well, isn't that strange?'

Etienne shrugged once again. 'I don't see why. I can take fingerprints, but I'm guessing it doesn't get cleaned very often, and anyone could have used it, so it wouldn't benefit us very much. Je suis désolé, I haven't found more. There doesn't seem to be a lot to go on, as far as I can tell.' He took a deep breath. 'However, there are a few other things which might interest you, but I'm clutching at straws here.'

Hugo leaned forward. 'Aren't we always? What did you find?'

'It's probably nothing,' Etienne reasoned. 'I've been looking into the past of some of our witnesses. The usual sort of misdemeanours, in most cases, nothing to be unduly concerned about.'

'Most cases?' Hugo quested.

'Yeah,' Etienne confirmed. 'Clementine Bonheur was busted quite a few times,' he added with a wry smile, 'mostly for drunk and disorderly, or being in possession of drugs, just weed, nothing heavy, and once,' he paused, 'for sexual impropriety with a sixteen-year-old boy.'

Hugo's eyes widened. 'She was certainly a character. Who was the boy? Anyone we know?'

Etienne shook his head. 'A tourist. By all accounts, he was a willing participant, but his family wasn't so happy about it, although he was about to turn seventeen. They kicked up a fuss. She was arrested, but only given a slap on the wrists because no crime had been committed. The boy is thirty now and a teacher in Belgium.'

Another dead end, Hugo thought glumly.

'Captain Comtois has a fairly good police service record,' Etienne continued. 'A few complaints on his file, excessive force, that sort of thing. Nothing was upheld or went any further. Most of the reports seem to show he's a pretty good, if slightly old-school sort of flic.'

Hugo nodded, not unsure if his own opinion was entirely dissimilar.

'Same goes for Dr. Jaques Oppert.'

Hugo nodded again.

Etienne continued. 'As for the rest of the suspects in Beaufort-Sur-Mer - no police records, nothing on any of our databases. As far as I can tell, they're all pretty clean.'

Hugo sighed. 'Then we have nothing.'

'I didn't quite say that,' Etienne replied with a smile. He tapped the notepad. 'I didn't fill you in on the investigations from Vincent Roche's suicide in Montgenoux.'

Hugo looked keenly. 'Is there anything there?'

Etienne laughed. 'I'm not sure. I'm *never* sure.' He paused. 'Mais, thankfully, you usually are.'

'Then tell me what you have.'

'When you told me about the awful thing that happened to Brigitte St. Pierre, I looked into her past,' Etienne replied.

'Pourquoi?'

'Because I always do, and I trust no one,' Etienne replied. He fluttered his eyelashes. 'Present company excluded, évidemment.' He glanced around as if satisfying himself they were alone. 'And I'm glad I did.'

Hugo's eyes widened. 'Pourquoi?' he asked again.

'Five years ago, when she was fifteen years old, Brigitte St. Pierre claimed a fellow student in her boarding school raped her.'

'Claimed?' Hugo questioned. He felt the hairs standing up on the back of his neck, knowing something important was coming.

Etienne nodded. 'There was no direct evidence.'

'Did she report it to the police?'

'Non,' Etienne replied. 'And the only reason I found it was because the family of the boy made the report.'

Hugo frowned. 'Well, that's unusual.'

'As far as I can make out, the family were friends with the Commander of the local Police Nationale,' Etienne continued. 'They contacted him because they claimed they were being blackmailed by Brigitte St. Pierre.'

'Blackmailed?' Hugo gasped, his forehead crinkling. 'Doesn't she come from a rich family already? I'm sure someone told me she did.'

'Her family is indeed rich. They mine diamonds in North Africa,' Etienne answered. 'Therefore, I checked Brigitte's bank details and, as far as I can tell, the family keeps her on a very tight leash. They pay her school and tuition fees and give her a quite modest monthly stipend, so she's not spoilt as far as I can tell.' He shrugged. 'It's not conclusive, but it might explain her motivation.'

Hugo sighed. 'None of this means she wasn't raped, then or now,' he said briskly. 'Rather, she might have realised no one would believe her, so she wanted to make them pay in one way or another.' He took a deep breath and lit a cigarette. 'What did the police do?'

'The family dropped off the blackmail money at a park,' Etienne continued. 'And the police were waiting for Brigitte when she came to collect it.'

'She was arrested?'

'Well, she was taken into custody, mais it seems the family declined to press charges. I guess they just wanted her warned off, and for the entire business to end. The police report says she was read the riot act and informed if there were any more problems, she would most certainly be arrested and charged.'

They lapsed into silence. The only sound was the breeze and Hugo gently inhaling and exhaling his cigarette. 'Whatever happened back then,' he began, 'can't really be related to what happened here this week. I can't imagine Captain Comtois has the kind of money which would attract blackmail, not if he's paid the same sort of salary as I am.'

Etienne flashed him a triumphant smile. 'I knew you'd say that, so just in case I ran his finances as well,' he added. 'And he has close to a million euros in his bank account.'

'A million euros!' Hugo exclaimed. 'Ah, that explains something that was troubling me. I got the impression he had money, but certainly not that much.'

'Yeah. And before you ask, I don't know where it came from.

All I can tell you is he appears to have had the money for some time. There was no lump sum paid into his account, certainly not recently.'

'Then it's not the money from Jasper Connor?' Hugo asked.

Etienne shrugged. 'I can't say with any certainty, other than the only monthly deposits in his account are his pay-check from the Republic. The money has always been there, it seems. I'll try to figure out where it came from, but it may take me some time.'

'Or we could just ask him directly?' Hugo contemplated. He sighed. 'Regardless of where the money came from, he had it, but it begs the question - how on earth would Brigitte St. Pierre know about it, unless…' he trailed off.

'Unless?'

Hugo scratched his head. 'Well, it's a little out there, but it might just be an explanation. What if Gregoire Comtois was actually involved?'

'What do you mean?' Etienne asked.

'We're dealing with a great deal of supposition,' Hugo mused. 'We only have Brigitte St. Pierre's word regarding her conversations with Gregoire. What if he saw a way to get out of Beaufort-Sur-Mer and live the life he wanted away from a father who was clearly embarrassed by him?'

Etienne gave him a doubtful look. 'I can't imagine how it would have come up naturally in conversation. Brigitte St. Pierre was hardly likely to have suggested it - *hey, I've done this sort of thing before, we can make a mint!*'

Hugo pursed his lips. 'Why not? If Gregoire told her he was gay and that he had to pretend to be straight to appease his father. It's not too far of a stretch he may have also mentioned he was only waiting for his father to die so he could get his money and leave. If Brigitte lied about the first rape for money, she may have instantly seen a chance to make some big cash from Captain Comtois. A plan could have been born from that conversation.'

'As you said, it's a lot of supposition,' Etienne replied with apparent doubt.

'One that might just make sense, though,' Hugo reasoned. 'Gregoire would have known his father would most likely readily pay to keep the secret hidden.'

'Then what went so badly wrong?' Etienne interjected. 'Because something did, and, as far as I can tell from the hospital report, it's clear that Brigitte was drugged and that she was sexually attacked.'

'I didn't say I had all the answers,' Hugo retorted. 'And I agree, unless I'm very much mistaken, Brigitte's reaction seemed very genuine to me.'

'She could just be an excellent actress. We've seen it before,' Etienne sighed. 'We've both looked straight into someone's eyes and believed everything they're saying, only to find out later they're vicious murderers.'

'Still…' Hugo took a long drag on the cigarette. 'Even if we can imagine such a scenario was concocted between Gregoire Comtois and Brigitte St. Pierre, and we further assume she was sexually assaulted. Then if her attacker wasn't Gregoire, we are back looking at there being a third person involved. This person raped Brigitte, then killed Gregoire and then posed his body on the boat. The question is - was Brigitte involved in that?' He paused. 'You mentioned you were glad you checked the criminal records. Was there something else?'

'The other student, Quentin Arquette, also has a criminal record,' Etienne continued. 'It's from when he was a juvenile so I had to… er… do a little digging, if you know what I mean.'

Hugo suppressed a smile. 'I won't use it. What did you find?'

'It seems he's always been a bit of a swimmer. At fourteen he swam from Calais to Dover and set a record for his age group, but he got into trouble with one of his teammates. She claimed he tried to drown her when she rebuked him.'

Hugo raised an eyebrow. 'What did he do?'

Etienne checked his notes. 'There wasn't much of an investigation. I suppose he held her underwater until she somehow got free. The police spoke to him, but the girl withdrew from the team. He remained, I guess because he was pretty good and they didn't want to lose him from the team.'

Hugo nodded. 'Merci. I'm not sure what to make of this, or how far it helps us to understand what's happened. It's all a bit of a mess, but I'm afraid I'm hard-pressed to understand what may or may not be relevant.' He rose to his feet. 'I think I'll talk again with Brigitte and Quentin, just in case.'

Etienne stepped next to him. 'I'll wait for you at the hotel and keep digging.'

They walked in silence together, slowly descending the steps. 'Oh, there was one other thing,' Etienne said. 'Remember the missing red towel?'

Hugo turned his head. 'The missing red towel?' he asked with a frown. 'Oh, I'd forgotten about that. The missing towel from the swimming pool in Montgenoux. What about it? Did you find it?'

Hugo recalled the cleaner who had discovered the body of Vincent Roche had mentioned seeing a red towel next to the pool. The towel, however, was not there when the police had arrived. Hugo had dismissed it as the cleaner misremembering seeing something because of the shock of discovering a body in the swimming pool.

'Non,' Etienne replied. 'Mais, when I went back to the pool, I found several red fibres in the area the cleaner claimed she saw the towel. I examined the fibres, and they were Egyptian cotton, which is what most towels are made of...' he trailed off. 'So, make of that what you will.'

Hugo shrugged. 'I don't think it's important, mais still, it's odd it disappeared, don't you think?'

Etienne chuckled. 'I think everything about my life is odd, so

I couldn't comment.'

'You're probably right,' Hugo said, staring straight ahead as the boulevard came into view beneath them.

trente-neuf

Hugo stepped carefully down the walkway which lead into the bay, as Quentin Arquette clambered out of the water, dropping his diving gear on the steps.

Hugo spotted Quentin's clothes piled neatly on the edge and picked up a towel, handing it to the young man. Quentin took it from him, wrapping it around himself whilst all the time regarding Hugo with caution and obvious concern. Moments later, Brigitte St. Pierre appeared from under the water and climbed onto the walkway. Quentin ran to her clothes and snatched her towel, handing it to her with a quick flick of his wrist.

Brigitte shook her head, spraying them all with an abundance of water. 'Désolé,' she called to Hugo after noticing him wiping the drips from his face.

'Did you have a nice swim?' he asked.

'We have to keep practising,' Quentin snipped. 'We still have heats to compete in when we get back to school. Speaking of which…'

Hugo nodded. 'I believe we can leave on Sunday,' he answered. 'You should be back in time for school on Monday.'

'Then… then it's over?' Brigitte asked gently, drifting towards him. She pulled a hoodie over her head.

Hugo was not sure what she meant. 'The investigations will progress,' he said, 'but I believe it can take place without us having to stay in Beaufort-Sur-Mer.'

'Then you're no closer to finding out who killed Gregoire and that painter chick?' Quentin asked with a haughty arrogance, which bothered Hugo immensely.

'I didn't say that,' Hugo snapped, immediately wishing he had not reacted. The fact remained, at that point, he was sure of nothing.

Quentin stepped towards him, his eyes flicking angrily over

Hugo. 'What's that supposed to mean?'

Hugo stood his ground. 'I'd like to speak with you both, if I may. Could I buy you a drink?'

Brigitte bit her lip. 'Could I get changed first?'

'Bien sûr,' Hugo replied. 'How about I meet you both in the bar in half an hour?'

Brigitte nodded. She tugged on Quentin's sleeve. 'Come on, Quentin,' she whispered.

Hugo watched as she dragged Quentin towards the boulevard. The young man appeared reluctant, glancing over his shoulder towards Hugo.

Hugo cleared his throat and took a sip of his drink. His fringe fell over his face and it afforded him a moment to study the faces of Brigitte St. Pierre and Quentin Arquette. He pushed it away, taking the moment to study the two young people.

What Etienne had discovered about them both was troubling, but, as Hugo reasoned, both events had transpired when they were much younger. And with no evidence directly to the contrary, he knew he should consider them to be youthful indiscretions, ones which they had hopefully learnt and grown from. He noticed also that the ice between the two of them seemed to have thawed. He supposed Brigitte had taken some comfort in the fact Quentin had stepped up following her attack and was keen to look out for her. If there was a shared anxiety between them, it was not obvious. Quentin, as was his norm, appeared bored and irritated. Brigitte appeared more relaxed to Hugo than she had before.

'I'm looking forward to going home,' Brigitte said, 'and putting all this behind me.'

Quentin nodded. 'The swimming championship is just what we all need to take our minds of all the shit that's happened.'

'Will it still go ahead?' Hugo asked, surprised.

'Bien sûr,' Quentin snapped. 'We just have to get one of the reserves up to speed, that's why we need to get back to practice with him.'

Hugo turned to Brigitte. 'And have you thought any more about what you plan to do?'

Her nostrils flared, and she angrily tossed her hair over her shoulders dismissively. 'It's over.'

Hugo shook his head. 'It can't be over, not until we discover what happened to Gregoire. The police are still going to have to speak to you about what happened.'

'I told you, I won't make a report,' she hissed through gritted teeth.

'It's not about that, necessarily,' Hugo responded. 'Mais, you will need to explain it, as you remember it. Whatever your feelings about it, this also concerns what happened to Gregoire.'

'The rapist pig, you mean,' Quentin interrupted.

'I made my statement,' Brigitte interjected. 'And that's where it ends. I can't add anything to it. I WON'T add anything to it.'

Hugo took a deep breath. He was not sure how to proceed. He had read her statement, and she had made no mention of the rape. Her narrative was vague. She remembered nothing after getting drunk and high. It was exactly as she had told him. But he knew it would not remain so. The hospital report would come out, and it would change everything, It was obvious Brigitte St. Pierre had been seriously sexually assaulted, but everything about it suggested the rapist had not been Gregoire Comtois, and it worried him that if Captain Comtois was to look further into the allegations, he too would discover what Etienne had.

'Mademoiselle St. Pierre,' he began cautiously. 'You were raped. I understand your reticence to come forward and ask for an investigation, and please do not take this the wrong way, because I am not trying to diminish what happened to you in any way, however, I feel as if I must warn you so you can prepare yourself that there is a possibility what happened in your past will come to light. It shouldn't, but I am afraid it could happen.'

Brigitte leaned forward in her chair, resting her elbows on her knees. 'What are you talking about?' she snapped defiantly.

Hugo held her gaze, waiting until the flash of realisation appeared in her eyes. It did not take long.

'Fuck!' she spat. 'How the hell did you find out about it?'

Hugo took a breath. 'It doesn't matter. What does matter is others can find out, too. I don't want it to be used against you, and that is why it is even more important we understand what happened to you that night.'

'What are you talking about?' Quentin asked.

'Don't you think I know that?' Brigitte cried. 'It's exactly why I didn't want to report what happened because I knew the first thing people would do was take two and two and come up with fucking fifty.' She stared at Hugo, her eyes imploring him to understand. 'It was years ago. I didn't know what I was doing.'

'What does any of this have to do with something that happened when she was fifteen? The two things aren't connected.' Quentin questioned Hugo.

Brigitte turned her head sharply to him. 'How the hell did you know what happened when I was fifteen?'

Quentin shrugged. 'I don't,' he huffed. He pointed at Hugo. 'But the fact he's brought it up means he thinks it's important.'

She gave him a doubtful look.

Quentin nodded at Hugo. 'Isn't that correct, Captain?'

Hugo ignored him, still directing his attention towards Brigitte. 'Again, it's not my intention to pressure you or bring up a past you would rather forget. The fact remains, I have to because other people will. They'll bring up what happened and try to use it against you.'

She slammed her fists on the table. 'What do you want from

me? I was raped, then and now. What I did five years ago is not something I'm proud of, but it doesn't change the facts.'

Hugo nodded. 'Can you tell me what happened?'

'I was raped by a boy I was in love with,' she stated matter-of-factly. 'He said it was my fault for leading him on.' A sob escaped her throat, and she laughed. 'He was an idiot. If he'd asked me, I would have slept with him, anyway. I was so in love with him, I would have done anything he asked. But not that. I wouldn't have done that. He held my face to the ground and had his way with me. And then he laughed about it and called me a whore.'

'Why didn't you report it to the police?' Hugo asked, knowing it was a stupid question.

'Because they wouldn't have believed me. They never do,' she answered. 'His father was a hotshot, and he told me that no one would believe a fat, ugly bitch like me. And he was right. I knew it.' She sighed. 'I knew he would never pay in the way he should, so I thought I'd at least get something out of it. If they were going to treat me like a whore, I figured I should at least get paid for it.' She laughed. 'I was stupid to believe I stood a chance against them. They made out I was some blackmailing whore. The police officer who interviewed me actually laughed in my face, called me a silly little girl, and that if I didn't crawl back under the rock I'd crawled out from, he'd throw my fat ass in jail.'

Hugo gulped. 'Je suis désolé, for everything you've been through Mademoiselle St. Pierre.'

She shrugged. 'What does it matter? People go through a lot worse shit in their life than I have.' Her eyes widened. 'Mais, I'm not lying. Not then and not now.'

'I believe you,' Hugo stated. 'Is there really nothing you can tell me? I understand why you may have kept quiet earlier, but now, now that I know about your past, peut être you don't need to be afraid.'

She looked at him desperately. 'I told you everything. I can't remember anything. I swear! I swear!' she cried, her voice rising sharply.

Quentin touched her arm. 'Come on, let's get out of here.' He grabbed Brigitte by the arm and pulled her to her feet. He glared at Hugo. 'Stop hounding her, or dammit, I'll make a complaint against you. She is the victim here.'

'Je sais!' Hugo called out desperately.

Brigitte allowed Quentin to lead her away. She stopped and turned back to Hugo. 'I just want to put this all behind me, Captain Duchamp. Please let me, I beg you.'

Hugo watched with inherent sadness as she moved away. He was only sure of one thing at that moment. It was not all over for Brigitte St. Pierre.

quarante

Etienne's finger moved quickly across his keyboard. He lifted his head momentarily and saw two people enter the hotel's crowded outdoor restaurant. He had never met them before, but he had seen them in a photograph, in an embrace. Jasper Connor and Avril Roche sat at the table next to him. They did not notice or even look in his direction, such was the intensity they focused on each other.

It occurred to him it was not an exchange between lovers, as it had appeared in the photographs. Something had changed, that much was clear. There was little warmth present between them. Etienne considered leaving but realised they had never actually seen him before. He decided to remain where he was, at least for a few moments.

'This is all too much, Jasper,' Avril Roche spoke in quick, hushed tones.

Jasper reached across the table and took her hand. He gestured to a passing server. 'Deux verres de chardonnay, s'il vous plaît.' His face tightened as he turned back to Avril. 'We just have to keep our heads down and wait for this to pass.'

'Wait for this to pass?' she shrilled, clearly exasperated by his response. She snatched back her hand. She looked at it dumbfounded because it was shaking so violently and placed it on the table, covering it with her other hand and pressing down on it in an attempt to stop it moving.

'Oui,' he said calmly. 'Duchamp will be out of Beaufort-Sur-Mer and everything will get back to normal, you'll see.'

Avril shook her head vehemently. 'Non, things will never get back to normal. Not after what we've done. Clementine is dead because of us, Jasper. She is dead,' she spelt out. 'What is it about that, that you don't get?'

He grabbed her hand, glancing around nervously.

Etienne quickly dropped his head and continued typing quickly on his laptop. He had hit the record button because he wanted to be sure he missed nothing of the conversation.

'Will you be quiet, Avril?' Jasper hissed through gritted teeth, hidden behind a fake smile. 'People can hear you, and we don't want what you to say to be open to… *misinterpretation.*'

Avril snorted but said nothing. She snatched the wine from the approaching waiter and drained the contents in a few gulps. Jasper smiled politely at the waiter, took the bottle and refilled Avril's glass.

'We should never have allowed her to get involved,' Avril whispered.

Jasper shook his head. 'It wasn't a question of allowing her to do anything,' he snapped. 'The damn woman was always in everybody's business, skipping around town in those godawful kaftans like she was a fairy or something. If she wasn't always flitting around, she wouldn't have seen what she did, putting us all in danger.'

'She didn't mean to…'

'She never meant to,' Jasper interrupted. 'Mais, she still always seemed to manage to cause trouble. Do you know what I think? I think she actually enjoyed stirring things up.'

'That's a despicable thing to say!' Avril sobbed.

'Non, it isn't,' he retorted, 'because it's the truth. She played the ageing hippy artist well, but that's all it was - an act. She was manipulative and actually pretty damn nasty. She encouraged you to have an affair because she knew you would keep coming back to her for reassurance, to talk to. She set herself up as your confidant because it suited her. She was in charge of you, she always was.'

Avril opened and closed her mouth rapidly, as if she was about to say something and then thought better of it. Finally, she spoke. 'She was my friend, and she was a good friend. She didn't deserve what happened to her.'

Jasper took her hand again. 'Bien sûr, she was. And non, she didn't deserve what happened to her. But the second she injected herself into all of our lives, she opened herself up to a whole world of pain. Being nosey never ends well.'

'Still...'

He squeezed her hand. 'Cherie, you have to put this all behind you now. We all have to. They're gone. Arthur. Vincent. Clementine. And that is sad for you, I know, mais you can't let them take us with them, or what was the point in it all? We <u>have</u> to move forward, and we can't do that by looking back. A lot of sacrifices have been made, and we owe it to them to make the best of it. We will run this hotel together and make it the best damn hotel we can. Je t'aime, Avril. And believe me, that's not what I wanted. I've spent my life running from love. I thought coming to Beaufort-Sur-Mer was just a quick way to make some money. And it was. After...' he lowered his voice. 'After what we did, and I was free. I could have left, but I didn't want to. Being with you taught me something I needed to be taught. To stop and to be happy. Je t'aime, Avril,' he repeated. 'Don't you love me?'

Avril rose to her feet. 'I'm not sure I do.' She stepped away. 'However, the fact is, we're tied together by the rotten things we've done.' She shrugged. 'And I think that's my punishment. To be shackled to you for the rest of my life.'

Etienne closed his laptop, watching Avril as she hurried out of the restaurant.

quarante-et-un

Hugo stared at Etienne's laptop. 'You realise, whatever is in this recording, we won't be able to use it, don't you?'

Etienne nodded. 'Oui. I didn't want to make it obvious I was listening, so I thought this was the next best thing. Besides,' he added, 'I don't believe they said anything incriminating enough for you to speak to them, or to use against them.'

Hugo tipped his head. 'Then press play and we'll pretend I didn't hear it,' he said.

Etienne moved inside Hugo's hotel room, sat down and pressed play, the muffled sounds of the restaurant filling the room. Hugo and Baptiste followed him. Hugo dropped onto a chair and lit a cigarette, training his ear in the direction of the laptop. He closed his eyes as he concentrated on what was being said between Avril Roche and Jasper Connor. They listened in silence until it was finished and Etienne closed his laptop.

'Are you sure they didn't know you were listening to them?' Hugo asked.

Etienne shrugged. 'Pretty sure. I don't think either of them has seen me before, so I doubt they know my connection to you.'

'What do you think they were talking about?' Baptiste asked.

Hugo rubbed his chin. 'I think it ties into what Captain Comtois told me, however, I don't see the connection between that and Clementine Bonheur's death.'

Baptiste frowned. 'There must be a connection, because it sounds like they're saying Clementine was killed to keep her mouth shut.'

'Mais, pourquoi?' Hugo asked. 'And more importantly, why now? This all happened long before we even came to Beaufort-Sur-Mer. I just can't see what the connection might be between it all. If her murder was connected to the blackmail and drug running, then why wait until now?'

Baptiste shrugged. 'Does it matter?'

'I think it does,' Hugo responded. 'It appears too random to me to exclude the possible connection between the murder of Gregoire Comtois and the subsequent murder of Clementine Bonheur because as far as we can tell, Gregoire Comtois had little to no involvement with Jasper Connor and whatever shady activity he was up to.'

'It doesn't mean there wasn't one, just that we don't see it,' Etienne reasoned.

'I know,' Hugo sighed.

Baptiste jumped to his feet. 'Well, it's almost 20H00, and I'm famished. What say we go and have supper?'

'You two go,' Hugo replied. 'I think I'd like to stay here. I'm not very hungry. I'll call Ben and then I'll turn in.'

Baptiste moved towards him. He touched Hugo's cheek. 'You look tired, Papa? Are you okay?'

Hugo smiled gratefully at him. He had never quite become used to people caring about him. As odd as it felt for him, the truth was, he had finally begun to enjoy having people around who cared about him. He ruffled Baptiste's hair, pushing the long quiff over the back of his head. 'Merci, fils, mais I'm okay. I just need to lie down. I don't believe I'll sleep, but I need to think because I hope if I am in silence I may just see what it is I'm missing.'

'You're sure?' Etienne asked.

Hugo nodded. 'Oui. Let's hope tomorrow brings us something we need. Clarity.'

Baptiste kissed the top of his head. 'If there's anyone who can figure this out, it's you, Papa.'

Hugo watched as they made their way from the room and flopped onto the bed. He closed his eyes.

quarante-deux

Dax Chastain threw a beer can into the water, roaring as it briefly bounced like a pebble before sinking. He thumped Guy Fallon on the back, waking him from a slumber. Night had descended on Beaufort-Sur-Mer and the twinkling rope lights lining the boulevard were swaying in the gentle night breeze, casting an eerie shadow over the harbour.

'Hey, welcome back!' Dax said cheerfully. 'How you doing?'

Guy stared at him, eyes crinkled in confusion. It appeared to take him a while to realise who was talking to him. 'I didn't even bother taking the boat out today,' he muttered, the slur of alcohol clear in his tone. 'I figured, what was the point? I mean, what the hell's the point in anything?'

Dax nodded and ripped open two beers, handing one to the fisherman. 'Aint that the truth.'

The two men sat in silence. Dax glanced over his shoulder, his attention drawn to a trio of drunken tourists stumbling from the bar towards the hotel. He smiled wistfully. 'That should be us,' he mumbled. 'That should be *all* of us,' he added. 'How the hell did this all get so fucked up?'

Guy nodded. He ran his hand across his chin and muttered something incoherent. 'Do you remember the time when…' he began before trailing off.

'Remember what?' Dax asked.

Guy shrugged. 'It doesn't matter. It could be anything. There are so many things to remember. So many times. So many…' he trailed off again.

Dax turned to him. 'What are we going to do?'

Guy moved his head slowly, slugging on his beer. 'About what?'

Dax shook his head. 'Not about. What are we going to do? What are we going to do without Vincent, without Gregoire, without,' he paused, lowering his voice, 'Clem?'

Guy finished his beer. 'How the hell am I supposed to know? We move on. What the hell else can we do?' He lowered his head. 'Désolé, that came out harsher than I intended.' He sucked the night air into his lungs and then pushed it out with a weary sigh.

'I'm not sure I can stay here,' Dax said.

Guy looked at him, surprised. 'What are you talking about?'

Dax shrugged. He was staring into the sea and, after a moment, he wiped his eyes with the back of his sleeve. 'There are too many ghosts here, don't you think?'

Guy gave him a puzzled look. 'I didn't finish school, kid, I have no idea what you're talking about.'

Dax stared at him. 'You know exactly what I'm talking about. I feel as if my life is sitting here, getting drunk and missing everyone, then it's going to be a pretty boring one. I'd rather try my luck elsewhere.'

'You can't leave!' Guy cried. 'Neither of us can!'

Dax shook his head. 'Why not? What the hell do we have to stay here for? It used to be fun, but now, well, how can it be fun again?'

Guy shrugged. 'We can't leave,' he repeated. 'Because they're still here. We'd be deserting them if we left.'

Dax snorted. 'You're wasted, idiot, but more importantly, you're talking crap.'

He shrugged again. 'Whatever,' he murmured. 'But it's true. We can't leave, for their sake's and ours.'

'Hey, guys!' Baptiste appeared at the top of the harbour. 'Can I join you?' he asked, clearly unsure what he had just interrupted.

'Sure,' Guy answered cheerfully. 'We have beers.'

Baptiste skipped cheerfully down the cobbled walkway. He reached out and took a beer from Guy. 'Merci.' He sat down between them, dangling his feet over the harbour wall. 'Can I ask a stupid question?' he asked with a faint smile.

'Non,' Guy and Dax answered in unison and then both laughed.

Baptiste sipped the beer. 'Can I make an observation then? Life is shit.'

Dax snorted. 'No disagreements here,' he laughed.

'And just when you don't think it can get any better,' Baptiste continued, 'it does.'

'At this moment, that's pretty hard to believe,' Dax hissed. 'And what the hell would you know about it anyway, with your perfect little life.'

Baptiste nodded. There was a flash of hurt on his face, but it passed quickly as if he realised where Dax's anger was coming from 'Yeah, it is pretty perfect,' he agreed. 'I have two fathers who seem to think the world of me. Dieu knows why. I seem to have walked into an amazing career. I literally pinch myself every day, because the truth is, my life wasn't always this great.' He gulped. 'There were times I thought I was done, finished, washed up when I was still a teenager. I had no one, and I had nothing, and then I had something... *someone*, and I thought, *wow, maybe it's not over for me*, and then... and then it was over, and it felt like I was back at square one, and it all felt so hopeless again.'

'What's your point, kid?' Guy snapped.

Baptiste smiled. 'My point is. One day I smiled again, and it wasn't the fake sort of smile we get used to putting on our faces to stop idiot people from asking how we are. It was real.'

Dax frowned. 'You're saying you got over what happened to you?'

Baptiste considered. 'I wouldn't say got over, exactly, more than I realised I wasn't going to be hurt and sad forever, that I *could*, or rather, I *would* move on.' He laughed. 'And that pissed me off even more, because I didn't really want to move on. Part of me still doesn't. But I have, and you will too. You'll probably remember what you've lost for the rest of your life, but at some point, you'll be able to remember it with a smile. A happy memory which will make the sadness seem just a little bit more bearable.'

Dax nodded. 'I hope you're right,' he said. 'Mais, I'm not sure if I can move on, not until I know what happened.'

'And why they had to fucking die?' Guy added.

'Je comprends,' Baptiste replied. 'That's all Vincent wanted, too. He wanted to understand.'

'I hate him,' Dax spat, before adding, 'for what he did.'

Baptiste lowered his head. 'I wish I'd understood how much trouble he was in,' he said. 'I have to live with that. He wanted answers, and I want to get them for him, but the longer this goes on, the more I see, I'm just not sure that's going to be possible. And that pisses me off because it means his death was for nothing. There were no answers which would have satisfied him. I should have tried harder to make sure he understood that.'

Guy agreed. 'I get you. None of this makes sense. I can't for a second imagine who would murder Gregoire or Clementine.'

'We're leaving on Sunday,' Baptiste stated. 'And I hate going home without knowing what happened.' He turned to the two men. 'Isn't there anything you can think of that might help finish this once and for all?'

Dax shrugged. 'Don't you think I would speak up if I knew what happened? Gregoire was a friend, and the worst part is, it was like he was finally getting a chance to break away from his damn father, and then this happened.'

Baptiste pulled himself straight. 'What do you mean by that?'

Dax shrugged again. 'Nothing, really. Just on the night he died, he told me he was finally getting out of this shit hole.'

'I didn't know that,' Guy Fallon interrupted.

'We've all said it dozens of times,' Dax reasoned. 'Usually when we're drunk or stoned, so I guess I didn't pay a lot of attention. Not until he was dead, and I was like, *see what wishful thinking gets ya?* He snorted, beer spilling down his chin.

'What did he say exactly?' Baptiste pressed.

'Who knows? More of the same old bullshit, that's all,' Dax replied. He frowned. 'Pourquoi? What does it matter now? He's gone, and it's done with. Like you said, time to move on. It's finished.'

'Maybe it isn't,' Baptiste conceded. He frowned. 'It's just the timing seems a little odd, non?'

Dax thought about it. 'Dunno.'

They lapsed into silence.

'Does it really matter?' Dax asked again.

'I don't know,' Baptiste answered. 'It just might. At the very least, Hugo should know. Can't you remember anything else?'

Dax balled up his fist and smacked against the side of his head. 'You were all there. It was the night he died when we were up at the fort.'

'I don't remember him saying that,' Baptiste stated.

Guy shook his head. 'Nor do I.'

'Are you sure?' Baptiste pushed.

Dax frowned. 'Yeah, I think so. We were getting a drink, and he wrapped his arm around me and gave me a kiss on the cheek. I remember thinking, wow, that's pretty forward. I asked him what was going on. I don't even remember what he said, really. We were all pretty wasted by then. I guess it was just a throwaway comment, something like, *I'll be out of here soon, once and for all, and I'll never look back. I hope you get the chance too.* I laughed and reminded him we all said the same thing all the time, but not of us actually had the balls, or the cash to do it. He laughed and said something weird. I can't remember, but it was something like, *I'll have everything I need soon.*'

'Everything I need soon?' Baptiste repeated.

Dax nodded. 'Yeah, something like that.' He narrowed his eyes. 'Is it important?'

Baptiste mulled it over. 'I just don't know, but I will mention it to Hugo.' He looked between the two men. 'Do you have any idea what he could have meant?'

'I suppose I thought he meant he was just going off somewhere with the boy he'd been hooking up with,' Dax answered.

Guy shrugged. 'It sounds like a stupid dream to me.'

'That's what I thought,' Dax said. 'And I suppose why I didn't think it mattered. We all said the same thing all the time. That's why we hated Vincent.' He gulped. 'Not hated, I mean, just that we were jealous he was the one who actually made it out of here. Gregoire said it, but I don't think he meant it.'

'Or he could have had a plan,' Baptiste mused.

'I had a plan to run off with an heiress once,' Dax replied. 'She said she would marry me and that her daddy would have to accept me because she'd say she was pregnant.'

'What happened?' Baptiste asked.

Dax shrugged. 'She woke up and told me to get my spotty ass out of her bed.' He laughed. 'Another beer?'

Baptiste looked at his watch. It was late. He wondered if he should disturb Hugo, but remembered Hugo had said he was going to turn in to try to make sense of what had happened. *Let him sleep,* he reasoned. He was sure it was not important and it could wait until the following morning. He smiled. 'Yeah, I'll have another beer.'

quarante-trois

Hugo had left the doors to the veranda open, pulling only the thin drapes across the windows. As he lay in the bed, cradling his cell phone, which was still warm from a lengthy conversation with Ben, the gently swaying drapes captivated him. They pushed the cool breeze across the room towards him as he lay on the bed.

He knew sleep would not be forthcoming, so he reached for a cigarette. Talking with Ben had soothed him, but it had not been enough to clear the fog in his brain. Ben's advice had been succinct. *Close your eyes and let your mind wander.* Hugo had joked he sounded like a cheap shrink. They had laughed together, and Hugo felt the pang of loneliness he was still unaccustomed to. In the past, such a feeling would have terrified him, but now he knew it meant there was something to return to. A life to belong to.

He allowed the cigarette smoke to lift gently towards the ceiling and he was reminded again he should not be smoking indoors. He climbed out of the bed and pulled on a robe, padding slowly onto the veranda. He reached over the ledge, peering down into the still bustling boulevard.

All signs of life were present. He watched a pair of young lovers who had stopped in front of one of the lampposts, entwined in an embrace. He hoped their lives were good, and not filled with the darkness which inhabited the lives of most of the people he met in his life.

At that moment, he wondered what it would be to live such a life, and it saddened him that he probably never would. He had decided to follow a certain path in life, and it was not one he had regretted. He imagined if he could help people in their darkest moments, then there was always an incentive to keep going. He stubbed out the cigarette and closed his eyes.

Hugo awoke with a start, jumping to his feet. His eyes darted around the darkened room, fixing on the shadows and slithers of light slicing through the gently swaying drapes.

He hurried across the room, panicked. He was unsure where he was, and it felt as if it was restricting his breathing. He yanked back the drapes and threw himself onto the veranda, desperately sucking in the air. His eyes slowly came into focus, and as they did, he felt his breathing regulating. The water lapping against the harbour was enough to bring him back. He remembered.

He sunk into a chair and lit a cigarette. His mind was clearing, and he was beginning to remember where he was and what he was doing. He was not sure how long he had been asleep, but he could hear no one below on the boulevard, so he imagined it was the middle of the night. He did not remember falling asleep, indeed he had grown bored and weary of staring at the shadows of a strange room, in a strange environment. The shadows told him no secrets and pointed him in no obvious direction.

And then he had opened his eyes, and he was no longer in the hotel room. He was standing again next to the swimming pool in Montgenoux. Vincent Roche was staring at him from the bottom of the pool, his left arm extended, drifting in the water, his hand gesturing to his right. Hugo knew he could not be pointing at anything. Vincent Roche was dead. His time for passing on secrets and clues had passed. Hugo moved slowly, his legs felt leaden. He kicked a red towel and frowned, picking it up and placing it on one of the benches which lined the auditorium.

And then he was gone. This time, he was creeping along the boulevard in Beaufort-Sur-Mer. He realised he was heading towards Clementine Bonheur's studio. He stopped and pushed open the door. It was just as he remembered it, but at that moment everything looked larger and brighter, as if floodlights had been placed around the room. He squinted, but he could not see them. Instead, he concentrated on what was around him. There was a vibrancy to the studio he did not remember from before, and the colours seemed to be much more intense.

He moved towards the hideous portrait, forcing himself to stare at the macabre painting. The slashes of red and the scratches on the canvas were as he remembered them. At that moment, he became aware and realised it was his subconscious telling him he had missed something. But in the end, he saw nothing, and felt nothing other than the sadness he had felt when he had first walked into Clementine's studio.

Moments later, he was in the water, being pulled down towards Arthur Roche's boat. He could barely see it. Everything around him was red, pulling him deeper and deeper. He felt as if he could not breathe and he began gasping for air and then…

Hugo opened his eyes again, wincing with pain. The cigarette had burnt down to his fingers. He shook his hand and lit another cigarette, hoping it would calm him. He took his time, inhaling and exhaling slowly. It troubled him that he had been so lost in his thoughts. It was unusual for him, and he imagined it was because he was alone in a strange environment. An environment filled with strangers whose motives he did not understand.

In Montgenoux, it had always seemed easier, because he knew there was someone always next to him. Not just Ben, but the team who had surrounded him and formed a team with him. It comforted him that at least Baptiste and Etienne were with him in Beaufort-Sur-Mer, but it was not the same.

He tried to clear his mind and focus on what he had seen in his dreams. But in the end, he was not sure it was anything at all, other than a tired, troubled mind filled with sadness and desperation. He closed his eyes and waited to see if sleep and realisation might finally come to him.

quarante-quatre

Etienne and Baptiste shared a concerned look over the breakfast table. Hugo was opposite them, staring at his feet. Baptiste elbowed Etienne, gesturing for him to speak.

'Are you okay, Hugo?' Etienne asked finally.

Hugo lifted his head slowly, his mouth twisting into a smile when he saw the concerned looks on their faces. 'Oui. I'm fine,' he answered. 'Don't worry. It's just I didn't sleep very well,' he paused, 'or you might say I slept well, but not comfortably.'

Baptiste frowned. 'Well, that explains it,' he laughed. 'Mais, you're okay?'

Hugo nodded. 'Oui, I am.'

'Did it help?' Baptiste wondered.

Hugo considered his answer. He glanced around. They were in the hotel breakfast room, and other than a foreign couple in the far corner, they were alone. He looked at his plate of eggs. They looked appetising, but he was not in the mood to eat. 'There's so much about what has happened here which makes no sense, so it's not surprising I'm having trouble piecing it all together.'

'What about it is bothering you the most?' Etienne asked. 'Try separating all the facts, rather than thinking they have to be connected. Imagine they're not, and then see where it leads you.'

Hugo laughed. 'You've been hanging around me too much! But I think you're probably right. It makes little sense because we're trying to connect too many things. Some which have no business being put together, and because of that, it is confusing everything else. This began with a suicide, and then another. And then two murders. All seemingly separated by periods of time, reasons.' He stopped. 'We have believed everything is connected and yet...' he shrugged again, 'there is no real proof *anything* is connected.'

'Then none of it makes sense!' Baptiste whined.

Hugo nodded. 'Oh, I agree,' He smiled. 'Or perhaps it is all making sense if we just look at it from a different angle. I mean, isn't that what we do? Find the possible in the impossible?' He turned to Etienne. 'Have you turned up anything else?'

Etienne shook his head. 'I'm afraid not,' he answered glumly. 'I'm waiting on a phone call from a buddy in the North about some missing records, but I wouldn't hold out on that being your smoking gun.'

Baptiste cleared his throat. 'I spoke with Dax and Guy last night,' he said. 'And this might mean nothing too, but Dax mentioned Gregoire said he was going to leave Beaufort-Sur-Mer like he'd come into money or something.'

Hugo's eyes widened. 'Why didn't they mention this earlier?' he snapped.

Baptiste shrugged. 'I don't know, I think they just thought he was going off with the boy he'd met.' He stared at Hugo. 'He said he didn't think too much about it because they've all been saying the same thing for years.' He shrugged. 'I used to say the same thing myself, I never meant it, it was just a foolish dream.' His mouth twisted. 'At least Gregoire had a dream of getting away. When you're in that dark place, hope is so important, trust me.'

Hugo nodded. 'Oui, je sais.' He moved the fork slowly across the plate.

'What is it, Papa?' Baptiste asked. 'Is it important?'

'I don't know, but it just might be,' Hugo replied. 'Because it reminds me of something else.' He dropped the fork, his face tightening. He opened his mouth as if he was about to speak, but he stopped, his attention diverted by the door to the breakfast room opening. Avril Roche entered. Her face extended into a tired smile when she saw them, and she moved across the room. Hugo noticed her face was pale and drawn, and she seemed to have aged in the short time since they had met. She walked slowly, and it was as if it caused her pain to move.

'Ah, good, you're here,' she blurted. 'I called your room, but there was no answer.'

Hugo rose to her feet. 'What can I help you with, Madame?'

Avril's eyes flicked over Etienne. Her mouth twitched as if she was having trouble placing him.

'May I present my colleague from Montgenoux?' he said quickly. 'This is Etienne Martine.'

Etienne stood and extended his hand. 'Enchanté, Madame,' he said. 'I'm sorry for your loss.'

Her eyes bore into his. She did not take his hand. 'Have we met before, Monsieur Martine?'

Etienne shook his head. 'Non, I don't believe so,' he answered.

Hugo cleared his throat, keen to direct her attention away from Etienne. 'You said you were trying to get in touch with me, Madame?'

She spun around. 'Oui. I wanted to talk to you about something.' She paused. 'I know you'll think it's inappropriate, but we're having a small memorial for Clementine this evening by the fort,' she stated. 'The timing is wrong, and under the circumstances, it is perhaps in poor taste, but in a town such as Beaufort-Sur-Mer, we have to act differently. We have to honour our citizens. It is expected.'

Hugo nodded. 'I understand. People need to do something at times such as these. It is normal.'

'Normal,' she sniffed. 'Let me tell you, she would have hated any kind of fuss, but it is what it is. She spent a lot of time at the fort, so I think she would forgive me for organising this on her behalf.'

She blew her nose. 'I know you're leaving tomorrow. That's why I have arranged it for this evening. I know it is not necessarily something which you would wish to attend, but after everything that has happened, and after everything we've been through, I really would appreciate it if you all came along.' She smiled at Baptiste. 'I know it's silly of me, but you all knew Vincent before he died. It would feel as if he was there somehow. And that matters.'

Hugo nodded again. 'Bien sûr, it does. And we'll be there.'

'Merci,' Avril replied. 'Well, if you'll excuse me, I must go. Our housekeeper is sick, and I'm afraid we're running out of towels and tablecloths.' She sighed. 'The mundaneness of daily life goes on, no matter what, doesn't it?' She smiled. 'I suppose it's a good thing. We must keep busy, or rather, we must appear to keep busy to keep ourselves occupied. I find people are uncomfortable viewing you if they think you are wallowing. Au revoir, Messieurs.'

Hugo watched as she left and sank back into his chair. With Clementine Bonheur gone, he desperately hoped Avril Roche would find someone to confide in and to share her time with. He turned his head. Avril had moved to the corner of the room and was struggling with a trolley laden with linen. One of the wheels was broken, twisting awkwardly as she tried to drag it out of the restaurant. He gasped.

'Are you okay, Papa?' Baptiste asked, touching his arm. 'You look like you've seen a ghost.'

Hugo stared blankly at him. A myriad of thoughts pressing against his skull. 'Etienne, I need you to double-check on someone for me, and then can you come with me to the forensic lab?'

'Sure,' Etienne replied. 'What's happened?'

Hugo's mouth twisted. 'I'm honestly not sure,' he responded. 'And it makes no sense, but I would just like to check something out and we can't wait for them to get to it. Not if we want to understand what happened here.'

Baptiste smiled. 'You've figured it out, haven't you?'

Hugo shook his head. 'Something has become clear,' he answered. 'But I hope it isn't what I think it is.'

quarante-cinq

The forensic technician opened the door to the lab and gestured for Hugo and Etienne to follow him. Hugo recognised the weariness of a public servant who was overworked and underpaid. He also imagined the intrusion of a pair of outsiders severely irritated him.

'What's your name?' Etienne asked.

'Martin,' the technician answered. His tone was surly and clear. *I hate you both.*

'I thought I recognised you,' Etienne retorted. His own tone was soothing. 'You attended the forensic anthropology seminar in Bordeaux last year, didn't you? I was one of the lecturers. I remember you clearly, because I thought you were one of the best students in the class. Certainly the one with the most brains and the most intelligent questions.'

Despite himself, a broad smile appeared on Martin's face. 'You really remember me?'

Etienne smiled. 'In a sea of faces of men and women who are only there for the free food and drink and the recreational hookups they might get away with, you tend to notice the ones who are actually interested in what you have to say. Your report was outstanding as well.'

Hugo stole a sideways look at Etienne. *You're good.* If he was lying, he was doing an excellent job of it, because the forensic technician was visibly thawing in front of them.

'You're here about Clementine Bonheur, right? I don't know what to tell you,' Martin said, moving across the room, 'other than I personally oversaw the examination of the deceased's studio. We missed *nothing*.'

'We aren't suggesting otherwise,' Etienne replied. 'I don't believe for a second you missed anything. Anything obvious, at least,' he added.

Martin raised an eyebrow. 'What do you mean?'

Etienne moved across the room. He stopped in front of a large canvas covered by a forensic bag. 'Can I remove this?' he asked Martin politely.

'Sure,' Martin replied. 'I've finished with it.'

Etienne carefully removed the covering, revealing the bloody portrait of Clementine Bonheur. Hugo moved to his side.

'The work of some sicko, huh?' Martin asked.

'You can say that again,' Etienne agreed. He leaned in closer to the canvas, his eyes moving slowly around it. He turned to Hugo. 'I think you're right.'

Martin looked between them. 'Right about what?'

Etienne gestured for Martin to approach. He pointed at the canvas and traced his finger around it. 'Tell me what you see - here, here and here, between the gaps where the murderer used the deceased's blood to paint.'

Martin bent forward. 'Scratches on the canvas?'

'That's what I thought at first as well,' Hugo interjected.

Martin looked surprised. 'And you don't now?'

'Dammit, you're right, Hugo,' Etienne sighed. He was peering at the canvas. 'There's a pencil drawing underneath the blood.'

'A pencil drawing?' Martin questioned.

'Oui,' Etienne nodded. 'If you follow the pattern, you can see the portrait in blood has been painted over what I imagine was a guide sketch in pencil underneath.'

Martin scratched his head. 'Maybe, but so what? What does that have to do with anything?'

'Peut être, nothing,' Hugo conceded, 'or maybe everything. You see, from the very beginning, I never understood the reason for the painting. It made no sense, whatsoever.'

'Psychopaths rarely make sense,' Martin reasoned.

'I agree,' Hugo replied. 'The point is - he took time to pose

le bateau au fond de l'océan

the body of Clementine Bonheur and then paint it. Time he most likely didn't have, because he risked being discovered at any moment.'

'Then why do it?' Martin asked.

'The only reason I can think of is that for some reason he had no choice,' Hugo continued. 'It could have been a compulsion, a part of the fantasy perhaps, or it could have been because it somehow incriminated him.'

'You're talking about the pencil drawing underneath?' Martin stared at the canvas. 'Even if it is a drawing, why not just take the canvas with him?'

Hugo took a deep breath. 'At this point, it's all supposition, but I would imagine he couldn't risk removing such a large canvas and taking it with him. For one thing, he risked being seen with it, but if he wasn't seen - where would he dispose of it in such a way that it wouldn't be discovered? Non, if there was something about the canvas, he may have done what he had to do to cover it up.'

Etienne tapped his chin. 'Then why not just destroy it?'

Hugo shrugged. 'For the same reason. If he slashed it, then he could have drawn attention to it, and we may have tried to put it back together. He could have tried burning it, I suppose, but again, he may have attracted undue attention to himself and prevented his escape, or risk being seen. I know at this point, I'm only guessing. But it seems to me, by painting over the canvas, he assumed we would be so appalled by it, we wouldn't even think of looking UNDER the blood.'

Etienne smiled. 'And he'd probably be right. Most people would ignore a few pencil marks.'

'We did,' Martin added.

'I don't blame you,' Hugo mumbled, 'and I'm still not saying there's anything to it, but at the very least, I would like to rule it out.' He turned to Etienne and Martin. 'So. You two are the experts. How do we see what's underneath?'

Etienne turned to Martin. 'Well, what do you think? We covered this in the 09H00 lecture. Most people were hungover and probably paid no attention. But, I'm sure you did.'

Martin pressed his hand against his chin. 'Well, we could try to remove the top layer of blood,' he stated.

'But wouldn't that damage, if not also remove whatever is underneath?' Hugo asked.

'It's possible,' Etienne replied.

Hugo sighed. 'Then there's nothing we can do?'

Etienne smiled again. 'I didn't say that,' he answered cheerfully. 'Martin, do you have an infrared light?'

Martin nodded and pointed to an anteroom. 'Ah, you're thinking of infrared reflectography?'

'Infrared reflectography?' Hugo repeated.

'Basically, normal light in our visual range isn't powerful enough,' Etienne began, 'but infrared light can penetrate the layers of pigments. To put it succinctly, we used infrared light and reflect it into a specially designed camera. When it reaches an artwork's underdrawings, we should, in theory, see an image of what is below the top layer.'

'And you have the equipment?' Hugo asked Martin.

Martin smiled. 'Oui.'

Etienne smiled and turned to Hugo. 'Give us an hour, and we might just have something for you.'

Hugo flicked on his glasses, narrowing his eyes to see the grainy image which had appeared on the computer monitor.

'I'm sorry it's not clearer,' Etienne sighed. 'Mais, it appears it was only a rough pencil sketch.'

'She was painting her murderer,' Hugo whispered. He shook his head. He felt sick. 'That's how he got close to her. That's how he had the opportunity to do what he did.'

'Then you know who it is?' Martin asked, staring at the image.

Hugo took a step closer to the screen. 'I can't be one hundred percent sure,' he pondered. 'And it makes little sense. But, I think it is him.'

Etienne moved next to him. 'I can't be sure, either, and I've seen him.'

'Then I doubt you'd be able to use this in court,' Martin stated.

Etienne chuckled. 'That's never stopped us before.'

'And hopefully, it becomes redundant,' Hugo added. 'Once we confront someone, it tends to have a snowball effect. One set of circumstances leads to another. We need to find more on him if we're ever going to understand why he did this.'

Etienne nodded. 'What are you looking for?'

Hugo shrugged. 'A wise man, *i.e. you*, once told me there is no such thing as a person being able to keep this kind of secret. There is *always* something. There is always a tell.'

'That's just my suspicious mind,' Etienne retorted. 'Mais, you're right. There must be something I've missed.'

Hugo glanced at his watch. 'We have an hour until Clementine Bonheur's memorial service.'

Etienne gulped. 'You want to do it then? We don't actually have any actual evidence yet.'

Hugo shrugged. 'I don't think we have a choice. I don't want to risk him getting away, or even worse, doing something else. He is very dangerous, and I can't risk him hurting anyone else.' He moved towards the door. 'Find what you can, Etienne, because you're right, we don't have very much, and I have a feeling he will not go down without a fight.'

quarante-six

Hugo was overwhelmed as he approached the top of the steps leading to the old ruined fort. He stopped and steadied himself on the handrail, Baptiste and Etienne appearing by his side.

Together they climbed in silence the remainder of the steps. Two enormous bonfires, either side of the fort were burning, and they had lined the crumbled walls of the fort with Clementine Bonheur's paintings, and in the centre, was a lifesize painting of her. Hugo stopped again and moved across the clearing to the painting. His jaw flexed as he wrestled with an emotion. He did not notice Avril Roche appearing by his side.

'It's a self-portrait,' she whispered.

Hugo nodded. 'It's very beautiful. Mademoiselle Bonheur was extremity talented.'

Avril nodded. 'She never believed in herself, the silly woman. Do you know she hated this painting? She called it the height of self-indulgence. She only did it because a lover asked her to do it for him. When she finished it, she was so embarrassed she covered it up and hid it in the back of her closet.'

Hugo studied the portrait in disbelief. He was not sure he had seen anything like it. It was almost a photograph, but the eyes were dark and sparkled as if they were inviting the watcher into a secret world. 'What a waste,' he said.

'She couldn't destroy it, of course,' Avril continued, 'then nor could she bear to look at it.' She laughed. 'Clementine once told me she felt as if it was some kind of modern Dorian Gray. She said she was terrified of looking at it again in case she had grown withered and aged, and no man would want her.'

Hugo shook his head. 'I'm not sure I've seen anyone look more beautiful.' He paused. 'Or free.'

'Free?' Avril questioned.

Hugo's cheeks flushed. 'Désolé, I sound foolish. I know

nothing about art.'

'On the contrary,' she retorted. 'I think you have quite the eye. What did you mean by free?'

He shrugged. He pointed at the portrait. Clementine Bonheur was standing straight, her gaze fixed firmly on the viewer, a hip jutting defiantly, one hand pressed on it, the other to her side, the fingers stretched. The eyes and the mouth belied a playfulness. He could not explain it, but to him, the woman in the painting appeared as if she was free of all burdens and restraints.

'I'm not sure I believe in an afterlife, but if there is one, I imagine that is what it looks like. We're free from whatever chained us in this life,' he offered.

Avril touched his arm. 'How lovely. And merci. Jasper told me I shouldn't put it out, but I wanted her here with us tonight, watching over us. I know it sounds stupid, but I wanted her to see us all here to pay our respects to her.' She took a deep breath. 'Merci, for making me think I made the right decision. I find I doubt myself more and more these days. This night must be just right.'

Hugo lowered his head, blond hair falling over his face. Now he felt even more guilty for what he was about to do. It seemed inappropriate to spoil Clementine's memorial.

Avril stared at him. 'What is it? You look upset?'

Hugo did not respond.

Avril pressed her hand into his, squeezing with such intensity it caused him to wince. 'You know what happened to her, don't you?'

Hugo turned his head slowly. 'I believe I have an idea.'

'Then why aren't you arresting her murderer?'

'I intend to, but there is a lot I don't understand. I need to be sure. Under these circumstances, it is always difficult to proceed. Proof is not always as easy to find as understanding. Once we understand, we must press for proof.'

'Then you understand?'

'Oui,' he replied.

She nodded. 'Then be sure and end this, for Clementine now.' Her face tightened. 'And the timing is perfect.' She pointed again at the portrait. 'And she is here to watch over us all. There has been so much loss, there has to be an end, and I would be grateful if the end is now.'

Hugo stared at her. 'No matter the consequences?'

Avril threw back her head and cackled. 'Be damned the consequences. Be damned us all who deserve it.'

quarante-sept

Hugo moved slowly around the fort. He knew it was important that he focused on what he needed to say because there was so much he still did not understand.

Before they had left the hotel, Etienne had filled him in with what Hugo hoped was the last piece of the puzzle. But it had not helped. It had only produced more questions than it answered. More importantly, it had shown him the gravity of the situation, and just because he did not understand exactly what had happened and why, it did not alter the fact he realised he was dealing with someone who was immensely dangerous.

He spotted Baptiste and Etienne by the makeshift bar and approached them. Etienne handed him a drink, giving him a quick nod. Hugo recognised it because it was a clear message of intent. *You have this, and I have your back.* Hugo sipped the drink, allowing the alcohol to swim over him. He did not want it to affect him, but at that moment, he needed something to steady his nerves. A series of grievous crimes had been committed, and he needed to be ready to bring the perpetrator to justice.

Avril Roche moved into the clearing. The flames of the fire illuminated her, grey strands of hair drifting in the breeze behind her. She smacked her hand against the side of her wine glass. 'Bonsoir, mes amis,' she shouted above the mumblings of disparate conversations.

'I want to thank you all for coming tonight. It isn't an easy time for me, or for any of us. When I was ten years old, I lost my father. At his funeral, I was perplexed by all the people, many I'd never seen before, who were so obviously distressed by his death. I asked my mother why all these strangers were as sad as we were about losing Papa? And she turned to me and told me that loss is not measured in proximity, more by the effect a person has had on other people's lives. She pointed to all the people at the funeral and said, *see, your father touched all these people and they are very, very sad to lose him. It's a different loss to the one you and I feel, but it's a loss we should not measure, but rather share. It is not a competition.*'

Avril turned slowly around the fort. 'And seeing you all you here, I am reminded of just that. It has taken me back to that time. To that funeral. To that loss.' She lowered her head. 'And, of course, to all the losses which have followed.'

She smiled at the people in front of her. 'We have all lost so much. Friends. Lovers. Sons. It is both unbearable and incomprehensible. Dax, Guy. You were friends to my son, to my husband, and Clementine. You loved them as family.'

Guy Fallon threw his arm over Dax's shoulder and pulled him close to him.

Avril extended her hands towards Captain Franc Comtois. He was standing at the back of the group, Dr. Oppert next to him, both of their faces stoic, as if they wished to be anywhere other than where they were now. 'And dear Franc,' Avril continued. 'Someone who can understand the loss of a son as very few of us can. Someone who, by now, also understands the unnecessary platitudes which do little to ease what we have lost.'

Captain Comtois stared at her but said nothing. His nostrils twitched as if he was stifling a sneeze.

Avril turned to the others. Hugo was standing in a line with Baptiste, Etienne, Brigitte St. Pierre and Quentin Arquette. 'And then we have the strangers to Beaufort-Sur-Mer. But these strangers brought my son home, and for that, I will be eternally grateful to them.'

Jasper Connor stood and made his way towards her. 'That's very nice, cherie, mais tonight is a night of celebration. It is what Clementine would have wanted…'

Avril raised her hand to stop him. 'Mais, rien. You knew Clementine for but a second. I knew her for all of my life, and I let her down. I let them all down.' She gestured to Hugo. 'Captain

Duchamp is going to talk to us now, and he is going to find a way for this to be over.' She noticed Hugo's impassive face and smiled. 'He doesn't know it yet, but I'm sure he is.'

Hugo moved toward the centre of the clearing. He stopped in front of Clementine Bonheur's portrait and raised his hand, moving it around the edge without touching it. 'Merci, Madame Roche.' He turned to face everyone who had gathered. 'A few moments earlier, I had thought tonight was the wrong time to do this, but in reflection, and after hearing what Madame Roche said, I realise it can only be the right time. Lives have been lost and lives have been destroyed and we must address it, and it must be addressed now. There can be no more hiding, for anyone.'

'I hope you will not do, or say something foolish, Captain Duchamp,' Jasper Connor snapped, the warning clear in his tone.

Hugo's mouth twisted into a smile. 'Probably. Mais, I believe we will leave here tonight understanding why three people died unnecessarily.'

'Three?' Jasper asked, his voice rising to a piercing tone.

Hugo nodded. 'Oui. I believe so. I believe two people died as a result of a person who sought to use a suicide as a cover for their own despicable motivates and urges.'

'You're not making any sense,' Jasper snapped.

Baptiste leaned forward. 'He's about to, so shut up, you arrogant prick.'

quarante-huit

'This all began with the suicide of Arthur Roche,' Hugo began, before adding, 'or so I thought.'

'What do you mean?' Avril asked. 'Of course, this began with Arthur. How else could it have started?'

Hugo moved away from the self-portrait of Clementine Bonheur. He turned back to face her. 'Your son, Vincent, was troubled by the loss of his father. I believe in his grief, he imagined a dozen different scenarios as to how his father died. It's not unusual. We'd all do the same, I would imagine.'

'He killed himself because of what I did,' she snapped. She stole a look around her. 'Everyone knows it, just few are prepared to admit it to my face.' She stared at the portrait. 'Apart from Clementine. She knew what she had done and owned it in a way which shamed me into owning my own despicable behaviour.'

Hugo took a breath. 'Your son was heartbroken by what happened here in Beaufort-Sur-Mer,' he continued. 'I don't imagine it was just about you, or your husband, or what happened between you. He was troubled because he didn't understand what could have driven his father to do something so drastic, and so final.'

'Arthur was a sore loser,' Jasper Connor spat. 'That's all.'

Avril Roche glared at him. 'Non, he wasn't. He was a good man who just lost his way.' She threw back her head and laughed. 'And that was the very reason our marriage ended. I thought he lost his way, and I betrayed him because of it.' She pressed her hands against her chest. 'And then I turned around and did exactly the same thing, only worse. Because I wasn't like him. I knew the difference.'

Jasper raised his glass and shook it from side to side. 'Cherie, I suspect the wine is a little strong for you, and mixing it with your grief, you're just not making a lot of sense. Mais, understand, we are all here for you. We're all here to save you.'

Her nostrils flared. 'I don't need saving. I can't be saved, least of all by you.'

'Arthur was a drunk,' Jasper spat.

Avril nodded. 'I know that. And that only makes it worse. But he was still a good man. The alcohol was a mask for the misery of his childhood, and I knew that, and that's why I stayed with him for so long. He had a streak of melancholy which passed on to our son. I left him because I was fed up with being a wife and a mother to them both. That's the truth, and I can finally admit it. I was a selfish bitch who wanted more for herself than cooking and cleaning in a damn hotel which was going down the tubes. Arthur was taken up in his own nonsense, and Vincent…' she stopped, her voice cracking.

'I believed Vincent would go away to school, and that would be that. He'd be gone, and I'd be right where I started. Alone with Arthur with nothing having really changed.' She shook her head. 'I'm a despicable person who thinks only of herself. No wonder everyone hates me. I hate me.'

'No one hates you,' Dax interrupted. He stood and hurried to her. He placed his hand on her shoulder. 'Vincent loved you both, he always did, and for what it's worth, he understood about his Papa.'

She turned to face him. 'He did? He told you that?'

'Sure he did.'

'Many times,' Guy chimed in.

'And he knew he wasn't perfect,' Dax added. 'And I can promise you this. He didn't blame either of you. He was worried, that's all. Right before he went away to school, he said he didn't mind you'd left Arthur. He was sad about it, sure, but he knew it was coming.'

Guy laughed. 'Do you remember what he did?'

'What do you mean?' Dax asked. He scratched his head. 'Oh, yeah, I forgot about that.'

'What happened?' Avril cried.

'He went to Arthur and told him that if he got himself straight and sobered up, then he could win you back,' Dax replied. 'Arthur laughed and said, he didn't stand a chance, and sobering up was not something on the horizon for him, and as far as he was concerned, you deserved a fantastic life, but he knew he wasn't the one to give it to you.' He turned to Jasper. 'And for the record, he said, nor were you.'

Jasper Connor shrugged nonchalantly. Whatever.

'Merci for telling me that,' Avril said softly. 'It means the world. I knew Arthur wasn't a wicked man. And I believe he killed himself because he felt he had no other choice, and after what happened, I can't say I blame him. The only person to blame is me because I should have known what would happen.'

She stopped, her chest was rising and falling with such rapidity, she appeared to be on the verge of a panic attack. She steadied herself on the fort wall, her eyes locking on Clementine Bonheur's self-portrait.

'Are you all right, Madame?' Hugo asked, taking a tentative step towards her.

'Oui. Ça va bien, merci. Or as well as I can be,' she answered.

'You said your son inherited his father's streak of melancholy,' Hugo stated. 'What did you mean by that?'

She shrugged. 'I knew he took his father's death badly. He wanted answers where there were none. I should have helped him more. Mais, I truly didn't believe he would do such a thing,' she continued. 'He was mad at me, with good cause, and I was ashamed, so I wasn't as present for him as I should have been. It was easier to feel his disapproval via his silence, rather than in his tone or the way he looked at me.'

She took a deep breath before emitting a long sigh. 'However, two days before he died, he rang me. One of the last things he said to me was all we had was each other and we would get through it together.' She looked at Hugo desperately. 'And that's why I never imagined for a second he would have killed himself. I knew he was devastated, but I thought he was strong enough to make his way through his grief and to find his way back to me, to us.'

Hugo stole a look at Etienne. He was not sure the truth would make her feel any better, but he knew she needed to hear it. He took a deep breath. 'Madame, there is no easy way of saying this, and I realise it is going to come as a terrible shock to you, but I'm afraid I don't believe your son killed himself.'

Avril's face froze in horror before she screamed and dropped to the ground.

quarante-neuf

Hugo and Jasper Connor pulled Avril Roche to her feet and moved her quickly towards a seat. They lowered her gently. She lifted her head. Her eyes were wild and confused.

'Bring me some water!' Jasper yelled to no one in particular.

Guy Fallon rushed forward and handed over a bottle of water. Jasper placed it to Avril's lips, and she gulped at it, splurging water down her chin. She wiped it away irritably. 'What did you mean by that, Captain Duchamp?' she asked breathlessly.

'That's not important now.' Jasper waved his hand dismissively. 'We need to get you to the hospital, right away.'

'It's the only thing that's important now,' Avril hissed. 'So, get your damn hands off me. I'm not going anywhere until Captain Duchamp explains what the hell he means.' She glared at Hugo. 'Well?'

Hugo stepped away. 'We all know Vincent was deeply troubled by his father's death, and that he was convinced it was not a suicide at all.'

Captain Comtois tutted. 'You keep going on about that, and I'll keep telling you the same thing. Arthur Roche committed suicide. There was no murder, and there was no coverup.'

Hugo nodded. 'I know, and I think you are probably right. But, for whatever reason, Vincent Roche didn't believe it, and I imagine he felt desperate. I can't say whether the idea was his, or someone else's, but I believe Vincent staged an elaborate suicide attempt of his own, in order to draw attention to his father's. I imagine he believed it would get a lot of attention, which would trigger another investigation into his father's death.'

'That sounds rather fanciful, and,' Jasper Connor interrupted, 'rather stupid.'

'Peut être,' Hugo conceded. 'And I can't be certain of all the facts at this moment. But we do know how sad and desperate

Vincent was. He believed you killed his father, Monsieur Connor.'

Jasper clenched his fists. 'I've warned you, I will not take baseless accusations from you, or anyone else for that matter,' he added, shooting an angry glare across the clearing. 'Not anymore. I've had about as much of it as I can stomach…'

'What'll you do, get one of your drug pals to finish us off?' Avril interrupted.

He gasped, staring at her with obvious disbelief. 'Avril!'

She shrugged him off. 'You know it's true.' She stared across the fort, her eyes locking on the two men. 'You brought those people into Beaufort-Sur-Mer and dragged us all into it. I will not keep lying or protecting you. Not now.' She looked at Hugo. 'What does this have to do with my son's death, Captain?'

'Well,' Hugo replied, 'I imagine Arthur told Vincent about something he discovered, something about you Monsieur Connor, and what you had done to corrupt others in this town.' He swallowed and then lit a cigarette. 'And I think that was enough for Vincent to believe his father's suicide was not what it seemed.'

Dr. Oppert toyed with a stray hair on top of his head. 'You suggested that Vincent's suicide attempt was meant to be a what… a cry for help?'

Hugo agreed. 'I believe so. A way to draw attention to what had happened with his father. He was frustrated by what he imagined was a cover-up. Especially because he believed the very people who were telling him his father's death was a suicide were the same people he believed were involved in a drug-smuggling scheme his father had told him about. Under those circumstances, Vincent didn't know who to trust, and in his grief, I think he just needed to talk about it.'

Baptiste took a tentative step towards them. 'He never mentioned this to me, I swear.'

'Je sais,' Hugo replied.

'Captain Duchamp,' Dr. Oppert continued. 'Far be it from

me to cast aspersions on your theory, mais, if what you are suggesting is true, then what on earth went so drastically wrong?'

'Because there was no damn plan,' Jasper interrupted. 'He just killed himself. He was weak like his father.'

Avril stood and raised her hand and slapped him with such force it caused him to fall backwards. 'Don't you ever speak either of their names to me again, you bastard. Not ever.' She turned to face Hugo. 'What are you basing this on, Captain Duchamp?' she asked with clear desperation.

'Several factors,' he replied. He began pacing in front of the ruined fort. 'Beginning with the disappearing red towel.'

'The-disappearing-red-towel,' Jasper spat out the words with incredulity. 'Have you lost your senses, you stupid man?' He looked at Captain Comtois. 'We may have police bordering on the senile here, but they at least live in the real world.' He smiled at Comtois, ignoring the glare he received back. 'What you are suggesting is… fanciful… lunacy…'

Hugo bowed his head. 'I agree, it is a little vague and doesn't really suggest much, but all the same, it troubled me, right from the very beginning.'

'What on earth could a red towel have to do with what happened to Vincent?' Dax Chastain asked.

'It may have nothing to do with it,' Hugo conceded, before adding, 'or it may tell us something.' He lit a cigarette, knowing it would calm him and allow him to continue. 'According to the cleaner, the towel was there, beside the pool when she discovered Vincent, but by the time we got there, it was gone.'

Dax scratched his head. 'Then she made a mistake, obviously.'

Hugo nodded. 'Peut être,' he conceded. 'Or it could suggest something else. If the suicide attempt was staged, then someone else must have been involved, someone who was supposed to jump in and rescue Vincent at the last moment.'

Dax gave him a doubtful look. 'Then why didn't they rescue him?'

'They could have arrived too late,' Hugo reasoned, 'or they could have other reasons for not rescuing him. We'll come back to that shortly.'

'What does the towel have to do with it?' Captain Comtois asked.

'I would imagine he was hiding somewhere nearby, and removed the towel before we arrived,' Hugo replied. 'He may have forgotten it because although he was *supposed* to use it to dry himself off, he never actually meant to use it because he had a completely different idea in mind.'

Comtois shook his head. 'That makes no sense. A stray towel lying next to a swimming pool is hardly likely to cause any suspicion, now is it? Even by your strange scenario, he could just have left it arousing no suspicion of note.'

'You're probably right,' Hugo agreed. 'Unless there was something specific about the towel which might link it to the owner. Whoever was helping Vincent is not likely to have wanted his or her name linked to what happened.'

'And the letters to me and the avocat?' Baptiste interrupted. 'Why would Vincent have done that, if he had no intention of going through with the suicide?'

'It was to make the suicide attempt look authentic,' Hugo replied.

Avril shook her head. 'Then was it an accident? Not a suicide?' she cried. 'I can't believe this.'

Jasper Connor sighed. 'What difference does it make now? Vincent is still dead.'

'It makes all the difference to me,' Avril shot back, 'and the fact it makes no difference to you gives me all the proof I need to know what a terrible, ridiculous mistake I made with you. My son died, and the fact you say it makes no difference to you proves exactly what everyone said about you from the second you moved into this town. You're a pig, and I hate you.'

Hugo gave her a sad look and continued. 'When we arrived here in Beaufort-Sur-Mer, I was dismayed there was no evidence of anything but a suicide in the case of Arthur Roche because it meant his son died in vain. But then everything else went wrong, and we were faced with a seemingly unrelated murder.'

'Seemingly?' Comtois asked sharply. 'You can't be suggesting my son's murder has anything to do with what happened in Montgenoux?'

Hugo sighed. 'I'm afraid that's exactly what I'm suggesting,' he stated.

'Then you're a fool.' He pointed at a smug-looking Jasper Connor, who was sitting with his arms crossed. 'As he said, you've lost your mind!' Comtois exclaimed.

Hugo shrugged. 'Sometimes I feel as if I have. For the longest time, I couldn't imagine there would be a connection, but something about it just didn't feel right. I don't know if you've experienced that sort of gut instinct yourself, Captain Comtois, but over the years, I've learnt to listen to it, and more often than not, that instinct has served me well.'

Comtois did not respond, instead gestured for Hugo to continue.

'The murder of Gregoire appeared to have been triggered by a horrendous attack on Mademoiselle Brigitte St. Pierre,' Hugo continued. He stole a look at her. She had lifted her head and was staring at him defiantly. Baptiste moved to her and placed his hand on her arm.

'Be very careful what you say next, Captain Duchamp,' Comtois hissed with the intent of a clear warning.

Hugo nodded. 'I don't believe your son raped anyone,' he replied. 'Instead, I believe he was tricked into a plan by someone very manipulative.'

'A plan?' Comtois questioned. He was clearly not expecting Hugo to suggest such a thing. 'What sort of plan?'

'The night of his death, Gregoire told his friends he had a plan to get out of Beaufort-Sur-Mer. A plan to be with someone he cared about very much…' Hugo stopped speaking, noticing the concerned look on Comtois' face. 'I have no interest in discussing anyone's private life. That isn't what this is about. What it is about, is the fact your son knew you had money, and I suspect he told someone about it. Someone who I believe is both incredibly manipulative, but also intentionally deceptive. The plan was to blackmail you, Captain Comtois, and to use your own personal reticence to force you to pay. Your son was to be accused of raping a woman, and your choice would be stark. Accept it, and risk him going to prison, or fight it using the truth. A truth you were not prepared to become public knowledge.'

'I was raped!' Brigitte St. Pierre screamed. 'Just because I don't remember it, doesn't mean it didn't happen, and it certainly doesn't mean I deserved it.'

'I'm not suggesting that for a second,' Hugo responded quickly. 'You were raped, and I'm so sorry for that. You didn't deserve it, but your rapist was not Gregoire Comtois. It was the person who entered into the blackmail plot with him.'

'But I'm not being blackmailed!' Comtois shouted.

'Not yet. I suspect the blackmail was forthcoming. Perhaps the blackmailer has photographs. I can't be sure at this moment. But I believe the blackmail plan would go ahead, just without Gregoire.'

'Then why kill Gregoire?' Dr. Oppert asked.

Hugo shrugged. 'For reasons which will become clear, I hope. But most likely because the partner didn't want to share the money, or rather, and as I suspect, because he is a deeply troubled sociopath.'

'And Clementine?' Avril asked. 'Why did she have to die?'

'Clementine claimed she saw nothing,' Hugo replied. 'But it occurred to me the murderer may have believed otherwise, possibly because, like me, they had been told several times that Clementine was always walking around Beaufort-Sur-Mer at all times of the day, even at night. She even told me herself she was an insomniac. So, it's not too much of a stretch of the imagination that she may have been around the night of Gregoire's murder.'

Avril shook her head. 'Clementine wouldn't have kept quiet about something like that. I've known her all my life, she just wouldn't.'

'I agree,' Hugo replied. 'And the point is, she may have seen something, but just not understood its significance. That's not to say she wouldn't have eventually, and for that reason, I believe the murderer couldn't take the risk she would recall what she had seen. So, he did what he had to do to get into her studio. He asked for her to paint his portrait.'

'Are you serious?' Avril asked.

He nodded. 'Oui. It was the perfect way to size her up, peut être to see if she remembered him, or what, in fact, she remembered about the night of Gregoire's murder. Maybe that's why he murdered her. When she was sitting there, she remembered something, or recognised something about him.'

Jasper Connor snorted. 'All I'm hearing from you, Captain Duchamp, is an awful lot of *what-ifs*, and *I imagine*, and *peut être's*. It's tiresome, and it's terrible, shoddy police work.'

Avril Roche glared at him. 'There's nothing tiresome about it, so keep your mouth shut, or I'll start opening mine, and you wouldn't like that very much, would you?'

'You wouldn't dare,' he growled.

She smiled. 'Try me.' She turned back to Hugo. 'Please continue, Captain.'

'I agree, Monsieur Connor,' Hugo continued. 'There is an awful lot of supposition because I'm afraid it is the nature of what I do. The people I deal with rarely tell the truth, and more often than not, they go to a great deal of trouble to make it very difficult for us to understand what they are up to. I am always a step behind, and I'm not embarrassed to say, I have to rely on the mistakes they make.'

'Mistakes?' Dr. Oppert interrupted.

'Oui,' Hugo replied. 'The mistake in Clementine Bonheur's studio was not obvious, but it was enough for me to notice it because it was out of place. I just didn't understand it, to begin with. As I said earlier, I believe Clementine's murderer sought her out using the guise of her painting his portrait. She would have begun by sketching him on the canvas, ready to begin the real painting. When we discovered her body, the painting troubled me. Why would someone go to all that trouble? To paint her portrait using her own blood?'

He grimaced. 'Obviously, I thought, we're dealing with a thoroughly sick individual, but it seemed a slow and deliberately nasty way to kill someone, and one most certainly dangerous and time-consuming. So, why do it? At first, I just barely noticed what appeared to be scratches on the canvas beneath the blood, and I didn't really think too much about it. It was only later I came to realise what it could mean.'

'A sketch of her murderer,' Avril whispered.

Hugo nodded. 'I believe he panicked. Removing the canvas was problematic because he might be seen, and then there was the issue of how to dispose of it. He could have destroyed the canvas, but if he had, it would probably have made us pay more attention - why would he have destroyed it? And we would have tried to put it back together. Instead, he decided to cover it with her blood, assuming we would have just believed it was part of a sick modus operandi.' He shrugged. 'And we almost did. The scratches, like the red towel, kept bothering me.'

'Putain! The red towel again!' Jasper snapped. 'Get on with it, man.'

Hugo smiled. 'You're right. It is time to end this, for everybody's sake.' He turned. 'Monsieur. I am placing you under arrest for the murders of Vincent Roche, Gregoire Comtois and Clementine Bonheur.'

cinquante

Quentin Arquette lifted his head slowly, his eyebrows knotting in confusion. The student pushed his hand through coarse black hair. He looked around him anxiously, staring at everyone.

'What the hell are you talking about?' he demanded. He turned his head with incredulity. 'Why are you all gawping at me?'

Hugo moved across the grass. He gestured for Etienne to stand in-between Quentin and Brigitte St. Pierre. Etienne moved quickly, pushing himself between them.

'This is ridiculous!' Quentin cried. 'I didn't know any of these people before this week. Hell, I barely knew Vincent, and I certainly didn't help him do anything. We weren't friends.' He laughed and shook his head. 'You've really lost it, Captain Duchamp.'

Hugo shrugged. 'It's fanciful,' he agreed. 'Mais, that does not mean it isn't based in fact. Let's go back to the red towel, and why I believe you had to remove it from the swimming pool. It was because it had your name sewn into it, wasn't it? When I met you and Brigitte the other day and you were swimming in the sea, I handed you your towel. It was red, and I noticed it had your name sewn into it.'

'And?' Quentin sniffed. 'My mother buys me monogrammed towels, so what? That hardly makes me a fucking killer, does it?' he snorted.

'The towel would place you at the scene of Vincent's death,' Hugo replied. 'I realise it would likely not have raised any concern. I mean, after all, you're on the swim team. It would be perfectly understandable for your towel to be next to the pool. Except at that point, on that night it would be out of place, and it might just place you at the scene of the crime, and you weren't prepared to take the risk of linking you to Vincent's death. Especially after what had happened in your past.'

'In his past?' Brigitte St. Pierre interrupted. 'What happened in his past?'

'My colleague Etienne Martine, as a matter of course, performs background checks,' Hugo replied. 'Etienne discovered Monsieur Arquette had a juvenile record.'

'So?' Quentin snipped. 'What does that have to do with anything? You shouldn't be able to just nose through my past. Especially when I did nothing fucking wrong, in the first place.'

'What was important about his juvenile record?' Comtois asked keenly.

'When he was fourteen years old,' Hugo replied, 'he attempted to sexually assault a girl on his swim team. When she started screaming, he tried to drown her.'

'She was lying!' Quentin screamed. 'It was her fault... she was a...'

'She was a, *what?*' Hugo pushed. 'What were you about to say, that she was a tease? That she deserved what she got?'

Quentin's face was stoic. 'I didn't say that, and if you think for a second it has anything to do with what happened here, then you really are as crazy as everyone is saying you are.'

'Peut être,' Hugo conceded again. 'Mais, just to be sure, I had Etienne look into the circumstances of your juvenile assault. The original statement was vague, so we tracked down the young lady. She spoke about how you not only tried to rape her, you tried to drown her, and that you were very obviously sexually aroused when you did so.'

'Lying bitch,' Quentin mumbled.

'I can't comment on that,' Hugo conceded. 'Mais, it is important that your school let you get away with it because you were their star swimmer. I know you are good at swimming in pools, but you failed to mention that when you were younger, you were a very accomplished swimmer and diver. In fact, you went to great pains to explain to me how you were afraid of going below the waterline and submerging yourself. You said you couldn't scuba dive because it terrified you.'

Quentin's mouth moved into a sarcastic, *et?*

Hugo continued. 'When Etienne looked into your past, he also discovered that in your high school, you won an award for deep-sea diving. And of course, you are an experienced and practised ocean swimmer. Why then would you tell me you were afraid of it and had never done it? I can only think of one reason.'

'That you wanted us to think you couldn't have been involved in moving Gregoire's body down to the boat,' Captain Comtois said, completing Hugo's thought.

'Here's what I think happened,' Hugo added. 'Somehow or other, you got talking to Gregoire Comtois. I don't know whether he or…' he stopped, stealing a look at Franc Comtois. Comtois lowered his head, nodding slowly, indicating Hugo could continue. 'I don't know whether you realised he was gay, or he told you, or even whether you instigated it, or he did, but somehow you came to realise his father had money and that you could use Gregoire to get it from him.'

'The fag was putty in my hands,' Quentin laughed. 'I knew the first second I met him who he was. You see freaks like that around the pool all the time. He took one look at me and it was like he was the cat and I was the cream.' He smiled. 'I let it play out. It took him like five minutes to tell me he was getting out of Beaufort-Sur-Mer one day, and that he just had to wait for his father to die and then he'd be rich.'

Quentin sighed. 'I grew up dirt poor, and honestly, after twenty years, it's pretty fucking boring. I looked at this spoilt queer kid, and I realised I had an opportunity.'

'What did you do?' Brigitte cried. Her mouth twitched as if she could barely put into words what she needed to say.

'Nothing weird,' Quentin sniffed as if he was offended by what she was suggesting. 'I didn't need to. I just had to pretend, and that was enough. I could see how turned on he was. It was pretty easy really.'

'Why did you bring me into this?' she asked.

'Because you never learned your damn lesson,' he answered matter-of-factly. 'You swanned around school as if you weren't aware of the power you have over men. You flirted with Baptiste. You flirted with Vincent. Dammit, you flirted with everyone but me. You were just like that bitch back home. Flirting with everyone but me, walking around, sticking your ass out and your tits forward. She needed teaching a lesson, and I would have if the damn swim coach hadn't had come back early.'

He smiled at her, his fingers toying with his clumpy hair. 'You were just the same. I've been thinking a long time about teaching you a lesson.' He moved away, staring down at the boulevard below. He laughed again, pointing at Baptiste. 'I actually thought it would be him to be the patsy to take the fall. It seemed genius. The weirdo fresh out of a nuthouse in Ireland, now living with a gay cop. The newspapers would have a field day.'

'You son of a bitch!' Baptiste hissed.

'Chill, freak,' Quentin retorted. 'You dodged the bullet. You can actually thank Vincent for that.'

'What are you talking about?' Baptiste shot back.

'I overheard you two talking in the changing rooms,' Quentin continued. 'Like another pair of fags.'

Hugo glared at him. As difficult as it was to listen to him, he knew he needed to give the young man the platform he needed to speak.

Quentin turned and faced Avril. 'And there he was like a whining little bitch, his Papa this, his Papa that. I watched as you left Baptiste and saw his reaction. He was resigned. He knew you would not help him, that you were just like everyone else, patronising and inadequate. That's the way my parents always made me feel, so I got it. So why didn't Vincent get me? He was like everyone, staring at me like I was a freak.'

He snorted. 'Like I was the freak instead of them. I think it was then I realised how much I hated him. He had the friends, everyone loved him, the girls,' he stole a look at Brigitte, 'the boys,' he glared at Baptiste. 'And the really fucking annoying thing about it was, he didn't care. All he cared about was his stupid drunk of a father who was dead. It was boring, it really was boring to see him like that.' He threw his hands in the air. 'The weak ones always get the life I should have had. The girls, the friends, the parties. It wasn't fair,' he cried.

'What did you do?' Hugo asked.

'I went to him. I *listened*,' he asked with a snort. 'And the more he talked, the harder it became not to just beat the crap out of him, but then he said something which caught my attention. *Maybe I should just drown myself like they say he did. Maybe then they'd pay attention.*'

Quentin slapped the top of his head. 'That was like a wow moment for me. I can help this kid, I thought. I went home that night and I couldn't sleep. All these thoughts kept going around in my head. When I finally fell asleep, I had a dream about his father drowning himself, and then I remembered Anna, the girl from school, and how beautiful she had looked and how much of a kick it was to see her life in my hands, beautiful below the water.'

He shrugged. 'Poor Vincent needed help, so I decided to give him it. I pulled him to one side the next day and told him I had a plan. A plan to make people stand up and finally pay attention to him.'

Hugo frowned. 'And he went for it?'

'Sure,' Quentin answered. 'As everyone keeps saying, the kid was fucked up in the head. He actually thought it was a genius move, and you have to admit, it was pretty damn impressive. I said to him - if you want them to take you seriously, then you've gotta get serious and creative.'

'Still, that was pretty out there,' Etienne interjected.

'Yeah, but it worked, didn't it?' Quentin replied proudly. 'And Vincent saw the sense in it.'

'Then the plan was,' Hugo continued, 'to stage a suicide attempt in the same manner as his father's, and your plan was to what, sweep in at the last minute and save him? Then as he's lying in hospital, the avocat comes forward with the letters, and then the police become involved and we have to look into his belief that his father was murdered.'

'Except he wasn't murdered!' Captain Comtois repeated. 'I don't know how many times you want me to keep saying that. No matter what I did, no matter what happened before, or afterwards, none of it had anything to do with Arthur's death.'

Hugo nodded. 'I actually agree. Arthur Roche committed suicide. But it doesn't mean that what you did had no effect on his decision.'

'That's unfair, Captain Duchamp,' Comtois spat.

'He's right,' Avril interrupted. 'You know it, and I know it, WE ALL know it.'

Hugo stubbed out a cigarette and lit another. 'And while the crime you committed went unpunished, and it is not necessarily relevant to the murders which followed, you should know I am preparing a file and will hand it over to the local Police Nationale. It will be up to them to decide what to do next and how to proceed with charges.'

Jasper Connor pivoted his head toward Captain Comtois. Comtois shrugged, the message clear on his face. *I had this coming.*

'What about my son?' Avril asked weakly. 'Tell me what happened to him. Was this really about what we did? The hotel? The drugs?'

Hugo searched her face. It was desperate and while he considered how best to approach her; he realised that in the end; it did not matter. All Avril Roche needed was the truth.

'The crucial point is that Arthur's death, whatever the reason, pushed your son over the edge,' he continued. As everyone has told me, he was already a little fragile, and obviously, it was all too much for him. Perhaps, in a way, he just didn't want to believe it was suicide, that there was someone to blame. I suppose that's what we all would do under similar circumstances. In grief, we take solace in anger, but it would have changed in time.'

'We'll never know now,' Avril sobbed.

Hugo faced Quentin. 'Monsieur Arquette. Did you ever actually intend to help Vincent?'

Quentin did not answer immediately. 'Does it matter?' he answered with a non-committal shrug.

Hugo nodded again. 'I believe so.'

Quentin turned his eyes slowly towards Brigitte St. Pierre. He recoiled as if the look she was giving him was more than he could stand. He shrugged again. 'Yeah, I was going to help him, but seeing him there, I realised how pathetic he was, and how he had gone along with such a stupid idea. Then the fact was he didn't deserve to live.'

'You never intended to help him,' Brigitte hissed. 'Just like that girl, you get off on seeing people in danger, you sick bastard.'

'I put a sick dog out of his misery,' he answered without looking at her. 'But whatever you say, I didn't set out to let him die. I figured I'd swoop in at the last second, drag him out and for once… and for once….' he gulped, desperately pulling air into his lungs. 'For once I'd get to be the hero, the one all the chicks dig and the one all the dudes looked up to.'

Baptiste moved away, angrily kicking his foot against a tree. 'That's what this was all about? You and your damn pride, some stupid ego thing? You were jealous because everyone liked Vincent?'

A gasp escaped Brigitte. She held her hand against her mouth. 'This was my fault, wasn't it?'

Finally, he stood and faced her. 'I was sick of you looking right past me, straight at him, so I decided to teach you a lesson.'

'Teach me a lesson?' she cried.

He threw back his head and laughed. 'Yeah, so I taught you a lesson, you dumb bitch. You'll never look past me again now, will you?'

cinquante-et-un

'So, you taught me a lesson by raping me?' Brigitte St. Pierre asked, as if she could barely get the words out.

Quentin stepped away, putting some distance between them. 'Well, with such a clever plan, I deserved a treat, didn't I?'

Brigitte jumped to her feet. Etienne and Baptiste grabbed her from either side and pulled her away.

Hugo stepped between them all. Raising his hands to try and diffuse the situation. He needed to end it and place Quentin in custody, but he knew he needed to keep Quentin talking because most of what had occurred was circumstantial, and he was never likely to get such an opportunity to talk to him again. Once the arrest took place, Quentin would receive legal advice and that advice would be quite clear. *Say nothing else.*

'Whose idea was it to claim Gregoire raped Brigitte?' Hugo asked. 'Did you always plan to murder Gregoire and rape Brigitte?'

'I'm clever, just not that clever,' Quentin quipped. 'I googled Brigitte a long time ago, so I knew about her attack five years ago. I figured I could use that. When Gregoire and I got talking, I told him about it, and how we could use it to get his father's money.'

'And he went for it?' Captain Comtois interrupted. 'My son was many things, but he wasn't so cold and calculating. And he wouldn't drag an innocent girl into it. I know this to be a fact.'

'As do I,' Dax Chastain added.

Guy Fallon nodded. 'Me too.'

Quentin raised his hands. 'Keep your panties on, big men,' he spat. 'And as for dragging innocent girls into his lies - hasn't he always done that? Pretending he was some big stud while all the time playing hide the sausage with the queers who roll into this godforsaken hell hole?'

'That was different,' Dax retorted.

Hugo stubbed out his cigarette. 'Unless you told him Brigitte was in on the plan,' he stated.

'I told Gregoire about Brigitte's past, and that we could pay her off and she would happily lie for us. I mean, she'd already done it once,' Quentin conceded.

'I'd never lie for you, you filthy pig!' Brigitte screamed.

Hugo shook his head. 'I don't believe you would either, but Gregoire may not have known that,' he responded. 'And I think he was desperate to get away.' He paused. 'But the most important point is that I know you were raped. And I know it wasn't by Gregoire, and I also believe he wouldn't have been party to it. Therefore, I can only think of one other explanation.'

Quentin clapped his hands. 'To kill two birds with one stone.'

Hugo noticed that Captain Comtois was becoming more and more agitated. He nodded at Dr. Oppert, silently telling him to stand by his friend. Oppert moved quickly to Comtois and placed his hand on his arm. 'Don't give him the satisfaction, Franc,' he whispered.

Comtois stared at him. 'I have patience. This isn't over.'

Hugo exhaled, realising time was not on his side. He needed a full confession from Quentin and he needed it soon, or he might not be able to control the outcome.

'What happened?' Hugo asked. 'Because I don't believe you actually even told Gregoire about the plan involving Brigitte,' he pushed.

Quentin sighed. 'Okay, I'll tell you, seeing as you're not smart enough to work it out for yourself.'

Hugo inched forward. This was progress. Quentin was warming to his story, and crucially, he was revelling in being the centre of attention. Believing he was smarter than anyone else would be his downfall.

'We were talking earlier,' Quentin began his recollection. 'And as I said, I knew he was a queer, and that I could probably get him to do what I wanted. He told me about the money and I told him the plan. He'd go down to the beach hut with Brigitte, and I'd meet them there later. I told him I'd slip her something extra in her drink, something that would knock her right out so that she'd pass out until the next morning and have no idea what had happened when she woke up.'

'And he went along with that?' Hugo asked.

Quentin nodded. 'Yeah. Listen, as far as he knew, he was going to get me for the night, and a million euros from his Papa, as far as old Gregoire was concerned, he was having a hell of a good night! The plan was, I'd go to his father the next day and say Gregoire had raped me and that I wanted to report it. I was worried old Papa Comtois would call my bluff, but Gregoire said that would never happen. He said his father would give every penny he had rather than have anyone know his son was gay.'

'Then if that was the plan, what changed?' Hugo pushed.

'Everything was going to plan,' Quentin answered. 'I made it to the beach hut, and by then, the drug had worked and Brigitte was out for the count. And then,' he gulped as if he was about to retch. 'then the pervert kissed me,' he whispered. 'Like he had a right to.'

He stepped across the stones. 'I hadn't thought about killing him, not really, not seriously anyway. It's messy, and no matter how careful you think you are, there's always something you miss, i.e. a fucking red towel,' he spat the words onto the ground. 'Anyway, a million euros is a lot of money, even if you have to share it. But when he kissed me, my first thought was repulsion, mais the second was, a million euros is a lot of money, especially if you *don't* have to share it. I smacked him with a stone and he was down. It took a second. And it was already done. It only took another second to make sure. And then I looked around the beach hut and realised I could have it all. I could have the money AND the girl.'

'Why go to such elaborate means to pose Gregoire's body?' Hugo asked.

Quentin shrugged. 'Because I wanted to make it look like just another suicide, or even if it wasn't, then I figured if he was down there, no one would really look at me, because I had nothing to do with him. And besides, I figured everyone would have just figured he'd topped himself like anyone else. I figured I'd whisper in a few people's ears that I heard he and Vincent Roche had been secret lovers and that he couldn't bear the loss.'

He smiled at Comtois. 'I figured once that rumour was out, you wouldn't have bothered looking too far, and certainly not in my direction. Getting rid of him wasn't difficult. It took me barely half an hour. I knew where the scuba gear was. The door wasn't even locked. I'd dived in the dark a hundred times, so it was easy just to drag him down and get rid of him.'

He wiped his hands together. 'Easy peasy.' He winked at Brigitte. 'I came back and claimed my reward. I made love to my girl. It was a good night.'

A silence descended on the fort, the only sound the wind and the gentle lapping of water beneath them.

'And Clementine?' Avril broke the silence. 'Why did she have to die?'

'Because you told me she often walked during the night,' Quentin answered. 'And when I climbed out of the sea, I thought I saw someone on the harbour. It was only a shadow, but I thought I recognised the long dress she wore blowing in the wind.'

'And you murdered her just because you saw a shadow?'

He shrugged again. 'I couldn't take the chance. Not after the towel. It was easy enough. I asked her to paint me. She said yes.' He laughed. 'I think the old whore actually thought I wanted to fuck her. I told her I already had a girl and I think she was disappointed, poor bitch.'

'And did she remember anything?' Hugo asked calmly.

'I don't know. I don't think so. But I couldn't take the chance. Not when I was so close to getting the money.'

Avril Roche stifled a sob. 'And my son? Is Captain Duchamp right in what he said?'

Quentin laughed. 'I hated Vincent. He was a snivelling brat, always bleating on about his dead father. He was weak and boring.' He stopped and glared at Brigitte. 'So, of course, that meant all the chicks were desperate to drop their drawers for him. Anyway, he kept going on about how he wanted to disappear, but how he wanted to get the police to take his father's death seriously, and he had no idea how to do it. I came up with the idea and all he needed was for me to come and find him and rescue him.' He snorted. 'He was as stupid as he was dull.'

Hugo spotted Avril Roche out of the corner of his eye. Her fists were balled and her face was tight, but she was staring at Quentin with a burning intensity. He imagined at that moment she was more interested in discovering how her son had actually died than anything else. 'You always intended on letting him die, didn't you?'

Quentin shrugged again. 'I told you already. I didn't give it that much thought. I was just gonna watch and see what happened. When he was down there, I suppose I figured it was better just to leave him, like some dull animal which needed putting out of his misery.'

The uncomfortable silence descended again.

'Why did you come here?' Avril said, her voice barely audible. 'Was it to rub our noses in it?'

He laughed. He pointed at Brigitte. 'My girl was coming here, so of course, I had to follow her.'

Brigitte slapped Etienne and Baptiste away. 'Don't touch me,' she hissed at them. She moved towards Quentin. 'Are you saying three people died because of some disgusting obsession you had with me?'

Quentin smiled. 'You could say that. Which technically makes everything that happened your fault, doesn't it?' He reached forward and kissed her cheek. 'But don't worry, I forgive you.'

She recoiled at his touch. 'Do you know the only thing that has made me feel safe these last few days?' she asked him. Quentin did not respond. She took a step closer to him. 'It's this.' She reached inside her blouse and extracted something. Quentin narrowed his eyes to see what it was. Moments later, the glint of the blade illuminated his face. Brigitte St. Pierre pulled back her hand and, with a quick lunge, plunged the blade into his chest.

cinquante-deux

It took only a matter of seconds for Hugo to sprint across the clearing. He threw his body at Brigitte, knocking her to the ground. 'Get a hold of her!' he called out to no one in particular.

Etienne and Baptiste grabbed her, dragging her away as she uttered a guttural scream. 'Let him die! Let the bastard die!'

Jasper Connor stepped over. 'It is the right thing to do.' He looked at Captain Comtois. 'Right, Franc?'

Comtois did not answer. He was staring at Quentin. He was convulsing on the ground, crying in obvious distress. 'He killed my son,' Comtois said. 'He doesn't deserve to live.'

Hugo's eyes darted over the wound. Blood was spurting from the gaping wound near his heart. He pressed his hands down as he attempted to stem the flow. 'We can't let him die,' he cried.

'Oui, we can,' Comtois snapped. 'You know as well as I do, if he goes to court, he'll likely get off, or else he'll plead insanity. Even if he gets convicted, he'll be out and living a normal life all too soon. And he'll do it again. He'll destroy another family, rape another woman, and then that will be on you if you let him live, Captain Duchamp.'

Hugo stared at him wide-eyed. 'We can't think like that,' he gasped. 'All I know is that if we let him die, the only people who'll suffer is you and Brigitte.'

He shook his head. 'And that means he'll be getting off easy. All we can do is make his punishment count. Make him live the rest of his life in the knowledge of what he has done - let everyone else know that. Make sure he never has a peaceful day again in his life - those are all things you CAN do. Letting him die is too easy. He gets off then, and you'll be the one who ends up rotting in prison. That makes no sense. Let him live and let him live with IT. Make sure he does. Never let him forget, never let anyone else forget. That's the best thing you can do for Vincent, Gregoire and

Clementine, and you and Brigitte. Don't let him win. Make him pay for what he's done.'

Comtois took a step forward. 'Non. He has to pay.'

Dr. Oppert pushed past his friend. 'I don't care who he is, or what he's done, Franc. I haven't worked this long to end it by giving in to base instincts. I am going to do what I can to make sure this young man survives, so he faces what he has done. If you don't like that, then you're going to have to stop me.'

Comtois stared at him, his face challenging.

'Doctor, I need your help,' Hugo called out.

Oppert stared at Comtois. 'You heard him. What's it to be, Franc? Are you going to make us all murderers?'

Comtois continued to wrestle with his emotions. Finally, he stepped aside.

'You have to save me,' Quentin gurgled. 'I'm dying! I'm dying!'

Hugo stared at the young man. 'Non, you're not. We're going to save you,' he said, before adding, 'even if you don't deserve it.'

Oppert dropped to his knees, his eyes scanning the wound. 'Stop being such a drama queen, young man. It's barely a scratch. I'm going to patch you up to make sure you live a very long life, in prison where you belong, where I hope your cellmate will be as kind to you as you have been to everyone else.'

fin

Avril Roche stepped out of the hotel, a tray of drinks in her hand. She placed it on a table and turned. 'I want to thank you all for coming this afternoon,' she began. 'Captain Duchamp, and his friends,' she addressed Hugo, Baptiste, Etienne and Brigitte. 'And my darling son's dear friends, Dax and Guy. Join me in a glass of champagne.'

She gestured to the tray and waited until everyone had a glass. 'I realise it is slightly unusual, but I wanted to say au revoir to our new friends, especially Captain Duchamp and his colleague, without whom we may never have truly understood what happened. Santé!'

Everyone raised their glasses and repeated. 'Santé!'

'Where is Jasper?' Dax asked.

She took a moment to reply. 'This morning I went to the police and made a statement. Jasper is now in police custody.'

Baptiste leaned forward. 'At the fort, you mentioned something about drugs. What was that all about?'

Hugo took a sip of his drink. 'At first, I wasn't sure how relevant, or irrelevant, it was, but I knew it was important. We discovered in the papers left by Arthur Roche that he had discovered what he believed was corruption in Beaufort-Sur-Mer.'

'And was there?' Baptiste asked.

Hugo nodded. 'Oui, but not as he imagined it.' He pointed at Etienne. 'Etienne discovered Jasper owed a lot of money to some very dangerous men, drug dealers. He realised that moving his operations to somewhere like Beaufort-Sur-Mer, with its small police force and a direct route from the Atlantic Ocean would keep those men satisfied. He planned on using Captain Comtois' crutch to blackmail him.'

'That his son was gay?' Baptiste shook his head. 'This shit again? Jesus, when are people going to realise it's 2022?'

'I'm afraid it was my fault,' Avril interjected. 'I was the one who told Jasper about Gregoire. I don't know why, I just did. I loved him, or at least I thought I was, but at the time, I would do anything for him. I DID do anything for him.'

'Anyway,' Hugo continued. 'Jasper, like Quentin would later, thought to use Gregoire's sexuality against his father. What he didn't count on was Franc Comtois hated being blackmailed, probably just as much as he hated his son's homosexuality. So, he thought the only thing he could do was to fight fire with fire. Jasper Connor was blackmailing him, and in return, Captain Comtois protected himself. And to all intent's and purposes, it worked, because neither side could use their blackmail or they would be exposed.'

Guy Fallon cleared his throat. 'Am I in trouble?'

'What does this have to do with you?' Dax asked.

'Jasper needed my boat to go out and meet the boat bringing the drugs in,' Guy replied. 'He knew I went fishing every night anyway, and that no one would think twice about it.'

Dax shook his head. 'And you agreed?'

'Non,' Guy replied, staring at Avril.

She reached over and touched his arm. 'Je suis désolé,' she said, her lips trembling. 'It was me. Jasper asked me to spike Guy's drink so he could take out the boat that night. I didn't want to, truly I didn't, but by then I felt as if I was in too deep. I'd already done so many bad things. One more didn't seem to matter all that much,' she added sadly. 'I do regret involving you, sweet Guy.'

He took her hand and held it against his cheek. 'I understand.'

'I told the police what happened,' she continued. 'They know you didn't even know about the boat being taken out that night without your consent.'

Guy exhaled. 'But I knew the next day. I saw the drugs. And Jasper told me it was too late, and that I couldn't do anything about it, and if I tried, no one would believe I wasn't involved in drug smuggling. It only took me a minute to realise he was right. Who were the cops gonna believe? Me, the ageing hippy fisherman who spends most of his days high and most of his night's fishing on the Atlantic, or him, "respectable" businessman. I knew they'd take one look at the situation and I'd spend ten to twenty in the nearest prison.'

'You won't face charges,' Hugo reassured. 'Not only because of Avril's statement, but I've also spoken with Captain Comtois. As well as retiring from the police force, he is also coming clean about his involvement with Jasper Connor,' he said reassuringly. 'And at this point, he is prepared to face the consequences, so long as he takes Jasper Connor with him.'

'What about all Franc Comtois money?' Baptiste asked. 'Did he lie about the drug drop only happening once?'

Etienne shook his head. 'Non. He was honest about that. I finally tracked down where the money came from, and I'm afraid there are no secrets there, just an inheritance. His parents had property in Switzerland, and when they died, he sold it to a clinic for a lot of money.'

'Gregoire probably knew about the money and grew frustrated because his father wouldn't do anything with it, or give any to him,' Hugo added.

Avril agreed. 'Franc isn't the sort of man to have his head turned by money,' she stated. 'Ironically, I think the reason he didn't want to give any of it to Gregoire was because he knew if he did, Gregoire would leave and that would be the end of it. Franc is a complicated man. He loved his son as much as he was embarrassed by him.'

The group lapsed into silence.

'Then it's all over,' Brigitte sighed. 'Quentin will rot in jail and we can all move on.'

'It'll never be over,' Avril interrupted. 'We have to live the same sentence as him, and from what I saw at the fort, I don't think he'll give us a second thought, whereas I will spend the rest of my life seeing his face every waking moment.'

Brigitte shook her head. 'Oh, I plan on living a full and fabulous life, in spite of him, not despite him. And more importantly, I plan on never thinking of him again. Unless some fool ass avocat tries to get him out of prison, and then he'll know my name again, they all will!'

Hugo smiled. 'I'm sure they will. And living your life for yourself is probably the best revenge you can have. Don't think of him, unless you have to.'

'Merci, Captain,' she breathed.

Baptiste pointed at his watch. 'We should be heading to the station. Our train is due in forty minutes.'

Brigitte jumped to her feet. 'Oui. We have two spots to fill on our swim team now.'

Baptiste turned to Hugo. 'You were such a natural with the scuba diving, Papa, why don't you join our swim team?'

Hugo looked towards the sea and lit a cigarette. 'Suddenly, I feel very, very old.'

Baptiste flung his arm around Hugo's shoulder as he headed towards the boulevard. 'Think of it this way,' he snatched this cigarette from Hugo's hand, 'a few less of these, and a few early morning swimming sessions, and if you practice hard enough, you could end up with one of these,' he lifted his t-shirt, revealing a perfect six-pack, 'and more importantly, you could live to be a very old man, fifty-years old even.'

Hugo rolled his eyes. 'Oui, Baptiste, that is *anci*ent.' He smiled and grabbed the cigarette back. He threw his arm over Baptiste's shoulder. 'Take your old Papa home.'

HUGO DUCHAMP WILL RETURN IN A NEW INVESTIGATION:

Chemin de

Compostelle

Printed in Poland
by Amazon Fulfillment
Poland Sp. z o.o., Wrocław
30 May 2022

85a40071-447d-4e20-a83d-ebbfd1624750R01